TO BLESS

or

TO BLAME

a novel by PAT MCGAULEY

Copyright © 2002 by Patrick McGauley

For information regarding this title, please contact:
Patrick McGauley
2808 Fifth Avenue West
Hibbing, MN 55746
(218) 262-3935
email: shatiferin@aol.com

Manufactured in the United States of America through Stanton Publication Services, Inc., St. Paul, MN. Published by Pat McGauley Publishing (Hibbing, MN 55746).

ISBN 0-9724209-0-8

The Library of Congress catalog identification number is pending
Copyright pending.

First edition, November 2002

In Appreciation

A STORY MUCH LIKE THIS ONE was written over several months in 1983. Despite many efforts at getting my book published, that original effort was much too convoluted and attracted only letters of rejection. I let the story sit in a cardboard box until January of this year when it was resurrected from the cobwebs on a basement shelf. I reread the pages then titled *The Giant's Ridge* and still liked the people and the place as much as I had nearly twenty years ago.

But this time I let the story tell itself and invited some help with the editing. I must thank Ed Beckers for walking through the history with me and for his help in keeping my characters consistent. From Ed I passed the manuscript to Kathy Serrano for more precise editing. Kathy spent countless hours giving the story her professional touch. Through three rewrites, Kathy gave the story its necessary polish. Both retired school teachers have been enormously helpful and supportive during my story telling.

Before the final rewrite, the manuscript went to my friend Nancy Erickson for her reading and review. Neighbor, Dave Wirkkula, is the artist who did both the cover graphics and insert maps. Another friend, Al Zdon is a newspaper man and published author. He assisted me with a thousand questions about publishing. I have learned that a book is not only about people but requires people to make it happen. For all of their help I am truly grateful.

The story, *TO BLESS OR TO BLAME*, is generally accurate in an historical sense. Although the major characters are fictitious, some others actually lived in the timeframe of Hibbing in the early 1900's. I must further express my gratitude to all of those who have worked diligently to preserve the history of Hibbing and of the Mesaba Iron Range. I have drawn extensively from their research and their memories. They have kept alive the spirit of those early days in this most unique corner of America.

DEDICATION

I was blessed with loving parents. My father Richard McGauley and my mother Madeline Myre McGauley Theodore are in my memory every day.

"I had Ambition, by which sin The angels fell;
I climbed and, step by step, O Lord,
Ascended into Hell."

—WILLIAM HENRY DAVIES
(1871–1940)

PROLOGUE

JANUARY IN NORTHERN MINNESOTA presents a challenge to those who are not properly forewarned. Winter's talons are at their sharpest during this season of shrunken days and long, frigid nights. This Monday afternoon hung like a sullen gray curtain across the white-clad expanse of mountainous dumps that proved a vivid testimony to the hungry appetite of iron ore mining. Spirals of chimney smoke rose from every rooftop in a city frozen by minus thirty degree temperatures swept along by fierce northerly winds. In every bitter aspect it was a day determined to drive this visitor away from his appointment with an erstwhile veteran of many Hibbing winters.

But once inside the old man's small living room, sitting across from some snapping birch logs, the tingling fireside warmth soothed his guest's negative attitude about this remote place enveloped in the bowels of January. Like healing fingers, the radiance conjured an optimism that promised to soften all thoughts of the blustery howl beyond the frosted window panes.

Heavy oak bookshelves covered two walls from floor to ceiling. A collage of yellowed photographs and maps were haphazardly cluttered on an opposite wall. It was an untidy and well worn room; yet its personality felt congenial. A sense of expectancy hung in the air like the scented smoke wafting from the kindling birch embers across the charred hearth.

The atmosphere of the room seemed defined in the framed, hand-printed transcription displayed by itself above the arched entryway. Its very position seemed to exaggerate the significance of the verse . . .

"Nothing that was worthy in the past departs, no truth or goodness realized by man ever dies or can die; but is all still here, and, recognized or not, lives and works through endless changes.

Thomas Carlyle . . . "

The man sat in a large overstuffed chair near the corner of converging bookshelves with his hands folded loosely on a plaid blanket that draped unevenly across his spindly legs. One of his books was thick and red-covered and lie half-opened on his lap. A tattered Webster Dictionary rested on the chair side table within an arm's easy reach. Every obvious trapping of a journalist's world found its casual expression here: the roll-top desk, Adler typewriter, stacks of tablets, and pencils strewn everywhere. In this unkempt but comfortable room there was an unspoken definition of the man in residence.

"So you've read my book." His smile was a wide crease across a narrow, angular face with the furrows of seventy-two years. He lifted the red-covered book, closed its pages, and placed it carefully atop the dictionary. "And it hasn't answered some of your questions about the history of this place." Claude Atkinson was the town sage—a newspaper editor for countless years as well as the local authority on almost everything—from Mesaba's geology and geography to Hibbing's people and politics. Mostly, Claude was an astute historian who had established a more than considerable reputation for himself throughout the state.

"You're right, of course. I'll not be defensive on that matter, nor will I allow my feelings to be hurt by the suggestion in your letter that I . . . 'had more to say about mining than miners'!" His piercing green eyes sparkled under thick, bushy, gray brows. "When I finished writing *The Red Country,* I believed that in every essential detail my manuscript was perfectly comprised. Not a smidgen of doubt in my mind about that!" Then, with an easy smile of self-amusement and a keenly sincere laugh, Claude leaned back in his chair. "Yes, without any reservations, I presumed that my high-minded portrayal was what this crude Mesaba Iron Range, and my town of Hibbing, were all about.

"Wasn't until that day—March of 1912, the eighteenth it was—that I became possessed of a disturbing realization. Something was wrong.

Seriously wrong! I had just sent my book off to a publisher in St. Paul, and it struck me like a blow to the stomach. Unmistakably, something vital was missing—and, that something was possibly the very life's-spirit of it all. Can you imagine my feeling? I had conceived my masterpiece and . . . " His clear voice wavered slightly, his eyelids drooped almost imperceptibly. "And in my heart I knew this marvelous child was stillborn!"

He shifted in his chair and leaned emphatically forward. "It really wasn't the history though—please God I captured all of that quite well I'm certain. And, I'd never want to say that my style was altogether lifeless—I've been writing all my life you realize. And, if I've learned anything, it's how to get an idea from my head to the page in front of me clearly enough. No, it was something far more important. It was the story! Or rather, how I chose to tell the story." Claude massaged his temples, then brought his long fingers down the sides of his face. His elbows rested on this knees, hands cradling his long face as he mused on what he had just said.

"Retrospect is sobering. In the footprints that trail her is that noble impossibility we call wisdom. Anyhow, I felt the story about this place and these incredible people had not fully been told."

Atkinson glanced toward the thick binding of his copy of *The Red Country* then placed a hand on the tome. His gaze fell absently upon the bulk of five hundred and thirty meticulously researched pages. His acknowledged masterpiece was a substantial work. For the first time in our conversation the wrinkle of a frown crept over his face, narrowed his eyes. "It was good . . . but certainly not good enough!" he communed in a voice soft with regret. "Before the book went out of print a few years back, I was beginning to make another effort. This time I had outlined a novel—something that would let me get into the heads and hearts of the people who made this town what it is. In writing historical fiction I could take whatever liberty I wanted in capturing their emotions . . . their motives and ambitions—their incredible spirit!" Claude stared into the fireplace with what seemed a contemplation of the remorse that is every person's unrealized dream. "But . . ." he cleared his throat, "I'd lost too much of the energy that this project would require . . . I guess. Maybe I lost some of the insight I needed, too. So I let that story fester in my thoughts without ever getting it onto paper in my Adler over there."

"There is something I can do before it's too late," his expressive eyes were animated again. "I'm feeling that story come alive as I sit here, and I'd like to tell it before my time runs out." He shrugged his shoulders. "We wouldn't want this book I didn't write—and surely never will—to share an eternal grave with me. That would be a shame, wouldn't it?" His hands opened as if he were appealing to his listener to get started taking notes. "I'll need to put some flesh on that skeleton of history— give it the vitality it needs to have. A story needs to breathe and to bleed. You came here to learn more about this place, and I damn well can't let you go home empty minded.

"This story's about some people I got to know back then—in the *old* Hibbing—just after we turned this new century. Strong people! But none of them out of proportion to this rowdy time and place." Inspired by the memories flooding his thoughts, Claude reclined in his chair while thoughtfully fingering his stubbled chin and focusing on arcane thoughts far beyond this room and this moment. Clearing his throat he smiled what seemed to be a challenge, "You'll have to listen carefully to this old man's ramblings, son. These people I'm talking about came over here at different times, you know. So, I'm going to jump around a bit and expect you to be forgiving. As a newsman all these years I've sharpened my memory on dates. Dates—they are the backbone of a writers craft." Claude's wan smile disappeared for a moment as his long finger pointed at the visitor much like a teacher might toward his student. *"Make sure you get the dates down in you notes and fix them in your mind.* Can you do that?" Then he closed his eyes and remembered.

"Certainly every story needs a heroine. Well, Mary Bellani was easily the most beautiful woman that ever graced our fair community. Strikingly attractive, eyes with a diamond's sparkle and a smile that would surely put our most splendid July sunshine to shame. And courageous! Like any other woman that ventured to these robust, masculine parts—she had to be strong! Mary came here from the Campania in Italy. I'm told she left her homeland with a heart set on finding a love here . . . and, she did of course. But that's a bittersweet story that I'll have something to tell you about.

"There was Tony Zoretek. What a tall, strapping, handsome fellow he was—and a gifted athlete as well. I'm not quite sure why that comes first to my memory—the athlete thing—because Tony was something much more than the finest ballplayer that I've ever had the good fortune to know. What exactly was it? Well, maybe Tony was the real arch-hero type. He possessed the character that powerful books are made of. And personable! Hard to imagine anyone not liking him . . . except . . . , well, that will surely come up later.

"And, I'll need more than a few hours to tell you about Peter Moran. He was an empire builder in those tumultuous days. 'Irish Pete' threw more weight around Hibbing than the legendary Paul Bunyan might ever have hoped to. It's almost ironic when I think about it; but, he came from a logging family too—the Moran clan. If I had to describe Peter in four or five words I couldn't do it. But, let me see: compelling, ambitious, headstrong, even ruthless at times . . . a very complex man in every sense of the word. Maybe his power was his poison! Nevertheless, it was Peter Moran more than anyone else who shaped the old town of Hibbing with his two manipulative hands. When all is told, this was *Peter Moran's town* in those days.

"So these are the three people through which most of my story is woven. I must use threads of many textures—strands of strength and weakness, honesty and deceit, love and hate. Senia and Steven and countless others are sewn into my story. Without them . . . ?" Claude smiled at his memories of the people he would warm his visitor with on this frigid January afternoon.

"I guess it is really as Mr. Carlyle so wisely observed . . ." Claude gestured toward the framed verse on his wall . . . *"Nothing that was worthy in the past can ever die . . ."*

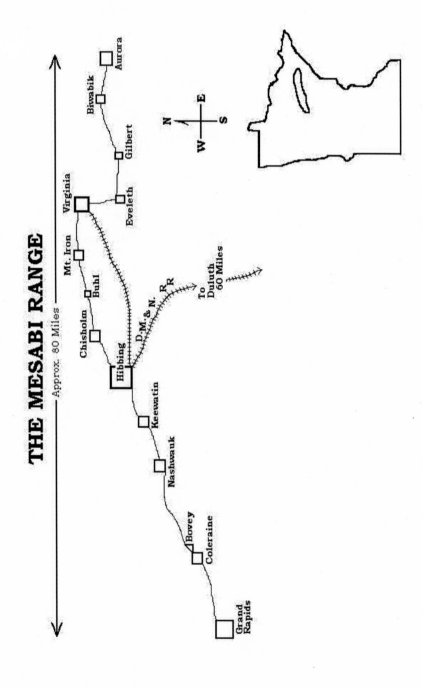

THE MESABI RANGE
Approx. 80 Miles

Aurora
Biwabik
Gilbert
Eveleth
Virginia
Mt. Iron
Buhl
Chisholm
Hibbing
D.M. & N. R. R.
To Duluth 60 Miles
Keewatin
Nashwauk
Bovey
Coleraine
Grand Rapids

N E W S

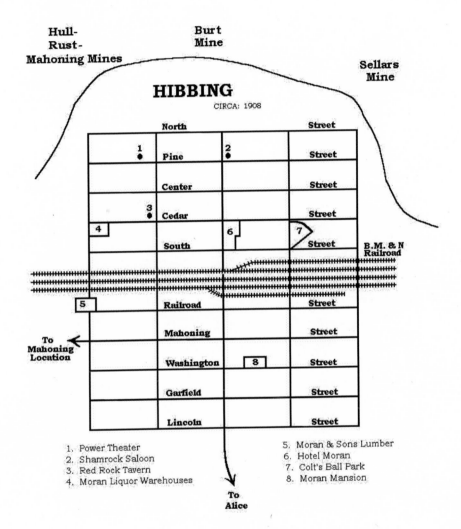

HIBBING

CIRCA: 1908

Hull-
Rust-
Mahoning Mines

Burt
Mine

Sellars
Mine

North   Street

1   Pine   2   Street

Center   Street

3   Cedar   Street

4   6   7   South   Street   B.M. & N
Railroad

5   Railroad   Street

To
Mahoning
Location   Mahoning   Street

Washington   8   Street

Garfield   Street

Lincoln   Street

1. Power Theater   5. Moran & Sons Lumber
2. Shamrock Saloon   6. Hotel Moran
3. Red Rock Tavern   7. Colt's Ball Park
4. Moran Liquor Warehouses   8. Moran Mansion

To
Alice

BOOK ONE

Hibbing, Minnesota

'DALY'S VISION'

October 1889

The ridge of mighty pines lined the hillside and veiled the autumn morning's sun. A father and his son stood in shadowed solitude. Beyond them to the west, as far as their eyes could see, was a tawny sweep of empty grassland.

"I ain't nothin of a religious man, son, but to look at these trees," he paused almost reverently regarding the stand of white pine, "It kinda makes one believe in God, a God that's taken pretty good care of us Morans over the years." Daly Moran smiled down at the boy, and placing a weathered hand on his shoulder, drew him close. How the boy had grown Daly realized, as Peter's shoulders brushed against his elbow. Daly clutched a pipe in his other hand using it to gesture toward the treeless field, fringed with clusters of aspen shedding their dead, yellowed leaves. "And, He's got a lot more timber just waiting for us out there. Somewhere."

But where? Where would they go from here the tall, red-bearded man mused to himself. A glint was in his eyes, "Gonna be going west, son, like we always done before."

The boy gave him a wide, expectant smile. "We leavin here, pa? We gonna find another place? Make a new camp?"

Daly Moran let the questions drift with the pungent tobacco smoke. Absorbed in his own thoughts and ambitions, Daly could feel the familiar pull of the western horizon. He turned the boy's gaze toward the bank of green timber towering beside them. "Not for a while, Peter. We still got us

3

some work to do here. Come winter we're gonna take all these pine down. One by one we're gonna cut 'em, strip 'em, and haul 'em outta here. With a little luck, we can stretch this here job for another year, maybe two." He gave his son a confident smile, relighted his pipe, coughed and spat. "Let's get back to work, son. We'll talk about moving some other time."

As Peter led his father on the way back over the hilltop toward their logging camp, he appealed as he'd done so many times before. "Pa, do ya think I'll be able to help with the cuttin this winter? Do ya think?" As always, Peter's plea held an equal mixture of exuberance and impatience. The boy desperately wanted to be more involved in his family's timber operations.

"Don't s'pect so, son. Your day will come soon enough. You just let your pa figger out when that's gonna be." Daly knew that much of his own ambition churned in the spirit of this son. Peter was his favorite. Daly often sensed that this was the son who would keep his vision alive. It was this love of Peter that gave rise to his dread of having his son join the lumberjacks in their perilous work.

"For now, you've got your book learnin to do," Daly uttered in an appeasing tone. "Besides, you're the only one in the camp who knows where everything is. You're too valuable to your pa in the office. Don't want you going out in the woods and gettin yerself hurt."

Daly Moran was a timber man. His was the third generation of loggers who started in the forests of New York, moved through Pennsylvania, along the Great Lakes, and into northern Michigan. Logging was both transient and dangerous. The Morans had jumped from stand to stand, and camp to camp, with an acumen passed from father to son. His own father, Liam, had been a victim of the precarious timber cutting. The elder Moran was pinned under an errant tree cut which crushed both of his legs. Liam Moran was forced out of the forest he loved, to a desk he despised. Liam refused to live a life that was only half-filled and died a young man not yet forty.

Daly maintained the family tradition with a fervor that kept him one step ahead of rival companies many of whom were larger, better financed and equipped. He hired good men and made timely decisions. He understood precisely when and where to move getting his first steps rooted as firmly as the trees he would cut.

To ensure his success, Daly gambled, sacrificed, and manipulated. His very nature seemed harnessed to his ambition. Anyone who could not keep pace with him was left behind including his wife and daughter in Warren, Pennsylvania. He seldom thought about them. His three sons were with him always, integrated into his timber operation: Moran and Sons. Each son, he believed, was destined to fit the mold of the Moran men before them.

His wife Kathleen had given him the sons he wanted, therefore fulfilling her obligation to their marital union. Although Daly could abandon his family, he could never shirk his responsibilities. Daly was generous with Kathleen. When the timber was sold, she received no less than one third of the company's sizable profits. When the season was over, usually in June, he and the boys traveled to Warren spending a month with Kathleen and Emily. The visits were often stressful. Kathleen wanted her sons to go to school and enjoy the social benefits of community roots she so painstakingly established. Daly was always adamant in his refusal to compromise the Moran business.

Another concession Daly made to his marriage was his fidelity. He loved Kathleen as best he could given the circumstances of long separation. The life that his father and grandfather had passed on to him, however, was his greatest passion.

Peter burst through the door and Daly's thoughts like a gust of wind. "Mr. Harney's back! Pa, he's comin up the road right now."

Daly rose from behind the crude desk in his makeshift camp office outside of Marquette, Michigan. The room was small, cluttered, and outwardly very disorganized. Portable wooden boxes, stuffed with business records, lined the walls and crammed the corners. Yet Daly, and thirteen year old Peter, knew the contents of every box. Daly often talked about his business with young Peter and was never surprised at how quickly the boy caught on. The boy loved numbers and the ledgers that kept an account of them.

Tom Harney was a veteran timber cruiser who had been with Daly and his father before him for more than twenty years. He was one of the few men who could match any Moran stride for stride. Tom looked Daly straight in the eyes. "Daly, I want you sitting down for this." He took

Moran by the shoulders, eased him into the chair behind the desk, then sat himself down across from his boss.

Peter found a chair off to the side and watched the two men he admired most in the world. Peter's business education consisted of listening to the men and sorting out in his mind the important from the trivial. This conversation, he knew from his father's restlessness lately, was important stuff.

"Holy Jesus, Daly! You shoulda seen what was out there. White pine . . . thousands of acres as untouched as a virgin. They was just punchin holes in them clouds!" Harney had just returned from several months of surveying the dense woodlands of Northern Minnesota. The enthusiasm in his voice conveyed more than words.

"Can't say I'm one bit surprised, Tom." Daly leaned back in his chair, swung his boots up onto the window ledge, and stroked his thick red beard. Daly measured his old friend's excitement, making an observation of his own. "Ya know, Tom, there's rumor that iron ore's up there in Minnesota, too. Some day that place could go crazy with the mining and timber. It'll be a hellava lot bigger than what we've seen in these parts the past few years." Daly had talked with Wellington Burt, a former Michigan Governor recently turned prospector. Burt had watched the rapid depletion of his native state's forests. Being an opportunist of some reputation, he had also been to Minnesota looking for new pine lands.

Daly banged the dead ash from his pipe on the floor, pushed away from the desk, and gazed out the window at the setting sun "Not that I give a logger's crap about iron ore, but it's gonna mean new railroads, boom towns, and construction 'til hell won't have no more of it. She'll be one powerful combination: lumbering and mining. I can't believe we could possibly miss by getting ourselves into that mix before our competition beats us to it."

Daly began a nervous pace about the room. "Tommy, the time to get in there is right now. Actually, yesterday!" When excited, Daly moved with the restless instinct of a caged animal. Upper Michigan was beginning to feel like that cage. Daly obsessed to be first. Harney's timber cruising had brought the Moran operation here four year's ago, and their timing had reaped huge profits for the company. But, the good years were clearly numbered now, and no Moran would ever be a scavenger. "Show me where ya been, Tom, I wanna get a picture of the place in my mind. Peter, where's them maps we was looking at the other day?"

Peter was off his chair in an instant, digging into a small box set on top of a larger one in the corner of the room. "Right here, pa. I already marked this box: 'Minnesota'." The boy eagerly spread the maps out on Daly's desktop. The two men smoothed the papers out, and spent another hour hovered over the topography charts sharing their trained observations and assessments. Next, they studied some land ownership records that Peter had filed in his Minnesota box. At his father's instruction, Peter always listed 'things to do' in his yellowed tablet.

"Don't unpack your gear, Tom. We've gotta jump into this thing with both feet runnin'. Take Denis and Swede Olson with you. You'll have to round up as many homesteaders as you can. There's lots'a Swede's people, and even more Finns up in Duluth." Daly's words spewed in rapid staccato. "Set up a bank account in Duluth. Let's be as tight as we can with the money and try not to go over a buck and a half an acre." Daly estimated his profits from this year's harvest in his head considering what he might be able to borrow on his good reputation. "Let Olson work the homesteading stuff. He's done that before, and I'll put Denis in touch with Ed McIntosh down in St. Paul. Ed can set up a land office for us in Duluth. He'll be able to take care of all the legalities." Moran gave Harney a heavy slap on the back and smiled at his wide-eyed son. Peter had written everything down as fast as he could get ink out of the bottle. Daly made another observation, "Mac's a smooth operator, and he knows how to go to bed with the politicians if he has to."

Daly knew that McIntosh, his lawyer friend, would give every essential priority to Moran's venture. Like his father before him, Daly had been through other land-grabbing schemes with McIntosh, and had made few mistakes in the process. Ed was like family.

"Don't let nothin hold you back but fear!" Daly concluded with one of Liam's favorite expressions. Tommy laughed easily at the familiar adage from a man who had no conception of what fear was. "I'll go find Denis and Swede. We can go over everythin with 'em tonight, get packed, and be off in the mornin. Do you want me to get ahold of Terrance for the meetin, Daly?"

Daly shrugged, "I'll talk to Terrance later. He'll have to mop up things here in Michigan and keep it all goin so I can get away to Minnesota as soon as possible. See ya later, Tom. We got a hellava lot to get done and damn little time to do it." Daly turned toward Peter who was putting maps back in the box. "We'll need those tonight, son. By the way, where did you hide my tobacco this time? I need a pipe fill." Peter hated when his father smoked. He hated the terrible coughing it caused his pa.

"Bottom drawer, pa." He set the maps down, headed out the door after Tom Harney. Later he'd listen to what the men had to say about his pa's ideas.

Alone at his desk, Daly contemplated his sons' places in the ambitious plans that would be made. At twenty-one Terrance was the oldest. He was also the most remote and disinterested of the three boys. As different as Terrence was from each of them, he was the one son that Daly best understood. Terrance was his mother's child. Slight, fine-featured, and sandy-haired, Terrance reminded Daly of Kathleen in every physical aspect. But he lacked her willpower and optimistic spirit. He possessed a melancholy that distanced him from the people who were an integral part of Daly's world. A bright lad and better educated than the other men in the company, Terrance attended to technical projects competently. Yet, Daly knew, this son disliked loggers and logging. To Terrance, the family business was a job and nothing more than his present source of income.

Terrance, never 'Terry', kept an apartment in Marquette near the public library where he spent most of his time. His various company responsibilities included equipment and supply purchases, and maintenance and transportation routes. Since these could be done in town, it was convenient for him to be gone from camp most of the time.

Daly intimidated his oldest son. He knew that when he relaxed the reins, Terrance would bolt like a horse through an open gate, probably back to Warren and his mother. Daly also knew that time would not be too far off. He would let his son handle this phase-out of the Michigan operation, and not force him to follow the business to Northern Minnesota. Daly would unlatch the gate.

Denis was now a man of eighteen. The second son was tall, barrel-chested, and as powerful as a bull. He was also short tempered. Denis was happiest when working with the lumberjacks facing the physical rigors of hard work. Featured with Daly's snarly red hair, large ears, and keen blue eyes, this son was a mirror of his father more than the others. It was his father he sought to emulate in everything he did, and nothing in his life was more important than Daly's attention. But, Denis was not his father. He was unable to grasp matters quickly, and he needed constant direction. Denis avoided any responsibility that required making a decision, because a wrong decision brought disapproval. Denis believed that he might best impress his father by being a dedicated lumberjack. Therefore, hard work became his life's focus.

Daly often complimented his second son's tenacious, bull-like strength in cutting the timber that was the company's livelihood. He often brought attention to Denis' enthusiasm for pushing himself to get one job done and another started. Daly made Denis a foreman, hoping to encourage more supervisory skill, and reduce his time spent on routine logging activities. He tried to motivate Denis by involving him in the business aspects of company operations. Despite his effort, however, Denis was reluctant to attempt anything that required paperwork or numbers. Matters demanding reading and writing were too difficult for Denis.

Daly believed he could change this son. He planned to push Denis into areas of the business where he might have an opportunity to build some self-confidence. Daly would include Denis in the Minnesota venture, and would take him away from the winter timber harvest.

Just the thought of Peter always put a smile on Daly's ruddy, weathered face. He sat at his desk and contemplated his youngest son. His pipe was clenched in his teeth as he reached down for his tobacco. Peter had confessed to hiding the pouch in the bottom drawer. "That little rascal," he though to himself. "Not so little any more," he mused. Even at thirteen, Daly sensed that his youngest was incredibly bright, curious, and ambitious as well. Peter was his shadow, sometimes following, at other times, out in front of his father. Of the three, Daly already realized that this son was destined for bigger things than he might care to imagine.

Daly remembered an exchange about five years ago, when Peter was only eight. The teamsters were unloading logs from their huge sleds into a nearby river.

"Where they goin now, dad?" Peter asked as the logs rolled over the bank.

"They'll end up at a sawmill down river, son."

"What'll happen at a sawmill, pa?"

"The mill will cut the big logs into boards."

"What'll they do with the boards?"

Daly considered the many potentials then gave his son a simple answer. "Probably build houses, Peter."

"Why don't we build houses, pa? That'd be fun."

"Maybe we'll build us a house some day. Would ya like that?" Daly asked the boy.

Peter had a frown on his face. "Only one house, dad? I want us to build a whole town of houses. What d'a ya think about that idea?" Peter said in earnest. A picture of a city with many different houses formed in his mind.

Daly could not contain himself and broke out laughing at his son's ambitious thought.

"What's so funny, pa?" Peter was offended by the laugh.

Confounded, Daly could only say, "Nothin' son. I mean. . . ."

The boy looked up at his father with an expression as solemn as an eight year old can make. "Ain't nothin' funny about that! Why couldn't we do that? You and me, pa."

This conversation with his youngest son was the best frame a portrait of Peter could have. Daly wondered if this son would build a city of his own some day? Damned if he couldn't if he set his mind to it.

"Ya know, son, sometimes I think that these boots I'm wearin' right now won't be big enough to fit ya when you've grown up to be a man. 'Build a town', now if that don't beat all."

Huddled around a lantern, the four timber men worked deep into the chilly October night. Every assignment was discussed, clarified, and refined in detail. Denis Moran would travel to Duluth with Harney and catch the train from there to St. Paul. He would work with Ed McIntosh on the land purchases. "It's an important responsibility, Denis, but I know you can handle it." Swede Olson would set up an office for 'Moran Properties' in Duluth, and Tom Harney would locate a preliminary campsite near a place on the crude maps called Rock Lake. From that site, the logistics of rivers and lakes, linking the site to the Mississippi River seemed plausible. Down the great river, Little Falls and Minneapolis were already well-established sawmill towns.

Daly, however, was thinking much bigger this time. Sawmills made the big money. Maybe the time had finally arrived for Moran to have his own mill. Somewhere within the large circle he had drawn on the map, between Rock Lake and Swan River, Daly would build his most ambitious lumber operation ever. Harney would investigate any viable railroads in Northern Minnesota that they might connect with and report back to Daly. None were indicated on the maps they studied. "If we gotta do it ourselves, we'll build the damn railroads!" Daly said. "I ain't gonna wait for no one else to do it for me." This endeavor would be of a scale beyond anything he had attempted before.

"We're gonna put 'Moran and Sons' on the map, fellas." Daly's company would be in a position to market their own lumber, and, if they had to, they would run their product over their own rails. This venture would require precise timing, and greater upfront expenditure than anything Moran had ever imagined. Daly was convinced, nonetheless, he could afford anything but patience; patience at this time seemed far too expensive. The footprints of both his family, and the timber industry, had been an inexorable push west. Daly could envision an end to the pine forests. Between Minnesota and the Rockies, a vast, treeless plain had sprung to life. The market, the future, the fortune lay west! "Am I thinking big enough, and moving fast enough," he wondered. Daly's instincts had never failed him. Time was his enemy.

"There are no problems, only challenges, gentlemen. We're gonna make it big for once in our lives. I've got this feeling in my gut that I ain't never had before. This is our time! Now, all of you get a good night's sleep." He met every pair of eyes, "I'm gonna be right behind all of ya, soon as I can tie things up here. Good luck."

Daly shook hands with each of them at the door. These men, he knew in his heart, would break their ass for him.

Out of sight of the men, Peter watched with wide eyes from his perch on a box in the corner of the room. His head throbbed in excitement over what he heard.

"I know you're there, Peter," Daly said without looking up from a strew of papers. "Off to bed with ya now."

Peter stepped boldly into the glow of the lantern and faced his father. "Pa, I wanna go with Tom Harney to Minnesota. Please, sir . . ." Peter had never called his father 'sir' before. "I'm thirteen years old, sir, and you're gonna be going up there as soon as ya can. There's nothing here for me anymore. Minnesota's where I need to be, pa. I gotta go."

Daly regarded his son. He realized that his Minnesota venture would require one more decision. A decision he had not contemplated having to make.

September 1901

The century had turned. Moran and Sons Timber Company had become the largest owner-managed timber enterprise in Northern Minnesota. Among the many competitors for a foothold in the red earth of the Mesabi Iron Range, Moran and Sons was the first with a lath mill, rail network, and statewide markets. Moran's lumber was building communities across the Mesabi, supplying the expanding mining companies, and providing the heavy timber for the massive ore dock facilities at the Duluth-Superior harbor. The past decade had brought wealth beyond the comprehension for those men who had shared Daly's vision from the logging camp near Marquette.

Profound change had swept across the lengthy span of Mesabi. The once mighty white pine forests had been largely cut over with a careless abandon. In the wake of the ambitious lumbering was a far greater appetite for mining. Iron ore enterprises had stripped the landscape, dug canyons into the earth, and created mountains of the ore's overburden.

The ravaged earth yielded its red treasure. Lon Merritt from Duluth, along with his brothers and other astute disciples of mining, had been right about the awesome iron ore potentials of Northern Minnesota. With the advent of this new century, Mesabi's hematite ore had attracted entrepreneurs like John Rockefeller, Andrew Carnegie, and James J. Hill. By this time, J.P. Morgan had molded a formidable consolidation that would become the United States Steel Corporation. The headquarters of the Oliver Mining Company, the corporate giant which managed more than a hundred mine operations on the Iron Range, was located in Hibbing.

Daly and Denis stood at a third story window in their Hibbing building which faced the south side of Railroad Avenue, overlooking their enormous lumberyard below. The room was plush with extravagant oak furniture and soft, expensive, imported rugs. This office belonged to Peter and appealed to his taste for luxury.

"We're gonna miss Ed McIntosh." Daly coughed into his handkerchief, turned away from his son to hide traces of blood, and quickly stuffed it back in his trousers. "He was a true friend. What stories I could tell ya about Mac and me, and the 'good old days'. I feel just terrible about not getting down to Duluth for the funeral." His tired eyes were moist, his complexion ashen, and his shoulders stooped. Ed McIntosh, one of Daly's oldest friends had passed away from pneumonia the week before.

"By the time word got out to us in Warren, it was too late to get here." Spending more time with Kathleen in Pennsylvania, Daly had distanced himself from the hectic Hibbing lumber operations. His wife was a comfort, and his body was tired from too many hard years of work.

"I couldn't get there either, pa. I guess Peter was the only one of us Morans ta . . ."

The door swept open and Peter strode into the room. He wore a fashionable new gray suit, and highly-polished leather shoes. "Hello, pa, and welcome back to you, Denis. I've missed you both. Really sad about Ed, God rest his soul, but he'd been in a bad way for more than a year. It was a blessing though, he passed well enough I'm told. Jimmy's taking it pretty hard though." Peter's welcome and his condolences were expressed in one, swift and cursory breath. Jimmy McIntosh was Ed's son, and had become Peter's closest friend, as well as his business associate. "But life goes on! Right, Denis. We get over these bumps in the road and forge ahead." Peter gave his brother a heavy slap on the back. "Don't look so glum . . . you two. It's a beautiful day. Look at that stockpile of lumber out there."

Peter moved between the two men at the window, draped his arm over their shoulders, and gestured widely at the yards below. The sight was impressive. Beyond the stacks of fine yellow lumber were mounds of black coal. At Peter's insistence, the Morans had diversified their operations to include coal. With all of the money he could accumulate, Peter had made shrewd investments in real estate and liquor distribution. Brash and forceful, he had made the name of Peter Moran synonymous with power in this town.

"Just look at it all, and I've got contracts for every stick of that pine. We'll make three thousand by the end of the week on lumber and another couple on the coal. Life is good. We're prospering!" Peter beamed boastfully. "Now, let's all sit down, have a drink, and catch up on things. What do ya think about some Irish whiskey?"

Denis had returned from Oregon the night before and Daly from Pennsylvania on Friday's train from Duluth.

"What do the traveling Morans have to say?" Peter dragged two chairs from against the wall and set them in the center of the room. He brought his own heavy mahogany captain's chair to a place between them. It appeared this was Peter's meeting, Peter's agenda. His aura dominated the room.

Peter went to the sideboard, set out crystal glasses, and splashed fine Irish whiskey over ice. "Come and get 'em," Peter beckoned his visitors to join him.

Denis and Daly turned from the window, accepted their glass of spirits, and sat down on either side of Peter. Despite Peter's show of hospitality, tension could be tasted in the space of the room. The whiskey was unlikely to take any edge off the estrangement that had developed among the Moran men over the past year. The pace in Hibbing which completely energized Peter was a weight on the spirit of the other two men.

"How's mother? Emily? Terrance? I haven't heard from any of them in months. I'm so damn busy here that I can't even find time to write them a letter." Peter sought to lighten things up. He'd start with family small talk before getting down to business. Peter hated small talk. "Cheers!" he toasted. His gaze focused on his father. He felt a sense of remorse about Daly. Life had changed his father and himself in ways that were likely never to be undone. Both of the men knew this to be true but left the matter largely unspoken.

Daly was nearing sixty years, but looked older. He knew better than his sons did that his health had greatly deteriorated. Doctor Hane had diagnosed emphysema three years earlier. Daly's looks, however, were deceiving. The family patriarch had not lost his keen sense of perception. Peter was the power broker; even Denis realized that. But Daly was not ready to be put out to pasture. He longed for a place where he might fit more comfortably, a place where he might revitalize a spirit that still persevered below the surface of his advancing age and ill health. He did not fit in this opulent office, in this new lumber and coal business, nor in this prospering mining hub. He did not find satisfaction in what had now become Moran and Sons. Logging blood still pulsed in his veins. The lure of the outdoors with the boisterous activity of the lumber camps, his life's spirit until recent years, still held an attraction for Daly Moran. These were places where he might reside more comfortably. Daly could not believe or accept that this place was the end of the line for him.

"Your mother's doin' just fine. Kathleen ain't never gonna change." Daly showed his first spark. "Emily's gone and made us both grandparents; a nice enough looking little girl she had. Named the baby after your mother, too. And Terrance, well he's done pretty well for himself back there. He's got himself a college degree, something like literature if I remember rightly, and got himself a contract to teach some classes in a high school out by Philadelphia." Daly stroked the side of his clean shaven face, coughed deeply again, and cussed to himself. "Let's hear what Denis has to say. You've been out there in Oregon for what-two months, son? And Tom, what in God's creation is going on with old Tom Harney these days?"

"Tom's doing good. Says to say hi to ya, pa," Denis blurted. "Don't want no part of Hibbing no more. He's 'bout as happy as a bear in honey out there in Oregon. Says that's where he's going to take his big nap when the time comes."

Denis leaned forward in his chair toward his father and away from his brother. "Pa, I gotta get you out there. Tom's dying to see ya. The place is just . . . I don't have the words to describe it."

"Green or maybe beautiful? How about fantastic?" Peter chided his brother with his sarcasm. Denis was neither bright nor well spoken, and Peter always brought attention to that reality.

"All that, Peter, and lots more. I just don't have the words, ya know. But I'd go back out there quicker'n a dog's flea, I tell ya."

"Then why don't you go, both of you for that matter? I can get along fine here. Jimmy and me got a pretty good handle on things. You guys ought to take a little vacation, catch up on things with Tom Harney, and get some fresh Oregon air."

"I think your brother's talking about going out there for good, Peter. And, you're right. We're not really needed here these days. Might be much better for my health out there, too."

Daly realized long before sending Denis out west that one last move might prolong his life by a few years. This hellish place belonged to Peter. It was Peter's ambition, more than anything else, that had made them all wealthy men. Peter thrived on the competition far more than even Daly had when he was younger. It seemed Peter had the touch to turn everything into gold. And Peter did not make mistakes that could be fatal in these times.

Daly reflected on the meeting with Ed McIntosh in Duluth, Minnesota, twelve years before. Mac had lined up 20,000 acres of virgin pine in the Rock Lake area and had pleaded with Daly to spend the extra money to get the mineral rights to all that land. Daly had balked at the idea. "I'm a lumber man, always have been, and that's all I'm ever gonna be," he told Mac. "You can speculate on them minerals with your own money. I'll be damn willing to bet, you'll go broke in the process, Ed." The senior Moran would never forget that mistake and its financial consequences. Daly Moran might have been as rich as Rockefeller if he had taken the advice. Besides Ed McIntosh, only Peter knew about Daly's foolish decision. Peter, however, never once mentioned it to his father.

"Yep, I think your old man's about ready, boys. One last shot as they say. Denis, do ya think we can make us a few bucks out there?" Daly put a hand on Denis' shoulder and raised a broad smile in his son.

Denis' thoughts were swept with lightheaded emotion. "Pa wants to go out west with me, only me and not Peter!" He stammered his elation over Daly's suggestion. "No doubt about that, dad, like you always said when I was a kid, 'can't let nothin hold ya back but fear', remember? We ain't afraid of nothin, are we, pa? We're Morans, and Oregon ain't seen nothin 'til us Morans get there. Ya told us once that everythin's west." Denis found his words exhilarating and looked to Daly for approval.

Daly stiffened in his chair. Now was the time he dreaded. A time he had put off for much too long. He looked from son to son, allowing a pause from all the words that had been said and unsaid. Pulling himself out of the chair and stuffing his hands in his trouser pockets, he began pacing across the room. Pausing pensively, Daly gazed outside. Pacing back toward his sons, he circled behind them, before returning to the window.

Whenever Daly paced, he was agitated by something, and both brothers knew that well. As he walked about the room, no one spoke. Daly turned from the window and sat against the lower ledge. Behind him, the brightness of the afternoon became a radiant frame. He presented a surreal image to his sons. From their perspective, he appeared much larger evoking an unnerving sensation.

Without realizing the impact of his words, Denis gave Daly's tired spirit a spurt of resolve. "Thanks for reminding me, Denis. Yes, I do remember that Daly Moran from back then. I still remember what he said, and what he believed in. I been thinkin more and more about the way things use'ta be. I remember sending you off to St. Paul to work with old Ed McIntosh. I can recall Ed telling me that you were never gonna be a businessman. 'Let him cut down your damn trees, Daly!' is what he told me." A smile creased his face at the memory.

"And that's what you did, Denis, lots of trees have gone down with your ax over the years. I'm proud of you, son, for all that hard work and devotion.

"And, Peter. Peter, my ambitious one." Daly's eyes were moist, but from his place by the window he knew that his youngest son could not see his tears. Daly looked across the space of years that had passed between them. So vivid was his memory of the boy at his side in a Michigan forest one October morning, that he could almost smell the scent of pine in the air again. His son once loved those trees as much as his father. Success, it seemed, had dulled Peter's appreciation of family roots.

And, how could he forget the eight-year old boy at his side on the river bank- the son who wanted to build himself a city. Where had father and son lost each other?

"I didn't even think to ask if you wanted to come along to Oregon, Peter. I'm sorry for that. I just assumed, I guess, that you really wanted to do things here by yourself."

Daly swallowed hard, retrieving his hankie. "But, to be as honest as I know how to be, I didn't ask you to come because I didn't want you along. You left me to come here with Tom Harney when you were what? Thirteen? It hurt me some to let you go, but if I held you back, you might never have forgiven me. Now it's my turn to go and leave you behind." Daly caught Peter's eyes across the space between them. They were cold, distant eyes. He turned away for a moment composing himself.

Peter felt the rising tightness in this throat. The man towering over the room from the window had been his sole role model. The very clay of his essence had been shaped by this once forceful man. Daly's ambition stirred him as a boy, and it was Daly's 'don't hold back' confidence that pulsed in his veins now.

In a voice unnaturally strained, Peter spoke: "You've got that right, sir. I'm staying here where I belong. I'm building a town like I always wanted to do." He would not allow himself any tears. "You and me . . . sir." Respect of this man would always be the essence of who he was. "You and me can work out something that is fair and square. I want 'Moran and Sons' for myself." Peter paused before completing the thought. "Leaving me behind is the way I want it too, pa . . . more than anything!"

Peter rose from the chair smoothing the wrinkles from his imported silk suit coat. He stepped in Daly's direction with his hand extended. "No hard feelings?" His confidence and composure were back. With their understanding, father and son had become equals.

Daly reluctantly accepted his son's handshake. He was insulted by the disrespectful tone of Peter's candid proposition but kept his shoulders square, head high. As his eyes met those of his son, he was struck by a realization stabbing deeply into his heart. When he left Hibbing, his eyes would probably never behold this son again, and his arms would never embrace him. Daly could not restrain the impulse to hug his son one last time.

"You work something out, Peter. 'Fair and square' as you say. Send whatever might be my share from all of this to your mother in Pennsylvania. Keep the Moran and Sons name if you wish, and rest assured there are no hard feelings!" Daly left the room followed by a dumbfounded Denis. Astonished, but feeling a sense of incredible satisfaction, Denis had his father—Peter had his town.

Over the following weeks, Peter carefully dismantled Moran and Sons. He sold his coal interests to the Remington Company and invested the profits in his liquor distribution operations. In the letter outlining a final settlement to Kathleen Moran, Jimmy McIntosh explained every detail in precise legalese. Every member of Peter's family was given an equal share of the Moran holdings.

Peter Moran was now unencumbered of any family obligations and free to begin building a dominion of his own. His credo, which would serve him well in the years to come was: Timing is everything; know the weakness of your adversaries; everybody has a price; and ethics are situational. Timing was on the top of his list. Peter had learned that back in Marquette from the father he had both respected and rejected.

Over the next few years, a new empire would be forged in the boom town of Hibbing by the firebrand who was Peter Moran.

'The Bella of Campania'

April 1904

The myth of an America with 'shores of gold' seemed most believable in the Campania countryside of Southern Italy. The pervasive poverty of the region was powerful motivation for peasant farmers to leave their agrarian villages and seek a land of far greater promise. By the thousands they left with inspired dreams of a new life, good paying jobs, and an abundance of good fortune.

Piedimonte was a tiny village nestled below the gently rolling Matese Mountains of the Campanian Appennines. A few kilometers south of the village and a short walk off a narrow road was the small farm of Angelo and Justina Bellani.

"It is such wonderful news!" Justina said as she kneaded the lump of thick bread dough on the table. "I want to laugh in my joy, and to cry at the very same time," she sniffled. "Truly, our prayers have found heaven, Angie."

Justina's emotion was triggered by her lifelong friend and neighbor, Lucia Depelo. Lucia would be making passage to America in two weeks.

"Lucia has been almost two years without her husband, and at long last, they'll be together again." The small-boned woman brushed her eyes with the back of her hand leaving traces of flour on her brow. "We'll surely miss her. When will it all end? So many of our friends have left Piedimonte in the past few years. "

Short and thickset, Angelo turned his wife toward himself, gave her a kiss on the forehead, and gently dabbed the smudge of flour. He remembered his pain when John Depelo had left. "There is nothing here anymore, Justina. If we were younger, I believe we might think about going to America ourselves. Anyway, we must go over to visit Lucia this very day, and offer her any help that we can give," Angelo said. He gave his wife a hug, while a smile creased his sun-weathered face. "She'll have the latest news from John. He's already purchased a house I've been told. What a wonderful place it must be, that America. In Italy, we must wait for our father to die before we can own a home of our own."

"I wonder who'll be the next to leave this place?" Angie asked his wife. "Maybe young David Malero." David had an older brother. Only the first born son had a future in the rural Campania. A man's oldest son would inherit his land, and with that land came the prospect of marriage. "These are difficult times, but it's surely God's will that things happen as they do. One day your tears will be shed over one of our own sons, Justina. Now, I must leave you alone with your thoughts; please make them happy ones, and pray for my work of this morning."

At the narrow doorway, Angelo bumped into four year old, Georgi, who was rushing into the kitchen. "Papa, where's Mary?" the boy panted. "She promised to take me with her this morning."

"Must I remind you, son, when your big sister goes to visit with Mrs. Samora she's too busy to be bothered by a little brother. Besides, Viola is teaching Mary her skills of sewing. Now, off with you before I find some chores to keep you busy," he chided playfully.

At seventeen, Mary was the oldest of the seven Bellani children. Her younger siblings were constant rivals for her time and attention. More fair complected than her parents, Mary's dark brown hair fell in springy curls over her delicate shoulders. From her mother she inherited wide oval eyes, high cheek bones, and a full mouth. Just as her physical beauty came from Justina, her confident, easy temperament, and animated smile, were from Angelo. Mary's loveliness was both inside and out. To those of tiny Piedimonte, she was 'Bella', the beautiful one.

No one dreamed brighter dreams than young Mary Bellani. In her mind and heart, life held only wondrous promise. Her spirits were filled with buoyant hopes this beautiful April morning. She was a woman in love. The man of her affection was Michael Samora. Today, for the very first time, Mary's romantic fantasy of being with her beloved man, held a glimmer of possibility.

Mary hastened along the narrow pathway through the date groves which lined the sun baked hillside between the Bellani and Samora farmsteads. She would have her morning sewing lesson with Viola Samora and an opportunity to share something so very exciting it made her heart leap. In her elation, she nearly stumbled into the sewing room behind the small kitchen of the widow Samora's house.

"Mama Samora," she called into the room, short of breath from the run and the excitement. "Do you know what day this is?"

Viola Samora was a seamstress of wide reputation throughout the Campania. Her unique artistry had been passed down from Samora women before her, and she was determined to assure the tradition would be preserved. The widow did not have a daughter of her own so was delighted to have Mary call her 'Mama'. For nearly two years Viola had taught Mary the delicate intricacies of her craft. She was convinced there was not much more which the lovely girl might learn from her. Mary was not only diligent in every detail of sewing, but also a delight for Viola to visit with every morning. "My goodness, child, your face is flushed. Give mama a hug, then sit down and catch your breath."

Mary was especially radiant this morning. She hugged the fragile, grayhaired woman, whom she loved as dearly as her own mother. "Mama Samora, do you know what day this is?" She blurted her enthusiasm.

Viola kissed Mary on her cheek and met the twinkle in her eyes with a knowing smile of her own. "Yes, my dear one, I know what day this is. Let me see. On my calendar it is the ninth day of April." She put aside the fabric on her lap, and gave Mary a puzzled expression. "Could this be someone's birthday?"

"Oh, you tease me so. How can you pretend not to remember?"

"I know, my bella." Viola said with understanding affection. "It is my Michael's birthday today."

Viola's only son, Michael Samora, had left Piedimonte more than two years ago. Both she and Mary remembered that March day with a sadness that was often shared in their daily conversations. Neither woman had heard very much about his new life in a place called Minnesota in America. Michael had not written any letters home for nearly a year. "I hope his day brings him a special happiness. I worry and I pray for my son. Why does he not write and tell us how he is doing?" Viola lamented. "Do you know what birthday this is for my Michael? Can you remember Mary Bellani?"

"Your son is now twenty two," Mary beamed affectionately. "About the proper age to be taking himself a wife don't you agree, Mama?"

Viola could not conceal her laugh at Mary's unveiled question. "Yes, you may be speaking the truth about that. Perhaps my Michael should be giving some thought to having a family of his own in that place called Hibbing in Minnesota. I only hope that it's not too cold there for people to make babies. What do you think?"

Mary grinned at Viola's shameless question, "Too cold, I cannot believe that. All that any man would need is a good warm-blooded Italian woman, and I know just the one for Michael. We would have many children, mama." Mary was emphatic.

"Let's get to our work, Mary, we can talk about this son of mine while we sew. I have a feeling that there is much more on your mind this morning. It's more than Michael's birthday that brings such a glow to your eyes. Am I right about that, my bella?"

"Can I not hide any secrets from you? Yes, there is news that has kept me from sleep for the past two nights, Mama Samora. Have you heard about Mrs. Depelo from the village? It's so exciting. She'll be going to America soon to join her husband John. Mr. Depelo is also in Minnesota, you know." Mary exclaimed. "Lucia will be going to a place that is very near to where Michael lives in Hibbing."

"That is true enough. I was told of Lucia's good fortune only yesterday. John has sent enough money to finally make her travel possible, and he's got a house for them to live in. I'm so happy for her, and for John as well," Viola said as she stitched a hem on the cotton apron she was making for Lucia Depelo.

During the separation of Lucia and John, all the neighbors had shared in Lucia's loneliness and helped her with her savings.

"I want to go with her! I must!" Mary gushed. "Oh, Mama Samora, you know how it has been my dream for so long. I must join your Michael. My heart tells me this is the time to go. I just cannot wait and hope that he might come back here some day. You do understand, don't you? It is as if from heaven, this marvelous opportunity. If only, if only Lucia could take me with her."

"We will see what can be done," Viola said. Returning her attention to the work in her lap she began humming softly, allowing a smile to rest within the wrinkles of her kindly face. Anticipating this time would come, Viola resolved to support the girl who had become like her own daughter. "Yes, my dear, I will speak of this proposal to your parents."

Before leaving Viola for her chores back home, Mary let her emotion flow. "Thank you with all my heart!" she sobbed on Viola's shoulder. "I love you so. Please do all that you can do. My mama will listen to you like no one else in the world."

Viola stroked Mary's long soft curls. "Be hopeful, my dearest. I will write to Michael as soon as we know that your plans are certain. I will visit with Mrs. Depelo later this day."

Michael Samora did not remember that this April day was his birthday. The dark, narrow-faced man limped along, behind the long oak bar. Amidst the boisterous revelry of drinking miners, he mopped spilled beer and the red grime from miners' boots which caked on the wooden floors. Michael despised his job in the tavern, shunned the swarthy patrons, and cursed his fate with every breath. Only the dim hope of another job, perhaps in the liquor warehouse, kept him working in this despicable place. He wanted desperately to get away from the stares of people who gawked at his limp and made jokes about him when his back was turned.

Michael wore the constant, anguished expression as he wore the filthy shirt on his back. He often winced from the pain that shot like fire from his hips down into his legs. He dragged his right foot to the bucket, pushed it feebly in front of him, and rubbed a bead of sweat from his eye. This Saturday afternoon in Moran's Red Rock Tavern was another reminder that hell was for the living as well as for the damned.

This month marked the second year of Michael's new life in the tumultuous mine town of Hibbing. Two damnable years! The course of his misfortunes had aged him well beyond his years. The melancholy of his present circumstance had brought a premature gray to the temples of his once raven hair. Excruciating pain had etched deep furrows into his once handsome face. Michael's eyes, once bright with optimism before his accident, were dulled by his dark and pervasive pessimism. His posture, bent from the shoulders, stole inches from the height of his youth. His limp would never be corrected. Michael Samora was a wretchedly self conscious man consumed by a loathing of his life.

Within days of his arrival in this red-streeted ore mining town, in April of 1902, Michael found a job without difficulty at the Sellers Mine. As a laborer, he thrived on the hard work, and delighted in any job that brought him around the mammoth steam-powered shovels. This was a dangerous place to work requiring constant alertness for the ore cars that rolled in and out from the noisy digging pockets of the ore body. Yet, the more he worked on the narrow gauged railroad tracks around the shovel, the greater was his desire to one day become an operator of the mighty machine that hovered above him.

Riley Gillespie was an Irishman, and a master shovel-runner. His experienced precision in shaping, digging, and loading the red ore made him one of the key people in the Sellers Mine. Michael Samora aspired to be as good as Riley some day. If he worked hard, listened, and learned, then he might make it through the progression required to become a 'runner' himself. He watched the 'craner' riding high up on the incredible boom, as the man working the pulley motors tripped the bucket loads into the cars awaiting the load below. He observed with envy, the fireman, stoking the huge boilers which enabled the Bucyrus-Erie shovel to bite deeply into the rich banks of blasted ore fragments. Michael's infatuation with the steam powered shovel consumed him, inspiring his determination to befriend the much idolized, Riley Gillespie.

One day, in the third month of his work in the pit, Michael hung around the dry house, and found an opportunity to introduce himself to Riley. "I'm Michael Samora from the crew below your shovel." He was one of ten or twelve men involved in the crew activity, and thought Riley might recognize him.

"What d'ya do, young man?" asked the barrel-chested Irishman.

"Just about everythin', sir. I'm haulin coal, and settin water pipes, but usually I'm one of the guys trimmin the cars 'round your shovel."

"And itchin to be up where I am, I'll betcha." Riley knew well that his job was the envy of most pit miners.

"Oh, yessir, very much, sir." His eyes widened at the idea.

"Well, I'll be lookin for ya on the job, now that I know who ya are. Remember to be careful down there, cuz there's times when a shovel runner can't see you guys very well."

From that day on, Michael sought out Gillespie at every opportunity riddling him with questions about the mechanics of the awesome machine. "How do you do that?", "What happens when?", "Why does . . . ?" Riley provided the young man with thoughtful, sometimes technical answers.

Gillespie, taking an easy liking to the 'Dago kid', brought him up into the shovel runner's compartment late one afternoon. Although a serious breach of safety, Riley always did as he damn well pleased. From this incredible vantage above the ore piles, Michael could watch the master at work.

"So, what d'ya think about all this?" Riley questioned while operating the sticks before him and centering the heavy bucket over an ore car.

Michael shook his head in wide-eyed incredulity. "It's very . . . very good!" He was often embarrassed by his broken English, but too enthralled with the moment for any inhibition. "You are very good too, sir." Michael's smile was contagious.

Riley laughed at the compliment and the affection it carried. "Just takes practice, kid. Takes a lotta practice to do it right."

That day was the experience of his lifetime adding a new dimension to the fire that was his resolve to one day be like the big Irishman who was the 'King' of the mine!

In the late fall, only a week before the winter shutdown, Michael was cleaning ore spillage from around the rails in front of Riley's shovel. The huge mound of ore to the right of where he was working had been deeply undercut from an hour of rigorous digging. Michael, noticing the ominous overhang of rocky ore, realized from experience that it was highly dangerous to work below it.

His spade dug into the last scoop of residual ore when the overhung bank loosened, roared, and then caved.

The avalanche of dirt was instantaneous! Michael stumbled away toward the safety of the shovel, but the heavy bank caught him in his second step, and threw him with deadly impact onto the iron rails. His startled scream was smothered in the heavy groan of the crushing slide. The instant plunge of tons of ore pressed its weight over most of his body. Only Michael's head and shoulders found cover under Riley's shovel bucket which was suspended between him and the bank. Michael was knocked unconscious.

The avalanche should have buried Michael alive. Spared a horrible death, his body was freed from tons of rock and dirt by several frantic pit laborers who had witnessed the ugly scene. Michael's legs were badly fractured, his hip dislocated, and the bottom half of his body a twisted aberration.

"You're a lucky young man," said Ambrose Hane, a skilled surgeon at the Rood Hospital.

"We've done about all that we can do. The rest is up to you. It will take some time for sure, but you will be able to walk again."

"They won't work, doctor. I ain't got no feeling from here down." Michael ran his hands along his hips, down over his thighs, toward his knees.

"Most of it will come back. You'll be able to feel some sensation and to walk again as well. Believe me. More importantly, believe in yourself, Michael. It'll be as much your attitude as it will be anything else. Despite all of your injuries, you can walk again."

"Walk where, and what for? I'm half dead, doctor. I'm lucky you say; well, I ain't feelin lucky."

"The only thing that is half dead is that kind of thinking, young man. As your doctor I'll tolerate none of that." Hane was red faced at his dispirited patient. "You have three choices; you walk, find someone who will carry you, or spend a miserable life on your back. It's that simple."

Michael's eyes narrowed at the surgeon. An anger seethed in him. "No one's gonna carry me nowhere."

"That's more like it. Get as damned mad as you have to, but make up your mind right now that you've only got one choice."

Doctor Hane had not been totally forthright with Michael. Hane could tell from his examinations that the young man would never be able to have children. He knew that any mention of impotence would only diminish Michael's resolve to accomplish the demanding physical treatment he had prescribed.

Through many months of confinement at the Rood Hospital, Michael worked without enthusiasm at this therapy. It was an agonizing process, and although his body gradually responded, his mind was poisoned with hatred of his infirmity. More often than not, he wished his fate had allowed him to die.

The following summer he was able to walk without the aid of crutches and began looking for employment. There were no jobs for a cripple in the mines. No hope that Michael would ever operate a shovel.

He considered returning to the Campania but was repulsed by the notion of a dependency on his mother. No one from home must ever see him in this debilitated condition. He had no savings, no confidence, and no aspirations. He would always be only half of a man. Michael's only resolve was to stay in Hibbing, despite the dismal prospect of ever finding fulfillment. Michael Samora was an immigrant Italian, stranded in a place where few, except those who spoke English, could secure decent non-mining jobs.

Riley Gillespie had witnessed the tragedy at the Seller's Mine, and during the months afterwards, frequently visited the Rood Hospital. The shovel runner felt a sense of responsibility for the accident. Riley had shaped the dangerous bank while pushing for a high production of ore tonnage that day. "You're comin' along fine, kid," he said encouragingly on every visit. "We're gonna find you a job when you get outta here. Just leave it up ta old Riley."

Riley tried desperately to find Michael a clerical job in the Oliver Iron Mining Company office but to no avail. His young friend was, in company judgment, too disabled for any employment.

Late one summer evening, when all was bitterly hopeless, Michael's depression brought him to the brink of suicide. Despite a long bout of heavy drinking, he was lucid enough to know what he wanted to do. The object of his glum contemplation lay on the table. The knife's blade reflected in the flickering lantern beside it. He sat with his wrist upraised from his elbow, overwhelmed by the meaningless life that pulsed in his veins. His death would be nobody's loss. His fingers curled around the handle of the knife.

Excited to share his news, Riley burst into Michael's boarding house room without knocking. Their eyes locked momentarily, but Riley understood the scene with painful clarity.

"I've found ya a job, kid!" Riley's words broke through the sinister silence. "Ya start next Monday morning. I'll come by and take ya there about eight." When Riley left the room, Michael pushed the knife aside and cried shamelessly.

Peter Moran owned the Red Rock Tavern on the corner of Cedar Street and Second Avenue in Hibbing's bustling downtown district. Riley, a fellow Irishman, was a longtime friend of Moran's. Peter had agreed to give the Samora kid a chance. It wasn't much of a job, he confided to Riley, but it was better than nothing. Samora would be the saloon's janitor, and if everything worked out, Moran promised to find Michael something that paid better in one of his many Hibbing warehouses.

"Yes, sir, I do wanna work." Michael assured Moran at their first meeting in the tavern that Monday morning.

"You're going to get your ass here every morning on time? I don't have any use for employees who aren't grateful for the opportunity to work. Do you understand that, Samora?"

Michael was caught off guard by the intimidating and aloof man, dressed in the fine clothing of wealth. Mr. Moran was both unfriendly and aggressive. "Yessir, I'm grateful." He nodded, and tried to make his broken frame as erect as was possible.

"It's only for Gillespie's sake, you know. I don't have many of your kind in my tavern. The 'Dagos' have their own places to drink, and this isn't one of them. Understand? Don't let me down, and don't make Riley regret asking me for this favor."

Riley was unsettled by Moran's references. He sensed the owner had some deep prejudice toward Italians or cripples. He could empathize with the anger in Michael's dark, brooding, deep-set eyes. "Do the best ya can, kid," Riley said giving him a handshake. "Remember if things work out you'll get somethin better'n this."

On this April Saturday, Michael had been working twelve hour days for nearly eight months. He had made no friends. Each night, in the seclusion of his small, unkempt room, he drank straight from his bottle of whiskey. He never drank so much that it might jeopardize his job but always enough to ensure him a serene oblivion.

Every tie with relatives and friends back home in Piedimonte had long since been severed. Viola's letters were rarely read and never answered. Mary's letters, once an inspiration, were also stuffed in a box he stored beneath his bed. If only he had not come to this terrible place. What might have been? Beautiful, cheerful, and vivacious Mary Bellani would have been his woman. The very thought of her, now that he had been destroyed, brought only anguish. He had written to her often before his accident. That was during a time, however, when his life held the glimmer of optimism.

Mary Bellani, like every other dream, was only a brief respite from the cold realities of his present life. She must never know. No one from Piedimonte must ever know of his misfortunes in America. To insulate himself from betrayal of his dark secret, Michael was careful to avoid any social situation where his countrymen might be found. Such was the circumstance of Michael Samora on the anniversary of his twenty-second year of life.

Angelo Bellani bowed his head for his family's mealtime prayers of thanksgiving. After their father, each of the nine at his table would offer a small blessing that was appropriate to their day.

Mary held her breath as each prayer was spoken. After her sister Theresa thanked the Virgin Mother for giving them Jesus, Mary blurted her own prayer of gratitude. "Thank you, God, for Lucia Depelo's good fortune at this time. You will soon bring her family back together in America. It is my prayer this evening that I may be able to travel with her."

After the last prayer and Angelo's "Amen," there was an unusual quiet at the table. Although it was understood that the children were to be silent during mealtime, Mary's prayer brought wide eyes to the faces of her siblings. Mary interrupted the quietude.

"Father, I implore with all my heart for your approval. I have no future in Piedimonte." Mary's eyes were moist, and she turned to her mother. "Can you possibly understand how I feel, mama?"

Angelo and Justina were already prepared for their daughter's appeal. Word about what was happening around the village traveled rapidly from one mouth to another's ears. The parents had learned about Viola Samora's visit with Lucia Depelo, and of Mary's visit with Lucia as well. Angelo realized that one of his children would ask for his permission one day. Both he and Justina had believed that the first of their children to leave would be a son. Nearly every family in the Campania had given of its flesh to some distant place in the many corners of America.

Angelo sent an understanding smile toward the daughter he so loved and would be so dearly missed. He would not refuse her request. Mary was seventeen and fully deserved this opportunity to begin a life of her own. Her father, however, held his approval in his thoughts for the moment.

"Tell me more of all this, Mary. Why is it that you want so much to go to America?" Angelo could have answered this himself.

"Papa, I have talked with Mrs. Depelo. She would very much like to have another adult to travel with her." Mary gave emphasis to 'adult', then continued. "I would be able to help her with young Armando. Lucia has a little extra money to help me, and I've been frugal all these years. I've saved almost eighteen dollars," she announced proudly.

Justina, sobbing, dabbed at her tears with a linen napkin. "Mary, my dearest, your father and I have talked about this many times these past few days. Last night, Viola and your Uncle Marco were here to visit with us about your going to America. We all know how important this is to you, and we discussed the money that would be needed for such a journey."

Angelo cleared his throat. His children sat in silent anticipation of what their father was about to say. Theresa, sitting in the chair next to Mary, squeezed her sister's knee under the table.

"May I say another prayer?" Angelo had everyone's rapt attention. "Dear God in heaven, we have been so blessed with this daughter, Mary, and thank you for allowing us to have her with us for all these years. Now, we pray that You will go with her as she leaves us. Bless her always with the happiness she deserves. Amen."

Mary could not contain her joy, and wanted to rush from her chair to give her father a hug. "Thank you, papa, for your prayer, and for your approval. I *will* find happiness in America."

Angelo got up from the table and stepping behind his wife gently kissed the top of her head. He looked at his oldest daughter, "We have borrowed ten dollars against our crop this year. It will be yours, Mary. Uncle Marco, who has always been so generous with our family, has promised to match that amount. Money should not be a problem, and the 'Nulla Osta' authorizing your travel will be sanctioned by the village magistrate," he said. "You have our blessing."

"One matter has not yet been discussed." Justina's eyes caught those of her husband, and there was a tease in her voice. "What of this Michael Samora, Mary?"

All heads at the table turned to Mary. She flushed nervously while her sister Theresa giggled. "I don't know." Mary stammered, "Mrs. Samora has written to Michael telling him that I 'might' be coming to Minnesota, but I don't know what will happen once I get there."

"Has there been any talk of marriage?" Justina asked. She had been aware of her daughter's affection for the neighbor boy long before Viola had confirmed it.

"No, Mama, there has not been. But, I promise both you and papa, if Michael will have me, I will get married as soon as that is possible. I love him very much."

"Then marry him, my dear. Viola has a special gift for you to take along. Something she has sewn herself for a very special occasion. She has it already packaged for you," said Justina.

That evening Mary and her parents were up late talking about America, Minnesota, and the boy who once lived in the house beyond the date trees. They would have only one more week together before Mary's departure to America.

On April 24, 1904, Mary Bellani said her last goodbyes. She would leave her native Italy a girl of seventeen, and arrive in Minnesota three weeks later, a woman of seventeen. Her strength and unwavering optimism inspired her friend Lucia, and enabled the weaker woman to withstand the hardships of their long journey.

'TRAINS OF INNOCENTS'

December 1907

Tony Zoretek was only eighteen, yet the last traces of youth had long since vanished from his face. Like other immigrants of his generation, maturity came swiftly and closed forever the brief chapter of adolescence. Tall, strapping, and ruggedly handsome, Tony believed that he was strong enough to deal with any adversity. He always had. The circumstances of this Sunday night in the solitude of his boarding house room overlooking South Street in Hibbing, Minnesota, however, gave him a sense of utter defeat. Both the time and place were grim realities that overwhelmed his confidence.

Sitting at the table, Tony fought his emotions. Outside, a swirling wind was whipping sharply, rattling the loosely fitted window panes. An icy draft was seeping around the heavily frosted frames, adding its dreary chill to the sparse room. The young man had never known a subzero cold like this December night. The gusting gale combined with minus thirty degree cold was a conspiracy which would freeze exposed flesh in seconds. The whirling drifts of snow howled across the dark lines of the railroad yard below his window warning people to stay inside.

Looking out the window and wringing his large hands together, he mumbled to himself, "I think this ice box has numbed me. Good God, even my thoughts are frozen."

Stronger men than Tony Zoretek might have been subdued by the misfortunes that had marked his life since his arrival in Hibbing several months before. But Tony was a survivor. He swallowed those feelings of defeat and the self pity that went with them. He would overcome the emotional turmoil of being homesick, alone in this despicable place, and estranged from all that was familiar.

Tonight he must write the letters that had been too long ignored. Christmas was only weeks away, and he would send his best regards to his family back in Slovenia. He would write to his mentor, Robert Jamison, as well. Tony contemplated the blank paper on the table before him. Once more he absently dipped his pen into the ink bottle. Droplets of blue spotted the white page, but the pen in his cold fingers felt awkward and reluctant. "I must tell them the truth. If I lie to my parents and friend, then I dishonor myself. More than anybody, they can understand my failures and my loneliness; they will love me even when I cannot love myself."

Tony, wrestling with what might be the first words, pushed away from the table. Combing his fingers through long dark hair and massaging the tightness behind his neck, he was struck with a sudden frustration. He kicked his wooden chair, sending it noisily across the floor and smashing against the wall. "Now, do you feel better, Tony?" He was able to laugh out loud at himself.

A wave of nostalgia reminded him of his youthful idealism only two years before in his village of Churile in the Slovenian hills. He remembered the first American he had ever met, and how that meeting had so inspired the journey his life had taken.

Tony met Robert Jamison in the small library of the village school he attended. Jamison, he learned, was a graduate student doing research on Balkan folklore for his degree in anthropology. The young man was small, delicately featured and had wispy, blond hair which he combed away from his high forehead. Outgoing and curious, Tony introduced himself, "I am Anton Zoretek. What is your name?" Jamison offered the tall youth his handshake. Tony puzzled at the gesture. "It's a custom in America to shake another's hand when meeting them," he said with a smile that was both disarming and contagious. "I am Robert Jamison, Anton. It's my pleasure to meet you. Will you join me?"

An instant friendship was born that afternoon. In the days that followed, Tony's thirst for learning about America became almost unquenchable.

The two men had an understanding which proved to be of mutual benefit. "I'll help you learn my language if you'll help me with my English," Tony proposed, and Jamison readily agreed.

"My uncle, Steven, has gone to a place in America, 'Manazzotta', I think. He has become an iron ore miner," Tony announced proudly.

"Minnesota?" asked Robert Jamison.

"Yes, that's it. Minnesota. Where is that place?" Tony asked.

"Well, Tony, let's look at my atlas again." Jamison pulled out the tattered book from his leather satchel on the floor. He opened to the colorful page of the United States.

"Now, where on this map did I show you the location of my university?" Jamison challenged the confident boy.

Tony quickly found New Jersey and put his finger on Princeton.

"Very good, now, " Jamison moved Tony's long finger across the page to Minnesota. "There it is. Can you see Minnesota? It's a great distance from Princeton and the ocean, isn't it?"

"Maybe a hundred miles?" Tony guessed.

Amused by his protege's miscalculation, Jamison only smiled. "Closer to a thousand miles, Tony. If you see Duluth here . . . yes, the United States is a very large country, don't you agree?"

Young Zoretek was bewildered by this place, America. The two of them spent hours together with the atlas of states, cities, rivers and mountains. Jamison told of American Presidents, important historical events, and geography. Young Zoretek was eager to learn about Mr. Teddy Roosevelt who was the leader of Jamison's huge country, and the most fascinating person Tony had ever studied. "You must tell me more about this Roosevelt, Robert. Maybe after I help you with some of your own studies," Tony said.

Tony helped Jamison with stories which he had learned about the time of the Turks and French in Slovenia, the Haiduk robbers, tobacco smugglers, and the rich tales of ghosts, gypsies, and magicians from his childhood folklore.

Tony thoroughly enjoyed school and excelled in his studies. The months he spent with Robert Jamison enriched everything he learned and swelled his resolve to see that fascinating America some day. Jamison, to Tony's dismay, had to move on to Zagreb in nearby Croatia to further his research.

The American student, however, gave his promise to visit Tony whenever he could find the time. Jamison kept his promise and visited Tony in Churile on several occasions.

"Thank God he's gone from here," grumbled Jakob Zoretek, Tony's father after Jamison's departure. "All that time you two wasted with those books. You've been most negligent in the chores of our farm, son. Books are for noblemen who've got nothing else to do. They're not meant for farmers like us," Jakob reproached.

Tony would not be discouraged by his father's reprimand, nor would he accept such reasoning. He gave more attention to his tasks in the field but continued to spend stolen hours with the books stored in the trunk near his bed. Jamison had left him a copy of Whitman's *Leaves of Grass*, and Tony was memorizing the lines of prose in English.

When the eve of his eighteenth birthday arrived in June, Tony asked his mother and father to stay up later than was usual for them. He had finished his schooling and was restless. "I have some very important things that I must talk with you about," he implored.

But, to his surprise, there were to be no surprises about what Tony wanted his parents to know. Tony was the middle son of Jakob and Helen. The reality that his older brother, Jake, would be heir to the family farm made their talk inevitable. Although Tony had requested the conversation, it was his father who initiated the strained dialogue.

"As you know, my son," his father spoke with an even voice, "some important decisions must be made. Your brother, Jake, has my name, and my property is his birthright. With God's blessing, this farm could provide for you, and for your younger brother, Rudolf. Our land has done so for seven generations. But these times are not good."

Tensions smoldered among the Austro-Hungarian states. Churile offered few opportunities, and agriculture held only marginal promise for those few who possessed land. Jakob did not have to explain the two options for his son: military conscription in a hopeless war or poverty. Every father in Slovenia was obligated to have this kind of conversation when his son reached the age of conscription. "Father, I have a confession to make to you and to you, mother," Tony said. "I've written twice to Uncle Steven in Minnesota. I have here a letter from my uncle that came only three days ago." He passed the envelope to his mother. Steven Skorich was Helen's younger brother.

"As you will read, there are jobs, many jobs with good pay in the iron ore mines there. Uncle Steven will take care of me and will send some money for my travel if . . ." Tony swallowed hard, "if you'll give me your blessing to go. I want very much to travel to America and to make a success with this life you have given me."

With the early June sunshine on his back, Tony walked up the hillside trail away from the farm and never looked back. He sensed with every step that these would be the last ones on this native soil. There were no tears, only confidence in the dark eyes fixed surely on the road ahead. He would lug his book-laden travel case on his back for twenty hours, through the pleasantly cool night, to Novo Mesto and would catch the mail coach that went from there to Videm. For the first time in his life, Tony would travel beyond the borders of Slovenia.

The creak of the opening door jarred Tony back into the cold reality of his room.

"Is everything all right, Tony?" It was the familiar voice of his friend, roommate, and fellow countryman, Lud Jaksa.

"I heard a racket." Lud noticed the overturned chair. "I wondered what was goin on upstairs." Lud had been on the floor below drinking beer with some of the other miners. The noise above them had caused the men to think that there might be another fight going on. With the rampant drinking on Sundays, it was not uncommon for fist fights to break out among the un-ruly miners. Sadie Dukich, the landlady of the boarding house, allowed liquor to be sold illegally from her cellar storage room. Her house was one of the many 'blind pigs' where such activity occurred. Hibbing was a town where men too often confirmed their virility with drunken brawling.

"No fights, my friend, except within myself. I'm fine now." Tony laughed. "I'll make some coffee if you'll join me."

Lud squinted. "You ain't been drinking, Tony?" His friend noticed that Tony's eyes were red but knew that Zoretek rarely had so much as a beer, and then only sociably.

"Don't tell me that you've been outside tonight!"

"God forbid!" Tony righted the chair and slid it toward Lud. "I'm not that foolish . . . but drinking?" Tony smiled. "Maybe so, Lud, drinking too much depression. This Sunday has been a miserable day for me."

Lud amused over the profound, sometimes poetic observations of his friend. Tony was different from most of the other guys.

"Damn, it's cold in here!" Lud rubbed his hands together. "I think old lady Dukich is cutting back the heat. And, by the way, I talked with her this morning. She's really upset about the money we owe her from last month. I think I smooth-talked her into giving us a little more time."

They talked in good humor about the alleged wealth of Sadie Dukich who, many miners believed, had hidden a small fortune from her boarders somewhere in the house. During the busy times of the mining season, she packed the house with men. Often the beds were shared; if a miner worked a day shift, he slept in the bed of another who was on afternoon shift. Also, there was her liquor money.

"I think I'll be out of here before January, Tony. I've got just enough money left to get me a ticket to my brother's place in Chicago. He's been a meatpacker there. Says that there's work for anyone who wants it, and they don't shut down the plants for winter. Why don't you come along? Nothin's happening here until the mines open next spring."

Lud talked, as he often did, about how much he hated working in the mines and wondered why he had come to Hibbing in the first place. "How stupid I was. Some steamship agent back home was a real recruiter. Anyhow, he only wanted warm bodies. He promised us jobs over here. Everybody else was going. Why not me? I'm a sucker for a promise every time. He even told us that this place was beautiful! Can you believe that, beautiful? If I ever meet that sonofabitch again, I'll set his ass out on one those snow drifts. Beautiful? Godallmighty!" Both men laughed.

"What he said about jobs was true enough, though. Old 'Uncle Oliver' was just waiting for me to get here. I'm probably better off than if I'd stayed back in Slovenia. I might have been drafted and got myself killed. Don't know, never will, I guess," Lud told his friend.

"So, what's your story, Tony? I've never really asked about how you got over here. Were you as gullible as your friend Jaksa was?"

"Much more so than you want to know, Lud. It's a story that makes me ashamed, but I'll tell you anyhow."

The voyage to America seemed endless. Even the young and strong were wearied from dizziness, nausea, and constant vomiting as the steamship swayed upon every heave of the turbulent Atlantic.

After eight days, the *Lasovoie* , slipped past the awesome silhouette of a majestic lady who towered over their destination at Ellis Island. The heady inspiration of their arrival was swiftly dashed by the overwhelming crush of humanity in the immigration facility which was known to many as the 'Isle of Tears' or 'Heartbreak Island'.

Tony Zoretek, dressed in his Sunday best that day, wore a blue shirt with its pocket sewn closed to protect the small sum of money his Uncle Steven had sent him. Around his neck an official had hung a sign that read, 'Anton Zoretek- to Hibbing, Minnesota'.

In the upstairs room of the main building, physicians scrutinized hands and scalp. Then they checked for trachoma by using a buttonhook to turn eyelids painfully inside out. After the physical examinations, they were ushered down railed alleyways to meet more officials and interpreters.

"Please speak English with me," Tony appealed.

A battery of questions and papers were another part of the tedious routine in the immigrant processing facility.

"What is your name?" an official in a gray uniform asked. Tony responded indignantly, refusing to point to the sign he wore as the others did. "My name is Anton Zoretek," he said clearly.

Many would be unable to pronounce or spell their names in precise English and would leave the island with a new or abbreviated version, an Americanized surname which they would carry with them for the rest of their life.

Hours later, they were crowded into a barge that would take them to the New Jersey mainland where busy railroad terminals awaited their arrival. From here they dispersed in every direction.

The train ride west revealed a vast, colorful countryside under the bright July sunshine. Tony marveled at the endless sweep of land that was

America. He imagined the long finger of Robert Jamison crossing the page of his atlas.

Chicago was in darkness, but the immensity of the place brought wonderment to Tony's eyes. He could not sleep, afraid that he might miss something of this incredible country. Duluth, at the end of the line, presented the weary travelers with a cool, damp, and overcast morning.

Duluth's immigration terminal hosted a confusion similar to their experience at Ellis Island. But, the people here were different. Almost all of the hundreds of bodies which crowded the long room, were young men like Tony. Many of them were Montenegrins who had just arrived in Duluth by way of Canada.

Several men climbed atop the wooden benches, gestured for quiet, and began to speak in different languages. A squad of uniformed police encircled the large group, and Tony felt a grip of apprehension inside. Then he heard one of the men translating in a crude Slovenian. Tony listened to both the English and the paraphrase of his own language from the interpreter.

"We have jobs for all of you. Yes, each of you in this room can begin your work this very day. You will work in a place called a mine." The interpreters relayed the message on cue. "We know that this will be a different kind of work for most of you, but everything will be carefully explained when you get to the mine. Do you understand what I have told you?"

Tony noticed that the others began to nod. He did the same. *Mine* was a word, however, that was already familiar to him.

"This will be hard work, and if you do not listen carefully to your bosses, if you do not do exactly as you are told, it can be very dangerous for you. Do you understand this?"

Again, all the men acknowledged their understanding. All of them appeared to be more bewildered by everything going on than Zoretek was. Tony's gaze was riveted on the many uniformed men who held rifles cradled in their arms.

"Now, hear this instruction. Stay together at all times. This is very important, stay together! You will be protected." Tony puzzled deeply over the strange command and the promise of protection. For what possible reason, he wondered, would he need to be protected in this great, free country? What could be so fearsome that guns seemed necessary?

"The Oliver Mining Company will be taking care of you until," the thickset man looming over them from the bench paused, "until you are settled. You will each be well paid for your work, and both food and lodging has already been arranged for you. Your relatives and friends will be informed of your arrival later. Do you understand?"

The official waited a moment, "Now, are there any questions? We are almost ready to go."

No questions were raised. Most men seemed consumed by their disbelief. Could all of what they were hearing be true? A job paying good money this very day with food and a place to live besides? All of this would be provided for them by the Oliver Company?

Having their complete attention and no questions to answer, the mining agent concluded. "That's just fine then. We are happy to have you with our company and wish you well. Now, before you board the train to Hibbing, which is waiting outside that door," he gestured toward the back of the cavernous room, "remember to stay together as a group at all times. That is the most important thing for your continued safety once we get you to your jobs."

It was mid afternoon when the train began its crawl into Hibbing. The scene that hailed their arrival was sobering and erased any trace of elation from the face of each man on board.

Throngs of men, maybe hundreds, were lined along the tracks. Between them and the train, several armed police in their blue wool uniforms stood poised with rifles ready. The mob outside was hostile, and their curses could be heard above the clatter of the noisy train. The men outside the train gestured their rage and shook their clenched fists. There were posters with strange words, red flags, shouts of "scabs, strike, go home, and don't work!" But the train only slowed down, and then proceeded through the outrageous choler of the demonstration.

Tony pressed his face against the window, absorbed by the ugly assembly, searching for that one face he might recognize. His Uncle Steven had been told of his arrival date and would surely be there to greet this train. But, could Steven be in that crowd?

"Uncle Steven!" Tony waved excitedly. It was surely his uncle, standing next to a tall blond man who was waving a red flag furiously over his head. The train passed gradually, and for a brief moment, Tony's eyes were locked in a deep blue stare from that handsome blond man who stood beside his kinsman. Again he waived at the window, but to no apparent avail. Steven had not seen him.

On board the train, an Oliver official passed down the narrow aisle with his pistol drawn protectively. Like the other Oliver agents, he seemed to be frightened and uncertain. The man wanted to calm the apprehension among his bewildered passengers.

"Don't worry. Hear me, all of you. This is nothing to concern you. These people are jealous about any new workers in the mine. They want all of the money to themselves; like pigs they are. Everything will be just fine. We will give them a few days to get over this bad feeling. Today we have work to do. Do you want to make money?"

The men appeared rallied by their anticipation of work and making money. A modified excitement returned to the car. Yes, they could reason, some men were greedy indeed.

Soon the steam engine began its gradual decent into the depths of the massive Hull-Rust Mine which gaped before their eyes like an unbelievable canyon.

Steven Skorich and his miner's union friend, Timo Arola, were among the dissenters that had formed this mob of protest against the trainload of immigrant miners. The Oliver Iron Mining Company would break the back of the Western Federation of Miners walkout with a combination of strike-breakers and the blatant intimidation of hundreds of armed deputies.

Steven watched despairingly, knowing in his heart that one of these trains brought his relative to this ugly place. Because there had been a series of trains the past few days, he could not know for certain which train carried Tony. He wondered if he would even recognize the young Zoretek. It had been three long years since he'd seen Tony who was only fifteen at the time. How could he ever hope to welcome this nephew if he was one of those who might take his job away?

The afternoon sun at its zenith spewed a suffocating heat into the dusty crimson depths of the mine. Rapidly divided into work groups, the men began their toil. They shoveled ore into cars, hauled heavy wooden ties, iron rails, and laid track into new digs. In the ore pockets, a gigantic machine gouged huge bites of dirt like a hungry monster from another world.

Tony had been detailed, along with about forty others, to a track gang that wrestled the heavy timbers into place and laid out the long sections of iron. The foreman worked alongside the new recruits, attempting to teach by example because of the language barrier. Tony, however, could pick up enough words in English to have a general idea of the conversations among the *Cousin Jacks,* as the bosses were called . He was also able to piece together an understanding of what was a very frightening situation. He realized he should not be here; however, he knew he was powerless to change the situation.

Because of his size and obvious strength, Tony was singled out for the bull work of hammering the spikes that would pin the rails to the ties. His tight muscles ached with every excruciating swing of the sixteen-pound sledge hammer. The sweltering heat was relentless and thick dust choked his parched throat. Yet, Tony worked without pause, arcing the hammer with force and accuracy, not even slowing to wipe away the salty sweat dripping over his brow and burning into his dry eyes.

Within a few hours, the gang was working with some semblance of precision which allowed the foremen to withdraw from the work and concentrate on supervising. The track bosses paced along the grade encouraging the men with "keep it up", "be careful", and "gotta keep going!" Taking only short breaks for a cup of putrid-tasting water, the track gang labored into the encroaching evening shadows. A fading sun dropped behind the steep pit wall on the western end of the crater, and still they were pushed on by the bosses who paced along beside them.

Tony's ungloved hands were raw and his face burned red, but he maintained a total concentration on his work. His mind blocked out the pain that raked his body. While others fell limp and exhausted or sick from vomiting, Tony persevered.

As dusk became a heavy veil, the victimized miners had put in their first day's work. The foremen were joined by a group of heavily armed Oliver deputies. "Let's get together now!" an official in suit and tie shouted. Another formed them in ranks of three abreast.

"We're going out this way!" The official gestured to the railroad grade that wound upward in a huge circle around the walls of the pit.

"Follow me and stay together!"

Like a procession of prisoners, the long column was conducted up the hill.

"When we get to the house, there's gonna be a good hot meal set out for you; all you can eat. And, after eating, there's a nice bed for each of you," announced the man in the suit.

Ten minutes later they reached the crest of the pit and headed down a narrow Hibbing avenue toward the boarding house. Along the way more security guards could be seen. Some were hiding behind trees like snipers.

Blocking their path only a short distance ahead was a throng of torch-wielding men. It looked like the same angry mob that cursed their arrival hours before. The miners began to murmur among themselves, terror stricken by the ominous sight. The immigrants clustered together, locked arms, and picked up their pace. Again the rancorous clamor of "scabs, strikebreakers, bastards, and Oliver whores" filled the night air. The deputies buffered around them, their long clubs at the ready to back off any over-zealous agitators. The boarding house sanctuary was only a block ahead.

Bewildered by the dreadful scene which he now understood, Tony lingered a few steps behind the rush of immigrant workers. Gazing into the crush of demonstrators along the side of the street, Tony spied the blond man again. The protester stepped out, screaming profanities and waving a dark object over his head. Tony watched in terror as a smaller man pulled the blond man back from the street and took the rock in his own hands . He saw a deputy, pistol drawn, step in the direction of where the two men had breached the security zone that the police had maintained along the sides of the avenue.

A voice rang out of the crowd, "Timo, watch out . . . Timo!"

Tony glanced ahead at the growing space between him and the others of his group and began running to catch up.

Suddenly something struck him. A forceful impact between his shoulders dropped him to his knees. His paralyzed arms could not break the fall, and his face smashed into the dirt of the street. Thrusts of pain raced into his neck. Fighting for consciousness, Tony got up on his elbows, then weakly to his knees. Another rock sailed past his head. Then Tony heard a crack, clearly a rifle shot, followed by a scream . . . "Timo!"

Tony was jerked to his feet by one of the guards who rushed back to help him. "You stupid 'Bohunk'! Do ya wanna get yerself killed?" The guard cursed as he half dragged Tony toward the house. The surrounding echoes of hatred were not from jealous men. Something far more powerful was behind the intensity of their wrath.

Once inside the boarding house doorway, Tony collapsed to the floor, the crack of a single rifle shot still pounding in his head. This had become a nightmare beyond belief. He could not help wondering if someone been killed in this madness?

Lud sat in stunned disbelief as Tony told his story. A frown was tightly drawn across his face. "You? I mean, honest to God, you were one of them scabs, Tony? I can't even imagine you got caught up in that terrible mess." He shook his head.

"Yes, me. I'm sorry to admit it. I'm sure my Uncle Steven knew. I'm almost certain of that. I wonder if I can ever make things right with him. Surely, he could tell me things about that time that I might otherwise never know. I still have nightmares, Lud. Something terrible happened that first night I was here. I can feel it in my gut. I fear someone was killed, and nothing was ever said about any death." Tony massaged his temples against the headache that throbbed from his memory of the strike.

"Don't be too hard on yourself, Tony. Don't think your uncle can't understand what you've just told me. Let me tell ya this, I've met Steven Skorich. He's a hellava guy. He was one of the key people during the strike. Everybody respected him more than most of the other leaders. Skorich was close to Petriella who was the one who called all the shots. Yes, Steven Skorich, he's a big man like you. They call him Korenjack, and I think he lives in Chisholm these days. Why not give yourself a Christmas present, Tony, and look up your uncle? It might be good for both of you.

'KITCHI GAMMI CLUB'

September 1906

Peter Moran prospered along with the Mesabi mining bonanza and gained the reputation of a dynamic entrepreneur within the growing Hibbing business community. His success, like that of his father, was due to good timing and a willingness to gamble. Unlike Daly, however, Peter preferred to make things happen behind closed doors where his brand of negotiating a deal was most effective. He was hard nosed and unscrupulous.

Hibbing had become a sizable hub because of its central location along the eighty mile long Mesabi. Most of the wealthy mine and timber barons, however, preferred to live some sixty miles south of the ribald mining activity. Duluth offered a relative calm and sophistication. The Lake Superior port city had among the highest per capita incomes in America after the turn of the century. Although Moran's commercial roots were deeply set in the red soil of Hibbing, his social life was closely connected to the Duluth scene. His new home on Washington Street was one of Hibbing's most impressive, rivaling many mansions on Duluth's waterfront.

Soon to be thirty-two, Peter stood nearly six feet tall with clear blue eyes and the chiseled jaw of a boxer. He enjoyed finely-tailored clothes, bow ties, and good Irish whiskey. Moran had expanded the family's lumber business and had also established the largest wholesale liquor business on the Mesabi Iron Range. Peter owned three of the busiest of Hibbing's sixty saloons and supplied both hard spirits and Fitger's beer to most of the others. Fortunately for Peter Moran, the Iron Range had become a long network of thirsty mine towns, and his liquor connections made him well known in Chisholm, Virginia, and twenty other mine communities. In the five years since taking over Moran and Sons, Peter had carved a financial empire.

Jimmy McIntosh was Peter's tandem in commerce. Mac owned a share of the mining action, a Hibbing bank, and various real estate holdings. McIntosh headquartered his business offices on Superior Street in downtown Duluth. He was Peter's age but taller and more slender. He, his wife Martha, and two daughters, lived near the Congdon mansion on Lake Superior. Jim was an avid golfer and belonged to the Northland Country Club. The two friends were as close as brothers sharing the same kind of sibling rivalries and jealousies. They had contrasting styles and philosophies but usually understood each other's motivations. Although Peter envied his friend's college education and the polish that went with it, the bond between Peter Moran and Jim McIntosh was almost inseparable.

The two men were sitting in McIntosh's Duluth office on this bleak afternoon in late September. "Tell me you like my idea, Jimmy. Just draw a picture of it in your mind. Imagine an elegant, European style hotel in Hibbing. It would have fine dining rooms and lounges. Then think of a fine theater to attract vaudeville performances from Chicago. Include a legitimate gaming room with slots and a variety of shops." Peter's latest proposed venture caused his friend to scratch his head over the extravagance.

Peter continued, "Hibbing needs what you've got down here in Duluth. The whole Iron Range needs more cultural stuff, more variety, and more class, Jim. Don't you agree?"

"It's not so much that I don't like the concept. Hibbing's a pretty rough place for sure, but why you, Pete? You've got enough going on as it is. Let me interest you in some solid investments I've just learned about. Then you can just sit back and watch your money work for you. God, you haven't slowed down in five years. Aren't you getting a little tired?" McIntosh chided. "Hate to tell you this, Pete, but I see some gray around your ears. Maybe what you need is a wife and kids like I have. That might give you a different perspective of what's important in life."

Peter ran his fingers through his wavy brown hair. He had, indeed, noticed the traces of gray, but found them to be rather distinguished. Most would agree that Peter's rugged good looks were not compromised by a touch of gray. Women conceded that the solidly-built Irishman was a most eligible bachelor.

"I believe a 'lady friend' will do me just fine for now, thank you. I don't need a wife. Since I have a lady friend, Jim, I want to concentrate on something I don't have, a hotel!" Moran laughed. The identity of his 'friend' was one of the few secrets Moran kept from McIntosh. "I'll let you sit back with your investments; I want to make my money the real way."

"You Morans are a stubborn breed. I remember my pa telling Daly, back when your father was setting up his first logging operation, to diversify his investments. How those two could argue, couldn't they? But, whether he was right or wrong, my father could never change Daly's way of thinking," McIntosh reminisced.

"On that point you are, unfortunately for Daly, absolutely correct. My dad was a mule," Peter conceded.

"All right, enough bullshit, let's talk about my hotel. I don't plan to start from scratch, you know. I've taken a good look at the Grande Hotel that's being built down on Third Avenue on the corner of South Street. It's just down the street from the ball park. Anyhow, the Grande's going to be three stories, brick exterior, with more than a hundred rooms. The builders plan to have it all done by next summer," Moran said.

"Yes, that's the Markman project, isn't it? He's got some St. Paul money, including some of J.J. Hill's fortune, I've been told. It's going to be a big place, but he hasn't planned anything as fancy as you've just talked about. There's no doubt he will make his money back. And Hibbing could use a nice hotel."

"I want to slow down the construction before it gets too far along and give myself some time to negotiate," Peter said. "Now, here's what I want us to do, Jim. Hear me out on this. I want to make a deal with Markman to buy the property, hire a new architect, and then expand the building half way down the block to the corner of Cedar Street. It'll be a hellava lot bigger and better than anything Markman has in mind." Peter leaned forward, "We can do it, Jimmy. Are you with me on this?"

"What do you want from me, Pete? I'm willing to do anything that's honest and ethical. You know that," Mac replied.

Both men laughed at 'honest and ethical.'

Moran explained his strategy. Through Mac's Merchants and Miners Bank in Hibbing, they would stall Markman's credit lines and create some cash flow problems. Moran would float the rumor that he was going to build a competing hotel. Markman would welcome a deal on Moran's terms within a month. "I can handle Harold Markman, Jim. He can find things to keep himself busy with down in the Cities. We don't need any of these out of towners in my city."

"I might be able to slow down some of his cash flow from the bank. Just don't go doing anything foolish on your own, Pete." Jim knew his friend only too well. "Stay in the background."

Peter moved to the window which overlooked busy Superior Street in Duluth's thriving downtown. "Someday, Jim, Hibbing might make this town look like a side show," Moran teased.

"Don't make any bets on that, Pete. Hibbing might not live long enough." Some of the Duluth businessmen wondered if the day might come when the rich ore that Hibbing was built upon might become more valuable than the city itself. "You know as well as I do that up there you're sitting on the richest iron ore lode in the world. Just sitting on top of it." Jim was amused by that very dilemma. "On that note, let me buy you a drink at the club."

In the opulent ambiance of the Kitchi Gammi Club, Moran and McIntosh enjoyed a prime rib dinner. The private club was a favorite of Moran, and a place to hobnob with Duluth's most elite citizenry.

John Allison, owner of the Fitger's Brewery, spotted Peter. "Hey, Moran, I heard that your village council just voted to make Hibbing a 'dry town'."

Peter stood up from his meal, pointing his finger toward the robust, bearded brewer, "If we go dry anywhere on the Range, it will be because the folks up there can't tolerate that skunk piss that passes for beer here in Duluth." Everybody enjoyed the good humor that the Range Irishman brought when he visited their prestigious club.

"Here, here, bartender," Allison rejoined. "Give everybody a round for that comment, but put it on Moran's bill. Let's keep some Hibbing money in Duluth."

Peter's weekly trips to Duluth were a mix of business and pleasure, but not necessarily in that order. Two years before he had met the 'lady friend' who gave a spark to Peter's single life. Miss Chevalier would be waiting for him that night when he got back to his suite at the Essex Hotel. Anticipating this evening's time with Barbara, Moran excused himself from the men at the club before it became too late.

"Gentlemen, I hate to disappoint you, but I have to leave now. As you must already know, the train to Hibbing leaves early in the morning," he called toward the fellows at the bar. "That's only because the folks down here in Duluth can't wait to get up to Hibbing. If you're lucky, I'll see you all next weekend and let you buy me a drink for a change."

As he left the Kitchi Gammi and turned west on Superior Street, Peter had a bounce to his step. During the three block walk, he remembered that night two years before, when he and Barbara Chevalier had met for the first time.

Barbara Chevalier had been raped by her drunken father when she was seventeen. The trauma of that experience after years of abuse caused Barbara to run away. She went first to an aunt in nearby Cloquet. Aunt Gretta, however, was unsympathetic. "Any decent girl belongs at home!" the spinster believed. Then she tried to find a place to stay at her father's parents in the West Duluth neighborhood of Morgan Park. Her Grampa Karl was a selfish man. His own children were grown and gone, and he liked it that way. Karl seemed to resent the beautiful girl's presence in his home and believed that only a very troubled child would ever leave her own family. "You can stay here for a few weeks, Barbara, until you get a job. Then find a place of your own," Karl told her.

There were no jobs for a single girl with no training or references. Grampa Karl introduced Barbara to his casual friend named Sam Lavalle. Lavalle told Karl that he had found good paying jobs for many young women who had some ambition. Karl's only knowledge of Sam was that the man worked at the prestigious Kitchi Gammi Club, and that impressed him. He assumed Sam was probably a manager there. Karl misjudged Lavalle and was naive about his jobs for young women. Lavalle introduced Barbara to prostitution.

Lavalle, long since fired from the Kitchi Gammi Club, had once been a Saturday night bartender there. He was a con-man and gambler with wide contacts among the disreputable elements in the West Duluth neighborhoods.

Lavalle knew several 'scarlet ladies'. Several of his women were local, while others were recruited from wide-open Hurley, Wisconsin. While working at the Kitchi Gammi Club, he was in a position to make confidential arrangements for any of the patrons who wanted a woman for the night. Peter Moran found occasion to have a drink with Lavalle before leaving the club on that night two years before.

Peter reminisced about that night as he continued on his way toward the Essex Hotel. He recalled the conversation with Lavalle at the bar and meeting Barbara for the first time. The relationship had grown between them these past two years.

"I've met a beauty, Mr. Moran," Lavalle spoke in hushed tones that night. "She ain't done none of this stuff before. I only met her a coupla days ago. For five bucks, I can have her up in your room in an hour." Lavalle glanced furtively around the bar for eavesdroppers. "Let me tell ya. This girl, her name's Barbara, well she's like nothin you've ever seen. That's for sure."

Lavalle made a phone call, and Moran left a five and a tip.

On the walk to her hotel appointment that night, a frightened and apprehensive Barbara Chevalier fought back tears. She believed she was about to begin the most hideous chapter of her life, and her stomach was a knot of anxiety. She wanted to run but had no place to go. She would sell her body to a stranger.

Once inside the lobby of the Essex Hotel, she grasped for a measure of composure, dried her reddened eyes, and primped her auburn tresses in the mirror beyond the entry way. She found the piece of paper in her handbag and reread the scrawled note she had been given by one of Lavalle's pimps. *Ask for Mr. Barker at the front desk. Tell Barker that S.L. would like you to have the key for room 412. Wait in the room.*

Trembling, Barbara went up to the spectacled clerk at the desk, got the key, and turned for the stairway to the fourth floor. "He's not in yet, m'am. Just go inside. He will be along shortly, I think," Barker mumbled discretely before she had taken two steps.

She waited inside the room. Her eyes were riveted to the brass handle on the door. An hour passed. Then, the knob turned, and the door slowly opened.

When Peter entered the room, he was stunned by the beautiful woman sitting rigidly on the sofa. Her loveliness and delicate features left him at a loss for words: "You must be Barbara Chevalier," he mumbled.

Barbara broke down sobbing. "I don't know, sir. Yes, I mean, that's my *real* name, but shouldn't I have another name for this kind of work? I don't really know."

That night Peter listened to her tragic story and felt an uncharacteristic compassion. This woman was not like the others in his past. Barbara might be a woman he would keep for himself.

She finished. "That's how I got here, sir. Please forgive me for unburdening my grief. You didn't pay for a sob story." Barbara stood awkwardly and began to undo the buttons on her blouse as she had been told to do. "I think I'm ready. Aren't you supposed to finish undressing me, sir?" she asked.

That night Peter found pleasure beyond imagination. He slept deeply and awoke much later than usual the next morning. There was no doubt in his mind, as he kissed the cheek of this infatuating woman asleep at his side, Barbara would be his alone.

While sharing a room service breakfast, Peter explained his proposition. "Stay away from that scum, Lavalle. He won't be working at the club after today. I'll see to that. If he tries to get in touch with you for any reason, I'll want to know about it. You won't be needing his 'work' anymore."

Confused, Barbara nodded. "What am I to do? I mean, after you leave?" she asked.

"You'll find some money in the dresser drawer. I'm sure it'll be enough for you to get through this next week very nicely. Buy some new clothes if you want, some jewelry, whatever you'd like. I'll keep this room reserved, and I'll find you a job a soon as I can. It'll be something that should give you a decent income of your own. Then we'll find you a nice place to live. Just let me take care of you. I enjoy being generous with people I care about."

Peter considered his intentions a noble gesture under the circumstances. His life was always business, and in business people had their price. "I'll be back in Duluth next weekend. We can go out and do something fun together. What do you say about that?" Peter kissed her softly on her cheek, gathered his hat and coat, and headed toward the train depot.

Since that first night two years before, their relationship had flourished.

In many ways it had grown beyond the mutually beneficial arrangement Peter had first intended it to be. Barbara had learned stenography then gotten a job in a West Duluth insurance agency. She became self supporting. Peter always treated her like a lady and was proud to take her to the finest places in Duluth. Barbara's life had a fullness and a meaning she could not have dreamed possible. She was a 'kept woman' and did not delude herself in that regard. But she was also a woman in love.

When Peter opened the door to his room on this September night, after leaving McIntosh at the Kitchi Gammi Club, he was met by only darkness. Barbara was nowhere to be found. Disconcerted, he turned on the lights. "Barbara . . . Barbara!" Surely she would not have forgotten. Frustrated, he tossed his coat on the chair, loosened his tie, and kicked off his shoes. "Barbara!" he tried again. He bit at his lip. Barbara was not there. Another man, he wondered? Peter was gripped with a fear that she might have tired of their relationship. He wondered if she might have found a man who could offer her the one thing she deserved most, and the one thing he could not give to her. Had Barbara found commitment?

Peter heard a slight rustle from the closet in the foyer. He was frozen. With a giggle, the door slowly opened.

"Barbara?"

"Surprise! Peter, my love. Happy birthday!" Barbara rushed toward him balancing a birthday cake in one hand and clinging to a bottle of champagne in the other. "Happy Birthday to you. . . ." she began to hum. "Happy birthday, dear Peter. Happy Birthday to you."

Embarrassed and relieved at the same time, he pulled her close causing her to let the cake slip from her grip onto floor. He kissed her passionately. A sparkle lit in his eyes, and he laughed heartily as he hugged her.

"Barbara, I forgot my own damn birthday!"

Back in Hibbing the following Monday morning, Peter moved swiftly to learn all he could about the Grande Hotel construction project. Harold Markman was building a first-rate structure of nearly the same dimensions that Moran had visualized for his own hotel. Peter and McIntosh reviewed the financial package that the builder had put together for the project.

Unfortunately for Peter, the proposal was a sound one, and Markman was an accomplished contractor. The hotel money, like Markman himself, came from St. Paul. Both credibility and management experience were well established in the venture. The situation posed an interesting challenge, but Moran reasoned, everybody had a price. Owning his own hotel had become an obsession with him.

Peter was on the phone with Jimmy McIntosh in Duluth. "Did you set up the meeting, Jim, at my place, next Tuesday? Great. Thanks, old buddy. It's time to make our move, Mac. You'll be here? Good. We'll wrap it up and send him packing."

McIntosh had given Markman the impression that their meeting would be more social than anything else, an opportunity to get to know each other kind of affair. He flattered the St. Paul businessman on the Grande project, and promised, "You'll enjoy meeting Pete Moran."

Pouring an Irish whiskey for everyone, McIntosh made the introductions. Peter was affable and flattered Markman at choosing a hotel site so near to the Hibbing ball park. Although he hated small talk, Peter would be congenial until the real purpose of their meeting was on the table. As a baseball fan, he informed his guest on the local team's most successful season. Baseball presented the men with a pleasant conversational diversion from local politics and from the growing tensions between miners and management on the Iron Range. Many people in Hibbing were worried that a strike might happen one day soon which would seriously undermine the local economy.

But Peter, tiring of these pleasantries, steered their attention to the hotel Markman was building.

"Mr. Markman, may I call you Harold?"

"By all means, Pete." Markman smiled graciously.

"Harold, let me be candid with you. I'm impressed with what you've got going at the Grande. What do you want for it?" Peter leaned forward in his chair.

Markman, taken aback, tried to laugh politely. "Why, Mr. Moran, we've hardly gotten started. We're only now working on the footings. We've got a long way to go."

"I know what you're working on, Harold. It's my business to know what goes on in Hibbing. I want to buy the Grande. So, what do you want for it? That's all I want to know," Peter persisted.

"I'm afraid that's quite out of the question." Markman met Moran's intense stare with his own. "I'm sure you can understand that my people intend to be good citizens of this fine community, and . . ."

Peter cut him off in mid-sentence, "I'm already a good citizen of this fine community, so let's cut the bullshit. Everyone, Mr. Markman, has a price. We both know that. So, what is your price?"

McIntosh intervened to calm the tense situation. "What Mr. Moran means, Mr. Markman, is that your project is a profit-making enterprise. Certainly, you and your group have calculated some substantial returns on your investment here in Hibbing. Mr. Moran is in a position to, shall we say, accelerate your return. That's all. Certainly this type of proposition is in everybody's best interest. Your group makes a nice profit up front, without having to do another thing."

"That much I can clearly understand, Mr. McIntosh. It is, however, very premature to make any determination of potential return at this time. As you know, we are highly optimistic about the Grande Hotel. We are very excited, as I was saying a minute ago, to become a part of this community. I must be adamant about your untimely proposal, I'm afraid. Our hotel is not for sale at any price, gentlemen."

Peter was intrigued by the tone of his adversary. Markman had some punch in him. "Harold, my friend," Peter cajoled the portly, finely-dressed contractor. "Just tell me what kind of money you folks have got committed to the project." Peter already had a good idea but wanted confirmation.

"That, Mr. Moran, to be blunt and conclusive, is none of your business. Now, if you will be kind enough to excuse me." Markman set down his half emptied glass and rose from his chair.

"Allow me to return your bluntness, Markman. I have some figures here." Moran took a paper from his coat pocket.

Irate, Markman stood up, "That will be quite unnecessary. As far as I am concerned, this conversation is over. I've heard just about enough!"

"Sit sown! I'll have something to say about when this conversation ends. You're in Hibbing, Mr. Markman, and we do things differently up here!" Peter fumed.

McIntosh pulled at his elbow. "Take it easy, Pete. I think that if both of you . . ." he smiled toward Markman, "settle down a bit and allow the matter to rest for now. Then, perhaps, Harold would be willing to discuss your interest with his colleagues. It's all rather sudden. Wouldn't you agree, Pete?"

"Thank you, Mr. McIntosh, for your sanity. Although your suggestion is well taken, I doubt that we'll have much more to say about the sale of our hotel. Now, I must be getting along." Taking his hat from the cloak rack, he moved abruptly to the door. Peter was inspired by the confrontation and could not resist getting the last word before Markman left his office.

"I've got some influence here, Markman. If I'm against your project, I think you will find absolute hell in trying to make a go of it."

Markman, however, gave Moran a sharp stare. "I regard that as an outright threat, Mr. Moran. In St. Paul we don't do things that way. By the way, Mr. Moran, I've heard talk that you were planning to build a hotel of your own in Hibbing. If that's true, I welcome the competition. Good day."

"Fuck you and your 'good day'! I want the location you've got right now. And, don't welcome my competition, Markman, because I never lose!"

McIntosh moved quickly to see Markman out of the room. "Let me apologize and extend the hope that we can find an amicable solution to this matter. We're all respectable businessmen after all."

Markman stepped briskly out of the room. Incensed, he blurted out, "With that arrogant and vulgar man? I'm afraid this matter is quite over with, Mr. McIntosh. I'll not talk to Moran again about it."

Late October graced the north country with a bright, crisp Indian Summer. Autumn brought a collage of color. The oaks and maples, resplendent in red, amber, and golden hues surrendered their leaves in the brisk westerly winds. Any sense of tranquility, however, remained elusive. The frenzied pace of life in the prospering village of Hibbing took no pause. Hibbing's population marched relentlessly toward ten thousand citizens as mining became the magnet for immigrant job seekers and entrepreneurs alike. Still a rowdy frontier community, vestiges of wealth and culture were discernible along stately Pine Street. The Power Theater, Merchants and Miners Bank building, Itasca Bazaar, and Hibbing Village Hall symbolized grandeur and stability. Clothiers, confectioners, cobblers, restauranteurs, and other diverse merchandisers combined to provide a commercial viability to the downtown area.

Yet, the essence of a mining town is ugliness. Saloons and brothels outnumbered churches by twenty to one. The masculine culture was pervasive. Women were only gradually making their way into the fabric of life as they joined their estranged husbands and began to rear children. North of the village, beyond the Oliver Mining Company headquarters, was the sprawl of open pit mining. The Mahoning, Hull- Rust, Burt, and Sellers Mines had already become gigantic craters in the earth. The blasts of earth and rock constantly thundered rattling houses like earthquakes and left the air saturated with a fine dust for miles around. The extraction of ore had no regard for the landscape or the people who lived on the Mesabi. The rich hematite ore was *red gold* to the Oliver and other mine owners.

Lines of ore-laden trains climbed out of the pits en route to the waiting ore boats at the harbors of Duluth and Superior. The mining companies of the central Mesabi had already moved hundreds of thousands of tons of iron ore toward the Eastern steel mills. The related earth stripping operations created an artificial range of mountains around the village. The locals called the huge mounds of earth overburden 'dumps', a simple reference to what the companies did with their waste materials. Hibbing was already becoming a peninsula as mining rapidly chewed away the earth to the north, east, and west of the city.

In his concerns about the ultimate fate of Hibbing, Jim McIntosh would prove to be prophetic. The hematite buried under the expanding city had more value than the city itself.

Peter Moran and Con O'Gara, a Duluth Mesabi and Northern Railroad manager, shared a bottle of imported Irish whisky at Moran's private table in the far corner of his Pine Street saloon. The Shamrock Saloon was Hibbing's finest drinking establishment serving a clientele of mostly wealthy and influential citizens. Here the talk was often of politics and community affairs. Con was a village council member who shared both ethnic and civic ties with Peter. A few other local politicians were numbered among Peter's friends. He liked the idea of having a few council members in his pocket.

The two men were waiting for Elwood Trembart, a local attorney and council president, and Jim McIntosh to join them later on this Friday after-noon. Mac had persuaded Moran to let him handle the Markman Hotel matter, and Peter was anxious to learn whether the week had brought any progress. O'Gara and Trembart were well aware of Moran's interest in the hotel but were never made privy to his strategies.

The past few weeks had witnessed a dramatic slowdown in Markman's construction. Structural timber and other basic materials arrived very slowly to the Grande building site. One large order of red brick was of such infe-rior quality that it could not be used and had to be returned. Cost overruns became a daily drain on Markman's strained budget. Then, on the previous Tuesday, an unexplained mishap had caused part of the South Street wall to collapse. A worker had been seriously injured in the accident and was in critical condition at the hospital. On the following day, Markman's project architect, a man named Jerry Sweeny, had withdrawn from the job for 'per-sonal' reasons and apparently taken a position in Duluth.

"If it weren't for bad luck, Markman would have no luck at all! Con O'Gara's observation brought a hearty laugh.

McIntosh and Trembart made their way through the crowded saloon stopping to greet patrons and friends as they moved toward Moran's cor-ner table.

"You've got your goddamned hotel!" McIntosh slapped Peter on the back and dropped a stuffed folder of papers on the table. "Sign on all the dotted lines, my friend." Jimmy was beaming.

Moran stood, holding up his glass. "Let's have a toast. Here's to my new hotel. She will be more than you can imagine. I'll assure you of that. I'll make her the finest in all of Minnesota," he boasted.

"'Tis the luck of the Irish, Peter, my boy. Damned if I thought you could pull this off. Here's to the luckiest man in Hibbing." Con O'Gara raised his glass.

Glasses clinked at the toasting of Moran's accomplishment. Trembart gave the Shamrock proprietor a peculiar look and commented, "Unlike Mr. O'Gara, I never had any doubts. Is it really luck Peter, or are you that damn good at getting whatever you want?"

"In all modesty," Peter savored the moment, "you're both right. Con, I've always had my share of good luck, and Elwood, I do get what I want. Let's drink to luck and destiny, my friends."

"Oh, and there's this, Pete," Jimmy said in an aside and discretely handed Peter an envelope. On the outside was his name and the sketch of a heart. At a glance Peter knew the note was from Barbara and slipped the envelope into his pocket.

"Are you keeping secrets from your best friend, Peter?" Jimmy smiled widely. "A lady left this with my secretary yesterday and asked her to 'please have Mr. McIntosh deliver this as soon as possible.' She must have known I was coming up to Hibbing today."

The men celebrated the luck of Peter Moran well into the night. Peter shared some of his grandiose plans for the hotel and bought several rounds of drinks for the house.

Later that night Peter would read his note.

'My Dearest Darling Peter. I must see you this weekend. All my love, B.'

Irony is often bittersweet. On this day of Peter's greatest triumph, half a continent to the west, Daly Moran passed away. The telegram from his brother Denis would arrive the following morning.

Daly didn't realize his share of Oregon's enormous timber profits. His emphysema worsened in the intolerable dampness, and he developed a case of pneumonia. His tired body and deteriorated health could not win this last fight for life. The spirit of Denis died with his father. He, together with a handful of Daly's crew, would maintain a modest timber business outside Eugene for a few more months. Embittered by his father's death, Denis turned to drinking. He would never forgive his brother for buying out their father's business interests in Hibbing.

Peter was too busy with the Markman project to travel out to Oregon for the funeral. Daly's wife, Kathleen, was sickly and his daughter Emily was pregnant. Neither would risk traveling such a great distance. His older brother, Terrance, now a college teacher in Philadelphia, would pay appropriate respects for the family which the patriarch had left strung-out behind him.

'A Letter To Churile'

May 1904

The sight of Hibbing was an absolute disappointment to Mary Bellani as she watched the ramshackle structures come into view from the window of the train. The early May afternoon was cold and drizzly. Rainwater had settled in the muddy ruts of the streets and formed red pools in the ugly mire. As the conductor announced their arrival, the train began a long screech until it halted at the station.

Mary concealed her disillusionment. Dreams which had been so exaggerated in her vivid imagination now were reduced to reality. "Look at all that red water on the street, Lucia . It is almost unreal." Mary pulled her shawl about her shoulders and neck as she stepped onto the platform of the depot. Four year old Armando Depelo clung to Mary's side hiding his face in her dress, and Lucia held onto her arm.

Mary looked all about searching among the faces of the crowd of greeters hoping she might see her man's face. Certain she would recognize his boyishly handsome features in an instant, she imagined the feel of his embrace. Would Michael be so bold as to embrace her in front of the Depelos? Was such a display appropriate in this new country?

"Do you see John anywhere, Mary?" Tears welled in Lucia Depelo's eyes as she watched the many joyful reunions.

"Not yet, but surely he's here somewhere in this crowd. Maybe he has been delayed by the rain, Lucia. Or, perhaps we have arrived too early." They both watched as the luggage was collected, and the platform emptied.

"Oh, Mary, where can John be? Shall we hire a carriage to Mahoning? I fear something is wrong," Lucia uttered in a distraught voice. The long journey had worn her down more than she would admit. Lucia was not a strong woman and relied greatly on Mary.

Mary hugged her and consoled, "Please don't get upset. I cannot find my Michael either. Maybe he and John are on their way here together. We must wait a while longer."

John Depelo was nearly an hour late, but quickly forgiven, as Lucia melted into his arms. Both cried in their happiness of being back together after nearly two years of separation.

"I'm so sorry, Lucia, my dearest." John apologized as he stroked his wife's face affectionately. "A wheel on my wagon had to be repaired, and I got my clothes so muddy that I decided to return home and change before meeting you. I shouldn't have done so, but I wanted to look my best." Both of the women laughed at John's vanity.

Mary was shocked by John's appearance. He looked so much older and thinner than she remembered. His skin, although clean shaven and scrubbed shiny, was marked with red ore in the deep creases of his brow. What would Michael look like after all this time she wondered?

Little Armando had waited patiently for his father's attention. The tall man was a stranger to him. But, John lifted the boy, and held him out in front of him, saying, "Armando, my son, how you have grown, and what a handsome young lad you are." John kissed the boy's forehead and re-marked, "As you've written, Lucia, the boy does have his father's Italian nose!" They all laughed and began to load the wagon John had borrowed for his travel into Hibbing.

Quite forgotten in the happy reunion, Mary kept searching for Michael. Could it be possible that her letter, and Viola's as well, did not reach him in time? Lucia finally apologized and introduced Mary to her husband, "John, you remember Angelo's daughter? I couldn't have made it all this way without Mary."

"My goodness yes, such a young woman you have become and beautiful like your mother, Justina. It's so good to have you with us, Mary. Now you'll be like a daughter of our own." John embraced the lovely woman who had been so helpful to his wife and son.

On the ride west of Hibbing along the rough red road to Mahoning

Location, a chilly darkness settled upon them. Mary was bewildered by the unsightliness of the landscape which had been so disfigured by mining excavations. The gigantic mounds of dirt resembled barren mountains. This was not the golden land of her dreams.

"I understand that you've got a fiancé here in Hibbing, Mary." John turned from the front of the wagon, "It's Michael Samora is it not? I only wish I could tell you that I've seen him, but since, you know . . ." John paused and frowned. "What happened was such a terrible shame, and since then, I have no idea of his whereabouts."

"Since when? What shame?" Mary cried, almost dumbstruck by John's disturbing words.

"Yes, what are you talking about, John? Has something happened to Michael?" Lucia expressed her own surprise.

"Mr. Depelo, please tell me." Mary's voice was tight. "I have heard nothing about Michael. What is wrong?"

John Depelo realized that he should not have said anything about Michael until later. When they were home, he might be able to tell the story more completely. "I'm very sorry, Mary. I thought you knew. Michael had an accident at the Sellers, a little more than a year ago as I remember. It was a pretty bad one."

"What happened?" Mary was wide-eyed, confused, and her stomach tightened in a knot. "Accident? Who is Sellers? What's he got to do with my Michael?" She found herself leaning over the trunks and cases between her and the front of the wagon. She grasped for John's coat sleeve. "I must know about this," she implored.

John's voice became stern. "Please be calm, Mary. Sellers is the name of a mine near here where Michael worked." They were nearing Mahoning Location, and the Depelo home. "This isn't a good time to discuss this matter. We're almost home, and you're all very tired from your travels. Later this evening we can talk more about it."

Despite her impatience, Mary would not be disrespectful of her elder and host. Mary sank back, her spirit and optimism drained in a rush of silent weeping. "Yes, sir," she choked.

Michael Samora considered throwing the latest letter from his mother away, just as he had done with so many letters before. Viola wrote of things that did not concern him anymore. She asked him questions that he would not answer. Yet, to his own surprise, he found himself peeling back the envelope.

"God damn, not Mary Bellani!" Michael cursed aloud, as he read his mother's words. He crushed the letter in his fist, tossed it against the wall across from the table, and reached for his bottle of whiskey. "Three damn weeks," he thought to himself as a panic seized him. His eyes focused on the calendar which was the only wall hanging in the dismal room and counted days in his head.

"I'm gettin' outta here. I've gotta find Riley. Maybe he can help me outta this mess. Maybe he can talk to Moran again. Moran's got connections everywhere. He can find me work in Virginia, Duluth . . . as far away as possible."

On that misty, gray May afternoon, however, Michael Samora found concealment in the shadows of a coal warehouse on Railroad Street across from the depot. The dampness aggravated the throb in his hips and legs. He paced, sipping at his bottle, and avoiding both the people and traffic at the busy station. He cursed his condition and his cowardice, but he must not be seen by anyone.

When the train pulled into the station, his eyes riveted on the opening doors while watching the departing passengers. There she was! Her beauty took Michael's breath away! "Mary Bellani, your loveliness is too overwhelming," he said to himself as he watched her move onto the platform. Her eyes searched about while Mrs. Depelo and the boy looked in his direction. Stepping back more deeply into the warehouse shadows, he slipped away across the coal yard and up the street to his apartment. He was almost unmindful of the pain as he dragged his legs into a run. He must never be seen by this beautiful woman from that long forgotten village of Piedimonte.

The days became a week, then two, but the torment of her memory would not go away. Michael could think of nothing else but that face. During those weeks, Michael realized that his pains were not as persistent as they had been for so long. Perhaps what Dr. Hane had told him in the hospital was more true than he had been willing to concede. He alone had the power to make himself well. All he needed was the resolve to do it. For the first time since his accident, Michael believed he had a reason to live.

Consciously he cut back on his drinking. The liquor no longer gave him his cherished oblivion. He began to go regularly to the public bath house across the street, shaved the thick beard from his face, and trimmed his long hair at the Italian barber shop. Using the few dollars he had stashed away, Michael bought some new clothing. The transformation in appearance and attitude gave him new confidence. Michael went to Sunday Mass for the first time since his arrival. It was the church where most of his countrymen worshipped.

But still he was deeply self conscious of his limp and the disfigurement of his hips. Nothing he might do could change the reality of what the accident had done to him. Michael realized that the avalanche of dirt had crushed his manhood and had left him hopelessly impotent. Was it possible that any woman could love a man who would be unable to give her physical pleasure or children? Could Mary Bellani ever love such a man?

John Depelo was a curious and a sensitive man. He perceived Mary's anguish since learning of Michael's accident. Determined to learn what he could of young Samora's whereabouts, John and his younger friend, Dino Madoni, entered the Red Rock Tavern and found a place at the crowded bar. From over their mugs of beer, the two men searched for one face among the many in the dark room.

"Excuse me," John caught the bartender's attention. "I'm looking for an old friend. Do ya know a Michael Samora?"

The bartender continued to draw beer from the keg behind the bar without looking up. "The name's familiar." He slid mugs down the bar with expertise. "Ya mean the 'Dago'?" Unmindful of his slur he continued, "The crippled guy? Ya, works here sometimes, he's a swabber."

"Yes, that'd be Michael," John acknowledged.

"Ain't been here today," the barman looked about. "Must be down at the warehouse. Whatta ya want with him, anyway?" His eyes narrowed curiously.

"Nothing important, we're countrymen of his and haven't seen him in some time," Dino clarified. "How's he been doing?"

"Do ya really want to know?" The barman tossed some nickels into a cigar box behind him. "Lemme tell ya this much. If he was workin here today, nobody'd know it. Guy's kinda creepy, ya know what I mean? No offense, but he ain't much for talkin to no one. Keeps to himself alla time. Nobody's never asked for him before you guys." He wiped the bar absently. "It's the legs, ya know. Bad legs. They's what make him the way he is."

"Yes, we know about that, a bad accident," John replied.

"Guess so, but he ain't gettin much sympathy from me or no one else aroun here." He placed his large left hand flat on the bartop. Three missing fingers made his point. "Lotsa guys get banged up. Take a look fer yerselves." He gestured toward a table. "See over there, sitting next to Ole Nord, the big cop?"

John and Dino spied the uniformed man. "Uh huh, I see," said John as he strained his neck.

"That there's 'lefty' Graff. The black powder got him. Just like it did me, an more'n a few others."

Both John and Dino were well aware of the hazardous blasting powder used in the mines. "Too bad." John shook his head at the armless man. "I'm sorry."

"Lemme tell you guys. Ya gotta live with it. Ya gotta play with the cards that comes yer way. Now this Samora you askt about. Ya, he got hurt all right, but," the bartender shot a hard stare at both of them, "he aint got the guts to play his hand. See what I mean? Nope, he just folded, cashed in his chips like they say." To this man, life was best defined in terms of a poker game.

John and Dino went from the bar to the warehouse but did not find Michael that day.

Splashing some lilac water on his freshly-shaven face, Michael made a final appraisal in the mirror he had just purchased. It had been more than a month since Mary's arrival in Hibbing, and he would rent a carriage for the drive out to Mahoning. Surely, Mary and the Depelos had expected to see him long before this day, but he would make up some excuse.

He remembered the letter from his mother and Viola's mention of Mary Bellani. She had hoped that the two of them would get married after she settled in with the Depelos. Michael had thought of nothing else these past weeks. Marriage. His obsession was almost as irrational as it was disturbing. The thought of her kept him awake at night and haunted his every thought. Had Mary been *promised* to him? Did their families expect they were to become husband and wife? Such promises, he knew, were taken with grave seriousness among his countrymen. He must, therefore, take her as his own. The thought of any other man possessing Mary had become unimaginable.

The late June sun was a lustrous ball hanging above this grand Saturday morning. Its warm radiance buoyed his spirits. The road to Mahoning Location was busy with families traveling east toward Hibbing for their weekend shopping. Approaching the small mining community, he hailed the driver of an ice wagon coming in his direction. "Say, I'd like to know where John Depelo lives," Michael pulled in the reins.

"Take a left at da second street. Den, lemme tink," He tipped back his cap, "Den it's da tird house on da left. Der's a swing on da front porch I tink. Tink John's at work tho."

Instead, Michael turned down the alleyway behind the second street and allowed the horse to pull easily while he looked out over the gardens in the back yards of the nearly identical wood framed houses.

"Can I help ya, mister?" came a voice to his left. An old woman was hoeing dirt among her vegetables.

"No thank you, m'am, Just passin by . . . nice mornin."

"Michael! Michael!" Crying out his name brought a rush of long repressed emotion. Mary remembered that voice from more than two years ago in the Piedimonte countryside. "Just passing by, is that all you're doing, Michael?" She was unable to reconcile her excitement with her frustration of these past weeks.

Michael was paralyzed by the voice he also recognized. From the other side of the alley came his name and a question. A lump choked in his throat as he tried to swallow. He turned in the seat and met the wide oval eyes of Mary Bellani.

"Michael, it is you!" Mary rushed from the clothesline to the fence in the backyard. In her confusion and surprise, she couldn't repress the angry frustration. "Coming out to visit the old folks from Piedimonte, finally? Or, are you truly just passing by in the back alleyway?" Her sarcasm could not be retrieved.

Michael was trapped. Speechless. Nothing could have prepared him for this situation. He looked dumbfounded and stammered a feeble answer, "I don't really know."

"I've been waiting, Michael, hoping you might come to our *front* door as seems fitting for a visit. I thought you might want to say hello to that little neighbor girl from the Campania or welcome Lucia and Armando to this new country." Mary stood with hands gripping the fence post regarding the man in the carriage.

"Oh, Mary, please. I know you deserve an apology, but Viola's letter, it didn't arrive until after . . ." Michael caught himself in the lie. "No, I must be honest. I did know you were coming with the Depelos, and that you were already here. I just couldn't. . . ."

"You were afraid. Are you still afraid, Michael? If you are not, then bring your carriage around to the front of the house and walk to the front door." Mary would test the mettle of the man she had so wanted to love but begun to doubt. "Michael, I've been told about your accident. Lucia and I will greet you at the front door." Mary picked up the laundry basket and headed into the house.

Michael spent the day, greeted John when he returned from work, and stayed for supper. Somehow he found the courage to tell his story and felt a sense of relief as he unburdened himself. Their conversation, although mostly strained, had pleasant moments when remembering times past in Piedimonte. The present, however, was more difficult for all of them to talk about.

Mary seemed pleased that Michael would be leaving the tavern and beginning a better paying job at a warehouse. But even in his apparent candor, Mary knew this man had been deeply scarred by his experiences. Despite his every effort at sociability, there was sadness below the surface that, she sensed, might never be soothed. Could she love this Michael? He was still a handsome man, and the limp was more distraction than disturbance. It was the melancholy, so deep in his marrow that she found most troubling.

"Thanks so much. I've enjoyed this day more than any I can remember for a long time." Michael was at the door. "And, yes, John, I'd be most pleased to join your family at the Italian picnic next weekend. Thanks for inviting me."

The Depelos left Mary alone with Michael, so she could say her own goodbye. Mary followed him out onto the porch. It was already late, but Mary invited Michael to sit for a moment on the swing.

Outside, the evening air was warm, humid, and still. The star-filled sky was like an umbrella over the enveloping quietude. Mary gave the swing a gentle push. The swing's squeak into momentum combined with the snorting horse at the gate, the bay of a dog in the distance, and chirping crickets from a swamp nearby, brought a soothing medley to the air.

"Look, Michael, a falling star! That's good luck, you know. Make a wish, quickly before it disappears."

Michael fumbled for her hand, held it in his own. "Mary, again I'm sorry. My wish is that I'd met you at the train."

"Oh, Michael, you don't wish over things that have passed; that's silly. You may wish only for things yet to come." She laughed for the first time that day.

"I've already had some good luck myself," she said. "My wish is that my new job will make me happy about being in this new country. Heaven knows that I haven't been so far."

Mary explained that she would begin working in the tailor shop of Luigi Anselmo next week. Luigi had been told of Mary's skill as a seamstress and was delighted to have some help at his busy shop. She would be moving to Hibbing and have a room of her own in the Anselmo apartment above the shop.

"And so, I'll be earning a salary and be able to make lovely new clothing as well. It's so perfect. Luigi is a fine, respected man, and his offer is a grand opportunity for me to begin a life of my own. I'll miss the Depelos though. They've treated me as their own daughter these past weeks."

Michael smiled over Mary's excitement and good fortune. Her eyes reflected the brightness of the stars. "I'm so happy for you. Luigi is the finest tailor in town. Would I be right to guess that my mother had something to do with your sewing skills?"

"Yes, she was the very best seamstress and a good friend to me as well. I still miss her very much, and I'm anxious to write and tell her that we . . ." Mary caught herself, "have met."

At the Society Gugielmo Marconi Picnic the next weekend, Michael was withdrawn. Despite the special effort of everybody to include Michael in the games and general revelry, he seemed mired in that same self pity of the past. The beer tent was a temptation that he avoided, knowing what might happen if he were to have a single glass.

John Depelo, Luigi Anselmo, and the other men tried unsuccessfully to interest Michael in playing bocce ball. He was content to watch the games at a distance. Mostly, he watched Mary. She was always in the center of activities: preparing the ethnic foods, organizing games for the children, setting tables, and mixing with everybody as she did so. Gregarious, animated, and turning heads wherever she went, Mary was happiest when with people. From a distance, Michael watched as Dino Madoni talked with her making her laugh. Jealousy consumed him.

Mary watched Michael as well. She observed his movement away from people and conversation, contented to be a spectator, never a participant. Mary would not allow herself to feel sympathy. She would not push him where he did not want to go.

Later in the afternoon, Mary saw Michael sitting at a table with John and Armando Depelo. She brought both men a glass of beer, the boy some lemonade, then sat down to visit with them.

Finishing his glass in swift gulps, Michael felt some of the tension leave his body. "You're so marvelous, Mary, out there meeting everyone and havin such a good time. It's still hard for me, ya know, with people. I only hope it's not too late to enjoy the picnic." He looked away from her eyes. "I see Luigi over there, and I've hardly said a word to him all day," Michael said pointing toward the tailor who was having a beer at the tent. "I should probably visit with him for a few minutes."

At the beer tent Michael was more at ease and sociable. He even told an off-color story he had overheard at the Red Rock Tavern some time ago, which brought hearty laughs from the men. Michael loosened up as he drank.

That night Michael walked Mary home in much better spirits. "The picnic was a wonderful time, Mary. I enjoyed seeing so many old friends." He lied.

At the back doorway of Luigi's shop where Mary was now living, Michael took her hands in his. "Mary, it was my mother's wish that we . . ." he cleared his throat. "This is so hard for me to say. But, I love you, Mary. I know that I can make you happy, if you'd only give me a chance."

Mary's hands tensed. She felt a cold shiver move up her spine. This was not something she expected to hear on this night. Was it something she wanted to hear at all? She felt a torment welling inside as she remembered so clearly the promise she had made to her parents that evening a lifetime ago. 'I promise I will marry Michael if he will have me for his wife.' It was her promise, her sacred word. She had made a similar vow to Viola when Mama Samora had given her the surprise package, the beautiful wedding gown that hung in her upstairs closet. Could she possibly love this confused and crippled man?

Michael bent to kiss her lips and pulled her close with awkward hands. He had never kissed a woman before.

Mary closed her eyes, and allowed her mouth to touch his. The kiss was a painful disappointment. From those deep and mysterious fantasies, she expected to feel something wonderful. There was, however, no flutter within her breast, no stir of emotion, no twinge of arousal.

Mary cried inside at that moment and cried throughout that sleepless night. Her promise was her nightmare.

Mary Bellani wed Michael Samora at the Church of the Immaculate Conception in October, 1904. Through the three months of their engagement, there had been times when Michael was open with her, but more often he was closed and distant. Always, she wanted to believe that she might change him. Mary allowed the confidence in her mind to dispel the doubt in her heart.

It was a small wedding. John and Lucia were reluctant participants in a ceremony that both opposed. The Depelos believed the blithe spirit of Mary Bellani might never be able to shine in the darkness of Michael's personality. Luigi Anselmo prayed for their happiness, but held little faith it might ever happen. Riley Gillespie, Michael's best man, found it difficult to kiss the beautiful bride who, he was certain, would never find fulfillment with his distant friend.

But, the promised nuptial was performed by a Catholic priest and the good news sent back to Piedimonte.

News of weddings and funerals, events and activities, good times and bad, made their way from the Iron Range to the Old Country. Hundreds of letters each week were packaged for shipment to those distant places which were once called home. By rail from Hibbing to Duluth, those letters traveled eastward to meet the returning ships on a transatlantic voyage to Yugoslavia or Austria, to Finland, Italy, and to more than thirty countries that had contributed their sons and daughters to the spreading Mesabi.

December 1907

Lud Jaksa left the chilly room and returned downstairs to join the miners for another beer. Tony Zoretek was left alone to write his letter home. He pondered the three empty papers on the table top and the words he must find to fill them. Little more than two weeks remained before Christmas, and he must get a letter back to his family in Churile, Slovenia, before the holiday.

A warm nostalgia crept into his thoughts. Christmas back home. Mother's foods and sweets, gifts shared by all, relatives and visiting the neighbors, Christmas Mass; everything that made that time of the year so very special in his memory.

Tony considered procrastinating. The young man was dispirited by loneliness and estrangement on this Sunday night.

"No!" He caught himself drifting toward self pity. "This letter will be written tonight."

He made the sign of the cross, rested his head on his arms on the table, and tried to relax his tension. Tony would pray for divine guidance in expressing words which might bring a measure of joy to his family as they celebrated their Christmas.

"Dear God, please help me to find the right things to say, and to be honest. As you alone can know, I do not want to hurt the feelings of my dear family. Bless me in my task, Amen."

Despite his good intentions, Tony would allow his pen to lie.

Dear Father and Mother, and brothers Jake and Rudolph:
Today is Sunday and very cold in this place so far north in Minnesota. Everything is covered with a snow that is deeper than even that of our own beautiful Mt. Triggav in the Julians. Here we have

no mountains but, with all of the mining going on, I believe that we will be making some by ourselves. I do not know how cold it is here today, but my feet become numb very quickly when I go out of the house.

Tony frowned over his words. Mother would be concerned about his health in such cold, and he did not want to worry her. He contemplated starting the letter over again, but had only three pieces of paper. He would need them all, and must be more careful . . .

But this cold is so very refreshing for me. I seem to breathe more deeply in this crisp air, and my cold feet tingle when I warm them by the fire stove in my comfortable room. Hibbing is not a very large city, but it is a very busy place. It has a library with many books, and you remember how much your son enjoys his reading. It also has large schools for the children to learn their new language and how to write in English. Only a short walk from my house is a very lovely Catholic Church.

The mention of a Catholic Church would very much please both of his parents. Tony felt a pang of guilt. He believed that his great sin during the strike was a *mortal* one and most displeasing to God. He found difficulty in a worship ceremony that gave thanks to the Almighty for the blessings of life. Since his arrival, Tony had attended Sunday mass only three times, two of those for the wrong reason. On that first Sunday, in October, he had seen a most beautiful woman in the church. She had long dark hair and a lovely, fair complexion. He took Lud with him the next Sunday, and Lud recognized her as the seamstress from a shop downtown. The next week he sat only two pews behind the woman in her black dress and was completely distracted from both the priest and the Mass he offered. The woman seemed to have a deep sadness in her heart, and Tony could see a melancholy in her eyes as she returned from receiving communion. He wondered to himself how a woman of such beauty could be so unhappy?

Tony scanned the last sentence on the page. What else could he write about Hibbing? This rowdy place of many nationalities and languages, of swarthy miners, gamblers and whores, of saloons and brothels. This 'melting pot' of every diverse and perverse element of humanity was his home in this strange new country.

> *I like this city because of the many different people who live here and come from everywhere in the world. My best friend lives in my house. His name is Lud Jaksa, and he is from Ljubljana not far from our village in Slovenia. People are kind and friendly to those of us who are new to their country. And the city grows larger by the day with fine new houses and buildings along the streets.*

Tony paused. He must now write the most difficult part of this letter. His parents would want to know about Uncle Steven. A pain throbbed at his temples over the lie he would conjure. Had his mother's brother told them anything about that time in July, when the miners went on strike? If his parents knew, then this letter was blatant hypocrisy . He must be careful.

> *I am hopeful that I will see more of Uncle Steven Skorich in this new year. I did see Steven upon my arrival here and again a short time ago. But we both have been so busy with our lives and our work that it is hard to get together. Steven's house is in Chisholm which is nearly ten kilometers from where I am living. Perhaps my uncle is pleased that his nephew is not a burden on his life.*

Tony had considered seeking out his relative many times but was so guilt ridden that he could not take the initiative. Steven had been one of the union's leaders during the unsuccessful strike and had paid the consequences for his involvement. His uncle had been 'blacklisted' by the Oliver Mining Company and would never again be able to work in the mines of the Mesabi. Tony, unaware at the time, had contributed to the ruination of the man who had paid for his journey to America.

Besides the one fleeting glance from his train window, Tony had seen Steven only one other time, and that was but a few weeks ago. He and Lud had attended a social gathering at the *Slovenski Dom* Lodge. Tony was certain that Steven had noticed him in the crowded hall, but before the two men might be forced to meet, Steven was out of his sight and not to be seen again that evening.

The job that I have is . . .

The rattle of a train in the yards outside seemed a welcome interruption to the stress he was feeling. Tony stood up from the table, stretched his arms, and moved to the frost-framed window. Icy flakes swirled in the frigid night. He cupped his hands around his mouth and exhaled warm breath to ease the numbness that had crept into his fingers. He returned to the letter.

. . . going very well.

Zoretek's layoff was into its seventh week, and his savings were nearly exhausted . He thought of the overdue rent. Could he possibly make it until spring with the eleven dollars he had tucked in his trunk? There was a timber crew working in the Grand Rapids area to the west of Hibbing, and some of the miners had been hired there. Lud seemed determined to go to Chicago and had his brother's assurance of a job when he got there. What would he do these next few months? Tony massaged the back of his neck to relax himself.

The open pit mine operations were seasonal because neither man nor machine could function in this harsh winter climate. The few remaining underground mines in the area continued to send iron ore to the stockpiles, but only the older and experienced miners held those scant year-around jobs.

I fear, however, that for a short while I may be without work. During this time of the year, the mines rest for a few months. This matter does not concern me because I have been careful with my expenses here and keep several dollars in the bank.

But why had no money been sent back to his family in Churile? Surely his parents would think him greedy and irresponsible.

When the spring comes, I will have much more money and will send some of it to each of you. My family may have another Christmas in just a few months. That will be a happy time for you.

Tony scanned what he had just written. Such a fabrication, but the ink was already dry on the page. He had one more blank paper to fill and was determined to end his letter in a manner that might assure his family of his happiness.

Earlier today, Mrs. Dukich, a woman from Croatia, brought me a hot bowl of stew and sandwiches of beef with cheese for an evening meal. It was delicious but, mother, your cooking remains a most pleasant memory for me. Do not worry that your son might ever become a skinny man with so much good food always to eat.

Tony's stomach turned in angry protest at the thought of food. He had not eaten since yesterday.

I know that all of you are in readiness for the Savior's Birthday. I will miss this special time with my family but will remember you with a special prayer at our Christmas Mass, and I shall light a candle at the church for all of the Zoreteks.

Tony could write no more. Already he had spent two tormented hours on the three pages.

I send every happiness and God's blessings to my loved ones . . .
                              Your loving son and brother, Anton

The letter to Slovenia found the proper hands, mail bags, and boats to reach the Zoretek family two days before Christmas. Helen saved the letter so that it could be shared with the whole family at their Christmas Eve meal. She could hardly contain her excitement as she handed the envelope to Jakob after his blessings had been spoken at the table.

The father read his son's letter without a trace of emotion.

"Oh, papa, our Anton must have money in all of his pockets, doesn't he, papa? What a wonderful place that Minnesota must be." Nine year old Rudolph was elated over the letter. "Will my big brother send money so that I can join him when I'm older?"

That night Jakob and Helen sat up late together. Neither had commented on the letter that both had read over several times. Tony's parents possessed the wisdom of parents everywhere. Their son could not conceal the truth of his life in that distant place. Jakob put his arm around his wife and caressed her shoulder.

"I'm afraid, my dear . . . afraid that our son has found very little happiness over there." His voice was strained.

Helen tensed. "I have the same feelings. He tried so hard to make his words pleasing to us. We must pray that everything will be better for our Anton," she sobbed.

'TIMO'S CAUSE'

Jurva Of Vaasa Province
(Finland)
1905

From behind the cluster of birch trees, she watched the man sitting on the large rock shelf which hung over the sky-tinted lake. The sun had risen, but an April chill lingered in the fresh morning air. He was a solitary figure whittling absently at a stick while dangling his bare feet in the icy water. He was as one with the quiet wilderness that surrounded his isolated hiding place.

Senia could not understand the passions that stirred within her husband. She was a strong-willed, intelligent, and perceptive woman. Yet, she wondered, how she could continue to abide a life so clouded by his dark privacy? What secrets were locked inside this intense man? Why did he no longer find any time to talk or to sleep with her in their bed? His remote introversion lately was of greater concern to her than even his many lengthy absences. Timo Arola had become a loner and shut his wife of three years out of his life.

But on this morning, Senia was determined to find some answers to these tormenting questions. For almost an hour she had been following him along a narrow deer path to this remote place deep in the forest beyond their home. She fought back her tears as she watched him pitch the carved stick into the lake shading his eyes to watch a hawk soaring high above the tranquil, glimmering water.

"You can come out now, Senia. I know you're there." Timo did not turn but kept his gaze fixed on the vast stretch of teal blue. "I know when I'm being followed."

"Timo." Senia swallowed hard and stepped over a fallen tree that crossed the path. "I'm not a very good tracker, am I?" She found a place to sit beside him on the flat surface of the rock outcropping and placed her hand on his thigh.

"Sorry to disturb you and your deep thoughts. Thoughts of what, however, I cannot imagine. That's why I came here," Senia explained. "I need to talk with you, Timo. I've needed to talk for weeks, even months. But you always keep me at a distance."

Senia had thought about what she might say while trailing Timo through the forest. "I can't help thinking that I have lost you to something, or to someone, but I just have questions without answers. Have I lost you to this hideaway in the woods, or to the world you live in and keep locked away from me? Please, I am your wife, Timo! I deserve some kind of explanation."

Timo squeezed her hand. "You do, and I'm glad you found me this morning, Senia. I knew you would one of these days." He smiled weakly, met her eyes. Senia had been patient through his trials of late and deserved to know the truth. "We do need to talk. It's time now." The knot in his stomach tightened. He so loved this woman. He knew how deeply he had hurt her with his long absences, cheating her with the lies behind his frequent travels.

A silence passed between them. The distant call of a loon brought its wondrous music to the air and relaxed the tension. Everything about this morning, and this remote place, seemed ideal for the dialogue which had been absent from their relationship.

"Senia, I've had many things on my mind, and I've had to keep them all to myself. They're disturbing, you must believe me." Timo turned to face her, cupped her chin in his hand, and gave her a light kiss. He had been thinking about this inevitable conversation, and how he might tell his wife. "I'm afraid there is precious little time remaining."

Senia pulled away releasing her hand from his. She was confounded. So little time remaining? Did he mean to tell her about another woman? Was there a job somewhere in Europe?" Senia wondered. Her face puzzled at her husband's strange words.

"What do you mean, so little time?" she asked him. "Is it a job? I know how hard you've been looking for a job. You've made so many trips to Helsinki that I can't count them all. Is that why you've been so distant from me, and why you always seem so troubled, Timo?" She took his hand back into her own. "I know it has been hard on you looking for something that suits your skills, but these are distressing times for everybody in Finland."

"I have a job, Senia. It's my job that has been the reason for everything, for all the time that I'm gone from you, and for all the lies these past months."

"Lies?" Senia was unnerved by the word.

Timo's travels had always been under the pretense of finding work. That explanation had always been his most believable deception.

"Please listen carefully, my love. What I am about to tell you will put a world between us," Timo began his admission. "Long before I met you at the university in Helsinki, for nearly five years now, I have been involved in . . ." he swallowed hard on his next words, ". . . . in the *cause*. That's what most people call the socialist movement these days. All of my time has been committed to this struggle against the Russian oppression of our people, Senia. This has been my life all these past months."

Timo explained his work, his friendships, and the ultimate purpose of his life. The Russification occurring in his homeland, the constant political turmoil and blatant oppression was an ugly story, but it was the story behind everything he had been doing. Timo had studied philosophy in college, written in the underground newspapers, and had become an important voice in the Finnish liberation. His oratorical skills had gained him a wide reputation and made him a marked man in the process. The tall, slender, blond-haired man had been avoiding capture for months.

"And now, after months of moving from city to city returning to our home in the country only to hide . . . now I am in serious trouble. My arrest seems imminent, and I don't want to be a martyr locked in some Russian prison." Timo realized that the General Strike in Finland would be repressed by the Russians, and that the Czar's reprisals would be severe to those who were known agitators.

"I must go away very soon, Senia. Already a plan is being arranged for my escape to America. While there, I can learn more about Socialism. I hope to return one day and help bring freedom to our beloved Finland," Timo explained.

For more than an hour, Timo told his wife about what was happening while fervently expounding both his beliefs and his goals.

Senia listened with rapt attention and could almost feel the fire from his piercing blue eyes. Her empathy for his torment welled inside. Timo was so intelligent, articulate, and passionate. These qualities attracted her to this man when they studied at the university.

"If you must go, Timo, take me with you. Let me be a part of your life for once. Whatever your suffering, let it be mine as well. I am strong enough for anything. More importantly, I love you. I don't want to be apart from you any more," Senia pleaded.

"No. That's not possible. I'm sorry, but this is something that I must do by myself. Plans are being made for me. Senia, wait for me. That's all I ask. I will return home one day soon. We'll have the lifetime together that we promised each other, but I must go to America by myself!" he said with finality. Getting up from the rock and offering his hand to Senia, he turned toward the pathway back to their house. "Let's go back to the house now."

Senia was indignant. She had put up with Timo's deceptions far too long. His pledge to return 'one day soon' rang empty in her heart. His selfish determination to steal away in the night and journey to that far away land greatly disturbed her.

"You can walk back by yourself. I'll be along later." Senia gave her husband a look of reproof. "I may follow you to America, Timo, despite what you say. If I do follow you, I'll do a better job of it than I did this morning." She claimed his place and his solitude on the ledge. Senia peered out across the blue water and imagined the Atlantic which her husband would soon be crossing. She could not keep Timo here, that much she knew. But, would she be far behind?

August 1906

"Where is the promise of America?" His strident voice rang over the assembled street corner meeting.

"There is a tyranny here! A fraud has been conceived by the money-hungry capitalists who seek to starve us of the justice and equality that brought us to this corrupted land. Oppression by the mining industry can no longer be tolerated under this disgraced flag."

The tall, blond man cast the American banner irreverently to the wooden walkway, placed his foot on the field of white stars, and hoisted a red flag above his head.

"Here is the only standard for all who seek to be free! Socialism is the only hope for America!"

His impassioned tirade was greeted with sporadic applause. People glanced from the orator toward several police officers who stood on the far side of Tapio Hall on Cedar Avenue. The Hibbing police watched the episode and those assembled. The policemen were more amused than concerned until the American flag was blatantly desecrated. One of the officers stepped from the sidewalk onto the street. "Who in the hell does he think he is? Any of you guys seen him before?" asked Ole Nord, the burly captain in charge of the surveillance detail.

The others only shook their heads.

"I don't know either, but that bullshit sounds like treason to me," said Nord in disgust.

The blond man saw Nord step into the street and defiantly turned to face him. "Go and tell your masters what I am saying. Tell them that we will seize those very rights inherent to all people."

His rhetoric was sharp, and he was unintimidated by the armed police guards. Turning back to the small, nervous crowd, he called out in shrill voice, "The right to an equal share of the wealth derived from the sweat of our labors is what we demand. We must let those manipulating mine bosses know that we will crush their disgusting system of class exploitation."

The all-out threat infuriated some of the officers, and they drew ominous black sticks from their belts.

"Get ready, men!" Nord called out loud enough for all to hear. "This guy's getting me damn mad. Any more of this 'system crushing' shit, and I'm gonna run the bastard out of town."

Near the speaker's elbow, the union leader, Tedfilo Petriella, whispered, "Be careful! Don't incite those brutes anymore. If you do, we're gonna have more trouble than we've bargained for. We don't need that. Maybe you've gone far enough."

The caution, however, drew a sharp glance from the speaker's penetrating blue eyes. "Just let them try to start something. I have every right to say what I believe to be true."

Timo Arola was an extremist. His frustration was deeply rooted in these troubling times in Hibbing and across the Mesabi Iron Range. Miners were organizing themselves against the managers, especially the leaders of the Oliver Mining Company whose vast operations dominated the mining scene.

Since his escape from Vaasa in Finland and the General Strike against the Russian Czar Nicholas, Timo had been espousing his brand of revolutionary socialism in Northern Minnesota. The brazen young Finnish immigrant was encouraged by the undercurrent stirred by his forceful speeches. He believed that one day soon his vision of a classless society would be realized, maybe here and maybe soon. So deep were his convictions, he had become fearless of any consequences. If necessary, he would be a willing martyr to the Socialistic reform that was his passion.

"That was one hellava speech this afternoon," said Martin Alto patting his comrade on the back. "You really let em know how it is here. Gave 'em something to think about."

Timo nodded. "The union people wanted me to tone it down some. Maybe they're right. We've got lots of work to get done this week. Confrontation will come soon enough."

Finnish Socialists from across the country were meeting in Hibbing to discuss the potentials of forming a National Federation of local units. They were joined by Petriella and other Western Mine Unionists for a seven day convention at Tapio Hall. The meetings promised to generate some lively philosophical debate and, it was hoped by many, a strong, organized front.

"I'll wager that we have a strike next summer." Timo Arola posed his challenge to Steven Skorich who sat beside him in the crowded local Temperance Society hall. The Monday morning session would begin shortly.

"Maybe so? If we have to, we will. But I'm hoping our union people can negotiate something acceptable without a strike." Skorich was an ardent disciple of the Western Federation of Miners but uncomfortable in the midst of these ardent Socialists. He puzzled over the fraternity of the two groups, wondering why his union's leadership embraced these radicals so casually.

"But, let's be realistic, my friend. We've failed every time before and have never gained a thing from our walkouts. My people have a gut feeling that a strike is both dangerous and hopeless." Steven shook his head, uneasiness gripping his stomach.

"Hopeless!" Timo shot a sharp glance toward the large Slovenian miner who was called Korenjack. "Don't use that word, Steven!"

Skorich, however, met the irate stare from Timo with his own level understanding of a situation he knew more about than did the recently-arrived socialist seated next to him. "Timo, 'hopeless' is an honest word, an attitude that many of us have come to live with in our struggles. Too many miners are afraid of any union. If they lose their jobs, they have nowhere to go. Don't get excited by what I'm telling you. We have a tough job to do, and we must do it together."

Timo locked his arm with Steven's and softened. "You are a wise man, my friend. You have seen much more of this than I have."

"Not yet wise, only learning. That's why I am with your group this morning. To learn and to bring back what I hear to those men I work with every day."

Timo sensed the uneasiness of his colleague. Steven was a non-violent man who offered a balance to his own inflamed spirit. But, more than anything else, Timo desired the confidence of this soft spoken giant of a man who was so widely respected.

"Steven, I want you to dream with me. Please keep your mind open to the promise of socialism." Timo paused in his thoughts then turned to meet the smile of his Slovenian friend. "Let's talk more later. I will be going to the lake after our meetings today. Will you join me?"

Timo had found a special place in the woods east of Hibbing. He went there often to think about things. The three mile walk put him in touch with his home in Finland and the wife he hoped to see again one day. Senia was often in his thoughts, but he never spoke of her to his friends. In the solitude of the forest near the lake, his spirit could connect with hers.

At this moment he recalled Senia looking for him in the forest near Vaasa and smiled to himself. Steven interrupted his reverie. "I'd enjoy that, Timo. Just the two of us. Your place at the lake is as peaceful to me as it is to you."

The mine workers had many legitimate issues with their employers. Among them was the long established practice of 'contract labor'. Bruno

Moscatelli was an Italian delegate to the Tapio Hall convention. The underground miner hoped to voice his anger over the deplorable Oliver Company practice of contract labor.

Sitting by himself in the back of the room, the diminutive man stewed about the system of bribes that the mine bosses used to exploit the men who worked for them. The contract arrangement provided pay based on the ore tonnage a miner loaded daily into the tram cars. To make decent money, a man needed to be assigned to a productive digging location because many of the underground drifts had large veins of worthless dirt from which no pay could be realized.

Bruno seemed lost in his own thoughts. Aside from Steven Skorich who sat near the front of the room, he knew only a handful of the people here and had no idea of what to expect from these meetings of miners and reformers.

Bruno Moscatelli's painful memory of an incident three months before, creased painfully across his face and stirred a bile in his stomach. He remembered as if it were only yesterday.

"Hey, Bruno, after this next blast we're getting into some sandy shit." Barton Wick was the shift boss of Bruno's crew and a notorious exploiter of the tram workers under his supervision. Over the years, Wick had learned to use his authority over other men in clever and wicked ways. His strong-handed intimidation had made him a despised and frightfully demented man.

"Near as I can tell now, there's only gonna be one decent pocket of digging. It should be lotsa money for a week or so." Wick's thin lips turned into a tight, devious smile.

Bruno could not contain his enthusiasm for an opportunity to get assigned to the rich ore. "Whatta ya want for a job in the good stuff, boss? Maybe a coupla extra dollars, huh?" The miner tried to smile but could not. "You know me, Mr. Wick. I'm always willin to pay. Ya just gotta tell me what ya want."

Sometimes Wick would put his snuff box out on a ledge and allow the men to put a coin or two inside. His silver box was not out on the ledge this morning.

"No, Moscatelli, it's not money this time. You save your money for your family." Wick was about to give his contract game a sinister and perverted new twist.

Bruno puzzled, "No money boss?"

At times, other miners had provided hams, chickens, or fresh garden vegetables to their bosses for good digging. Bruno would be pleased if his bribe was not money this time. His wife Maria was saving every dollar to help pay for her sister's passage to America.

"Moscatelli, tomorrow I can get you an extra afternoon shift. You understand?" Bruno nodded. A change in a miner's work schedule, or an overtime shift was not uncommon and easily arranged by a foreman.

"You see, I was thinkin that maybe you could tell your pretty little wife, Maria, that a very nice man will be stopping by the house while you're here at the mine."

Bruno felt a rage; his fists clenched tightly. In his outrage, he stepped toward the burly foreman. "No! You're a filthy pig, you bossman!" His eyes held a fire. "You're the scum of this company." He stammered his anger. "What kinda man do ya think I am? Let ya take my Maria to our bed?"

"Cool down, 'wop'! Don't get so damn excited and don't start somethin that you'll regret." Wick taunted the smaller man with his clenched fist, then smiled and shrugged his huge shoulders. "I was only suggestin. Thought that you needed to keep yer money."

"Damn you! I know what you wanted. Never, do you hear me? Never!" Bruno turned away, took his shovel, and moved toward the bank of dirt where he was assigned for that day's shift.

For three weeks Bruno and his partner toiled in the worthless dirt of the Utica Mine's fifth underground level to no avail. Their combined tonnage of ore was yielding the miners very little pay.

"I can't unnerstan dis assignment, Bruno." Eddie Koski was deeply frustrated. "I gave Mr. Wick money to get outta dis dirt, just like I done so many udder times, but we been gettin da worse places ta dig every day." The Finn was perplexed, either he or Bruno must have done something to rankle their boss. But what, Eddie wondered?

Bruno could not confide his problem to his partner of more than a year. It pained him to realize that Koski's family of six children were suffering because of Wick's treachery.

"Ya gotta try to find another partner, Eddie. I'm sure as hell that Wick's got it in for me."

Eddie rested for a moment from his shoveling. "I'm sorry to tell ya, Bruno, but I already asked Wick lottsa times. Wick ain't gonna let me get no new partners. I jus don't know what ta do 'bout it."

Bruno Moscatelli was a proud, compassionate man, but under this stress he was weak as well. One night he confided his dilemma to Maria. With tears in his eyes, he told his wife that he must quit his job in the mine. Maria's plans of paying for her sister's trip to America would have to wait, unless! He begged Maria to do this despicable thing just one time.

The following week Barton Wick defiled Maria Moscatelli during the afternoon shift he had arranged for her husband. When Bruno returned home late that night, he heard Maria's sobbing behind their closed bedroom door. Bruno was devastated over what he had allowed to happen. His Maria had paid the disgusting price of his cowardice. The damage to his relationship with Maria would never be undone. Their bedroom door would never be open to him again. But, Bruno would avenge his disgraceful act.

The mutilated body of Barton Wick was discovered near the railroad tracks below South Street. Wick, it appeared, had been run over by a late night ore train. Several puncture wounds on the neck and face, however, belied the report of another accidental death in Hibbing. The victim had been robbed of a large amount of money he was reportedly carrying in his wallet.

Maria Moscatelli never found her butcher knife. She thought it must have been lost somewhere in the small vegetable garden where she had used it last. Bruno's wife would never know the identity of the benefactor who had left an envelope with thirty dollars tucked under the front door of her small house, but it was enough for Maria to pay for her sister in Italy to join her in Hibbing.

Bruno snapped out of his self-loathing contemplation. He heard the call for attention from the front of the room. The meeting was to begin. Steven Skorich introduced Tedfilo Petriella to the audience.

September 1907

"Honestly, Senia, I think this whole idea of yours is craziness. Absolute futility!" Red faced, Henry Reivo shook his head at the sister seated across from him.

"I thought that by now you would have let go of that strange man. It was a mistake from the beginning. Surely, you know that. And what have you heard from him since he's been gone? Nothing! Nothing in what, nearly two years is it now?"

"Timo is my husband, Henry. I love him even if he doesn't write. We have a vow that I take seriously, and no, it was not a mistake. You never tried to understand him. You never even liked him."

Henry lit his pipe while regarding Senia. "Let me tell you what I do understand. You are a young, attractive, and educated woman. It won't be long before our bank in Vaasa offers you an accounting position. Hell, you know as much about the bank and finance as I do. Don't waste that opportunity, Senia."

Henry had spent months priming his sister in the intricacies of accounting procedure and often brought ledgers home from the bank for her instruction. "Your whole life is ahead of you, not behind." Henry appealed for his sister's logic.

"Nothing you say will change my mind, Henry. I must find him. You can't understand how tormenting it is not to know where he is or what he's doing. I don't sleep at night, and I won't until I know." Senia would not cry in her brother's presence. She knew that she was bright and reasonably attractive as well. Tall for a woman, Senia had the blonde hair and blue eyes so typical of southern Finns. She and Timo might have passed for brother and sister as easily as husband and wife.

"It's your life!" Henry sighed in resignation. "You will do what you want to do. You always have."

"Let's not argue. I have received a letter from Mrs. Niemi in Hibbing, Minnesota. Timo has been there for some time now. It's not that I don't know where to look for him. Mrs. Niemi will gladly let me stay in her home once I get there."

"Yes, I know." Henry put his pipe aside, reached across and took Senia's hands in his own. "And, I know many Finns have settled in that area. Minnesota is very much like our own country with the forests, the lakes, and even the climate." He smiled. "I only hope that you don't like it so much that you'll want to stay there very long. Find Timo if you must, and bring him back home where both of you belong. Let me know if I can help you."

"My goodness, Senia, such a lady you have become." Elia Niemi could not conceal her surprise over the comely woman she had not seen since Senia's childhood. "Let me help you with all these bags. Come in now and make yourself comfortable. This will be your home for as long as you wish." The widow led Senia into the small living room beyond the front door.

Later, and far into the evening, the two women talked. Mrs. Niemi was active in the Finnish Temperance Society and familiar with the diverse affairs of Hibbing. "Yes, he used to stop by here quite often, usually when he was half starved." Elia smiled over the memory. "But I think the last time was . . ." She searched her memory, "Sometime in July. Uh huh, it was just after this American celebration of Independence."

Elia's expression changed to a serious frown. "He had been making speeches that day. Timo and his Socialists were having a grand picnic in the fairgrounds, and there was much talk about the miner's strike at that time."

"I am not surprised, Mrs. Niemi, that's the kind of thing that Timo most enjoyed, making speeches. He had lots of trouble back in Vaasa with his activities. Has it been more of the same here?"

"Timo was very involved, my dear. His reputation, can I say, was quite notorious in these parts last summer." Elia explained the dramatic events of recent months as best she could remember them. She had attended some of the rallies while participating in Socialist activities, so she had some insight concerning Timo's involvement.

"But it was all to no avail, Senia. The strike was a failure. Those who were involved have been fired and forced to scatter all over the country. Some of them were even jailed in Duluth. Finns, who were suspected of supporting the strike, have suffered greatly in reputation here." She sighed in her despair.

"Many Finns will never be hired again in the mines and have gone into the countryside trying their hands at farming. It has been a hard time. We are now beginning to organize food cooperatives so that our people can survive this next winter."

"But Timo, what has happened to my husband? It has been since July you said. That's three months ago."

Elia looked beyond Senia and framed her thoughts: "Only rumors, I'm afraid. But, now you are here, and we can find out for certain."

"What rumors?" Senia asked.

"They are far-fetched I am sure. I was told your husband returned to

Finland, then that he's in Wisconsin or Michigan or even Montana where they mine coal. Who can begin to know what is the truth? But, Senia, you must stay here in Hibbing for a while. He may be in hiding somewhere nearby. I have heard that rumor as well."

Trouble, running, and hiding. Senia was reminded once again that the patterns of Timo's life were dangerous and transient.

"You are probably right, Elia. May I call you that? I must stay here. Perhaps together we can find out the truth."

But, as days became weeks and autumn a portent of winter, Senia learned nothing more than the rumors that Elia had already mentioned. The mystery of Timo Arola remained a frustration, and Senia realized that she must find a job to help Elia with the expenses. Her pride would not allow her to write home to Henry and ask for money.

"Yes, my dear, I must be painfully honest with you. It would help a great deal if you could earn some money. Already I worry about coal for the winter, yet work is so hard for a woman to find in this town."

"But I am skilled in accounting and banking, Elia, and I speak English quite well."

"That is true, but you are a woman, and Finnish besides. I fear that domestic work is all you might hope to find. Even that will not be easy for a woman with the name 'Arola'.

"Excuse me, Elia." Senia laughed. "My name is *Smith*. Senia Smith. What do you think of that?"

Senia found Peter Moran's grand colonial style house on Washington Street and strode confidently to the front door.

"Yes, madam. I am Miss Smith. I have an interview with Mr. Moran for the domestic position." Senia's English was crisp and articulate. "Perhaps I am early."

Moran's domestic, Mildred Graham, was a sour-faced woman of few words. "I'll bring ya to see him."

Senia was escorted through the spacious living room and, after a knock on the heavy oak door, into the library. The huge room was expensively furnished and held impressive shelves of books. "Mr. Moran is a man of considerable wealth," Senia thought to herself.

Peter Moran looked tired behind the stack of ledgers and scattered papers on his desk. He had just picked up the phone and glanced absently at Mildred. The maid cleared her throat and introduced the well-dressed, attractive blonde woman beside her in the wide doorway. Although most of the hiring in his enterprises was left to underlings, Peter would personally interview those applying for employment in his home.

"This here's Miss Smith, sir," said Mrs. Graham as she curtsied.

"Oh yes, please sit down." Moran gestured toward a chair beside his desk and continued with his phone conversation.

"Sweeny, get your ass over here! These books of yours, my personal account stuff, everything's a damn mess! I can't understand your figures. What do I pay you for anyhow?" Moran impressed Senia as being obnoxious and short tempered. "You're damn right I'm mad." Moran was obviously frustrated and his language blatantly vulgar in the lady's presence. "Right, half an hour, then. Don't make me wait!"

Moran slammed down the phone with a short, "Sorry . . .

"Now, Miss Smith, let me see. I have your letter here somewhere in this clutter." Moran fumbled, found the paper and quickly scanned the meticulously typed page. "I'm impressed. Did you type this yourself?"

"Yes. And, if I may be so forward, sir, I could not help but overhear your conversation. Those ledgers . . ." Senia gestured toward his desktop. She was astute and recognized an opportunity. "I have had considerable experience with bookkeeping and have a great interest in financial matters. Perhaps I may be able to . . ." Senia let her words drop, "I am sorry," she apologized. "That was very presumptuous of me."

Moran's eyes narrowed on the attractive woman. Something about her clear articulation and demeanor made an immediate impression on him. "This woman is not domestic material," he realized.

"Experience with bookkeeping you say. Where? Tell me about it will you please, Miss Smith. I see nothing about that in this letter." Leaning back in his chair, Moran dropped the paper onto his desk. "Yes, tell me about it. Sweeny at the hotel confounds me sometimes with all his high minded numbers. As you probably heard, it frustrates the h . . ." he caught himself, "makes me awfully mad!"

"In Europe, sir." Senia had a spark in her eyes. "I studied bank accounting at university for two years." Senia realized she must be careful about what she said but recognized potential advantage in this man's predicament. "I am quite good with numbers and may be able to help you, sir, Mr. Moran."

"Where in Europe?" Moran asked.

Senia took a chance, "In Vaasa, sir."

Moran puzzled.

"A city on the coast of Bothnia," she said. Senia hoped that Moran might not know that Bothnia was in Finland.

Moran had no conception of European geography. "Yes, I know of the place," he lied. He pulled a chair beside his desk. "What do you make of all this?" He slipped a thickly bound ledger in front of her. "I'd really like to know what Sweeny is up to with all this crap."

Senia spent an hour in Peter Moran's office. Sweeny was kept waiting outside.

"I'll be damned! 'Commingling' you say, the hotel finances with my personal expenses? That sonofabitch." But Moran was smiling. "Miss Smith, you work for me, beginning tomorrow, if you can. And, not as a domestic, I assure you. We can work out the details later, but I think you will like it here. This is the first time I've had any idea about what my bank account balance is. Now . . ." Peter rose from his desk extending his hand to Senia. "Will you tell the man waiting outside that he can come in? I'll be damned!" he repeated as he escorted Miss Smith to the door.

Little Bernie Ducette had his first taste of America on the train ride from New Jersey to St. Paul, Minnesota.

"Chocolates! Here! Take some chocolate candy for the children." A blue-suited man passed out five cent packages to the immigrant passengers in the crowded car.

Seven year old Bernie delighted at the rows of round chocolate in the opened box the man held out toward them.

"*Merci, merci beau coup,* I mean, thank you!" Bernie's mother said as she returned the smile of the vendor.

"Oh, mama, surely we are in America now." The boy bit into the lush candy. "Delicious!" His face and fingers were quickly smudged with sticky brown as the chocolate morsels were hastily eaten.

Minutes later the man returned from the forward car and walked down the aisle again. This time, when he reached their seat, he held out his large hand.

"For the chocolates, Ma'am. Pay me please." His face and voice were stern. Gone was the toothy smile of minutes before.

Mrs. Ducette reached deeply into the handbag on her lap. Two gold dollars were all that she possessed. Her face was marked with the anxiety she felt.

She held out the two coins in her delicate hand. "How much money do you need for the small box of candy?" she asked.

"Thank you," the man took both coins and stuffed them into the deep pocket on his blue jacket, turned from them and walked away.

Hungry and tired, Madeline Ducette arrived in St. Paul two days later without a penny to her name.

Bernie was enrolled in a 'Frogtown' neighborhood primary school soon after their arrival. Madeline Ducette was determined that her son would learn the language of this new country and one day become a citizen.

But the youngster struggled miserably in school. The teacher intimidated him, and fellow students seemed to grasp the English grammar with relative ease. Mostly, he hated the spelling and vocabulary which were so vital to the recitation of his language lessons. Every day in school brought another headache, and every headache seemed to throb more painfully than the one before.

"Bernard, it's your turn now." Miss Scranton's hard stare was fixed on the nervous boy in the front desk.

"Yes Ma'am," he said politely.

She held up a picture "Now, pronounce the word and spell it."

"B . . . O . . . T . . . ," Bernie smiled confidently.

"No, try again, Bernard," the woman reproached.

Bernie heard a snicker behind him, then a whisper. "The dumb 'Frog' will never learn to spell nothin . . ."

Distracted, he tried again . . . , "B . . . O . . . T . . . E . . . ,"

At his second mistake, the same boy in back laughed, louder this time. It was a hideous laugh and cut Bernard deeply.

Miss Scranton shook her head. Bernie tried to concentrate every fiber of his mind, "B . . . O . . . O . . . T . . . !"

His tormenter scoffed again, "Let me spell it, Miss Scranton." The voice in back appealed. "Let me do it. It's such an easy word."

"No!" Pointing a finger at the boy, she insisted, "One more time, Bernard. Spell the word in the picture."

Embarrassed and dispirited, tears spilled from his eyes down his cheeks. "I cannot spell it!"

Frustrated by Bernard's giving up on his word, Miss Scranton berated him. "Then why are you in school, Bernard? Our desks are for children who want to learn, not for quitters."

The word 'boat' would never be forgotten nor would the laugh and taunt of the boy in the back of his classroom. Bernie never remembered the face or the name of the boy who had caused him to drop out of school. However, the teacher who had embarrassed him that day lived near his neighborhood. One morning Miss Scranton awoke to the smell of smoke in the air. The teacher found that the outhouse in her back yard was a charred ruin.

As a youth and into adulthood, Bernie drifted from job to job. He was a street hustler and a petty thief, but his biggest thrill was always a fire. When he was discharged from the stockyards in South St. Paul, he left a familiar reminder that he had been there. Arson was the trail he always left behind.

One night Bernie Ducette was quietly drinking a beer in a 'Frogtown' saloon. Down the bar three men were talking. One of the men laughed loudly. Startled, Bernie felt a flush come over his face. He remembered that cruel laugh over the space of the thirteen years since he left the primary school. His memory was vivid, and the hatred it inspired throbbed in his heart. It was the same peculiar voice of that taunting boy.

To his list of countless petty crimes, Bernie Ducette added the most heinous one. Neither his victim, nor anybody else, would ever know the reason for an apparently senseless murder in the alley behind the saloon.

From St. Paul to Duluth to Hibbing, Bernie was on the run. In Hibbing he found a job at a local liquor warehouse but was fired by the owner only months afterward. His one friend in town was killed in a freak accident, and Bernie felt the urge to move again. Maybe he'd go back to Duluth and the ore docks where he worked before. Then, something happened to keep him in Hibbing.

Life had been a cruel ordeal and America a land of empty promises for the illiterate Frenchman. Neither those terrible headaches from his school days, nor his antisocial attitude ever went away.

For a time, though, Bernie Ducette was inspired by a hope. A vision enflamed him while he was attending a picnic on a spring Saturday afternoon. The people at the fairgrounds were most friendly to him, and the food settled well in an empty stomach.

"There will be a better tomorrow!" the man was saying. "We will find justice and equality in this wretched place. Yes, nobody will have any more than anybody else. Can you imagine that? The great wealth of this land will be shared by one and all in equal measure. We will rid ourselves of rich and poor!"

The words were like seed in his fallow mind. Clearly, this man spoke the truth. His passion and conviction made a powerful impression on Bernard. Yes, there seemed no doubt, the ideals expressed by the tall blond man were everything he had ever hoped to believe in. He moved forward toward the front of the gathering, clapping and cheering with a newfound fervor.

After the speech, a woman, Mrs. Neimi, came around with a collection box for the Socialist cause. Bernie offered two dollars; it was all the money he had in the world.

"I want to meet that man," he told the woman who thanked him for the generous contribution. Bernard gestured toward Timo Arola, "That man who promises us equality and justice."

From that day forward and for many months, Bernie was near the side of Timo Arola. Although he could not comprehend the complex issues about the miner's strike, his passion has been stirred by the prospect of a better tomorrow. Tirelessly, he marched and paraded with the red flag held high above his head. And, when the trainloads of scabs came rolling into Hibbing, Bernie was in the front lines shouting his curses, "Oliver whores!" Everything that Timo believed was like a sacred ideology to the zealous new French disciple of Socialism.

"Let's get one of them, Timo." Gripping large stones in both hands, Bernie was eager to incite the scabs.

The two men stood in the shadows of the sweltering July night, watching the procession of immigrant strikebreakers walking down the dark Hibbing avenue toward a boarding house.

"This is a strike!" Bernie shouted like all the others. "Go home, you filthy bastards. Oliver whores!"

Bernie stepped into the street and threw a heavy rock at one of the scabs, hitting him squarely in the back dropping him to the street.

"No, Bernie, get back here!" Timo shouted as he grabbed his friend's arm. "We don't want to start something. They've got guns." Timo was into the street restraining his friend.

Bernie saw the cop swing his rifle in their direction, "Timo! Look out!" Bernie screamed as a sharp crack split through the darkness behind the marchers.

Bernie Ducette was one of a very few who knew about Timo's murder that night. Steven Skorich and Martin Alto buried the inspiration of Bernie's life near a remote lake that was a favorite place in Timo Arola's troubled time in Hibbing. The gravesite was under a tree, near a rock ledge, overlooking the quiet water. Timo had taken Bernie there once to talk about the hopes and dreams that both men shared. With the death of his friend, Bernie Ducette was left without any hope of a better tomorrow.

BOOK TWO

The Hotel Moran

'The Mesaba Ore'

DURING THE EARLY MONTHS OF her marriage, Mary spent all of her tears. She no longer dwelt in the abyss of Michael's cruel deceit. This union had defiled her womanhood. She had not listened to her heart, nor had she listened to the good advice of her closest friends. She had honored her promise.

Mary Bellani Samora was too strong willed to be consumed by depression for long, and her optimism would prevail over her sorrow. Her employment with Luigi Anselmo had been rewarding, and his tailor shop had flourished since her arrival. Luigi had specialized only in fine men's clothing but now catered to women's fashion as well. Also, Mary found satisfaction in the activities of the Italian Society, and a spiritual renewal brought further involvement in activities of the Immaculate Conception Catholic Church. Mary was determined to build a new life from the remnants of her broken dreams.

It was late, and Mary stared from the apartment window at the blustery December night. The wind blew snow into drifts across the street below. Even the soft glow from the lamp outside failed to soften the harshness of Mary's first experience with a Minnesota winter. Michael was late again from the liquor warehouse where he now worked.

It was nearly midnight when she saw him coming out of the shadows of the alleyway and down the deserted street. He plodded through the snow with his head bent down against the fierce wind, dragging his feet in awkward prints across the white blanket. Mary could detect a stagger through the limp and understood why he was so late. Annoyed, she turned away from the window. Her revulsion was tempered by her sympathy for this pathetic man.

When he was inside, Mary hung his coat and brought him a steaming cup of black coffee. Without speaking, Michael sank heavily into the worn sofa and threw his head back so that he could stare at the ceiling and elude the eyes of his wife.

An uneasy silence hung in the room. Each waited for the other to speak.

"I'm sorry." Michael's speech was slurred as he leaned forward and sipped at his coffee still avoiding Mary's eyes. He shook his head absently, "I shouldn't have stayed out so late, but this new guy at the warehouse, Bernie, he wanted to buy me a coupla beers, and I thought you'd be sewing tonight anyhow."

Michael was always sorry . . . sorry about his drinking, sorry about his appearance, sorry about his negative attitude. All of these sorry's were symptoms of the consuming anguish of his impotency. "I won't let it happen again," he said.

Mary would not be caught within Michael's web of frustrations, problems, or apologies. They both knew his resolutions were as empty as their life together.

"Michael, I have made a decision," Mary breathed deeply. "I cannot live here any longer."

Her words brought him to his feet in an awkward stance. "My God, Mary, I promise I won't . . . ," Michael sniffled, rubbing his sleeve under his nose. Inside, he knew that Mary's decision was inevitable. Why had she put up with him as long as she had? Yet, his voice trembled, "Oh please, Mary, don't do this to me. Don't leave me."

"No, Michael, sit down before you fall down. It's not what you're thinking. I wouldn't leave you, even if you deserve it." She sat down on the far end of the sofa away from his sour, liquored breath. "It's this apartment. We're almost living with the Anselmos. God bless their generosity, but we need some privacy. What must they be thinking right now? I'm sure you woke them up again when you stumbled in the door." The time for her to show her resolve was now. She was not asking this time; she was telling her husband what she needed. "I have looked at a house down on Garfield Street."

"A house? A house for just the two of us? That's foolish, Mary. We're living almost rent free here. God knows we can't afford it. No, I've gotta get a better job first, make more money. It don't make any sense." Michael tried to assert himself on the matter, despite the relief he felt about the meaning of her 'leaving.' "No, I'm sorry."

Mary would not be discouraged by the husband she once vowed to honor and obey. She had already sacrificed too many of her dreams; perhaps her spirit would find space to grow in the quiet neighborhood of Garfield Street.

"We can certainly afford it!" Mary declared. "Have you any idea of what I am making in Luigi's shop these days? Do you know what I've saved? Your mother's generous wedding gift was supposed to help us buy a home for our family." Mary had never once cut into the delicate fabric of her husband's impotence and would not do so now. "We can afford it! I have already made an application at the bank. The Anselmos will guarantee the mortgage for us."

Luigi had arranged a Friday afternoon appointment with James McIntosh. The president of the the Merchants and Miners Bank lived in Duluth but usually spent two days a week attending to his business interests in Hibbing. "Don't be nervous, Mary," Luigi smiled his confidence. "He's a fine gentleman. You'll see for yourself. Everything will go well, I'm sure."

The bank president was congenial. "Please make yourself comfortable, Mrs. Samora, Mr. Anselmo." McIntosh shook their hands, offered them chairs, and sat down behind his desk. "I've already reviewed your loan application, ma'am."

Mcintosh was as distracted by the lady's comely beauty as he was puzzled by the absence of her husband at this meeting. He continued, "Mr. Moran's secretary has verified your husband's employment and income, and I have a salary figure from Mr. Anselmo." He nodded toward Luigi. "The down payment you have indicated is more than adequate." The bank president looked down at the numbers on the papers in front of him. It was highly uncommon to be discussing a mortgage transaction with a woman. "I can't see any problems with the monthly payments, but . . ." He looked up and met Mary's eyes. "How long do you expect to be employed?" He posed the question, looking from her to Luigi seated next to her as well.

"I hope to be working always, sir. Mr. Anselmo's business has expanded greatly these past few months." Her voice was confident as she smiled at McIntosh, then Luigi. "My husband and I will *not* be having a family, sir!"

The woman's candor impressed him. "Well, some things are never known for certain," McIntosh replied.

"This is not one of those things, sir." A trace of pain crossed Mary's face.

One month later, the Samoras moved into their house. Neither the new house, nor the prospect of a new beginning to their marriage, would alleviate Michael's habitual drinking. Both his attitude and demeanor continued in hopeless decline. He now drank openly, without apology. While Michael chose to sink into his self debasement, Mary chose to survive. Their lives had become as separate as the bedrooms in which they slept.

March 1905

A clear March morning spewed refreshing sunshine from the eastern sky, melting the snow and red mud in the streets into a slushy mixture. Stan Cleary, the liquor warehouse supervisor, stood in the large doorway off Railroad Avenue enjoying the freshness which rushed into the stagnant air of the building. Cleary, a sturdily built man, was not well respected by those who worked for him. He was neither bright nor motivated. As the liquor business grew, so did Cleary's frustration with his work.

Soon the Duluth train would be depositing its cargo of kegged Fitger's beer at the terminal across the street. It was the largest shipment Cleary could remember. Moran's business was expanding beyond what the existing distribution facilities could accommodate. Some temporary storage racks had just been constructed along the east wall of the warehouse, and Cleary had doubts about the workability of his makeshift solution to the storage problem. He reasoned that saving a few dollars might impress his employer. Cleary told the carpenters to use two by four lumber when they had recommended two by sixes.

"They're only temporary," reasoned Cleary. "In a coupla weeks we can tear 'em down and build something better."

Lars Udahl was the carpentry foreman and did not like the flimsy construction Cleary had ordered. Udahl shook the framework with both of his huge hands. It seemed sturdy enough. "I'm still worried. Just be careful not to overload them."

Stan Cleary supervised the unloading of the beer wagon and storage of the heavy oak kegs on the upper rack some twenty feet above the hardened clay floor. The casks were piled in a precarious pyramid. "Don't put no more onna top row. Start a new stack down below," Cleary instructed the workers while looking toward the open doorway.

"Hey, you . . . Samora . . . you're late!" he shouted toward the man who was slipping through the doorway. "One more time and yer down the fuckin' road."

Michael's head still pounded from a drinking bout with his friend Bernie Ducette the previous night. He saw Bernie sweeping the lumber scraps below the rack and hastened to join him.

Michael shot an apologetic glance at Cleary. "I'll work late tonight, make up the time. Sorry."

Cleary shrugged; the Dago kid and his Frog partner irritated him. Cleary shook his head as the two men worked slowly at their chores. He'd talk to Moran about getting rid of the two half-wits who were most likely involved in the missing liquor on his inventories. He also suspected they had something to do with a small, suspicious fire in a nearby storage building weeks before.

"Hey, Mr. Cleary, we're done sweepin here. What'ya want us to do now?" Michael dragged his leg up onto the beer wagon where the others worked unloading kegs. "Lemme give you guys a hand."

"Not your job kid! Better get your ass down and find some cleanup work," one of the men said as he spit out a plug of tobacco. Some of the brown juice splattered on Michael's pants.

Michael cursed the man under his breath.

"Get off that fuckin' cart, you crazy wop!" Cleary shouted as he stepped quickly in that direction. "That's men's work up there. Get down and find your goddamn broom."

Incensed, Michael rubbed at the pant stain and cussed, "Fuck you, all of ya. A man's job ya say!" Before anyone could stop him, Michael grabbed onto the keg that was being hoisted by a burly man nearby.

"What'n hell ya think you're doing?" the worker bellowed pushing him away with his elbow.

Michael's shoulder was already positioned underneath the heavy barrel. He leveraged his body and heaved. The weight was more than his weak legs could support. The oak keg slipped from his grip and slammed forcefully into the vertical timber supporting the upper tier of the rack. There was a sharp, splitting crack.

"Look out!" Cleary screamed. "The top row's gonna fall!"

Near the ceiling, the stack of kegs had begun to tumble.

"Jump!"

The two other men on the cart leaped and rolled across the floor away from the roaring crash.

Michael stood paralyzed. An earlier scene flashed in his mind . . . a huge bank of red ore . . . an avalanche of dirt in a deathly slow motion above the drone of the huge steam shovel . . . the deafening roar throbbed in his ears. The memory was lucid, overwhelming his every sense.

In that final instant, Michael's arms uplifted as if in fateful expectancy. Some imperceptible words escaped his twisted mouth, and his laugh was a shriek heard above the crash. It was his final laugh at the ironic twist of fate.

The first barrel to hit his head killed him instantly. Michael's body, crushed under several splinted kegs, was mutilated almost beyond recognition. Bernie Ducette would later swear that the last words he heard his only friend utter were, "Thank God!"

"He just stood there, Mr. Moran! As God is my witness, he didn't move. It was crazy. I couldn't believe my fuckin eyes. What more can I say? If only he'd jumped, tried to get out of the way, he mighta made it then." Stan Cleary tried to explain Samora's tragic death to his employer as the two men talked in Cleary's warehouse office. "One'a the guys said it was almost like suicide. Tol' me he thought the kid wanted to die right then and there. Said Samora was even laughin 'bout it, sir. Just crazy like I told ya it was."

Moran shook his head, his jaw set in angry disbelief. "I had a feeling about that wop the first time I laid eyes on him, but that damn Gillespie twisted my arm. Does this Samora have any family, Stan?"

"Has a wife, ain't got no kids though," Cleary remembered from the personnel records he kept.

"Send the widow a check for a hundred bucks. That should cover the funeral expenses. Send a sympathy note along with it and sign my name."

"Whatta ya want me do 'bout that Ducette?" Cleary asked his boss. "He's 'bout as loony as that Samora, Mr. Moran."

Moran had a vague recollection of the little Frenchman whom Cleary had hired as a janitor. "Go get him now. Send him here to the office. I'll fire that puny, sonofabitch myself. In the future, Cleary, let's not be hiring immigrants. I'm not really comfortable with people who weren't born here."

September 1906

Claude Atkinson was a journalist of considerable reputation. Claude was the owner-editor of Hibbing's *Mesaba Ore,* a daily chronicle of life in the rowdy mining town. Claude sat at his desk pondering an article for the Friday issue. The editor had been known to intermingle his personal commentary with reporting the news. His colorful style had endeared Claude to his many readers. The newsman had just learned that the injured bricklayer from the Grande Hotel construction site died of complications at the Rood Hospital. The man had been crushed beneath a wall that caved in during work on Tuesday of that week.

The recent accident evoked a vague memory of the young man who had been crushed to death at one of Peter Moran's warehouses about a year and a half before. "Hell of a way to go," he thought to himself. His Friday story, however, was not the construction death itself but what had caused the strange collapse of the building's south wall. He had tried to get Harold Markman to comment on the accident, but the contractor had been rather distant and aloof in recent weeks. 'Sabotage' was all that the St. Paul businessman would say about the incident. Markman's statement was 'off the record'. The word *sabotage,* however, seemed a strange choice. By whom and why Claude wondered?

Atkinson also learned that Jerry Sweeny, the project architect, had resigned his position with the Grande Hotel project. Sweeny had moved to Duluth to take another job. Nobody seemed to know what that job might be. Atkinson's contacts in Duluth were unable to provide any insight either. The hotel project, which started off so well, was running far behind schedule. Rumors were widespread that Peter Moran planned to build a new hotel of his own. There was a story here, but Atkinson was at a loss about what it might be. "Sabotage!" He was intrigued.

Nevertheless, Claude would report what his facts supported adding some of his own thoughts as well.

Many of us have wondered about the curious delays and mishaps at the Grande Hotel construction site. It has been speculated that last week's unfortunate collapse of a major wall was either an architectural error in the footing specs or the mortar used on the wall was of an inferior quality. This reporter, however, noted that all of the footings were poured under the same specifications. The team of bricklayers had been working on all three walls at the same time with the same materials. Nobody in a key position with the St. Paul financed venture would comment on the investigation into the accident. An unnamed source, however, seemed suspicious of foul play.

Local businessman, Peter Moran, assured this reporter that rumors of his intention to build a new hotel to rival that of the Markman group were groundless. The hotel concept, however, was a very good one according to Moran. "They just beat me to the punch on this one," the affable entrepreneur confided. "Whatever is good for Hibbing is all right with me. I wish them every success," Moran added.

The name of the construction worker killed in the mishap earlier this week has been identified as Billy Herrick, a St. Paul mason. The Mesaba Ore will follow the investigation closely and report our findings. We cannot help but believe that the word accident *has a hollow ring to it.*

The autumnal mildness of recent weeks was swept away by a piercing northerly which pushed an Arctic cold front over Northern Minnesota. The Saturday morning emerged sullen, shrouded in those drab gray-browns that threaten winter's arrival. Fallen leaves were whisked from beneath the naked trees whose branches clicked in the stiff breeze as if to applaud their coming dormancy. The abrupt seasonal transformation offered a bleak promise of too many long and colorless months to follow.

Appearing haggard from a restless night and apprehensive about his unexpected summons to Duluth, Peter Moran sat by himself in the executive coach of the train. Barbara's note held an urgency that caused Peter to contemplate. Good news, he believed, would wait; bad news always required immediate attention. This was bad news, Peter was certain of that.

Distractedly, Peter picked up his copy of the Friday newspaper and caught the front page story on the hotel. Atkinson told him he would be doing a story when the two of them talked the day before. Claude's article amused him. The quote attributed to Hibbing's 'affable Moran' was perfect. "I'll have to visit with Claude when I get back from Duluth, and let him know that I've just bought the place." Peter smiled to himself over the triumph which he and his colleagues celebrated the night before.

Peter would call McIntosh when he arrived in Duluth. He didn't want to wake his friend from a hangover before leaving Hibbing that morning but wanted to check on Jim's feelings about hiring Jerry Sweeny. In the afternoon he would drive out to Barbara's house in West Duluth.

After arriving, he headed straight for McIntosh's Duluth office to use his phone. "Peter here. I'm sitting at your desk as we speak. Hope you don't mind my using the key to get into your office. I had to make a quick, down and back trip to your fair city this morning."

"My office?" Jimmy was still groggy. "In Duluth? What the hell are you doing down there on a Saturday?"

"Among other things, I thought I'd visit with Sweeny and let him know that we're ready to go with my new plans," Peter said. "He won't be surprised that everything's happened so quickly."

"Are you sure, Peter? I don't have good feelings about that guy. Somehow, I don't trust him." Peter could visualize McIntosh's frown at his end of the line.

"We've had him in on our plans from day one, Jim. He's helped us make this happen as fast as it has. You know that, Jim," Peter reminded his friend.

"I know, but we've paid him well. I think we ought to just let it go at that. He sold out Markman; he could just as well do the same to you some day. He's a Judas, Peter." McIntosh had been against many of Peter's tactics in bringing down Markman's hotel project. He believed things had been going on behind his back. Consequently, Mac had regrets about his own role in the matter.

"Aren't we all, Jim?" Peter's observation disturbed McIntosh.

"I refuse to believe that, Peter. By the way, did you read Atkinson's article in yesterday's paper? What do you know about the hotel accident? This is the first I've heard about it." Jim was curious.

"Accidents happen, my friend, that's all there is to it."

The carriage ride out to Barbara's house on Wadena Street in West Duluth was uncomfortably cold. Peter stopped at a flower shop on Grand Avenue and bought a dozen roses. As he approached the front door, he felt an apprehension creep through his body.

"Peter, my love, I knew you would come right away. I'm so happy to see you." Waiting at the door, Barbara rushed to embrace him. "The roses, they're beautiful. How thoughtful of you, darling." They kissed briefly in the foyer; then Peter hung his coat and hat on the cloak rack.

"What is it, Barb? Your note caught me by surprise. Why didn't you call instead of going through McIntosh? I wish you hadn't used Jim." Peter's 'lady friend' was one of the secrets he kept from his friend. "I was in the middle of lots of things; then this note came. I dropped everything, of course. My first thought was that something might be wrong with you, but you look fine to me."

"I am just fine, Peter, my love. I'm wonderful! But just look at yourself, my handsome man. Are you feeling well? Barbara frowned then smiled, "Come over and sit down so I can tell you our wonderful news." She had prayed that her positive attitude would help to soften the blow which was to come. God, how would Peter handle this?

"Just give me a minute to thaw from this cold." Peter tried to smile, then walked over to the liquor cabinet and poured a scotch straight up. He retrieved a cigar from his coat pocket in the foyer before joining her on the sofa. While Peter fixed his drink, Barbara set the lovely flower arrangement in a crystal vase on a table near her front window.

"I just couldn't wait until next weekend to tell you, Peter. I hope you'll be as happy as I am." Although she had thought for days about what she would say, her confidence deserted her. Barbara no longer held her emotions in check and she began sobbing. Her whole body heaved as she sank her face into Peter's chest, pulling herself close to him. "Peter, I'm sorry. Sorry about the note, about this crying like a schoolgirl, and sorry about . . ." She let her words drop and clutched at his jacket.

Peter's worst nightmare seemed confirmed by her emotional outburst. He held her close, "Now, now . . . don't cry, Barbara. We can take care of this."

But Barbara pulled away, looked him in the eyes. "Take care of what, Peter?"

"You're pregnant, aren't you?" Peter held her shoulders in his hands, giving her a knowing look.

"Yes," she rubbed the tears welling in her eyes. "Doctor Dorsher says about three months. Peter . . . I can tell . . . you're upset. Please, my love, don't be . . ."

"Upset? Why wouldn't I be upset? Did you think I would be happy about this?" Peter stood, downed his drink, and walked to the cabinet for another.

With his back to her, he swallowed hard at the words he would say and the pain he knew they would bring. Peter had too many things going on right now; Barbara's pregnancy would be an unacceptable complication in his life.

He turned and met her eyes across the room. "I know of another doctor, over in Superior; he can take care of this for us."

"What? What are you suggesting, Peter? Don't even say that word. I won't hear it!" She was sobbing heavily now. "No . . . no . . . a thousand times no!"

Peter returned to her side on the sofa. "I know how you feel Barb, but I won't have this. You've got to understand. No, you can't possibly understand the stress that's going on in my life. I don't want any kids. That's final!"

Barbara rose abruptly and glared at Peter. "What do you mean by *final*? This baby will live, Peter! I don't give a damn about all the stress going on in your life. It's always you and your life that matters. Your secret life up in Hibbing, away from me until the weekend comes, then you want your loving girlfriend. Is that all I am to you, Peter, your mistress in Duluth?"

Barbara screamed. "How selfish can you be, Peter? This is your child in me. How can you even think . . . ?"

"Me? Selfish?" Peter's guilt was tempered by his outrage. He got to his feet. "Do I have to remind you where the money for this house came from, and that diamond necklace you're wearing, and your whole goddamned wardrobe? I'm selfish? You've never had it so good, Barbara, and you damn well know it. Don't talk nonsense."

Barbara ripped the gold chain from her neck and threw it at Peter's feet, then ripped open the bodice of her dress in uncontrolled contempt. "Do you want this dress back too? How about the furniture you gave me?" In her rage she pushed an expensive lamp off the table and sent it crashing to the floor. "Peter, these are only things. They're meaningless! I am talking about a life, a child. Now, get out of this house!" she pointed toward the door. "And, don't come back until you can be a man. I've never been so hurt in my life." Barbara ran from the room and up the stairs, leaving Peter speechless.

On the train ride back to Hibbing that afternoon, Peter wallowed in his misery over the confrontation which may have destroyed his relationship with Barbara. She could not even begin to understand his feelings, his business stresses, nor his complicated life. Was he any more selfish than she? A baby would only separate them, destroy the carefree arrangement that both of them so enjoyed when they were together. Having this baby was selfish of Barbara. What would he do? Barbara was beyond anger when she demanded that he leave her house. Peter realized that he would never convince her to have an abortion.

"What the hell," he mumbled under his breath, "I'll come up with something." Was McIntosh right when he told Peter it was time to settle down and have a family? Maybe it was time. Peter would think about it. Barbara was a great lady; but a wife? Mrs. Moran?

Claude Atkinson was a picture of confusion as he peered out his window watching the afternoon sun bury itself behind the western horizon. He leaned back in his chair and chewed on his pipe. Atkinson had just returned from a meeting with Peter Moran. The Hibbing businessman called shortly after lunch inviting him to drop by his office for a 'scoop' about a new development concerning the hotel project.

What was most puzzling to Claude was Moran's demeanor. The usually ebullient Irishman seemed subdued and distracted. Moran explained his purchase of the Grande Hotel from the Markman group. "I felt I had to bail them out of their financial mess," Moran had said.

Atkinson looked over the notes he had spread on his desktop refreshing his memory of their conversation. Some quotes from Moran stared back at him.

"I've always believed that Hibbing needed a fine new hotel . . ."

"I had no idea that this opportunity might present itself to me.."

"Markman's a real gentleman . . ."

"So many unfortunate problems . . ."

"I'll have to find an architect to go over all the new plans . . ."

Then, Moran went into great depth on his plans for the new project that would bear his name: *The Hotel Moran.* But even as he outlined his concepts of a vaudeville theater, ballrooms, gaming rooms, and various shops, the new owner's emotions seemed at odds with his ideas. Moran was conflicted. Again he looked at his notes. On the left side of the paper, he had listed other specific quotes and to their right his own observations from their conversation.

"I'll want at least a hundred and fifty rooms . . ."

"We'll expand down the street . . . four stories tall . . ."

"A news and tobacco shop on the main floor, slot machines . . ."

On the left of his notepad, Claude had noted:

Moran leaves his desk again . . . paces to the window . . .

Moran lights a second cigar with one already started in the ashtray . . . laughs about it . . .

Moran spills coffee on some papers . . .

Moran's hands are jittery . . . he wrings them often . . .

Claude did not have the story he wanted, not yet. He would write a story about the change in ownership and the new plans Moran had outlined. It would be an interesting article and sure to get Hibbing talking about one of its favorite sons. Who could doubt that this new venture was an ambitious one? It would stir far more excitement than the Grande Hotel might have ever done.

Yet, something was troubling Peter Moran; Atkinson was certain of that. He wondered aloud, "How can a man buy a hotel on a Friday and have a grandiose, detailed plan on Monday without an architect or contractor?" Everybody in Hibbing knew that Moran was enterprising and driven, but was he something more than that?

Claude remembered Markman's only comment on the past week's disasters . . . *sabotage.*

Barbara was in her eighth month of pregnancy when she felt the hard cramp in her stomach. In panic, she tried to brace herself against the kitchen countertop but could not break the fall forward onto her stomach. When consciousness returned, she saw blood pooled on the floor. Crawling to the phone only a few feet away, she got Dr. Dorsher on the line, weakly speaking through her pain and fear.

Dorsher was at her house in minutes, but Barbara's hemorrhaging had steadily worsened. He knew the woman was Catholic. "I must call Father Foley at Saint James, Barbara. This is very serious, I'm afraid." Dorsher tried to comfort the frightened woman as best he could, concerned she might go into shock. " Try to relax, Barbara. I'm going to save this baby!"

Barbara was still lucid when Foley arrived. Dorsher gave the priest a few minutes of privacy to administer his last rites of extreme unction.

"Barbara, I'm Father Foley. Do you have the strength to talk?" He realized Barbara was weakening quickly.

"Father," Barbara whispered toward the priest who hovered over her bed. "I am in sin . . . not married . . . ask God to forgive me, please."

"You are forgiven, my child." He blessed her with the holy oils and prayed softly. When he finished, he asked in a hushed voice, "The father . . . Barbara can you tell me so that I can reach him?"

"He lives in H. . . ." Barbara moaned in pain.

Dorsher was back in the room. "You must know, Father, we're losing her."

"I would like to know about the father," Foley pleaded. "He'll want to take care of his child."

"Father, I must take the baby." Dorsher was desperate. He knew that only minutes remained for the cesarian section which might save the unborn child.

"Peter. . . . Peter Moran . . . he lives in Hibbing, Father."

Foley assisted Doctor Dorsher with the difficult procedure. In minutes, the bedroom quiet was pierced by the scream of new life.

The boy was born on February 13, 1907. Barbara, aware of the birth, whispered . . ."Kevin . . . my baby's name . . . Kevin Peter."

That name would be the last words of Barbara Chevalier.

'A Standing Ovation'

PATRICK FOLEY, NOW IN HIS MID-FORTIES, had been in the Duluth Diocese since leaving County Clare, Ireland, as a newly-ordained priest. Over many years and varied assignments, he had been a good shepherd in countless lives. One of his assignments six years ago had been the Blessed Sacrament Church in Hibbing. The name Moran was a familiar one to the priest. Daly Moran, though not a regular churchgoer, had made some generous contributions to the parish. He remembered that Peter was Daly's son and a very successful businessman in Hibbing.

Foley's efforts to get the Chevalier family involved in Kevin's care had failed miserably. No one in Barbara's family would have anything to do with the child, and only Barbara's mother attended the small funeral at Saint James. Foley had placed the infant with the Schmitz family in his parish until he could come up with something more permanent.

When Patrick Foley called at Moran's pretentious colonial home on Washington Street, it was already late in the evening. He felt an uneasiness in this mission and said a prayer before knocking on the heavy door.

Moran's domestic, Mrs. Graham, ushered the priest inside respectfully. Foley apologized, "No, ma'am, I do not have an appointment. I hope that Mr. Moran will see me all the same. The matter is most important!" The priest's failure to make an appointment by phone, before his arrival, had been deliberate. Foley believed he learned more about people when they were unprepared.

Peter was working in his library when Father Foley was introduced. A priest late at night usually was cause for concern. The tall, black-clad man with the Roman collar was an imposing sight. Patrick Foley was well over six feet and broad framed.

"Father Foley?" The name was vaguely familiar to Peter. He extended his hand, offered the priest a chair, and joined him in the small lounge area away from his desk.

Foley took in the elaborate room exchanging appropriate pleasantries. "My sincere condolences. Your father was a fine man and generous contributor to our church," Foley said upon learning of Daly's passing. "I will remember him in my prayers."

Foley, much like his host, tired quickly of small talk. "I'm sure that you are wondering why a priest is calling at this hour, Mr. Moran. I'm afraid I must bring you some very sad news."

Foley explained the reason for his untimely visit. He told about Barbara's struggle for life during the birth of her son. With her final words, she had named him Kevin Peter. Peter remained dry eyed, but felt terrible pain inside.

"Before she died, Mr. Moran, she had a moment to tell me that you, sir, were the boy's father."

Peter had anticipated the priest's statement. "We were friends, Father. We had a relationship. That's all there was to it. How could she have been certain about this? There must have been other men in her life. She was a good looking, single woman."

"I didn't know Barbara, Mr. Moran. Her employer knew very little of her life away from the job, and she was estranged from her family. She was not a member of my parish. Barbara's neighbors simply described her as friendly and to herself. Other men? I seriously doubt that." Foley paused, trying to read the expressionless face of the man across from him.

The priest finished his thought. "It would seem that all I know for sure is that she gave me your name. That's why I am here this evening, Mr. Moran."

"What do you expect, Father? I had no idea she was even pregnant," Peter lied. "If there are any expenses, you know, I'll take care of them. She was a good friend, and I feel bad about what happened."

"You had no idea? When did you last see Barbara?" Foley was agitated finding the man across from him cold and unsympathetic. The priest did not believe what Moran had told him.

"I can't really remember for certain, but it must have been months ago."

Foley left Moran's house deeply frustrated. Moran pledged financial support for the child and agreed that Kevin's placement with the Schmitz family was a proper arrangement. Foley was determined to find the truth before visiting Moran again.

Peter saw the overstuffed teddy bear perched on the bookshelf near his desk. He had bought the toy for his child only weeks before. Picking up the bear, he hugged it in his strong arms and cried softly into the velvety head. The impact of the tragic news finally hit him. Beautiful, loving Barbara was dead. His own son passed on to strangers in another city. What kind of person had he become in his quest for wealth and power? He *was* his father's son he realized. Daly sacrificed family for ambition. When he was honest with himself, however, he would admit that his father loved people. Peter always struggled with that emotion.

Luigi and Tina Anselmo were frequent visitors to Mary's attractive little house on Garfield Street in a quiet southern neighborhood of Hibbing. It had been one year this week since Michael's tragic death. The three of them were joined by John and Lucia Depelo for a Sunday dinner. They talked about the coming spring gardens, the Italian Society's plans for the upcoming Easter Mass, and other activities in the busy community.

While talking about community events, Luigi suggested that the new hotel Peter Moran was building would surely bolster his business. "What will we do, Mary? We're already swamped with work. Maybe I can expand into the empty space behind our shop toward the alleyway. I've measured the property at thirty feet long and about twenty feet wide. An addition of that size would be perfect. It would be expensive, but maybe it's what we need to do."

"Oh, Mary," Lucia interrupted their conversation, "the dresses you are making have become the talk of the town. Just the other day, Mrs. Godfrey was bragging to a lady in the confectionery that her new dress was made by Mary Samora. She said it was one of a kind and worth every penny she paid for it."

Mary blushed at the compliment. "Thank you, Lucia, I'm so enjoying my sewing. Luigi's provided me with the loveliest fabrics. I can't help but make beautiful dresses. We've been getting some fine materials from as far away as New York."

"Speaking of dresses," said Tina Anselmo, "it's been far more than a year since Michael's passing. Maybe you should make some smart new dresses for yourself, Mary. Your time of mourning is no longer necessary. Let me suggest that you put away those black dresses you've been wearing once and for all. Better yet, why not burn them?"

Tina's candor evoked a gasp from Lucia. "Tina!"

"Don't *Tina* me, Lucia. This beautiful girl has had enough black in her life, and I'm not only speaking of the past eighteen months when I say that. I pray daily that she'll find happiness in her life one of these days. She certainly deserves it."

"Here . . . Here." John held his wine glass up. "Let's toast to that. Mary's next year is going to be the best of her life. I have a feeling that a fine young Italian man will come along. Here's to Mary. May God bless her with happiness." Everybody laughed with John Depelo and toasted their beloved Bella.

"Thank you, all." Mary was buoyed by her friends' good wishes. "Would you think me a terrible woman if I did burn my black clothing? The color is absolutely dreadful on me. Maybe a yellow chiffon would turn a man's head."

Later in the afternoon, Luigi told Mary about the invitation he had received from Peter Moran in the mail on Friday. "Mr. Moran is asking all of the merchants to join him for an important meeting next month. He believes, as I do, we need an organized plan for Hibbing. The new hotel will be a great help, but so many other things need to happen here. McIntosh, at the bank, feels we need to get low interest loans out to businessmen so they can expand," Luigi explained. "I might be first in line for a small loan to build the addition we need."

"Don't forget I've had my eye on a new sewing machine from the catalog, Luigi." Mary held his fragile hands in hers. "Can we get one? I could do twice the work in half the time."

"First thing Monday morning, my dear. We'll write up an order and get it in the mail," he said squeezing her hands.

Mary gave Luigi a kiss on his cheek. "Oh, Luigi! You have just won my heart. You're the nicest man I know, and I'm not just saying that because of a sewing machine."

Luigi choked up over Mary's display of emotion. "Mary, you have become like a daughter to me. Your good nature and humor have been a delight in my life since that first day I met you." His eyes sparkled, "I just want you to know that you're very special to me, too."

"I know, my dear Luigi." Mary, sensing Luigi's strong emotion of the moment, smiled her brightest smile. "And I love you as I do my own father. May God bless him always." The two of them hugged.

April 1907

Peter's grief over Barbara was distracted by immersion into the hectic activity of the hotel project. The ownership transition and the countless modifications Moran had planned moved everything further behind in his ambitious timetable. He regarded the calendar on the wall. The Markman deal had closed last October and now, six months later, so many modifications remained to be done. He stewed. The prospects of a 1907 completion seemed highly unlikely given the progress of the work thus far.

Moran was looking over blueprints with Jerry Sweeny in his Railroad Street office building. His sleeves were rolled up, and an expensive Cuban cigar dangled from the corner of his mouth.

"Damn it, Jerry! If we can't get her all done by September, then it's going to be next spring. There's no way in hell that I'm going to have the grand opening in winter." Moran imagined a Northern Minnesota blizzard as he shook his head. "No way!" he thumped his fist on the cluttered table to vent his agitation. "Not in the fucking winter."

Jerry Sweeny nodded his agreement. He had proven to be a competent architect and was amenable to Peter's whimsical suggestions for the lavish European style hotel. Sweeny coordinated design and construction with skill, taking care of all financial aspects of the project as well.

The HOTEL MORAN would be the Hibbing landmark. No expense was spared in design or materials. When everything was completed, Moran's capital outlay might exceed two hundred thousand dollars. Peter's *lady* as he often called the hotel, was destined to be a monumental tribute to its builder for generations to come.

Grateful for the excellent support that he had received from public officials and civic leaders in his business ventures, Peter was anxious to become the catalyst for other new commercial endeavors. He realized the more he could make happen in Hibbing, the better it would be for his own prospects.

Peter paced from his desk to the large window overlooking the lumber yards below. "You know, Jerry, what this town needs now, more than ever before, is an active commercial club to bolster some of the confidence we've shown in building this hotel. We have to get everybody pulling together here, like they seem to do in Virginia. Hibbing's got to be more aggressive and more competitive, or folks in Virginia are going to steal our future away. The Iron Range can have only one hub, and it concerns me about what's going on just twenty miles down the road."

Virginia called itself the 'Queen City' and, like its rival Hibbing, was growing rapidly along with the mining activity in her district. Virginia city officials were stressing economic development as a high priority, and their downtown's main street, Chestnut Street, was alive with activity.

"You're the one man in this town who can make something happen, Mr. Moran, and I agree, now is the time to get things going within the merchant community. Sometimes they get complacent and need to have someone put a fire under their feet." Sweeny agreed with everything Peter Moran suggested. The wispy, balding architect respected his employer's ambition but respected the fruits of that ambition even more highly. Moran had money, and Sweeny liked money!

The germ of this idea began to fester in Peter's thoughts, distracting him from the tedious plans on his desk. He realized the hotel would not be completed to his absolute satisfaction before the end of this year. He would, therefore, refocus his energy on civic matters and let the hotel find its natural course to completion. The concept of creating a means to the ends of his ambition held an immediacy, and he felt inspired by it.

Moran dismissed Sweeny. "Let's get together again next Monday, Jerry. We'll do some on sight inspections, and I'll want a temporary office in the hotel building by next week so that I can be more on top of things there."

Moran spent the afternoon drafting an invitation letter that could be mailed out to all of Hibbing's merchants and civic leaders. In two weeks he expected to have all the arrangements in place.

Two weeks later the Power Theater on Pine Street was the setting for an evening meeting of Hibbing's most prominent citizens. Moran had been a whirlwind of activity in organizing the occasion. The gathering of more than sixty people generated a feeling of excitement and expectancy. Peter's invitation had been as emphatic as his conviction: *"If you care about the future of Hibbing, you won't want to miss this meeting."*

As he mixed with the community dignitaries during the cocktail social, Peter was in high spirits. He moved through the large room offering handshakes, slapping backs, and greeting everyone including Elwood Trembart and Con O'Gara from the council, merchants Tom Godfrey and Max Friedman, and officials from the Oliver Iron Mining Company who were even more influential than Moran himself. These were the activists in this community on the rise in 1907.

As he mingled, Peter looked for Jimmy McIntosh. His inquiries met with shrugged shoulders. No one had seen Mac that day. Soon the assembly moved on to the theater. It was seven o'clock, the time that Moran had set for his presentation.

Striding confidently, Moran crossed the stage toward the podium waving hellos and reveling in the attention. He was in his element and thoroughly motivated to inspire this crowd. Dressed in a new navy pinstriped suit and bright red bow tie from Luigi's shop, Peter Moran cut an imposing posture.

"Thank you, my friends." Peter gestured a hush to the crowd sitting below him. "I'm delighted at our wonderful turnout tonight and on such short notice at that. It's really encouraging to see that when the call is made, our community responds.

"Let's give a nice hand to some of those people who worked with me to make this meeting happen." Peter turned to the four men seated on the stage behind him. Jim McIntosh's chair was conspicuously empty.

Peter introduced Claude Atkinson, the newspaper editor, Elwood Trembart, council president, Tom Godfrey, owner of Hibbing's finest men's department store, and Fred Bennett of the Oliver. Each of the men stood when introduced, nodded at their host, and waved at the crowd, which applauded at Moran's encouragement.

"And, our colleague, Jim Mcintosh . . . well, I guess Mac will be along later. He must have been tied up with business in Duluth." Moran tried to cover his displeasure. Jimmy had been rather distant for the past several months, ever since Sweeny had been hired for the hotel job.

"We've got a lot of ground to cover tonight. Where do I start? I might raise the issue of the empty storefronts over on east Center Street, and what we've got to do in order to get something going on there. Or, I could gripe about interest rates on loans for business expansions. We all know how tough it is to finance new projects in this town. Let me tell you what I overheard this morning at the coffee shop. Godfrey was there and heard it, too. A paint supply shop just opened in Virginia. Not in our fair city, gentlemen, but over there. And why, I ask all of you, did that happen?" He paused for effect to his question, then gave the answer.

"Because a Virginia banker gave the proprietor a better interest rate than any Hibbing bank was willing to give. Don't you think that shop would look pretty damn good over on Center Street? Well, my friends, I'm afraid we missed the boat on that one. Let's not let that happen again." Peter struck the podium with his fist. The assembly clamored their approval of Peter's pronouncement.

"As I said a moment ago, we have much to talk about, and we'll get to the heart of things in a few moments. First, allow me to make a timely announcement."

Peter looked into the audience and spotted the Honorable Judge Tom Brady, manager of the Hibbing independent baseball club. In Hibbing, summer meant baseball, and Brady's Colts were the toast of the town. For three years in a row his team had captured the Northern League's highly contested championship. The May opener was only weeks away, and already the baseball talk was heating up.

"Give us all a wave, Mr. Brady." Everybody hooted their recognition of the popular community figure.

"Back to my announcement. I had to hire myself a carpenter for the lumberyard the other day. My new man has never held a hammer, I'm told, and couldn't tell a two- by- four from a railroad tie, but down in Des Moines,

Iowa, it's said that Billy Breen can throw a baseball through a wall." The laughter echoed through the hall. Brady saluted the stage celebrity.

Peter continued to charm his audience. "And, I'll have another novice carpenter down at the warehouse. He starts work next Monday at a pretty decent salary, I might add. The guy's name is Walter Spragg. But, most of you know him as Moose Spragg." The revelation drew 'ahs' from the crowd. Moose had led the league in home runs while playing for Duluth during the past season.

"I'm told that Moose will be good for my lumber business." Moran paused again for effect, "He'll be knocking down those old wooden fences at the ballpark all summer." As expected, Moran's good humor brought down the house.

Tom Godfrey, Hibbing's noted clothier, stood up from his chair, anxious to have his share in the enthusiasm being generated by Moran. "Gentlemen, our fine host must not forget to mention that Brady's club will be the talk of the league this season. Yes, not only for their formidable talents, but for the finest looking new uniforms ever to attire an athlete in Minnesota." Whooping greeted Godfrey's timely remarks.

"And, the stylish white woolens are compliments of none other than our own . . ." Godfrey strode over to Moran's side, raising his arm like a prize fight winner.

Peter reveled in his friend's unexpected recognition and basked in the warmth of peer respect. This was his town and these were his people!

"Thank you so much, Tom, and friends. All of this is nothing more than an investment in a community that I believe in, and that's why we're here tonight." Peter maneuvered his captive gathering into the more serious purpose of the meeting. Using his most eloquent oratory, he professed the need for a viable economic life along with new and expanding businesses. He emphasized the competition of neighboring communities, especially Virginia.

Questions about how to aggressively attract business, how to have greater voice on decisions of the village council, and how to get tax dollars for improving the streets in the downtown area were raised. Everyone shared in the discussion, and all were resolved to boost business in the mining hub of the Iron Range.

In closing, Peter proposed the development of a new Commercial Club.

"Yes, my friends, we must face tomorrow today; with every confidence in our diverse community assets, with every resolve to initiate necessary enhancements, and with a solid commitment from each of us to promote the 'iron ore capital of the world!'" His voice was a high pitched crescendo. "And this can be done with all of us working together. Let's hear your support for a 'move it along' organization like I've proposed to you this evening."

A standing ovation followed the speech.

"Sorry about missing your meeting, Peter, but I had to take Martha to see the doctor yesterday," Jim McIntosh apologized as he joined Peter for a morning cup of coffee in Peter's office. With offices in both Duluth and Hibbing, McIntosh often wished he could be in two places at the same time.

"That's all right, Jim," Peter replied coolly. He was upset with his friend and tried to mask his feelings. "It went quite well, I think. I'm really getting the ball rolling. It's like I've told you before, Hibbing's going to make Duluth look like a small town.

"You're determined to make a believer out of me, aren't you, Pete?"

Peter elaborated on all of the happenings of the previous night's meeting at the Power Theater. Then switching topics, he discussed the progress of his new hotel. McIntosh noted how Peter's every sentence was liberally punctuated with the 'I's' and 'me's' of his inflated ego.

"I'm going to shake up this town, Jim. I'm not going to sit back and let any opportunity pass me by!" Peter boasted. While Peter talked, McIntosh regarded his friend with a gnawing annoyance. He realized an unmistakable change in Moran's behavior. Lately, Peter's arrogance seemed exaggerated, as did his cockiness and endless boasting. It seemed that Peter was dangerously absorbed in his own self importance. Peter had passed beyond the confident person McIntosh once knew so well. "What had brought on the change?" he wondered. Was it the hotel that made him feel so almighty important? Or, was there something hidden in his guarded personal life? He remembered the note from the woman in Duluth months before.

Jim also realized that Peter had not inquired of Martha's health. Didn't he have any concern at all about her illness? Feeling emptiness, McIntosh left his meeting with Peter Moran.

July 1907

The *Mesaba Ore* characterized the man of dark complexion as an "Italian Vagabond" and further, as "an anarchist with bloodletting tendencies."

More than anything in recent memory, the presence of Tedfilo Petriella was cause for grave concern in the Hibbing business community. Petriella was a fomenter of unrest and the seditious organizer for the growing Western Federation of Miners. From his office in Hibbing, Tedfilo had spent many months promoting his union of mine workers. He traveled across the length of the Mesabi Iron Range spewing his provocative rhetoric of striking against the tyranny of the mining companies. The Italian leader was creating a groundswell of tumult in every work location and town he visited in his tireless campaign. But Hibbing, at the heart of the mining district, was the most conspicuous powder keg of discontent.

A disquieting reputation of fierce and sometimes bloody labor struggles preceded Petriella's Federation to Northern Minnesota. It evoked memories of Coeur d'Alene, Idaho, or Leadville, Colorado. The city nestled on the edge of the gapping Hull-Rust Mine seemed on the edge of an anticipated labor upheaval as well.

People met openly at ethnic lodges, street corners, and picnic grounds for every opportunity to hear the speeches and rousing union rhetoric. Every social occasion seemed to galvanize a dangerous undercurrent among immigrant miners and their families. The repercussions of a massive strike by thousands of workers would be suffered statewide. Nearly every aspect of life in Hibbing was in wariness over the ominous, methodical consolidation of workers from a hundred different mines strung along the eighty mile body of ore.

Peter Moran assembled a full meeting of the Commercial Club membership at the Power Theater. Emotion hung like a dark cloud over the somber room.

"There's a number of radicals causing this trouble." Moran's voice was strained. "Nowhere in this great country are the workers treated better or paid higher wages than right here."

The businessmen were squarely in support of the managing companies and wanted to show their unity in the event of any trouble. Fred Bennett from the Oliver Iron Mining Company, along with Elwood Trembart, shared the stage with a concerned Peter Moran.

"If necessary we will call upon our esteemed Governor John Johnson and demand a call-up of the state militia. We will not be victims of this radical crusade of Finns and Bohunks, or of any other immigrant group that has lined up behind that lunatic agitator, Petriella. We will not be intimidated!" Moran spoke vehemently.

Impeccably dressed, Fred Bennett came forward. The mining official was a distinguished, gray-haired figure. "Businessmen and friends, indeed you are both. Let me provide you with some idea of what we are up against. I do not come before you because my company will be a principal target of this union's unholy strategy. Rather, I am first and foremost, a citizen of this fine community that we all call our home."

Bennett was respected by his listeners in the theater. He continued, "Allow me to quote to you from the preamble to the Constitution of this Western Federation of Miners." He put on his spectacles and read from the document he held in front of him: "I quote this verbatim, *'The class struggle will continue until the producer is recognized as the sole master of his product'...*"

The silence was deafening. Bennett paused for effect. "Need I say anything more? I believe that this manifesto contains the very seeds of treason and anarchy."

Elwood Trembart interjected his thoughts on a strategy for the businessmen. "There cannot be any credit extended, nor charity given to any striker. You folks at the banks had better foreclose on any note that becomes delinquent, and we of the legal profession will prosecute every outstanding debt in this town. We've got to be shoulder-to-shoulder through this critical time. We cannot let them succeed because if they do, we're sunk, each and every one of us in this room." Trembart stepped away from the podium.

After a few more pro-mining company speeches from the audience, Moran prepared to close the meeting. Peter had presented a bold confidence and optimism these past several months. Beneath an assured persona, however, his life was in turmoil. He wondered if the burning in his stomach was ulcers. Barbara's death still tormented him, his own son was an like an orphan, and his closest friend seemed estranged these past months. In addition to the stress in his personal life, he feared the economic consequences of a strike. Surely saloons would have to close their doors. As a result his liquor distribution enterprise would be greatly impacted. If the strike were prolonged, there was no doubt his lumber business would suffer. The hotel project was behind schedule, and construction cost over-runs were almost a daily occurrence. Peter's financial resources would be precariously strained. Where was his Irish luck these days?

"Gentlemen, thank you for coming today and showing your support. My dear father once told me that in life 'there are no problems . . . only challenges'. So, in that spirit, let's go back to our places of work with confidence we can handle whatever comes out of this radical conspiracy against the mine owners."

A dock strike hit Duluth's port with a sudden percussion that shot waves all the way north to the Mesabi mines. At Mountain Iron, the Oliver discharged hundreds of union members. The lines were becoming rigidly drawn between management and labor.

"Oliver wants a confrontation; all the companies do. Believe me, comrades, they are gonna have one!" The dark-featured man spoke in a thick Italian accent, "I didn't expect this dock strike to happen right now, but we'll take advantage of the situation it's provided us with."

Petriella looked grimly around the table at his trusted lieutenants. He had organized this union very effectively with an astute recognition of the various ethnic groups that composed the working classes of the Iron Range.

To Petriella's left sat Steven Skorich, a huge miner who brought the various Slavs—Slovenians, Croatians, Serbs, and Montenegrins—together. Bruno Moscatelli had spent months among the Italians from Aurora and Eveleth to the east; Virginia, Chisholm, and Hibbing in the heart of the Mesabi; and Keewatin and Coleraine to the west. Timo Arola, more than anyone else in the room, had incited a spirit of commitment from the large Finnish community across the Range.

Timo was an orator, an agitator, and an ardent disciple of Socialism. His energies seemed bent on overturning the entire system of private ownership in the mines. Even more than Petriella himself, Timo was an obsessed revolutionary.

"We will call all of our miners off the job next Monday. We'll need to have rallies, parades, and every possible show of unity. We'll need numbers, thousands of men, women, and children as well."

Petriella waved a telegram, "Here's some great news that'll really fire everybody up. 'Ma's coming here early next week."

Ma was none other than the mother of the American labor movement: Mary Helen Jones. Her presence would certainly bolster the Federation effort. Along with many of the top Western Federation leaders now en route from Denver, the union would present a formidable front which could not fail to intimidate the mine owners. The Italian organizer envisioned a long siege and hoped to focus national attention on his strike in Minnesota. When the issues became widely publicized, it would be easier to draw a Bill Haywood or even Eugene Debs himself to the Iron Range.

"I will issue our union demands here in Hibbing tomorrow. Everything is being printed at this very hour. We can have a blanket distribution of our position next week. The newspapers, damn them all, will twist everything. Atkinson, and those other sons of bitches, have become so pro-company that they reek of the same stench.

"We can expect Governor Johnson to come up here, maybe as early as next week. He doesn't worry me so much. The Governor's a politician first and foremost, and when he sees our numbers, he's gonna have second thoughts about whose side he wants to be on.

"And, I don't think that Moran's pack of merchants can buy the Governor over to their side. Make sure your women have lots of food stored up so we can boycott all those bastard businessmen." Petriella had done this kind of mobilizing before and had a depth of knowledge that none of the others possessed.

"The only thing that would turn Johnson against us is violence. Remember, he can call in the militia at a moment's notice, and they'll be itchin' for a fight if we make any mistakes. We've gotta stay away from any physical confrontation. No fights! Back off when the owner's goons try to get you fightin with them. We can make it difficult enough with our demonstrations." The union leader cast a stern look at every man at the table.

"No weapons, no fights, you guys gotta make sure of that. Make no mistake! Oliver's police will provoke you every chance they can. I'm told they've got a thousand deputies on their payroll right now."

Steven Skorich gestured his heavy arm for Petriella's attention. "What about strikebreakers? That's what's got me worried. If Oliver can keep the mines going, then we're really done for." The Slovenian miner dreaded the company's use of scab labor more than anything else. Steven knew the local scene better than Petriella and had a large following within the union.

"Sure as hell they'll have scabs, hundreds of them," Petriella replied. "But the Oliver can't ship nothin' out of here. The docks are down, and I'm hoping the railroad workers will walk out and support us. They've got their own issues, but they're working stiffs just like us," Petriella reasoned.

"It might be to our advantage now, but the companies are going to give in to the dockers and railroad guys as fast as they can. It's the miners they want to bust," Skorich said. "We're the ones that they're afraid of, so we'll be the ones they'll go after."

"All right men, we've got lots to do and damn little time to do it," Petriella said as he looked at each man. All of them were dedicated, intelligent and capable. He focused on the handsome blond man across from him. Timo had been unusually quiet during the meeting.

"Timo, be careful. Try to lay low as best you can these next few days. You're a marked man around here, don't forget that, and, Timo, remember, absolutely no violence of any kind." Petriella was insistent.

"Don't worry," Timo assured through tight lips. He was convinced that violence was inevitable and smiled at the thought. Under his breath he said to himself, "I'll give my blood to beat those bastard capitalists." Timo Arola had been on the run for years and realized that one day his footsteps would be silenced.

He had been distressed in recent days. In his heart he believed that a successful strike would not bring about the socialist order he advocated. His ends, and those of the union leadership, were not in accord. Steven Skorich and Timo had discussed this issue between themselves on several occasions. Skorich, more than anyone else in the room, was honest and forthcoming.

Maybe, Timo thought, when this was all over he would go home to Senia. She had been on his mind often. He had been gone from Finland for more than two years, and now it might be safe for him to return. Despite his philosophical reservations, he would give Petriella's strike effort his first priority. Then it would be time to think about returning to Senia.

Petriella got up to leave. The leader was confident of success regardless of overwhelming odds against his union. This was not a small walkout in some obscure location. This time he would have fifteen thousand miners up against the largest management arsenal in the country. Winning this would strike a blow for organized labor in every corner of America. A victory would bring Tedfilo Petriella the national reputation he aspired to achieve.

'Call the Hospital!'

CLAUDE ATKINSON SCANNED THE ARTICLE before sending it to the *Mesaba Ore* printing room. His newspaper maintained a strong bias toward the mining management position during the Mesabi strike. In this editorial Atkinson would offer his commentary on Petriella's ill-fated and impotent strike. His denunciation read:

> *There will never be a place in this great nation for red flags or what they represent. It is a flag of anarchy, and those who marched under her furl have not prevailed. They shall never prevail! Indeed, those misguided black hearts who led the insurrection should be deported and their followers blacklisted from our mines forever . . .*

It was inevitable that the Western Federation of Miners would fail in their fervent endeavor to erode the iron-fisted control of the industry. The union's advocacy of Socialistic precepts failed to inspire widespread support across the Mesabi Iron Range. Facing a prolonged economic hardship, the strikers soon became disenchanted with the union's cause and with its leadership. Fears of lockouts by the companies combined with the belief that strikebreakers would take their jobs and livelihood became rampant among the miners. But, mostly, the men wanted to work and were willing to work the long hours at the wages that prevailed before the walk out.

Claude was pleased that the Oliver and other companies were quick to reopen their gates to workers, and that an atmosphere of normalcy had returned to Hibbing. The strike had not been as bad as most had expected, and in spite of frequent clashes and arrests, Claude was unaware of any life lost in the unfortunate episode. The radicals who provoked the strike had dispersed to places beyond the Mesabi Iron Range.

Atkinson's commentary concluded on a positive note:

> *With that ugly chapter in our history now behind us, let us all come together and dedicate ourselves to making our community an even better place to live and work. God has blessed Hibbing's diversity of peoples with rich natural resources to sustain us for generations to come. Let us all be thankful as we go back to our work and our lives.*

December 1907

Monday afternoon brought sunshine and respite from the frigid weather of the past weekend. With the mines in winter shutdown, and most of the miners still struggling from wages lost during the strike, this Christmas season was slow for the Hibbing merchants. Construction at the Hotel Moran, however, continued through the blustery subzero weather of the past week, and today a shipment of Italian granite was being carefully unloaded at the site.

Peter called home from his temporary office on the floor above the workers. "Senia, I forgot to mention to you this morning that I'd like you to send an extra hundred dollars to Art Schmitz along with a nice Christmas card." He had never met the family that cared for his son Kevin and had only talked with Father Foley once on the phone since his visit months before. "And, send a check for two hundred dollars to Father Pat Foley at the St. James Church in Duluth." Musing over his Christmas list, Peter contemplated his generosity. Each of his friends and associates would receive something personal and all of his employees a sizable holiday bonus. He had given Senia a list of ideas for the gifts and given her the chore of doing much of his shopping.

Senia had been reconciling Moran's personal account ledgers that afternoon after doing some of her employer's shopping during the morning. "I'm glad you called, sir. Luigi Anselmo made some beautiful ties for Mr. McIntosh and Mr. Sweeny and stitched monogrammed handkerchiefs for several of the other gentlemen on your list. Would you like me to pick them up for you, sir?"

"Not necessary. I'll pick them up on my way home from the hotel. Did you ask about the new suit that Tom Godfrey sent from his store to Luigi's shop for alterations?"

"Yes, sir, it's packaged and ready for you. And, Mr. Moran, I located the file you have labeled 'Santa' with the names of employees who are to receive bonus checks. I've made the drafts from various business accounts rather than from your personal account as you did last year."

"Great! I was going to ask you to do that and forgot. I must be getting old!" he replied laughing easily.

Although employed only a few weeks, Senia had impressed Peter with her self-assurance and meticulous efficiency. Miss Smith developed a quick grasp of Peter's financial affairs even offering several suggestions on selling stocks and expanding his bond holdings. Since May, after a national financial panic, the American economy had been in a depression. Senia understood the intricacies of investments and saved Peter thousands of dollars. The confidence he so easily entrusted to Senia was a surprise to him. The skeptic in Peter's nature made personal relationships difficult, but Senia had a sharp intellect that was quickly gaining his respect.

Hanging up the phone, Peter looked outside at the approaching dusk. December days in Northern Minnesota darken early. This day, however, had been pleasant for a change, and he looked forward to hearing one of Luigi's Italian jokes that afternoon. The tailor was one of the few of his nationality whom Peter did not regard with an unreasoned contempt. Luigi had shown foresight and ambition when planning an expansion to his shop next spring. Peter would inquire about his plans and give him a nice Christmas gratuity for his work.

Inside the tailor shop he looked about for the small, mustaciohed proprietor. "Luigi, Peter Moran here!" His call toward the back of the room was hardly audible over the hum of a sewing machine. The hum stopped, and a woman stepped out from behind a rack of clothing.

"Mr. Moran. I'm sorry, but Mr. Anselmo is ill this afternoon. I do have your new suit and the ties packaged for you. If you will excuse me for a moment, I'll get them for you." The woman's wide smile revealed straight, beautiful teeth. As she disappeared into the back of the room, Peter stared at her remarkable figure with mouth agape. Never before had he seen such flawless beauty! Her wide-set dark eyes, creamy complexion, and long dark curls tumbling over slender shoulders caused his heart to race.

Returning with the packages, she gave him a polite and respectful smile. "Thank you, Mr. Moran. The suit is most attractive, and I know you'll like the ties Luigi made for you. Please do have a Merry Christmas, sir."

Peter stammered his response smiling awkwardly. "I'm sure I'll like them . . . the ties, I mean and Merry Christmas to you. Excuse my asking, but you are. . . . ?"

"Mrs. Samora. Mary Bellani Samora, sir."

"Yes . . . well, Merry Christmas, Mrs. Samora," Peter said and turned to the door. "Samora," he thought to himself. "I've heard that name somewhere before."

Outside, the rush of cold air failed to restore him from the intoxicating loveliness of the seamstress he had just met. "*Mrs.* Samora. She's married damn it all!" Peter struggled for a handle on the name as he stepped absently off the wooden walkway to cross the street. In his distraction, the heel of his shoe caught the corner of a plank.

The carriage driver screamed at the top of his voice, "Look out! I can't stop!" He pulled tightly on his reins trying to gain control of the spooked horse, but his rig was going too fast to swerve.

The sudden collision was horrifying. Hooves and wheels trampled the man who had slipped onto the street, raking his face and smashing his head.

Peter Moran was unconscious even before his head hit the frozen clay of the street.

Once outside the post office, Tony Zoretek heaved a sigh of relief that hung like a frozen cloud in the air. Daylight was surrendering the little warmth it held to the late afternoon cold, as the sun began dropping in the west. Pine Street was in the gray shadow of the early December dusk. "I'm happy that's over with," he said to himself. "I only hope it gets to Churile before Christmas." Writing the letter had kept Tony up late the night before.

Looking across the street and down Third Avenue, he plunged his hands deeply into the warm wool pockets of his trousers. Earlier that day, Tony had followed his friend Lud Jaksa's suggestion and stopped by the Moran and Sons lumber yards to inquire about job possibilities. He met a most unpleasant man named Cleary and was told that Moran's company did not employ laid-off miners, and would consider only experienced carpenters for employment. Another dead end. If only Grand Rapids were not so far away, he'd check on a logging job over there. "Maybe tomorrow," he thought absently to himself, "something will come up one of these days." He had a new found optimism now that his letter was posted.

Walking down Third Avenue, Tony passed the livery and a small cafe that was nearly empty. He thought of a hot meal or even a cup of coffee as he fingered the few coins in his pocket. He knew, however, that he would have to watch every penny. Crossing the street, he noticed the row of saloons. On the corner of Cedar and Second was the Red Rock Tavern. He heard the noise of a boisterous late afternoon crowd and breathed in the pungent smell of tobacco smoke, sweat, and beer. Rounding the corner, Tony put his head down against a gust of wind.

A scream up ahead startled him to attention. "Look out! I can't stop!" He saw the rig running out of control as the horse tried to pull away from the raised walkway that bordered the street. The driver's warning pierced the crisp afternoon air. It was too late! Tony saw the well dressed man in a long wool coat with packages tucked under his arm fall helplessly under the heavy carriage. Tony began running as fast as he could to the horrible accident scene only yards ahead of him. The collision happened so quickly the man had no chance to get out of the way. As he raced forward, the rig turned on its side with one wooden wheel shattering. The stunned driver had jumped to safety and appeared confused but uninjured.

Tony bent over the unconscious man. His face was bloodied from a profusely gushing nose and a deep gash along the hairline at his temple. His lips were already swelling and purple. Tony's hands moved quickly over arms and legs searching for fractures. He was certain there were no broken bones but wondered about the man's ribs. He listened for breathing difficulty. His mind raced, the hospital!

A dark-haired woman called from a doorway, "What happened? What can I do?"

Without looking up he hollered, "Call the Rood Hospital! I'm going to try to get him there as fast as I can. Tell them to have a doctor at the back door."

Behind Tony was an alleyway that would shortcut to Center Street three blocks away. "Let's go, fella." Tony lifted the limp and battered body from the street. "God, I hope I don't kill him, but there's no time and nobody here to help me," he mumbled half aloud. Although the victim was sturdily built, Tony was able to get his own solid shoulders under the man's midsection and lift him onto his back.

Down the slippery alley across Second Avenue then to First, Tony strained under the limp weight but did not lose a step. The three blocks were covered in minutes. He spied the back door to the hospital, summoned a last breath, and stumbled the last fifty feet.

"This way . . . hurry!" The doctor was holding the door open.

Every ounce of his energy was spent when Tony finally lunged into the hallway. He dropped to his knees and lowered the man carefully onto a strecher set out on the floor.

"Good God, it's Moran!" Doctor Hane gasped. The physician attending to the patient nudged Tony to the side. He did a superficial check for broken bones and listened to the victim's breathing. "What the hell happened?" Hane dabbed at the bloodied face, inspected the deep laceration, opened the coat, and moved his hands expertly over the body. "Let's get him to the emergency room as fast as we can." Attendants were already lifting the stretcher and heading toward the hallway beyond the door.

"He was run over, doctor, a horse and cart out of control! Got him here as quickly as I could!" Tony exclaimed breathlessly.

"You shouldn't have moved him." The doctor was visibly agitated. "Damn, I hope there is nothing internal."

Doctor Hane turned to follow the two men who were moving Moran to the emergency room. "I'll talk to you later, young man. Nurse!," he called back to the nurse who was standing aghast, "Get this man's name and an account of what happened for me." Tony sighed his relief. The man, Moran, would get excellent care in the hospital. He gave the nurse a report, his name, and address; then left.

Back at the Dukich boarding house, about twenty minutes later, Tony found a note slipped under his door.

I thought about our talk last night and asked a few questions. Steven Skorich lives upstairs of Nolan's Confectionery on Lake Street in Chisholm. I won't be back until tomorrow night, and I'll be off to Chicago on Wednesday. We'll talk later but I didn't want to forget to give you Skorich's address. . . . Lud

In the quiet of his room, Tony reflected over the note, Lud's leaving for Chicago, and the events of only an hour before. Everything swirled in his head. "Moran? I know that name, the lumber yard. Moran owns the lumber yard! He's a really important man in this town," Tony thought to himself. He remembered the doctor's admonishment. "I hope I didn't do something wrong." Tony looked at numerous blood stains on his jacket. "I hope the guy's okay, but the way my luck has been, I don't know."

"Thanks for the ride!" Tony called to the beer wagon driver who had given him an early morning transport the six miles to Chisholm. The man waved back as Tony's glance turned to the building on the other side of Lake Street.

He climbed the wooden stairway which crawled up the back side of Nolan's store. From behind the heavy door Tony heard the muffled voices of several men. He listened for a few moments before knocking.

A small man with no right arm slowly pushed open the door, "Whatta ya want?" His question was brusque and suspicious as he squinted against the outside brightness.

"Who's there, Lefty?" A voice called from inside the room.

"My name's Tony. I'm looking for Steven Skorich. Does he live here?" Zoretek called over Lefty's shoulder.

"Korenjack, someone's here. Name's Tony." The diminutive man spoke from the side of his mouth without looking behind. A huge form loomed over Lefty. Steven's eyes glared straight into those of his nephew.

"Anton Zoretek, well, I'll be . . ." The bearded man put his muscular arms around Tony and hugged him like a bear. "Finally! It's been so long, Anton. We'll have much to catch up on, won't we? Just give me a moment . . ." Steven led him into the room. Several men were playing cards. The room reeked of acrid cigar smoke. From the kitchen doorway Tony's quick scan revealed the place was filled with sleeping mats, old strike posters tacked to the walls, and heavy drapes drawn against the morning light. Several men were either at the table or lazing about on the floor. They gave him absent, fleeting appraisals. Tony guessed the apartment was a sanctuary for blacklisted miners, the outcasts of society. He waited awkwardly, not knowing what to say or do.

Steven grabbed a red-plaid wool jacket and tugged heavy boots over his stockinged feet. "We're going out for a cup of coffee; I'll see you guys later," Steven said as he led Tony back outside. "I'm so glad to see you, Anton. It's been much too long."

The two men walked across Lake Street to a small, dimly-lit restaurant. Once inside they found a corner table. Steven sat with his back to the entryway so passersby might not see his face.

"I'm very happy to have found you, Uncle Steven. Forgive me for taking so long." Tony's swallowed hard on his words. "There have been too many months and too many problems between us, Uncle. As you might have guessed, I was on one of those scab trains back in July, " Tony confessed with deep emotion in his voice.

Continuing, his face wore a mask of seriousness. "I did not come here to apologize for something I knew nothing about at the time. We were all innocent victims. I have come to see you, my uncle, because Christmas is near, and I want to have my heart at peace with you." He choked out his words nervously.

Steven laughed loudly. The full-bearded giant of a man had a sparkle in his deep set, green eyes. His quiet, gentle nature contradicted his imposing appearance. "Tony, you are here, and I am here. That's all that matters." His smile was contagious and Tony relaxed. "All that has happened is history now. It does us no good to get into what you did, or what I did for that matter." Steven's large hands reached across the table and came down upon Tony's. "I cannot believe how much you have come to look like my sister Helen, and your mother had all the good looks in our family. How is she? Tell me about your family, Tony; I haven't heard anything from back home in many months. I do miss them, and the old country as well."

The two men talked of Churile in Slovenia, not the Iron Range strike. They talked about Tony's work in the mines, not about how he came to be employed. The warm, pleasant conversation was long overdue.

After nearly an hour, Steven's eyes became serious. "You have heard about me and my activities, I am sure, Tony. It's probably all true. I have become somewhat of a fugitive, you might say. And the *cause*, if you want to call it that, has failed. We are the losers, and losers suffer the consequences."

"Uncle Steven, as unpleasant as it might be, please tell me your story. I want to hear it from you, not from someone else."

Steven told his nephew everything. The story was far more complex than Tony might ever have imagined. Steven was modest about everything he did, yet Tony could not help but form an heroic impression of his uncle in his mind.

"I didn't like Petriella. Personally, I despised the man. His mission was a selfish one, and we were probably used by him to make a name for himself. But, I did learn much about unity from his Federation and from my colleagues in the walk out. We were truly comrades and strongly believed in our grievances."

A strange sadness came into Steven's eyes, and he said nothing for a few moments. Tony could feel his emotion.

"I buried a man. A close friend of mine who was murdered for his convictions. Very few will ever know of that tragedy." Steven cleared the tightness in his throat. That memory was a nightmare which had haunted his sleep for months.

Tony leaned over the table, tension lined his face. "Was that man named Timo?" Tony remembered that frightening night in July as though it were yesterday.

Steven appeared shocked. "How could you possibly know?"

Tony told his story of that night in the street while the immigrant scabs were being led to the safety of the boarding house. Steven was fascinated by Tony's interesting perspective of events. The failed strike had many faces he realized.

Deeper into their conversation, Tony asked, "But why, Steven? Why all the secrecy about this man's death? I don't understand."

"Any word of Timo's death would have brought a blood bath. The Finns and hundreds of others would have taken on the state militia. If that happened, my God, I hate to think about it. So we decided to keep the truth among ourselves. As far as everyone was concerned, even Petriella, Timo went into hiding. We spread lots of rumors; he had gone back to Finland, to Michigan, to anywhere and everywhere."

"I am truly sorry, Uncle," Tony offered.

It was approaching mid afternoon and Tony would return to Hibbing. "Before I go," he gulped, "did you tell any of this to our family in Churile?"

"I have not written to anybody in more than a year," he said. I think my last letter to Churile was addressed to you. And, the money I invested in your trip to this country has finally given me a happy return." Steven smiled.

In the alley behind Nolan's store, the two men embraced again. Tears welled in Steven's eyes. "I have eased your mind, haven't I, Tony? Everything that has happened is between the two of us alone." He took his nephew's hand, "One last thing, Tony, you must be very careful about seeing me, or even mentioning our relationship to anyone else. Because of my union activities, I am considered a dangerous man. I don't get to Hibbing often since it's not a safe place for me."

Tony understood. "God bless you, Uncle Steven, and Merry Christmas." The two men parted with a promise to visit with each other in the new year.

On Friday, Tony walked over to the Rood Hospital to inquire about the condition of the man he had brought in the previous Monday. He learned that Mr. Moran had been released the night before. " A bad concussion, broken nose, and some facial trauma," the nurse told him. "He wanted your name, Mr. Zoretek, and I expect he will want to thank you personally," she added.

When Tony returned to the boarding house, Sadie Dukich was waiting anxiously at the doorway. Sadie told him that a Miss Smith had been by earlier and left an envelope for him. She handed him the letter and watched him read it. "It's from Mr. Moran," he told the curious landlady looking over his shoulder. "He wants me to visit him at two o'clock tomorrow at his house on Washington Street."

"Peter Moran!" Sadie was astonished. "What in the world have you done, Tony? Do you know who he is?"

Tony told her about the accident.

The Moran mansion was set well back from the street on a large, fenced, wooded property. The colonial style estate was more elegant than any Tony had ever seen. A carriage way looped through the grounds and widened in front of a huge wooden porch that supported heavy white painted Greek columns. Tony took a deep breath at the front door. "This should be interesting," he thought to himself.

From the marble-floored foyer, Tony was escorted to an elegant, book-filled library by a fashionably dressed and strikingly attractive blond woman. Once inside the spacious room, he recognized the sturdy man exhaling a billow of rich cigar smoke. A wide bandage was over his temple, and his nose was still noticeably swollen.

Moran, quickly out of his chair, moved toward Tony with an out-stretched hand. "Come in and make yourself comfortable, I'm Peter Moran. Can I get you a cigar?" Peter's greeting was warm and his handshake firm. "I'm having an eggnog with about two fingers of Irish whiskey. Can I interest you in the same?"

Tony, smiling, declined both the cigar and drink. "You look much better than I imagined you might, sir. I am Tony Zoretek." He introduced himself, met Moran's smile, then glanced over the man's shoulder at the impressive room.

Peter noticed the young man's deep-set blue eyes as they swept across the shelves of books along the back wall of the library behind him. He regarded the tall, handsome, strapping man. "Do you read?" Peter asked. The man's name Zoretek and his complexion belied his Austrian nationality. His clothing, although clean and pressed, were unmistakably lower class apparel.

"Why yes sir, I do. Like yourself, apparently, I love books. Your collection is most impressive. May I . . . ?" Tony stepped closer to the stacks and scanned the titles and authors. "Some of the very best literature. Do you enjoy Edgar Allan Poe, sir?"

"Poe?" Peter was embarrassed because he had not read any of the rich, leather-bound books. They were simply a part of the room's decor. "He tells a pretty good story, Poe. I enjoy him," Peter lied.

"Forgive me, Mr. Moran. How rude of me, but when I saw so many books, I thought I was in the public library." He laughed at himself and returned to the chair that Moran had set out for him. "I'm pleased that you have recovered so quickly. I was worried that there might have been some internal injury, and I might have done you more harm than good."

Moran sat back. This Zoretek carried himself with confidence, spoke in sharp, clear English and read books. Peter's stereotype of Austrian immigrants was undermined. "If you see any books you like, just help yourself," he gestured toward the wall. Moran sipped at his drink and began a recollection of the accident. "I still can't believe what happened. I must have tripped. It wasn't the carriage driver's fault. I'm sure of that. He tried to pull his horse back. But, what what you did, Mr. Zoretek, really impressed me. I weigh two hundred pounds, and the hospital was four blocks away?" Peter regarded the man's shoulders and frame. "But, now, meeting you, I can see how you were able to carry a man of my size. Regardless, it was quite a thing you did."

Tony laughed easily. "Just Tony, sir. Nobody ever calls me mister, but I'd be dishonest if I didn't say that you were quite a load."

Moran enjoyed the humor. The two men talked of the accident, the efficiency of the hospital staff, and Dr. Hane's attention in particular. Moran was struck by the easy pleasantry of his conversation with a young man who had been a total stranger only an hour before. Zoretek was amiable and well spoken.

Miss Smith knocked then entered the room. "I'm sorry to interrupt, Mr. Moran, but you said one hour. You have two calls to return, Mr. Atkinson and Father Foley." Senia felt bad about the intrusion because Moran was in very good spirits with his guest. "And, you wanted to know about that name, 'Samora', sir. I've found a record in the files."

Peter realized that he and Tony had been talking for much longer than he had expected, and that he had much to catch up on from his week spent in the hospital. At the same time, he was most curious about the woman from Luigi's shop, and Senia had found some information.

"Excuse me a minute, Tony, why don't you find yourself a book? This will only take a moment." Senia stepped beside her employer with her notepad open for him to see, and Tony wandered over to the bookshelves.

"The Samora I found in your files was Michael Samora. He was killed in the accident at your liquor warehouse back in April of last year," Senia explained. "He was first hired as a janitor at the Red Rock and then assigned to Cleary's warehouse. You noted on the file, 'favor to Riley Gillespie.' The widow, Mrs. Mary Samora, on Garfield Street was sent a check for one hundred dollars."

Peter remembered the dago cripple and the terrible accident. Twelve kegs of Fitger's beer had been smashed at considerable cost to him. His frown brought deep furrows under the bandage across his forehead. Peter could not imagine that beautiful seamstress having been married to that disfigured immigrant.

"Thanks, Miss Smith. We'll talk more of this later, and I'll get to the calls shortly. Give me a few more minutes here with Tony." Peter dismissed Senia and called over to the young man. "Did you find something you like?"

Tony returned with an unread copy of Stevenson's *Treasure Island*. He was smiling over his find. "I sure have, sir." He showed Moran the volume.

"Tony, I want to show my appreciation." Peter took out his wallet and fumbled for a twenty dollar bill. "It's the Christmas season, and I'm a most grateful man." He offered the bill to Tony and smiled. "Something for you and your family. You were, what does the Good Book say, a good Samaritan?"

Tony, knowing the Biblical parable, had a pang of conscience. "I can't take the money." He declined the offer before realizing what he had done. Twenty dollars!—that amount would get him through January.

Moran showed his surprise. "But I insist." The young immigrant, he was certain, had not seen a twenty in months, probably not since the mining shut downs of late fall. "You can use the money, Tony, far more than I can. And, I'd be offended if you don't take this." He offered the bill again.

Tony was quick to recognize an opportunity. "Yes, Mr. Moran, the money would be nice, no doubt about that, but . . ." Tony swallowed hard at what he would say next. "I can't take any money for what I did. But I would like to ask a favor of you."

"Name it," Moran insisted.

"I have been looking for a job, sir," Tony said.

Moran measured the young man and his request. He recalled a similar situation in this very room only months before. Miss Smith, also a foreigner, had made an appeal to him. Senia had proven to be his most trusted employee. Maybe, he thought, Tony Zoretek was also worth a chance.

"Tony, how would you like to learn to be a carpenter?" Moran smiled and extended his hand.

As Tony walked back to the Dukich boarding house, he realized how swiftly fate had changed his life. He would have an opportunity to learn a trade and have an income during the winter months. Mr. Moran had told him to report for work on the following Monday. He would introduce himself to a man named Lars Udahl. The idea of working with his hands, using his intelligence, and being creative was the best Christmas gift he could ever hope to receive.

'A GLASS OF LEMONADE'

THE CHRISTMAS SEASON WAS DIFFICULT for Senia. The mystery of Timo's whereabouts, her holiday homesickness, and the tightrope she walked each day, were all distressing. Being Miss Smith had proven an awkward charade and further hampered her efforts to locate her husband. Senia avoided the large Finnish community in Hibbing for fear that her identity be discovered. She had become estranged from the very people who could be of the greatest assistance in her search. Her friend, Elia Niemi, remained involved in the Finnish Tapio Hall Society and continued to make careful inquiries on Senia's behalf.

One bit of information brought a glimmer of hope to Senia's new year. Elia had picked up a lead from a man that had been involved in last summer's strike. Elia was at the Finnish Society's New Year's Eve party two weeks before and overheard a conversation about some strike leaders still in the area. Elia suggested that Senia try to find someone named Steven Skorich, the man called Korenjack, who probably lived in Chisholm. Somehow Senia would follow up on the name Elia had given her.

Despite considerable frustrations, Senia began the new year with a positive outlook. Peter Moran had been very generous to her. He had set up an office for his secretary in a pleasant upstairs room in his spacious home. The room overlooked the back yard gardens and was furnished to her particular taste. Down the hallway from the office, Moran had provided her with an apartment. In the short span of her employment, Moran had given her increasing responsibilities and increased her salary. Her work became a welcome diversion and challenge.

Senia was on her phone to Mr. Jim McIntosh at his Hibbing bank office. "I know it's highly unusual, Mr. McIntosh, but Mr. Moran is insistent on the matter." Moran had been investigating someone himself, and Senia found both her boss's behavior and instructions confusing. "Mr. Moran wants to pay off the mortgage balance on the Samora note."

"Has he told you why, Miss Smith?" McIntosh was puzzled as to why Peter personally had not called him.

"All I know is that Mr. Samora was an employee of Mr. Moran's and that he was killed in an accident. Mr. Moran said he felt a responsibility, or to quote him more accurately, an obligation to take care of the man's widow."

"I remember the accident," McIntosh said. "I also remember Peter was more distressed about the beer he lost than he was about the guy who got killed." Jim McIntosh was finding it more and more difficult to understand his old friend. "So, he wants me to make a transfer from his personal account, then he wants you to come by and pick up the ownership deed. I'll take care of it for you . . . or rather, for Peter." The banker sighed to himself, "Can't figure this one out though. Okay, I'll see you later, Miss Smith, and my wishes for a happy new year to you."

"Thank you, sir, and the same to you," Senia responded warmly. She liked Jim McIntosh.

On a gray Saturday afternoon in late January, Peter Moran was dressed in a new suit which Luigi had altered perfectly. He sent a note in advance and would pay a visit to the Samora residence on Garfield Street. The beautiful widow had become somewhat of an obsession with him, and he was determined to make a most favorable impression on her. He thought of bringing flowers but decided against the idea. He hoped there would be occasion for a bouquet on another day. Peter's usual confidence was tempered by his realization that most of his relationships with people were bound to the influence of his wealth. On this afternoon he remembered Barbara, and how he had taken care of her during their good times together. Any material thing she wanted, he gave her.

At the door of Mary Bellani Samora's house, Peter removed his stylish felt hat and knocked. In several moments the door opened and a smile nearly melted his composure.

"Mr. Moran, it is so very nice to see you again. Please do come in." Mary looked radiant and wore a velvet dress of a rich purple fabric. "I must admit that I was surprised by your note." She led him into her small but neatly furnished living room.

The small talk was easy. Peter complimented the home with its simple, stylish furnishings while Mary inquired about Peter's recovery from his well known accident some weeks earlier. She was pleasant to her guest but confused regarding the purpose of his visit. Not knowing what to expect, Mary took advantage of a pause in their conversation. "So, Mr. Moran, what brings you out on this unpleasant afternoon? Your note was rather vague, something about my deceased husband, Michael. There was a matter that you wished to take care of, I think you said. What might that be, sir?"

"Michael was a fine man and a valued employee. I had grown quite fond of him. As you might imagine, I was quite devastated by his. . . ." Peter let the sentence drop.

"Are you talking about my Michael, a fine man?" Mary was befuddled by Moran's apparent high regard of Michael. Surely he was trying to make her feel good. "This is most surprising. It has always been my understanding that Michael was a loner. I had no idea that you even knew who he was. You must have many employees . . ."

Peter nodded but did not reply.

Mary recovered from her confusion of the moment. "Anyhow, I was most appreciative of the check that you sent for funeral costs. It was helpful at that difficult time." She remembered both the $100 and Moran's absence at Michael's funeral. Other than her closest friends, only a man named Bernie attended the small ceremony. "I honestly did not realize your fondness for my husband. If I had known, I most certainly would have mentioned so in my thank you note after the funeral. I am sorry," she apologized.

"We are all like family, my employees, I mean. That's why I am here, Mrs. Samora. The check you received was a mistake or an oversight, I should say. I only learned about my oversight the other day when I was looking through the personnel records of my company." Peter gave Mary a grave look. "It is my practice, when I lose an employee to an accident on the job, to take care of the man's family." He leaned forward. "The check was supposed to be followed up with my personal condolences. I don't know why I didn't do so at the time and, for that, it is I who must apologize, I'm afraid."

Mary tried to smile at the contrite man and his strange commentary. "That is all in the past, Mr. Moran." She wished she knew of some way to bring a conclusion to this uncomfortable situation.

Continuing his elaborate discourse, Peter explained the company policy of paying off any existing mortgage that a deceased employee might have. Once again he stressed that his business was like his family. "Like yourself, Mrs. Samora," he said, "I have not been blessed with children. So I take care of my workers and their families as I might my own children." He finished his improbable explanation by taking the deed from his coat pocket and holding it out to Mary.

Unsettled, Mary kept her hands to her side. Moran's personal comments about her not having children seemed inappropriate and the company policy was not believable to her. "I cannot accept this, Mr. Moran. However well intended, my home is my own responsibility."

Peter was disappointed by her refusal. He had no way of anticipating this turn of events. "I am sorry that you feel this way, Mrs. Samora. Perhaps if you just think about it. You might even talk to Mr. Anselmo about my proposal. Then we might find another occasion to talk further. I know that this good fortune has probably caught you quite by surprise."

Sensing her agitation, Peter rose from his chair and offered an excuse that might hasten a conclusion to her discomfort. "It has been my pleasure, but I must be getting along. My new hotel has kept me so busy that even my weekends have been tied up. I would like to give both you and Mr. Anselmo a tour one day before we open to the public." Peter left his invitation at the door as he stepped out into the cold afternoon.

Peter might send flowers to Mrs. Samora one day soon and extend a more formal invitation to visit the hotel. He might even enclose a note of apology. He realized that his meeting with the widow had turned sour at some point. She appeared agitated and confused when he spoke fondly of her late husband. Yet, what had he done that deserved an apology? He sensed her annoyance when he left her house. Mrs. Samora's goodbye was strained and parting smile unnatural. Why was she so offended by his generous offer? Nothing in his experience enabled him to understand this beautiful woman.

After Peter Moran's departure, Mary stared in disbelief at the thick envelope that Moran had left on her coffee table. She was resolved to see Mr. McIntosh at the bank and reinstate her mortgage. Mr. Moran's money could be returned to his account. Reviewing the strange conversation in her mind, Mary wondered what this wealthy, prominent man wanted. Was his visit the obligation of sympathy, or were his intentions more social? Nothing in her experience enabled her to understand this wealthy man.

Mid-March brought a refreshing thaw to Hibbing's long winter season. Peter's spirits were elevated by the morning sunshine. Progress on his majestic hotel added to his bright mood. From the far side of South Street he peered at the impressive facade. His satisfaction brought the crease of a smile. The wait was certainly worth the frustration. Despite his frequent impatience with Jerry Sweeny, the architect had done a commendable job in keeping abreast of Peter's constant demands.

The grand opening gala had been set for June. Plans for the event were going splendidly. In about ten weeks, Hibbing would be the center of statewide attention. Determined the event would be like nothing his town had ever seen, Peter gave his personal attention to the publicity and invitations. The Hotel Moran would be his zenith! His 'lady' would grace the city of Hibbing with her grandeur.

Recently, Peter had been visiting the lumber yard more frequently. One Tuesday afternoon in April Lars Udahl, the carpentry foreman, greeted his boss. "Well, Mr. Moran, good to see ya again. How's the crew doin at the hotel? The place is really takin shape," Udahl said. "My guy's just can't believe the different kinds of wood you've brought in for the job. They've never worked with anythin like it before." Udahl marveled at the expensive imported mahoganies, teaks, and oaks that Moran had special ordered. "Are ya checkin up on my new carpenter again?" he continued.

Peter put his hand on the short, robust Norwegian's shoulder steering him off to the side. "Just between you and me, Lars, how's the kid doing?" Moran asked.

Lars knew that Tony Zoretek had somehow become a favorite of his boss, and it wasn't at all surprising to him. Zoretek was one of the most likable guys in the warehouse. "Let me tell ya, sir, Tony's unbelievable. I mean, honestly, I can't teach him much more than I already have these past coupl'a months. He's a natural. I'm sure that don't surprise ya none. Ain't I right about that, Mr. Moran?"

Peter smiled and nodded affectionately. "Where is he now? I want to talk to him!"

Udahl hollered for Tony over the noise of saws, gesturing for him to come up front. The three men talked a few minutes before Moran turned to go. "Tony, stop by the house after work. I've got something I want to show you," Moran said.

In his first letter to Churile since Christmas, Tony had good news and money to send to his family. The past three months had been a complete reversal of fortune for him. With exuberance, Tony began his second letter to Slovenia:

Dear Father, Mother, Jake and Rudolph,

Many wonderful things have happened in my life since the last letter I sent to my dear family in Churile before Christmas. I hardly know where to begin.

I am no longer waiting for the mines to open in the spring because I have a new job. Father, you will be pleased to know that your son is learning the trade of being a carpenter. I am working now for a large lumber company in Hibbing. There are many skills to learn, but Mr. Lars, who is my boss, is a very patient teacher. With all the new buildings needed for a growing city, we have been very busy these past three months. The owner of the lumber company is a very important and generous man. He is pleased by the progress I have made and has invited me to his large home many times.

Tony reflected on the man that fate had placed in his life on that December afternoon. Peter Moran had gone far beyond grateful attention and treated Tony almost as a son. After only a month on the job, Tony was working with the experienced crew at the hotel. When a special job came up, Lars Udahl would often take Tony along as his partner and used these opportunities to teach him more about the intricacies of his trade.

Just this afternoon at Moran's invitation, Tony had a marvelous experience. Peter had purchased a shiny, new, black Buick automobile. Along with Miss Smith and Mr. Sweeny, Tony was taken for a ride out to Mahoning location and back to Hibbing. People along the road had waved and shouted as they passed by in the beautiful machine. Tony felt important and honored.

There were many other instances of Moran's favor toward Tony. A box of new tools, books from his library, and gifts of fine clothing were only a few of the tokens of Moran's affection. Tony accepted the gifts graciously and returned the kindnesses with his warmth, dedication, and loyalty.

Tony continued his letter:

Here on my new job I have also found many new friends. One of them is so large that he is called Moose. The two of us have so enjoyed our companionship that I have moved from the home of Mrs. Dukich. I am now living with my friends in a house near the downtown of our city. Moose is Walter Spragg, and he is a very good player of the American game called baseball. He is determined that I should learn this very popular sport and be on the Hibbing team with him.

Walter Spragg and Tony started their jobs at the lumber yard only days apart and had become immediate friends. Both worked under the watchful eyes of Lars Udahl at the shop, and both found an easy companionship off the job as well. At Walt's invitation, Tony joined the group of men, most of them baseball players on the Hibbing Colts team, in a large Fourth Avenue house near the ballpark. Larry Zelner and Ben Goryl had jobs in the Agnew mine, Tommy Pell worked at Khort's Grocery, and John Ostergaard, the only non-player of the group, was a bartender at Moran's Red Rock Tavern. John might have been a ballplayer had he not lost his fingers in a mining accident. Johnny O was easily the catalyst for most of the men's good humored activity. He was a poker shark and his two-fingered shuffle had become a famous act. To Johnny, life was a poker game, and he spun his life's philosophy within the context of the risk of gambling.

Moose's buddies had a reputation as hellions always looking for a good time. A good time was usually drinking and women. Tony, an abstainer from most of the men's escapades, stood up well to the teasing and taunting of his friends. All of the guys had come to accept his peculiar interest in books and the cultural events that came to Hibbing on the weekends. Moran often gave Tony tickets to the entertainment at the Power Theater. He enjoyed getting dressed up in his new wide-lapeled suit.

And Mother, I have visited your brother, Steven, many times since my last letter. We have become more like friends than uncle and nephew. Often we talk about our good memories of Churile. He has asked that I send you and all of the family his affection. Like your son, Uncle Steven no longer works in the mines. He has a job with a railroad company and is very happy to be working the whole year. Steven is even bigger than you might remember him, mama, and he has a beard that is even more bushy than papa's.

Steven recently found a job with the D.M.N. Railroad Company. The Duluth, Mesabi, and Northern operated the busy line between Duluth and the Iron Range. On Sundays, while his buddies slept off their hangovers, Tony frequently found a ride to Chisholm so that he and his uncle could spend time together.

In Hibbing I find many things to do. Last week I watched a stage play called 'Peggy from Paris'. It came to our city from Chicago many miles away. The music in the play was excellent. When this summer arrives, our city will open a beautiful new hotel that will have the name of my employer. We are all very excited for that day to come.

As you can see, this is a wonderful time for your son. I do not remember that I enjoyed life quite so much when I wrote my last letter. But now I am looking forward to the summer and building new houses. I may even try this game of baseball.

Tony reread his last paragraph. He did not know how he might better explain his optimism of the moment. Never in his life had the future seemed so full of promise. In December he was on the edge of despair, and so very close to leaving this place for Chicago with his friend, Lud. Now, fewer than four months later, he had dreams and ambitions he could never have imagined. One day he might be building a home of his own, with his own two hands. Also, he was learning how to throw a baseball and gaining a familiarity with the concept of the complex sport. Most importantly, Tony Zoretek had a savings account now up to three figures. How proud he was to write the final lines of his letter. . . .

I send a deep-felt love to my parents and to my fine brothers as well. I know that you are so much help to our father on the farm, Jake. And I know that you are getting the best grades in your school, Rudolph. With every happiness I am pleased to send this bank draft of twenty American dollars to my family. I hope that the money will help to make your Easter celebration even better than I fondly remember it to be.

Until my next letter, you have my prayers.

Your loving son and brother. . . . Anton

May was unseasonably warm and dry. Colorful red-breasted robins were making their nests in the budding trees. The yellows and browns of winter dormancy were being replaced by a manifestation of green with a rich freshness hanging in the air. Spring in Northern Minnesota was more than a mere transition out of winter; it was an infusion of new life which exhilarated man and gave a luscious transformation to the natural world around him.

"Atta boy, Tony! It's really hummin' today!" Moose Spragg and Tony were playing catch in a narrow corridor between stacks of lumber in the yard behind the warehouse. "Get your hips into it! You're still using too much arm. Follow through like this," Moose demonstrated a wind-up lifting his left leg high, turning his upper body, and arcing his arm in a smooth overhand delivery. "Try it again."

Tony gripped the horsehide ball tightly between his thumb and fore-fingers and began another motion toward Spragg. He pivoted easily on his right foot, spun forward, and brought his arm down in a fast arc. With his forward thrust he could feel the extra force as both his hips and arm were in perfect coordination. Tony released his grip and sent the ball whistling straight and hard.

"Wow!" Moose dropped his leather glove, waving his stinging hand in the air. "Almost took my hand off with that one, Tony."

Lars Udahl stood on a lumber stack nearby and watched the two men toss the ball back and forth. "It's after eight o'clock, fellas. All my other men have already gone ta work. It could be they wanna get paid on Friday," the foreman laughed. "Moose, I want you at the hotel today, and Tony, I've got something else for you. Meet me in my office."

Lars had blueprints spread out on the long table in his cluttered work room in the back of the building. "You want to be a carpenter or a baseball player, Tony?" he chided.

"Both, but a carpenter first, Mr. Udahl."

Lars regarded the handsome and likable young man. Zoretek, he knew, was already accomplished in carpentry. He was more proficient than some trained craftsmen at reading prints and anticipating every step in the build-ing process. Moran had suggested that Udahl give Tony a job of his own. He wanted Lars to evaluate the young man's potential at being a crew fore-man one day soon. Udahl had no doubts that Tony was capable and sup-ported the idea with an enthusiasm of his own.

"Tony, I've got a small job here. The prints just came in. Let's take a look at them together," said Udahl. The foreman carefully reviewed the prints, his fingers moving across the papers before them. "The footings and slab work are going in today. It's sixteen by twenty feet, and basic two-by-four framework. Nothin different from what you've done a hunnerd times before. You'll go out through the back and widen this here doorway toward the alley." Lars pointed out the location on the prints to Tony.

Tony listened to his mentor and quickly grasped the design plan.

"Mr. Anselmo wants this wall to divide the space. He's gonna have two sewing machines over here, and this area will be for his fabric racks." Lars had already done a walk through while discussing the details with Luigi

Anselmo. The tailor was enthusiastic about his new expansion and anxious to get the job completed. Udahl had assured him that he would have the project done by midsummer.

"It looks pretty basic to me," Tony said. "I'd love to do it, Mr. Udahl. When would I start?"

"Today. I want ya to introduce yourself to Mr. Anselmo, take these prints along with ya, and let him explain everything to ya same way as he did me. Okay? He's s'pecting you this morning, Tony." Udahl rolled up the prints, "Always make a good first impression."

Tony left the warehouse for Luigi's shop, quickly surveying the plot of land in the alleyway before going inside. The cement contractors were already digging and planning to pour concrete that afternoon. Tony did some visualization. Everything needed to come together in his mind's eye of perfection. He bent over the stack of lumber already on the site to straighten some boards that had fallen to the side.

Mary Bellani Samora watched the tall, dark-haired man through the window at the back of the shop. His face was familiar, but she could not place it immediately. "How could a woman forget that face?" she wondered to herself. Then she remembered. As she saw him bend over the stack of lumber, it struck her at once. He was the man who beckoned Mary to call the hospital as he picked up Peter Moran in the street after the accident. She remembered her admiration of the man's determination and his strength.

Inside, Tony introduced himself to Mr. Anselmo and talked over the job. The tailor was warm and engaging with a quick sense of humor. Tony liked him immediately.

"I won't be able to start outside until they're through, but . . ." As Tony turned toward the back window and gestured at the concrete workers, he saw Mary. It was the woman from the Catholic Church. Tony made the instant connection. Lud had told him she was a seamstress and worked in Luigi Anselmo's shop. How could he have forgotten that? She was even more beautiful than he remembered. Tony gasped to himself and lost his train of thought for a moment.

"I know, it will be a couple of days yet." Luigi brought him back.

"Yes, sir." Tony turned away from his stare at Mary and smiled.

"But, as I was starting to say, I can come by this afternoon and start on the back of your shop. I'll cut out the existing doorway and open up the wall. There will be a little mess and some dust, Mr. Anselmo. You might want to move some of your machines and fabric away from the back."

"Please call me Luigi, and I'll call you Tony. We'll be seeing a lot of each other over the next several weeks."

Tony looked at Mary one more time and found that she was returning his glances. "Yessir, I mean, Luigi, sir, we will at that." The dark haired woman had distracted him again. He smiled at the tailor. "I will see you in a few hours, Mr. Anselmo." The two men shook hands.

After lunch, Tony brought his tools into the back door of the tailor shop to begin his first project.

"We haven't met, but I do remember seeing you before." The lilt of her voice was a perfect match to her features. "I am Mary Samora." Her smile was enchanting.

"Tony . . . Tony Zoretek, ma'am. I'm here to make a mess of things, I'm afraid." Tony met her smile, offered his hand, laughed easily. "And I've seen you before, at the Immaculate Conception Church last fall, I think."

"That is my church; are you in our parish?"

Tony flushed. "I should be, but I haven't been, you know, going to Mass like I should." He realized at that moment that Sunday Mass would be a priority on the coming weekend.

Luigi interrupted the awkward moment. "Tony, is there anything I can do before you get started? I have moved the machines away from the back doorway as you suggested."

"No, sir, I'm ready to get started."

"I'll look for you at Mass, Mr. Zoretek. I am pleased to have met you." Mary smiled and went to the front of the shop.

Over the next two weeks, Tony shaved every morning before going to work at the Anselmo project. The work was progressing well and the addition to the shop completely framed in. Luigi was most pleased with the development. Tony had very little opportunity to talk with Mary, who was busy at her machine most of the time. Nevertheless, he was always aware of her presence just beyond the back wall of the shop. Her face was a picture in his mind.

One hot afternoon Mary brought the shirtless and sweating carpenter a glass of lemonade. Tony was happy for the break and a chance for some conversation.

"Mr. Zoretek, Luigi insists that you're working too hard in this heat," Mary said handing him the glass. "He also insists that I step outside for some fresh air, so, you're stuck with me and a glass of lemonade for a few minutes." She smiled and sat down on the stack of lumber a few feet from Tony.

"May I use your first name as Luigi does?" Mary asked.

"Sure, Mary," Tony smiled and met her eyes.

"This is from heaven." Tony took a huge swallow from the glass. "Your company, I mean." He laughed, wondering if his comment was too forward. He had been thinking of her all day, every day, and couldn't help saying what he did. "When you work by yourself for hours on end, you start talking to yourself. Your company, Mrs. Samora, I mean Mary, is a welcome break for me," Tony recovered.

Mary enjoyed the compliment. "I don't think I've had a chance to tell you where I had seen you before you came here for this job." She recalled that December afternoon and Moran's accident in front of Luigi Anselmo's shop.

Tony told her about everything that had happened, at the hospital and afterwards. He expressed wonderful things about Peter Moran and his generosity. "If it hadn't been for Mr. Moran's bad luck, I wouldn't have the good fortune of being here this afternoon. I would be down in the pit of the Agnew Mine laying track in this sun. That accident changed my life in so many ways."

Tony noticed the trace of a frown on Mary's face when he spoke of Moran and sensed that she did not share in his enthusiasm for the man. He wondered at the attitude yet did not question it.

Mary puzzled to herself. Since Moran's visit to her house back in January, she had received flowers from him on two occasions and an invitation to a theater performance once. She had politely declined and sent a note to that effect. Tony's characterization of Mr. Moran made her wonder if she had seriously misjudged the man. Tony held Moran in the highest regard and seemed to have a father-like affection for him.

"So that's the story, Mary." The two of them visited for almost twenty minutes.

Mary, realizing the time, responded, "You must excuse me, Tony. I have very much work to finish." She took his glass. "I've enjoyed our visit, and . . ." How would she finish the thought? Mary had enjoyed listening to Tony's deep voice, observing his animation while he spoke, and inspecting the muscles in his arms and shoulders. "We'll have to pick up our conversation another time. Soon, I hope."

Every day after work Tony practiced throwing balls into a padded wooden box he had set over an improvised wooden plate behind the lumber shop. The box was sized according to what Spragg had called a strike zone. Each day he found that the velocity and control of each pitch improved. Tony found it challenging to throw every pitch into the box, placing the ball in the corners of the crate with some consistency. Tommy Pell had taught him a wrist-snap and a rotation that caused the ball to break down sharply just before it reached the front of his target box.

Hitting the ball was another matter. His early attempts at swinging the bat were futile. But Tony was as persistent with his batting as he was with everything else. When he did make solid contact on one of Spragg's pitches, he felt a great sense of satisfaction.

When Tony left Luigi's the following afternoon to play ball, he had Mary on his mind. Their past conversation replayed in his thoughts. He was critical of himself for monopolizing the conversation and wished he had given Mary more opportunity to talk about herself. He wondered about the unusual frown that came to her face from time to time. What had he said to cause this expression?

When he arrived at the lumberyard ball park, Spragg and Tommy Pell were playing catch with a new guy at the yard, Billy Breen. Spragg had constructed a mound of dirt and put in a wooden plate sixty feet away. It might be another week until Brady's Colts would be able to have regular practices at the Hibbing baseball park.

"Take a few swings, Tony," Moose invited. "Billy needs to throw some pitches, and Tommy'll catch. I'll watch your swing and try to give you some batting tips."

Billy Breen looked unhitable to Tony.

"Crouch a little more . . . keep the bat up higher . . . eye on the ball!"

Spragg instructed. But, try as he might, Tony could not get his bat to connect on any balls Breen threw at him.

Tony stepped away, wiped at his forehead, refocused on the right-handed pitcher who stood on the mound. "One more, Billy, as hard as you can!" Tony challenged.

The crack of Tony's bat split the air as the ball soared far over the wall of lumber toward the railroad tracks some four hundred feet away.

May 15 was opening day for the Hibbing baseball club. The grandstand and bleachers were filled to capacity when the Colts took the field in their new, white woolen uniforms. A thunderous roar erupted when manager Tom Brady doffed his cap from the Hibbing bench.

Tony sat with Peter Moran in choice seats behind home plate. His excitement could not be contained. "They will never be able to hit Billy Breen, Mr. Moran. Never! And, Moose, he'll knock one over the fence, I'm sure of it. Mr. Brady's got a fine team this year."

"Fargo's got a pretty fair team of their own, Tony my boy. They beat us once last year and almost cost us the league pennant," Moran reminisced. "You know most of the guys out there, don't you, Tony?"

"Yes, sir, I live with a couple of them, and I practice with them most of the time—not at the ballpark, of course, but back in the yards. This is the first real game I've ever seen." Tony's eyes were glued on field.

"There will be a lot more of them. Maybe you'll be out there playing with your buddies some day." Moran had been given some glowing reports of Tony's lumber yard pitching activity. He was less interested in the game, however, than he was in the huge building less than a block away. Towering over Center Street was his nearly completed hotel.

"I can't hit the ball, Mr. Moran. I can throw pretty well, but . . . hitting?" Tony acknowledged, "Hitting the ball is something else."

Hitting was all that Fargo would do that Sunday afternoon. The local nine was shelled by the visitors. Breen could not get a batter out in the second inning and went to the bench early. Moose Spragg struck out three times.

No one in Hibbing was a bigger baseball fan than Claude Atkinson. The opener had left him both sick to his stomach and dispirited. After the ball game, Claude went to his office at the *Mesaba Ore* to write his article for the next day's paper.

"The Hibbing baseball club opened its 1908 season on a discouraging note this Sunday afternoon. The Honorable Tom Brady's team was dishonored by the visiting nine from the North Dakota border city by a score of 9–1. Our lofty expectations were dashed and our lovely afternoon ruined by a display of ineptitude seldom witnessed by Hibbing's partisans.

The wonder of our national pastime, however, is that there is always another day. Let us all remain hopeful that 'another day' will come soon."

Claude finished his article on a positive note, shut out the office light, and headed home for a stiff drink and some aspirin.

'A Gala Grand Opening'

PETER MORAN SHIELDED HIS EYES from the late May sunshine reflecting off the huge windows on his hotel across Third Avenue. Peter stood with Jerry Sweeny and Senia Smith. The three of them watched the window cleaners bring a sparkle to the glass, and the painters touch up the wooden borders of the red brick structure.

"It is truly magnificent," said Sweeny. "Hibbing has its landmark, Mr. Moran, and I'm truly grateful to have been a part of it all."

"You must feel very proud, Mr. Moran," added Senia. "There is nothing that compares with your hotel in all of Northern Minnesota."

"You've done very well, Jerry. Senia, the final touches you've added are just splendid. What are they, and where did you find them all?" Moran asked as he gestured toward the plethora of flowers which added resplendent color to the walkways around the building. A hundred planters and hanging baskets graced the perimeter.

"I ordered them from Minneapolis, and they arrived earlier this week. The flowers are some of my favorites. The red ones are begonias, the pink and white ones in the baskets are petunias, and the purple ones in the planters are lobelia. My grandmother in Finland had the most beautiful flower gardens. . . ." Senia realized her mistake as soon as she said it. "I am so happy that you like them."

Senia's reference to Finland was not picked up by an absorbed Peter Moran, but Jerry Sweeny gave her a puzzled look. Sweeny said nothing, however, but filed the remark for future reference.

"Jim's waiting at the hotel," Peter said. "Let's meet him and go over our plans one more time." The Grand Opening was set for the first weekend of June which was only five days away. Peter was a bundle of nerves.

McIntosh was already in Peter's office when the three of them walked in. Peter crossed the room and embraced his friend. "Where have you been keeping yourself, Jim? I haven't seen you in two weeks. You always accuse me of being too busy," he laughed. "How's Martha doing, Jim? I'm told she's been having trouble with pleurisy again, but I didn't hear it from you. I had to call her myself to find that out." Moran had called Mrs. McIntosh the night before to confirm Jim's birth date. Peter wasn't sure if it was today or tomorrow.

Both men worried about their strained relationship. Each attempted in awkward ways to patch the damages. Peter's effort at reconciliation would be the recognition of his friend's birthday. He had forgotten about it last year. Jim was a family friend with roots back to the days when Daly and Ed McIntosh, Jim's father, had been business associates. Peter realized that without Jim he was a friendless man.

McIntosh had a surprise for Peter, too. Being fully aware of the importance of the hotel's opening to his old friend, Jim had sent news of the event to Peter's family: his mother Kathleen, in Pennsylvania, and brothers Terrance and Denis. Of Peter's family members, only Denis had responded to Jim's invitation. All that Denis had said to McIntosh was 'maybe'.

Preoccupied with his own thoughts, Peter did not pay any attention to Mac's news about the invitations. "That big package is for you, my friend." Peter pointed to the gift-wrapped box in the corner. Senia had wrapped the new set of golf clubs earlier that morning. "Happy Birthday!" Peter beamed.

Embarrassed, McIntosh opened the box and marveled at the beautiful clubs. "Don't tell me, Peter," Mac laughed, "your next project is going to be a new golf course in Hibbing."

"Don't be surprised if I do that, Jim."

Pleasantries aside, Moran called on Sweeny to review the copies of the itinerary for the grand opening festivities. Sweeny was flawlessly organized. He summarized the scheduled events one by one. On Friday evening there would be a five course banquet served in each of the hotel's three European motifed dining rooms. The menu would include filet mignon and walleye entrees, as well as exotic delicacies unheard of in Hibbing. A nationally-acclaimed chamber orchestra would perform contemporary music in the four hundred seat theater. There would be ethnic dancers, magicians, and comedians performing throughout the weekend. In each of the two ornate lounges, champagne would flow freely for more than three hundred invited guests.

"We'll be serving from six until midnight on both Friday and Saturday, but I don't expect things to slow down until three in the morning. And, Sunday will be the 'family picnic day' with food and beverages for everybody in Hibbing," Sweeny explained.

The hotel manager looked at his notes and saw an item he had underlined. "Back to the banquets for a moment, Mr. Moran. The head table will be in the Emerald Isle room as you requested. Let me review the head table guests: Mr. McIntosh, Mr. Trembart and Mr. O'Gara from the council, Fred Bennett, and your friends from Duluth, Mr. Allison and Mr. Parker. Have I forgotten anybody, sir?"

Moran puzzled. "I had thought we had ten dignitaries at the table. I only count seven. Who's missing?"

Jerry Sweeny's shoulders shrugged at the question. His name had not been mentioned, and his feelings were stung by the snub.

"The wives!" Senia spoke for the first time. "I think, Mr. Moran, that the wives ought to be seated with their husbands."

"I thought that was to be understood, wasn't it, Jerry?" Peter questioned. Then added, "Maybe Claude Atkinson, maybe Tom Brady, and their wives." Peter emphasized *wives*. "Let's set things up for twenty, Jerry. I'll give you the other three names you need by . . . say . . . tomorrow?"

They talked for another half hour about media coverage and the final touches to the hotel itself. "It's really going to be a thrill when the lights go on at midnight!" Peter said with a broad smile. He had erected a massive sign on the top of the building that would be seen for miles. At midnight on Friday, he would throw the switch on twelve high voltage lamps. *HOTEL MORAN* would illuminate the skyline of Hibbing, Minnesota.

The meeting ended with the four of them going their separate ways. All agreed to get together again on Friday morning. Jim left with his new clubs over his shoulder, Senia with dread over her earlier slip of the tongue, and

Sweeny with a knot in his stomach from the slight of not being seated at the head table. Peter left their meeting with Mary Samora on his mind.

Peter had sent her flowers two weeks before and invited her to the gala reception at his hotel. He had not heard a word. Not even a thank you note. In his fantasy, Mary would be at the head table seated by his side. It became clear in his mind, however, that Mary would not be there for his finest hour.

Claude Atkinson had been given a tour of the Hotel Moran on the Thursday before its opening festivities. Sweeny conducted the walk through as Peter was preoccupied with a thousand details. Claude was honored by Moran's personal invitation card providing the journalist with a seat at the head table. He wrote a front page story for Friday's issue of the *Mesaba Ore*.

> *HOTEL MORAN TO OPEN*
> *The entire community of Hibbing salutes the dynamo that is Peter Moran on the magnificent occasion of the Grand Opening of the hotel that proudly bears his name. The Hotel Moran is a splendid landmark that graces our fair city with a grandeur beyond the imagination of even a dreamer like this reporter. More importantly, the hotel is testimony to its far-sighted builder.*

Peter had sent Claude a personal note requesting the reporter to include some of his ideas, " . . . grace the city with her grandeur." Peter liked the feeling of the phrase. Claude had no problem with Peter's request. Claude's story continued:

> *Peter Moran has carried the concept of previous planners, (the former Grande Hotel was purchased by Moran in September of 1906), to dimensions far beyond their original mediocrity of scale. Moran's vision of a first class European style hotel is now a reality.*

Claude Atkinson reflected back on that strange meeting with Moran on a September afternoon almost two years ago. Claude's investigation of the circumstances surrounding the sudden purchase of the hotel and untimely death of the worker had been a dead end street. Both episodes were shrouded in mystery that stymied the reporter. The original builder Harold Markman would never say more than that one word off the record, 'sabotage.' Atkinson, however, would not give up searching for a reason for the word *sabotage.*

This reporter was privileged to have had a tour of the incredible hotel only yesterday. Stepping from Third Avenue onto the walkway of nearly two blocks on either side of the building is like stepping into a veritable Eden of flowers. The array would rival the gardens of Como Park in our state's capital city. Inside the massive carved oak doors, this visitor beheld a wall of white Vermont marble, embellished with French plate glass, golden antique oak wall panels, and hundreds of fancy electrical lights. The three dining rooms have an exquisite Dutch, French, and Italian decor. Chandeliers of Belgian cut glass and walls of weathered Flemish oak adorn the hotel's hallmark room, the Emerald Isle Room. Mirrors and heavy beams span the arched ceilings above each of the these ornately appointed rooms.

There is a billiard hall off the spacious main bar and lounge, a nickel arcade, a three chair barber shop, a tobacco and newspaper stand, and several professional offices. The four hundred seat theater will host vaudeville acts throughout the season. Below the main level of the four-storied structure will be a swimming pool and a bowling alley. The two hundred room Hotel Moran is like a city within our city.

Claude completed his story with the itinerary of events planned for the two day celebration, a list of the honored dignitaries attending, and an appropriate quote from Peter Moran:

"Hibbing is the mining capital of the world and the foundation of America's steel industry. My hotel will give our city the class it deserves."

Superlatives were profuse the evening of the Grand Opening. Every aspect of the gala went off as smoothly as Peter had planned. People were awed by the pretentious elegance of the hotel. The sumptuous banquet was prepared by chefs who traveled to Hibbing from the Kitchi Gammi Club in Duluth for the special occasion.

That historic night, Peter Moran sat like a crowned Napoleon on his throne. The supremely confident host socialized, mingled, and absorbed the incessant tributes from hundreds of his guests.

Jim and Martha McIntosh were enjoying their champagne in the main lounge with the Bennetts and the Trembarts when a disturbance erupted near the end of the long oak bar. "Fuck you! Lemme alone. I wanna see my brother!" the unruly man shouted above the hushed conversation of the room. "Hey, Peter, where the hell are ya, Peter, you ole sonofabitch?"

Jim McIntosh recognized the disheveled, plaid-shirted vagabond and rushed over to the disruption. "Elwood, somebody, go find Peter, and get him here as fast as you can. We've got a little problem."

Despite his intoxication, Denis Moran recognized Jim McIntosh immediately. "McIntosh, if it ain't my asshole brother's ole buddy." Denis threw his arm over McIntosh's shoulder, messed his hair, and slurred, "How the hell are ya, Mac? I made it to my brother's big affair after all. Thanks for invitin me."

Jim McIntosh realized that sending Denis an invitation was a big mistake on his part. How could he have known? What would Peter say? Mac's mind raced in his frustration over this embarrassing dilemma. He tried to settle Denis down and move him away from the crowd which had gathered. Denis pushed him away, spilling his glass of champagne on Mac's new suit. Then clenching a menacing fist in his face he slurred, "Lemme alone, Mac. I jus wanna say hello to my brother."

A panicked Peter Moran rushed into the barroom and spotted the shaggy red-bearded man at the center of the ruckus.

"Let's get him out of here, Jim. I've got Ole Nord and another security cop coming." Peter seized one arm while Mac grabbed the other and began shoving Denis toward a doorway behind the bar.

"Denis, what in the hell are you doing here?" Peter gasped as his brother struggled to free himself.

"My dear, rich, little asshole brother." Denis belched a reek of liquor and stumbled in his drunkenness. "Where you takin' me? Lemme go, you guys. Let's have a drink. Let's get ourselves good an' drunk for ole times' sake. My brother's buying."

The immense bulk of Ole Nord wrapped Denis Moran in his arms and carried him out of the room.

"I'm sorry, everyone," Peter apologized. "There's always one in every crowd. Ole will sober him up and send the man packing. Let's all of us get back to our celebrating." Moran grabbed a glass of champagne and toasted, "To my wonderful friends on this wonderful night."

Under his breath Peter told the huge police captain, "Give the bastard a good going over, Ole. I'll let you know later what we're going to do with him."

The merriment of the party lingered on well into the morning hours, and the episode in the bar was soon forgotten by most of those celebrating the occasion. Jim found a moment to explain and to make an apology. "I am truly sorry, Pete; I thought it might be a great surprise for you." Jim was visibly pained by the disturbance.

"A little embarrassment, Jim, that's all. Your heart was in the right place I'm sure. I'll take care of the matter and make certain that my brother doesn't give anybody any more trouble. There's no room for that rabble-rouser in this town." True to his word, Peter quietly ran Denis Moran out of Hibbing.

Denis Moran could not survive long without the constant attention of his father. During his years in Oregon, he had married and divorced a prostitute, bankrupted the business Daly had left him, and slipped into a pathetic pattern of drinking and whoring. Defeated and broke, Denis Moran had nowhere to run except home.

He had not been back to Hibbing in years and looked forward to an opportunity to confront the brother he despised more than his former wife. Since Hibbing was on the route back to Pennsylvania, a stop might produce a loan from his wealthy sibling. Maybe, if prospects were good in Hibbing, he would stay on for a while. His plans were as uncertain as his purpose in life.

On Peter's instruction, Ole Nord worked over his drunken brother, breaking a rib in the process. Then, he sobered up the despondent Denis Moran and arranged for a bath and a new suit of clothes. Peter had given Nord fifty dollars to put in the brother's pocket and told him to get Denis on the morning train out of town.

At the depot the next morning, Denis told the police captain, "Tell my brother I won't forget this. I'm gonna kick his ass good next time I see 'im. Mark them words, cop." Denis, slumped over in excruciating pain, was happy to get on the train to Duluth.

Peter slept late the following morning and did not see his brother off at the depot. He hoped that his pathetic brother was out of his life for good.

The Hotel Moran was filled to its capacity that Friday night. Most of the invited guests planned to continue their celebration through the weekend. Saturday's activities, although more subdued, brought hundreds to watch the theater performances. Public tours of the hotel were conducted hourly with many from the community taking advantage of the lavish foods and entertainment.

Peter enjoyed playing host to the local population. With the formal ceremony behind him, Saturday's atmosphere would provide Peter with a better opportunity to relax and savor the good feelings of those around him. In the afternoon, he served hors d'oeuvres and cocktails for Commercial Club members in his Emerald Isle room. As he mingled, Peter looked for the Anselmos. He found them at a table with the Godfreys in the back of the huge room. Luigi hailed Peter to join their group.

Tom Godfrey stood, shook hands with Peter, and offered extravagant compliments and congratulations. Luigi, introducing his wife Tina, voiced his own praise of the impressive facilities.

"You'll soon be having an opening yourself, Luigi. I'm told that your expansion project is going very well." Peter smiled as he found a chair next to the tailor and Tina Anselmo. "Your dress is quite lovely, Mrs. Anselmo," he complimented.

Flattered, Tina said, "Thank you so much, Mr. Moran, Mary Samora made it special for this occasion."

"It is unfortunate that Mrs. Samora couldn't be with you today. I'm quite certain that she was sent an invitation." Peter was more than 'quite certain'. He had sent a personal note and flowers the previous week. He wondered if the Anselmos knew that.

Luigi said good things about the work that Moran's young carpenter was doing. "I've come to really enjoy Tony," he said. "He's a hard worker, that man, and so considerate of our inconveniences."

The five of them visited for nearly twenty minutes before Peter excused himself to welcome some of the other guests who were arriving late.

On Sunday, the festivities were mostly outside the hotel on the wide walkways and into the street which had been cordoned off to traffic. On this day, a community picnic was planned. Free foods and beverages were set out on some thirty tables, and local musicians entertained at ends of the street. Sweeny had made all of the arrangements and told Peter to expect a thousand or more people. These estimates were easily surpassed.

Later that afternoon, Peter needed a few minutes of solitude to collect his thoughts. The exhaustion from all the activity, pent tensions, and too little sleep had taken a toll. He locked the door of his private hotel office and poured himself a drink. Sitting back in the leather chair at his desk and loosening his tie, he contemplated his personal accomplishments. When he allowed himself to relax and reflect, his thoughts often returned to the man who had shaped his ambition. Would Daly be proud of what I've achieved? Peter wondered about his father's sense of values. "Pa, I *bless* you for teaching me to always push myself to the limit. And, push I have these past few years. You should be in this room having a drink with your son this afternoon. You should be toasting a hotel that has your name on it . . . sharing my pride." Peter swallowed his drink and refilled his glass.

"But I *blame* you, too. For getting old and weak, for quitting what we had going here. Why couldn't you share my vision . . . like I shared yours? Why did you go back to ma when we had so much going on here in Hibbing? Why did you want to leave me and die out in Oregon? When you left, it pissed me off more than you ever knew, pa. I wanted you here . . . you should have known that. You just let me have whatever I wanted without so much as an argument. Why, pa?"

Peter would never resolve these questions. An hour later, he was back with the crowd on Third Avenue, walking with Jim and Martha McIntosh, and talking about the successful weekend. "Do you ever wonder what Daly would think about all this?" Mac asked.

Peter did not reply.

Peter slept until mid-Monday morning. The Grand Opening had been a resounding success, yet his restless ambitions were already stirring inside. Peter wondered what might be next as he lay in his bed gazing out of the room's large window into the cloudless blue sky. The expense of the weekend events, coupled with recent hotel cost-overruns, was staggering. On several occasions, Senia had cautioned Moran to be more conservative with his spending. Peter's extravagance, however, usually prevailed over her concerns. If Sweeny's projections were accurate, the hotel would be profitable within two years. But, if Miss Smith's analyses were closer to reality, Peter's overextended finances might not find black ink for more than five years.

Despite Senia's dire predictions, Peter resolved to let Sweeny keep the reins at his hotel. He was determined to give more attention to his social life in the weeks ahead. Mary had haunted his thoughts more now than ever. He had used several approaches of flowers and invitations but had not seen her since January. McIntosh had informed him of the mortgage issue. Jim encouraged Mrs. Samora to accept the payoff that Peter had arranged for her, but the widow was adamant in her desire to pay her own bills.

On this morning, Peter made up his mind to try again.

"What am I to do, Luigi?" Mary Samora was distraught as she watched the tailor read the note she had received the day before. "This is the third invitation, and I didn't even answer the last one he sent."

"Do you think you might have misjudged the man, Mary? Mr. Moran's offer concerning your mortgage was most generous. Perhaps it's a touch of your Italian stubbornness. I gladly accepted his offer to discount the cost of my lumber for the shop project. Maybe he's just a generous man."

Luigi had always found Moran to be amiable and generous. "Perhaps he's a little insecure with himself and finds happiness in giving to others. I don't know if that's such a bad thing, Mary. Maybe money doesn't make people as happy as we think."

Mary pouted. "Luigi, you remember what I told you about Michael . . . I mean what Mr. Moran said about Michael? He said he was fond of him and told me Michael was a valued employee."

"Yes, but would you have been more pleased if this man, a stranger in your house that day, was to have spoken badly of the deceased? He was being overly considerate, perhaps, but his intentions might have been well meaning."

"I think he lied," Mary responded.

"There are good lies and bad lies, Mary. You know that. Anyhow, Mr. Moran has always been pleasant to both Tina and me. And, Tony has always had good things to say about his employer. Just the other day . . ." Luigi told Mary about their visit at the hotel reception and how gracious Moran had been to both him and Tina.

"I know. You've already told me about that and the compliments he gave to Tina. But, Luigi, what am I to do about this invitation?" Mary pleaded.

"That, my dear, is something that you must resolve for yourself. I wouldn't encourage you to ignore this invitation as you have done with another in the past."

Mary sensed that Luigi was quite done with this conversation. It was, as he said, her own decision to make. Moran was a wealthy and important man and handsome as well. She certainly had no romantic stirrings for Peter Moran, but, she decided, she would not be rude to him again. Mary wondered, "What would Tony think?" Her heart fluttered when she thought of Tony Zoretek.

Peter opened the letter from Mrs. Samora with a small measure of dread. Despite several advances on his part, he hadn't seen or spoken to her in months. He expected the note would be another rejection.

Dear Mr. Moran,

Thank you for your kind invitation to join you for an excursion to the countryside in your new automobile. I have never ridden in an

*automobile before and would most welcome the opportunity. I will
expect you at about ten on next Saturday morning.*

Most sincerely,
Mary Bellani Samora

Peter's heart raced in anticipation. "Finally!" he said aloud.

The June Saturday was splashed with radiant sunshine and a sapphire blue
sky. Mary had made herself a riding duster to cover her yellow taffeta dress.
Her wide-brimmed bonnet was a perfectly matched yellow with stylish red
feathers. She did not quite know what to expect from Peter's vague invitation indicating . . . 'a ride in the countryside and picnic lunch'. She was excited and nervous at the same time.

Peter appeared at her door ten minutes early and greeted Mary with a
wide smile. "You look absolutely stunning, Mrs. Samora." Mary returned
his smile and reached for the cotton duster outfit she had made. "I am a
novice at touring, Mr. Moran, but I have been warned about all the dust
from the roadway. So, I made this from a catalog pattern in the shop." Mary
allowed Peter to help her put the outfit over her shoulders.

"Are you excited? I expect you'll find it to be quite an adventure!"

"I can't wait, Mr. Moran. I have imagined the ride all week. Where shall
we be going?"

Peter explained his plans and sought her approval. His idea was to drive
into the countryside south of Hibbing and show her some land that he had
recently purchased in an area called Alice Location. "An investment in the
future growth of Hibbing," he informed Mary. Then to a picnic in Mesabi
Park which was located near the city ballpark north of Railroad Street. In
the park he wanted to show her a new fountain he had built and donated to
the city. Afterwards, he suggested a personal tour of the hotel which Mary
had not yet visited. Peter's itinerary was clearly designed to impress!

"It sounds like a most exciting day, Mr. Moran. I'm quite ready to
begin."

The ride in Peter's fancy new '08 Buick was a thrill. Peter managed the
driving with considerable skill as they passed horses and carriages along
bumpy Third Avenue which traveled out of the city to the south.

For someone who hated small talk, Peter proved to be an engaging conversationalist and most pleasant companion on that Saturday morning. Moran's Alice property was on good, high ground that had been cut over by loggers years before. "High ground is important for building and drainage," he told her. As he walked over the one hundred twenty acre tract of land with Mary, he reminisced about his family's history in the timber business and about becoming established in Hibbing with their sawmill and lumber yard. Peter spoke fondly of his father, Daly. He characterized his father in glowing terms. It was all most interesting to Mary, and she asked many questions about his family and the early days of the village.

"Are you close to your mother in Pennsylvania?"

"Oh, yes, we correspond quite often. I was disappointed that her health prevented her from being at my hotel opening, but I'm sure she will come and visit me again one day soon," Peter lied easily.

In Mesabi Park, Mary was enthralled by the many flower gardens and the large gazebo at the center of the grounds. She loved flowers and was able to identify many of the blooming varieties to her most attentive companion. Peter's fountain was the largest and most spectacular of several in the park. The picnic basket Peter provided contained a variety of sandwiches, assorted fruits, and sweet cinnamon and chocolate dessert pastries.

In the afternoon, Peter was anxious to give Mary a tour of the hotel. The hotel manager, Mr. Sweeny, had been informed of the visit in advance and was at the front entry to greet his guests. Every attention and courtesy were extended, and Mary was made to feel like a princess in a castle. After the lengthy tour and Mary's many questions, they retired to Peter's private table in the lounge. Mary accepted a glass of wine. Peter had recommended an Italian Rose, a perfect choice.

"I have never tasted a wine this exquisite. Is that a proper word for a wine, Peter?" For the first time that day, Mary had used his first name. She flushed at the realization and tried to recover quickly. "I am afraid, however, that I must decline another glass, Mr. Moran. It's getting late, and I must admit, I'm a bit tired from all that we've done today. It's been a wonderful day, and I thank you so much for everything."

"Thank you, Mary." Peter had caught her slip and tried her first name. "I have thoroughly enjoyed myself as well. It's been my great pleasure. I don't get out like this very often. I must admit I work too much for my own good." He was in no hurry to end their time together.

"Are you sure that I cannot interest you in dinner? Our chefs are the finest, if I may be boastful. Maybe even the best in Minnesota and that includes the capital city and Minneapolis as well. Their seafood is marvelous, especially the walleye."

Mary declined the invitation. "Perhaps another time, Mr. Moran. As I said, I'm weary from all the walking we've done today."

Peter gave her a smile. "Before I take you home, I would like to give you a small token, something . . ." He was nervous and stammered. "Something you might consider as a remembrance of the day we've spent together."

Peter took a small gift-wrapped package from his jacket pocket and handed it across the table to Mary. "I'd be pleased if you opened it now," he said.

Mary was caught off guard. She had not expected any gift. Was this appropriate on their first time together? Her first inclination was to refuse the package, but Mary considered that might be rude. She did not want to give the impression that she had not enjoyed his attentions that day.

"My goodness, I just can't." Mary hesitated before taking the gift that Peter held out over the table.

"Sure you can. It's just something small. I would be offended if you didn't accept it as a small token," Peter insisted.

Mary opened the gift box that held a lovely cameo necklace on a gold chain. She knew immediately that it must have cost more than twenty dollars. Mary had never been given such an expensive gift in her life. Feeling discomfort and regret she replied, "Something small? Mr. Moran, it is beautiful beyond words, but . . ." She attempted to hand it back to him, but he would not allow her to do so.

"I can just picture you wearing it, perhaps with that purple velvet dress you have." He remembered that dress from the Saturday afternoon in January. That day had been miserable for him, but this day was superb. "A beautiful necklace for a beautiful woman," Peter smiled in his perceived triumph of the moment.

That night, Mary tossed and turned. The entire day was relived in her thoughts, washing over her with an incredible guilt. Throughout the day her thoughts and desires were with another man. While riding in the car, Mary wondered if Tony might one day have such a machine to take her touring. In the country on Peter's property, she imagined Tony building a house and herself planting gardens. At Mesabi Park she pictured walking with Tony through the flowers in the moonlight. Peter had provided a courtship experience for a third person he was unaware of. Her first thought of wearing the cameo necklace was, "Will Tony find it beautiful?"

Mary was in love. Every day she watched as the tall, handsome, well-built man worked on Luigi's project—his compelling eyes, strong jaw, perfectly white teeth when he smiled. His smile. More than anything else, Tony's smile. He smiled quickly, and often. He loved to laugh and enjoyed making her laugh as well.

Mary remembered an afternoon a few weeks before. It was the second time she had brought Tony a glass of lemonade. He had been roofing the building when she waved him down for a break. Tony jumped to the ground and turned his bare back to her while he grabbed for his shirt. He quickly pulled on the shirt and buttoned it part way up his chest.

When he turned to face her and accept the cold glass, he smiled awkwardly. "My boss, Mr. Udahl, would take me off the job if he saw me talking with a beautiful young woman without a shirt on my back. It's just not proper, he'd tell me."

Mary didn't know how to respond. Was it really his boss, or had Tony been embarrassed by his nakedness? She had enjoyed seeing him shirtless but would never admit it. She remembered her own mild embarrassment from the earlier afternoon.

"Just kidding you, Mary," Tony said as he laughed. "The last time you brought me lemonade I got caught without a shirt, and I saw a little flush in your cheeks. I didn't know whether to get my shirt or just sit there. So, I just sat and felt a little embarrassed myself."

"It didn't bother me!" she lied. "I didn't even think about it at the time, Tony." Mary said with a false bravado in her voice.

Tony laughed his deep full laugh and teased, "Now that just is not the truth, Mary." He enjoyed the first name basis of their conversations which came about naturally for both of them. "Mary, I embarrassed you as much as I did myself."

"It is not so, Tony Zoretek. How can you say that?' Mary pursed her mouth a cute pout. "I am not some silly girl who would blush at such a thing, you know."

They both laughed heartily at the earlier episode. Each of their conversations held some humor as well as some seriousness. Both were of rural, Old Country heritage, and both were learning a new culture. They had common experiences from growing up in a world so different from this new place. In sharing their lives with each other, their friendship was enriched and their relationship given new depth.

Mary finally fell asleep. It had been one of the most interesting days of her life, and in a strange and puzzling way, she had enjoyed Peter Moran. His boastfulness annoyed her at times, but he was a most interesting and complex man. However, he had spoiled the day with his extravagant gift. Moran's generosity?

Was it as Luigi had assumed, a cover for some deep-set insecurity? How could a man of such wealth and prominence in this community have any lack of self-confidence, especially with a poor immigrant woman with so little social experience?

'A Garden Party at the Mansion'

"Have you ever seen a more beautiful morning, Senia?" Peter stretched his arms and breathed deeply of the day's early freshness. The eastern sun was peeking over his lushly flowered back yard gardens. Purple martins were singing their salute to the day, and a gurgling fountain shot a misty spray over the shallow blue pond only feet away from where he sat. It was Sunday, and Peter was enjoying a cup of coffee with a splash of Irish whiskey for sweetening. Senia had been invited to join him. "I'm going to see if I remember how to relax," he yawned. Peter planned the gardens as a retreat, but their tranquil pleasures were something that his pace seldom allowed him to enjoy.

"It's simply gorgeous out here," Senia said sitting across from her employer under the shaded verandah. Peter had requested that she bring bring a notebook along. "You must be pleased with the work your gardener has done, Mr. Moran. The yard is perfectly groomed." On this golden morning the property was a veritable abundance of splendid summer colors.

"I am pleased. The gardens have never looked better, Senia. That's why I've asked you to come out here this morning." Peter looked toward his attractive secretary. Miss Smith had been entrusted with most of Moran's personal affairs, and from her office in his home, she oversaw his financial matters. "I'm so pleased with the grounds I was thinking of having some of my friends over so that I can show them off. My yard is as lovely as Mesaba Park."

"That would be fun, sir," Senia agreed.

"In two weeks we've got our Independence Day holidays. Are you

familiar with our American history, Senia? It's not something that they celebrate in . . . where was that again? England? Where you're from, I mean?"

Senia did not correct her employer about where she was from. She had
already made one slip of the tongue in that regard. She had studied her
United States history diligently. Recently, Senia was taking Americaniza-
tion classes at the high school and knew that the Fourth of July was a favorite holiday in Hibbing. She picked up on Peter's question. "American
Independence is probably not something that the English people care to remember," she answered.

Peter gave her a quick overview of the significance of the independence
Americans celebrated. It was history as he understood it and a very inaccu-
rate version! He confused the American Revolution with the Civil War and
mentioned Abe Lincoln many times.

"Anyhow, I was thinking of some people I'd like to have over for a party
on the Fourth," Peter continued. The Fourth was on a Sunday and the community had many events planned for the weekend. Peter had given his employees the following Monday off from work so that they might enjoy the
midsummer occasion. "Will you write down some names I've been thinking about and then get invitations out tomorrow morning? Add an RSVP so
that we'll know how many plan to come."

Senia nodded and put her notebook in her lap.

Peter's list would be his strategy and hopefully accomplish some of his
personal ambitions. Only the day before he had taken Mary Samora on
their delightful excursion. His thoughts were still swimming with the events
of yesterday, and he hoped to continue his initiative to impress the lovely
widow. Picturing her in his mind as he had so often done, he imagined her
with the black on white cameo necklace around her slender neck. His party
would be an opportunity to show Mrs. Samora his house and gardens and
perhaps, inspire her imagination even further.

"We haven't had Tom Brady over, Senia. Write him down and find the
name of his wife." He had a small favor to ask the baseball manager, and
this would be a way for Brady to pay him back. Brady was fully aware of
how much Moran had done to help his ball club.

"Elwood Trembart and Millie. He's kinda sore at me. He thinks I stole
that Alice property from under his nose. I did, of course, but the race belongs to the quick, and Elwood was too slow to get his paperwork done."

Peter knew Trembart was negotiating the land transaction and what he was prepared to pay. Behind his friend's back, Peter made a better offer and signed the deed. Elwood was enraged when he learned the news. "I'll make it up to El. He'd have done the same to me. Anyhow, let bygones be bygones."

"I'd like to have the Anselmos, Luigi and, I think, Tina. Would you check that out, too, Senia? Thanks. They're nice people." Peter smiled at the thought of making a favorable impression on Mary's closest friends.

"I haven't seen Riley Gillespie in months. Let's invite him and the missus. The old shovel-runner used to be one of my dearest friends in Hibbing." Peter was aware of Riley's connection to Mary through her late husband. Gillespie had convinced Peter to hire Michael Samora a couple of years before. If Peter hadn't done Riley a favor, none of this would be happening. This party, as he planned it, was going to be step two in his courtship of Mary Samora. Peter would get all the parts in place. He puzzled over the man who had been Mary's husband and shook his head. How could that have happened?

"Lars Udahl." Peter recalled that Udahl had worked with Luigi on the tailor's expansion plans. Lars was also one of his most trusted employees. "And Mrs. Udahl, Florence is her name if I remember correctly."

Senia was beginning to understand her employer's motivations. This was an unusual assortment of people for a social gathering at his house. Senia knew of Peter's Saturday excursion with the widow Samora and had ordered the flowers that Peter sent to her on previous occasions. She guessed that Mrs. Samora would be next on his list.

"Mrs. Samora," Peter said.

"I probably should invite Sweeny. He's still upset about not sitting at the head table for the hotel opening. How do you and he get along, Senia? I'd imagine that your paths have crossed quite often on hotel expenses and now with our revenues. Am I right about that?" Peter inquired.

Senia did not like Jerry Sweeny nor his financial procedures. The hotel manager liked to keep his own books and balked at Senia's inquiries. On one recent occasion, Sweeny had told her that a matter was, "none of her business." Senia had considered telling Moran about their rift but thought better of it. She would be doing an audit at the end of the month and would make it *her business* at that time.

"Let's keep the get-together small. Who am I missing?" Moran mused.

"I don't want the same old crowd. I've had the Bennetts and Godfreys over here before. How about Claude Atkinson and his wife? It's always good to have the press on your side." If Peter Moran was intimidated by anybody in Hibbing, it might be the newspaper editor. Atkinson had a quick and probing intellect, and the editor had a large following in Hibbing. What Claude printed in his paper was gospel to his readers. Peter remembered his discomfort months ago when Atkinson had interviewed him about his recent purchase of Markman's hotel. The newspaper article, however, was quite favorable.

"Yes, the Atkinsons, and, I'd like it if you and Tony Zoretek would join me and the other guests. The two of you seem to get along well together; don't you?" Peter questioned. He had seen the two of them talking about books in his library.

"Tony's a wonderfully bright young man. Who wouldn't like Tony? I do wish I knew him better than I do, but maybe I'll have that chance at your party, Mr. Moran." Senia could relate well to Tony Zoretek's intelligence, his love of books, and interest in Hibbing's cultural events. They often talked about plays they had seen and novels they had read. Tony was easy to talk with. His sense of humor and easy smile were endearing. Senia had not, however, talked to him about something very important and was resolved to do so one day soon. Senia knew that Tony was Slovenian. The name of Steven Skorich, also a Slovenian surname, continued to linger in her thoughts.

Senia looked back at the list on her lap. "Let me review the list, Mr. Moran: the Bradys, Trembarts, Anselmos, Gillespies, Udahls, Atkinsons, Mrs. Samora, Jerry Sweeny, Tony Zoretek, and myself. What about Jim and Martha McIntosh, sir?"

"I'm sure Jim gets tired of the trip up from Duluth, and Martha has not been feeling well. I don't think so. They've been here many times before and probably have plans of their own."

"Should I invite your guests' children, sir?" Senia posed one last question before taking her leave.

"You might include Molly, Trembart's daughter. They never go anywhere without her. Tony's invitation can include a guest. He'll probably bring one of his roommates because he doesn't seem to have any girlfriends that I'm aware of. Kids? No, they just get under foot running all over the place destroying the garden."

The thought of his own son, Kevin, slipped into his thoughts as he often did. If, someday, he and Mary . . . ? Maybe, a time would come when he might want to take his year old son back from the family in Duluth. What did the boy look like, he wondered? Some day he would have to pay a visit . . . but, he was too busy for that now.

"That should do it, Senia. Will you take care of the arrangements? I'm going to take a little nap." Peter gulped the last of the whiskey from his cup, closed his eyes, and remembered the wonderful day before.

On Monday morning, Peter was on the phone from his lumber yard office with Tom Brady. The two men discussed the disappointing start to the baseball season and what might be done to improve the ball club. "Pitching!" Brady said with emphasis. "Pitching is what the game's all about. We're scoring enough runs, but my pitching staff has been something less than mediocre."

"That's why I called you this morning, Tom," Peter said. "I've got a proposition for you to consider."

"I already know what your proposition is going to be, Pete. It's that kid at your lumber yard, Zoretek. My catcher, Tommy Pell, told me about him. They're good buddies, I guess." Brady went on to remind Peter that his team, despite a slow start, was not a 'bush league' outfit. He wasn't about to do any experimentation at this point in the schedule.

Peter became impatient. "Look, Tom, all I'm asking is that you give the kid a chance."

"Sorry, Pete, I don't want to send the message that we're looking for help from off the streets. I'll get things turned around with the players I've got." Brady was emphatic. "I've got to say no to the idea, Pete. Sorry. I know I owe you, but this won't work."

"Let me propose a bet to you, Tom." Moran wagered that Zoretek could strike out three of any five batters that Brady might send against him at their practice that afternoon. "I've got five dollars," baited Moran. "Just for the hell of it. What do you say?"

Although Brady was not a betting man, he saw an opportunity to put an end to this Zoretek business once and for all. The team's mentor was tired of all the advice he was getting. No kid was going to accomplish what Moran had proposed, he reasoned. "You're on, Pete; I can use an extra five."

Tony was at the lumber warehouse getting supplies for the nearly completed job at Luigi's shop when Peter arrived. Shaking hands, Peter asked Tony to join him for a minute in Udahl's nearby office.

"I've got you a tryout with the team, Tony. Brady wants you to come to his practice today. What do you think about that?" Peter was enthusiastic about the opportunity he had arranged for his young friend.

"Not interested, Mr. Moran. I'm planning to stay late at Anselmo's; the job's nearly finished and he's anxious to get things back to normal. Thanks anyhow." Tony had seen how much time his friends spent with their baseball activities: practices, games, and weekend travel. "Sorry, but I don't have the time or interest right now."

"What do you mean, not interested? Tony, I thought this was a chance you've been hoping for. Why else would you have spent all that time throwing balls into that stupid box you've got out in the yard? No, this is something that I want you to try. I insist!" Peter was annoyed by Tony's attitude and asserted his will.

"I beg your pardon, Mr. Moran." Tony met Moran's eyes with a cool stare. "I said that I was not interested, sir. I want to be a carpenter, a good carpenter at that, and I've committed this afternoon to Mr. Anselmo. This is the first project that I've done completely by myself, sir, and I want to be proud of it."

"You 'committed' did you? Then uncommit. I told Brady that you'd be there. I'd look like a fool if you didn't show up, wouldn't I?"

Tony fought to control his anger over Moran's intervention into his personal affairs and his insistent attitude as well. "What do you mean, uncommit? I don't want to disappoint Mr. Anselmo. No sir, with all due respect, I feel that I must. . . ."

Peter found Tony's refusal both ungrateful and insubordinate. "Tony, let me remind you of something. You work for me. Let's just consider this tryout as a job I have assigned to you, a priority assignment, if you will." He realized he was smiling over his little power play. "Luigi is an understanding man."

Peter Moran had drawn a line, and Tony recognized it. "All right, sir. I'll ask Mr. Anselmo if he'd. . . ."

"You will *tell* Mr. Anselmo not ask him; there is a difference! Practice is at five." Peter closed the conversation. "Good luck, Tony. I'm betting you'll turn some heads."

Tony reluctantly shook hands with his employer when Peter offered his hand. "No hard feelings, Tony. You'll thank me for this later."

Tom Brady called Peter Moran at his home later that night. "I owe you five dollars, Pete. The kid sure can throw a baseball. Is he always that angry? When I teased him about our little wager, I thought he was going to punch me or you in the nose. He sure wasn't happy about the bet we made."

Moran was pleased by the news. "When are you going to give him a chance to pitch in a game?" he asked.

"Sunday, the Fourth of July. We've got an exhibition game. We'll see what he can do in a real game situation with a big crowd out there watching. The kid hardly knows the game of baseball. It's simply amazing to me." Tom Brady could not remember hearing a fast ball actually whistle before Tony Zoretek's arrival that afternoon.

Mary reached Peter Moran at his hotel office on the telephone Luigi had installed in the new addition to his shop.

"Mr. Moran, I received your invitation just this morning and want to thank you for the kind gesture, but . . ." She paused, not sure what his reaction might be so soon after their outing. "I must give you my regrets I'm afraid."

Peter, devastated, swallowed hard. "What's the problem?"

"A conflict, sir. You see, I have been working for the past several weeks on the Independence Day picnic with the Italian Society. It's one of our biggest events. I have the children's games and twenty other things to do, so I just couldn't." Mary sensed his hurt feelings. "I'm so very sorry."

Peter knew he would not change her mind. "Mary," using her first name, "is there any way you could slip away from your picnic early? It would be a wonderful opportunity for you to meet some of my friends, and the Anselmos are going to be here, aren't they?"

Mary knew that Luigi and Tina had agonized over their invitation. Tina was involved in planning the Italian picnic and did not want to go to Moran's party. Luigi, on the other hand, believed that many of the Commercial Club businessmen would be there and did not want to snub the affair. Tina reluctantly agreed to attend the party. The future success of the family business was more important than their social obligations to the Italian Society.

"Yes, I believe that they'll be at your party, Mr. Moran. I've agreed to take over some of Tina's jobs at our picnic. If I can get away early, I'll join your guests, but I cannot promise anything. Besides, I'll probably be exhausted from the children's activities."

Tony was finishing the final touches of his six week job. He had offered to do some painting that was not in the original work contract. From where he was working, Tony could see Mary talking on the new wall telephone, visibly stressed over the call. After placing the receiver back on the hook, Mary looked in his direction. For some time she had been hoping for the courage to ask Tony to join her at the Italian picnic. "If he would just take a break from his painting," she thought to herself, "I would ask him right now."

Tony sensed Mary's discomfort over the conversation and wondered what might be wrong. Putting his brush in the bucket and wiping paint smeared hands on the side of his trousers, he decided to take a short break.

"Something wrong, Mary?" Tony sat down on an old chair across from her. He wished he had the courage to ask her to Moran's party. Although they were good friends, he had never asked her for a date of any kind. "If I can just get her to smile, I'll ask her," he resolved in his thoughts. Tony smiled, "You look as if you've just lost your last friend in the world," he said.

Mary smiled widely at her friend's concern. "Life is so complicated sometimes, Tony."

With Mary's smile, Tony swallowed hard and cleared his throat. "Something I've been meaning to ask you, Mary." He felt the tension rise up his back. "There's this party coming up at Moran's place. I got an invitation, and it said to bring a guest . . . so, I was wondering, you know, if maybe you could . . ." Tony found his words getting stuck somewhere in his throat, "go with me to the party, I mean."

"Tony, you dear, I would; I mean I wish, but I can't go." Mary explained her obligation to the Italian Society. "I wanted to ask you if you would join me for our picnic, but both are at the same time."

Tony was amused by their circumstance and laughed easily. Did I hear an invitation, Mary?" he said. "If I did, then I'm going to my first Italian picnic. I probably should show up at Mr. Moran's, but I will only stay for an hour or so. Is that okay with you? I mean, if I meet you at the picnic?"

"That would be just perfect. I'll be finished with the children's games by mid-afternoon," Mary beamed. The stress of a moment before was washed away in her excitement. "Thank you, Tony. You don't know how much . . . ," now it was her turn to stammer over how to complete her thought, "fun you will have at our picnic."

Both were embarrassed by what they had wanted to happen for so long. "I'd better get back to work before Luigi sees me slacking on the job again. Thanks, Mary."

Back at her own work, Mary realized that she had not told Tony of her own dilemma over Moran's invitation. Tony didn't know anything about Moran and her. Was this a deceit on her part? Mary struggled with her feelings of happiness and guilt. She was going to be with Tony at her picnic, and that was all that really mattered to her now.

Peter Moran stood at his dining room window and stared at a midmorning downpour falling from the steel-gray sky. He sipped his glass of whiskey in gloomy contemplation of the day ahead. Everything would have to be moved indoors for this afternoon's Fourth party. 'Irish luck?' he thought to himself. Without Mary, the whole idea of celebration seemed insane. He'd rather get drunk in the privacy of his library than try to be a gracious host to people he was not particularly fond of. Maybe she would come, he thought. Surely the rain would ruin the Italian's picnic. Yes, maybe this deluge was a bit of Irish luck after all.

By noon the heavy clouds were gone, and the afternoon's radiant sunshine brought fresh splendor to Moran's colorful gardens. The staff had dried off the tables and began setting out the foods when Senia joined Peter on the clay-tiled patio in the back yard. "It's going to be a lovely day after all," she smiled. "Mr. Abe Lincoln himself has smiled upon us from somewhere up there." Senia enjoyed her memory of Moran's history lesson two weeks before.

Moran was depressed, however. "I guess so. Everybody's plans for their ethnic picnics and whatever . . . they'll all be outside enjoying the afternoon."

Senia detected Peter's sarcasm and understood the reason behind it. Mary Samora would not be coming to the party. "We'll have a good time here today, sir," she consoled. The combination of invited guests and their interactions, however, gave her reason for concern. The mix of people was supposed to center on Mrs. Samora.

As Senia expected, socialization was strained that sunny July afternoon in Peter Moran's lovely gardens. The Gillespies sent regrets earlier in the morning. Riley, the shovel-runner, told his wife, "I ain't goin' to that Moran thing this afternoon. Haven't heard from that sonofabitch in two years, and now this invitation? Makes no sense to me. We didn't get no invitation to his big hotel hoopla. We ain't gonna give him the pleasure of our company for this garden party of his. What'd he ask us for anyhow?"

Tony was gregarious conversing easily with everyone. He introduced his guest, Tommy Pell, to Molly Trembart, and the two of them liked each other at once. Tony spent some time with Lars and Luigi then sat back with a glass of milk and visited with Senia in the afternoon shade.

The Anselmos felt out of place among Moran's guests, and aside from the luscious barbecued pig, found little enjoyment. Luigi and Lars Udahl talked about the addition which had been completed the week before. Both complimented Tony's work. In less than an hour they ran out of conversation.

Florence Udahl, self-concious of her thick Norwegian accent, spoke few words and smiled sparingly. Mrs. Udahl spent most of her afternoon wandering through the flowers, while her husband sat mostly by himself in the gazebo.

The Bradys and the Atkinsons spent most of their afternoon as a foursome. Claude and Tom talked of Sunday's exhibition baseball game with the renowned St. Paul Colored Gophers, who were an aggregation of players from several famous Negro ball clubs combining for a summer tour. Brady was confident, but Atkinson was highly doubtful of the outcome. "Going to give the Zoretek kid a chance to throw for an inning or two tomorrow," Tom Brady told Claude.

Elwood Trembart and Jerry Sweeny huddled off to the side for nearly an hour and talked disparagingly about their host, Peter Moran. "He really pulled one over on me," Elwood complained. "I'll never trust that bastard again."

"I'm only going to be with him for a few more months," Sweeny confided. "He treats me like an errand boy most of the time, and he's been giving 'Miss Smith' too much control over the financial stuff. I don't like that woman."

Both businessmen agreed Moran was always out for himself and used people to his own ends. In addition, both men believed Moran's exploitations would all catch up with him sooner or later, and that sooner was better. "I, for one, won't shed any tears if the guy falls on his ass someday," Trembart said to Sweeny.

Moran was enjoying his whiskey more than his guests that afternoon. The host managed, nonetheless, to spend a little time with almost everybody there.

Jerry Sweeny needed to confide. "Mr. Moran, we've got to talk about something, maybe next week. I'm having trouble getting along with your Miss Smith. She's on my back all the time about every damn penny; payables, receivables, daily expenses. It's a never-ending headache. I can't take all the probing. It's like she thinks I'm not competent or doesn't trust what I'm doing."

Claude Atkinson probed. "Pete, I didn't see Harold Markman at the hotel opening. Sweeny told me that Harry had been invited. How are you and Markman getting along? I'm still amazed about his selling out to you; it all happened so fast. We'll have to visit more about that one of these days. Make an interesting story I think."

Elwood Trembart responded to Moran's shallow apology with indignation. "Thought we were better friends than that, Pete. It's hard for me to believe what you've told me. Where would McIntosh get the idea that I wasn't interested in the land anymore? Why didn't you talk to me yourself before you made your offer? I hate to say I feel like I've been stabbed in the back, Pete, but that's exactly how I feel."

Peter would have to call Mac and ask his friend to cover up his lie to Trembart. McIntosh knew nothing about Peter's land grab. "Tell you what, El, I've got some land over near Stevenson Location. It's damn good property too, and I'll make you a deal on my forty to square things up with you."

The baseball manager had his gripes as well. "Pete, you promised us last year that you would renovate the grandstand. Those support beams aren't strong enough for five hundred spectators. One of these days the whole structure's going to collapse and then what? We'll have a law suit like I can't imagine."

Senia asked Tony if he would step inside the house, away from the guests, for a few minutes.

"Tony, I hope I know you well enough to confide something that I've been hiding for months. I feel I can trust you."

"Sure, Senia. Anything at all. It'll go no further than the two of us. You've got my word." Tony puzzled at first, then smiled assuringly.

"You are a Slovenian, aren't you, Tony?"

"Thanks for not using the word *Bohunk*, I'm getting pretty tired of that by now. Yes. Why do you ask?"

"Without going into detail now, I'm trying to locate and make contact with, one of your countrymen. His name is Steven Skorich, but some call him Korenjack. Do you know him?"

Tony was astonished. "He's my uncle! I see him every week. He lives over in Chisholm. Why do you ask?"

"I am looking for my husband, Tony. That's all I can tell you right now. I am told that Steven might be able to help me."

"Senia, I had no idea you were married." Tony shook his head in disbelief. "Does Mr. Moran know? Has he tried to help you with this?"

"No, Tony. He must never learn about my situation," Senia said. "I fear it might cost me my job if he were to know anything about my past. I haven't been totally honest with him, I'm afraid."

Tony promised Senia he would make arrangements for a meeting. "Can you get over to Chisholm, Senia? My uncle stays close to home since he was one of the leaders in the. . . ." Tony hesitated at his disclosure of the un-popular strike.

"I know, Tony. I've heard he was a hero to many people."

Tony did not ask Senia who her husband was but confirmed what she said of his uncle. "Steven would never consider himself a hero. He's quite modest about things. He's a wonderful man, Senia. I love the guy. I'll ask him to call you if that's all right with you."

It was nearly four o'clock when Tony found Peter and thanked him for the good food and a wonderful time. Although he was still upset over their confrontation of two weeks ago, Tony did not hold grudges.

"Where are you off to, Tony, baseball practice?" Peter sounded a bit tipsy.

"Going to meet a girl this afternoon, Mr. Moran," Tony bragged.

"Good for you, my young friend. Have a great time. I'll be at the ball game tomorrow to see you pitch. Good luck. And, bring your girlfriend over here if you want to. I'd enjoy meeting her and we've still got lots of food."

Tony stood for a moment on the corner of Cedar and Second Streets watching the Italian picnic festivities in the large grassy park area across the street. He spotted Mary almost instantly. She was surrounded by several children who were tugging at her pink and white dress and eagerly appealing for her attention.

Tony approached and called over to her, "Do I join in and play with the kids or rescue you?"

"Thank goodness, you're here. The little ones have me all worn out!" Mary smiled and reached for Tony's hand. "Take me away, valiant prince!" she sighed, then got the protesting children involved with another activity.

Mary led Tony toward the gathering of adults near the center of the park. "I have so many people for you to meet today, and I've warned every one of them about you," she teased.

Throughout the afternoon and early evening, Mary watched Tony mingle with her Italian friends. He was so outgoing and comfortable with people, always in the middle of conversation with men and women alike. John Depelo took a special interest in Mary's friend. "Tony, with that dark hair of yours you could pass as one of God's chosen Italians," he kidded.

Tony was quick to respond. "Do you think I might fool some real Italians if I were to say my name is . . . Tony Zoretelli, John?" Both men laughed at the ethnic bantering.

Mary remembered an afternoon long ago when she had brought Michael to meet her friends at an Italian picnic. Knowing it was unfair to compare the two men, she could not help doing so. How different they were in every respect. It was after that picnic, Mary recalled as she rubbed the tears welling in her eyes, that Michael made his marriage proposal. That was a lifetime ago. She was happier now than she had ever been. Michael's tragedy had given her new life and inspired her dreams of love.

The sun had fallen beyond the mountainous dumps to the west, and the picnic area crowd was thinning out. Mary found Tony helping Lucia Depelo with her cleanup while he tried to explain the game of baseball to young Armando. The boy hung on his every word.

"This man has talked us all into going to a baseball game tomorrow," Lucia shook her head skeptically, "and I think we will want to take you along with us, Mary."

"I've got housework and laundry tomorrow. Sorry." Mary gave her cute pout and caught Tony's quick frown over her teasing.

"You'll do nothing of the sort, Mary Samora!" Tony scolded. By now, he had his girlfriend's humor figured out. "I'll need all the fan support I can get. And, I'm counting on you to cheer me on."

Tony knew that Mary had come to the picnic with the Depelos, so he asked Lucia's permission to walk Mary home. "I don't know the custom for this," Tony shrugged his shoulders awkwardly. "Should I ask Mary's permission first or . . . ?"

John Depelo overheard Tony's question and smiled. "This is America, young man. It's up to Mary."

On their walk toward Garfield Street in the quiet, star-filled evening, they held hands while talking and laughing at the events of the day. Tony spoke of Moran's party and how the Anselmos appeared to be ill at ease among the guests. "I don't think anybody was having a very good time," he said. "I'm glad I joined your picnic instead of staying longer at Moran's. I had a great time with all of your friends, Mary. Thank you for asking me."

Mary did not want to talk about Moran's affair and was thankful that her picnic had provided a convenient excuse for not attending. She did not want to speak about Peter Moran any longer.

"I've heard so much of this game, baseball, but I don't understand any of it. What will you be doing tomorrow, Tony?" Mary changed the course of conversation with her question. "Will you be hitting the ball?"

Tony laughed at her questions. "I don't know the game very well myself, but I can tell you a few things." He tried to explain the concepts of three strikes and four balls and pitchers and batters and fielders and innings and outs. The game, he confessed, was impossible to describe.

At her door, Tony held her delicate hands in his own and looked into her wide-set brown eyes. This was a moment he had anticipated for so long. At the same time it was a moment of awkward anxiety. Tony had never kissed a woman before.

Mary, sensing his apprehension, did not want the night to end without a kiss. She lifted her head and leaned forward into his chest. "I would like you to . . ."

Their lips met and then opened naturally. The quiver in Mary's spine rushed down to her knees, and she clung tightly to his strong shoulders. She felt a deep pleasure as her breasts pressed into his body. Her breath came in trembling gasps. Mary realized at that moment that she had never experienced a man's kiss before.

Tony sensed their emotions were in perfect harmony. His hands moved over the small of her back and drew her warm body tightly to his own. After their kiss, he breathed in the fragrance of her dark hair and whispered, "I love you, Mary." He spoke his words so softly he could not hear them himself.

Duluth's more than seventy thousand citizens celebrated Independence Day 1908 with parades, marching bands, ethnic festivities, and fireworks on the sandy lakefront at dusk.

Jim McIntosh, with his Kitchi Gammi Club friends, met at the Northland Country Club for an early morning round of golf. Jim used his new birthday clubs for the first time on the front nine. He shot terribly and went back to his old 'sticks' to get his erratic game back under control. His second nine score was much improved.

Mac spent the afternoon with his wife, Martha and their two teenage daughters. He enjoyed his family and regretted all the time he needed to spend away from them on his many trips to Hibbing.

"I wish you didn't have to be gone all the time," thirteen year old Anna complained.

"Now that Mr. Moran's hotel is done will you stay in Duluth more often, Dad?" questioned her older sister Colleen.

The issue had become a strain on the family these past two years, and Jim was resolved to curtail his twice weekly trips to Hibbing. He was certain that his Merchants and Miners Bank could be sold to local interests at a nice profit, and that his other business arrangements could be handled from his Duluth office. Maybe, he considered, now was a good time for him to put the bank on the market. McIntosh would discuss the matter with his bank vice president, Harvey Goldberg, next week.

Father Patrick Foley spent the Fourth with his parishioners, Art and Sarah Schmitz, in their West Duluth home. Visiting with the Schmitz family was always a fun time for the St. James parish priest. Eighteen-month-old Kevin was a delight that brought the pastor to the Schmitz home often.

When the boy went down for his afternoon nap, the three adults talked as they had done many times before.

"Father, have you heard back from Mr. Moran? We are so anxious to get the proceedings going." Art Schmitz felt stymied by an adoption system he didn't understand and had relied on the priest for direction. "Is there anything we can do? It seems pretty clear that Moran has no interest in this child."

Foley had done some investigating on his own and was losing patience with Moran's refusal to return his phone calls. The priest would be going to Hibbing next week for another unexpected visit. He had no doubts about Moran's paternity. He learned that Peter Moran had purchased Barbara Chevalier's Wadena Street house for cash. It was obvious that Barbara's salary at the insurance office would not have allowed her to purchase the furniture, clothing, and jewelry she had accumulated in only one year's time. Peter had taken good care of Barbara. Although circumstantial, his findings were convincing. The priest could not fault Moran on the financial support he provided to the Schmitz family, but it was time to find a reasonable closure to this matter.

"I'll have some answers for you in a week, Art. I'm going to talk to Moran about the paperwork we'll need to get done for an adoption through the county. I don't know any reason why he'd want to block our efforts. He must realize what wonderful parents you and Sarah have been to Kevin," Foley said. "I'll remind him of that when I see him on my visit to the old parish up in Hibbing."

Open illegally on the holiday, Sam Lavalle's small tavern on Central Avenue in West Duluth served its regulars. The local cops left Sam alone for the favors he offered them. It was late in the afternoon when one of Sam's pimps came in the back door and motioned him away from the bar.

"We've gotta problem, Sam. Lily's got herself beaten up over at her place on Raleigh Street. Some drunk from out of town done it. He's passed out now; whadda ya want to do 'bout it?" Sam had an assortment of women who worked the western part of the city. Lily, new to the prostitution business, was vulnerable.

"Frankie, take care of the bar. I've gotta run for an hour or so." Lavalle was out the back door with his pimp and on his way to Lily's place five blocks away. Raleigh Street was a tough neighborhood, and Sam had discouraged his women from hanging around there.

Lily's face was bruised, but the woman was more frightened than hurt. She led the two men up the stairs to her apartment on the second floor of the shabby house.

Inside the room, Lavalle grabbed the man's shock of thick red hair pulling the half-dressed drunk from the couch where he slept. Once the man was on his feet, Lavalle kicked him savagely in the groin and watched him roll over in pain on the floor.

"What the hell! Ya wanna ruin me, you sonofabitch!" Denis got up on one knee, cupped his aching testicles in his hand and threatened, "I'll break yer fuckin neck for that." He struggled to his feet and lunged for Lavalle's throat.

The two men easily subdued the disheveled and bearded man.

"Tell me why ya beat up my girl," Lavalle insisted, "or you'll wish to God you'd never been born."

Denis Moran began to sob. "I paid yer whore. I gave her two bucks, then I caught'er going through my pants, tryin to rob me she was. Honest to god, I don't want no trouble with you guys."

Lavalle would check out his story with Lily later. "Who the hell are ya? Where ya from? I ain't seen you out in West Duluth before." Lavalle wanted to know about the people who came into his territory.

Denis Moran regained some composure while holding his throbbing groin. "Name's Denis Moran. I ain't from 'round here. Came in here from Oregon, a coupla weeks ago."

"Only Moran I've heard of is from up in Hibbing." Lavalle said. "And he's one sonofabitch. Had me fired from the best damn job I ever had. I'd like to kick him in the balls like I just did to you. Sure you ain't from Hibbing?" Lavalle looked for any resemblance between this Moran and the Peter Moran he despised. With the thick beard Denis wore, he could not recognize any similarities.

"Gotta brother up there. A no good, selfish, rich bastard of a brother. He told my pa to go to hell once. I ain't never gonna forgive him for that. Then he had me beat up by a cop and runned me outta town. That was a coupla weeks ago. I'll get the sonofabitch back though. I told the cop that too. One'a these days I'm gonna get my revenge fer what he did ta me . . . fer what he did to my pa."

"Peter Moran?" Lavalle was intrigued.

"The one and only," Denis spit onto the floor.

Lavalle laughed and extended his hand to the man slumped on the couch. "We've got somethin' in common, Denis. Let's the two of us go down ta my place and have us a drink. I got lotsa things swimmin in my head."

BOOK THREE

To Bless or To Blame

'THE WINNING PITCHER'

A DAMP CHILL SETTLED UPON this Sunday afternoon, but Hibbing's baseball fans still packed the grandstand to near capacity. Brady's team had seen a comfortable four run lead disappear in the seventh inning. Billy Breen, the Colts' starting pitcher, was tiring and manager Brady handed the ball to his young rookie, Tony Zoretek. "Don't be nervous; just focus on Tommy Pell's mitt out there," Brady instructed.

Tony had never felt so alone as he stood on the mound in front of nearly four hundred people. He caught a quick glimpse of Mary, five rows up on the third baseline of the grandstand where she sat with the Depelos. The game was tied at six runs each, and the St. Paul Negro All-Stars had only one out with runners on first and second base.

Behind the plate, Pell signaled for Tony's fastball. Tony concentrated on his pitching basics then delivered his first pitch. "Ball one!" The umpire shouted. Three pitches later, the bases were loaded, and Tommy went out to settle Tony down.

"Just imagine you're in the lumber yard throwing into your box. Block out everything else," Tommy Pell suggested. "This is just a game, Tony; try to have fun, and don't squeeze the ball so hard."

Pell's mound conference gave Tony a new resolve. The tall right-hander erased everything from his thoughts. In Tony's mind, Tommy became the familiar wooden box behind the plate, and all else was in a shadowed oblivion. Tony placed his pitches in all four corners of that box with increasing velocity, and the Colored Gopher batters swung at balls they couldn't touch.

As Tony focused on his box behind the batters, Peter focused on Mary opposite his reserved seat. He watched her cheer as Tony put down the opposing batters one after the other. "I'll have to introduce her to Tony after the game," he thought. Then, maybe, I can talk her into joining me for dinner at the hotel. He smiled to himself. It may have been just as well that she had missed his party the day before. His celebration was a failure, he realized, and most of his guests were gone before early evening.

Moose Spragg hit a long blast off the center field wall in the bottom of the ninth inning to score the winning run for the local team. Following a standing ovation for the victorious Hibbing nine, several of the fans came onto the baseball diamond to congratulate the players. Tony shook hands with many of his new admirers as he made his way over to the grandstand to see Mary.

"You did wonderfully, Tony!" Mary was as excited as those who clustered around her at the wooden railing between the stands and the field. Everybody wanted to congratulate the winning pitcher.

"You were so good!" she exclaimed reaching down to hold his hands. "At least that's what everyone around us was saying." She had no idea why he was a hero to the fans, but she reveled in his success just the same. "Did you hear me shouting at the top of my lungs, Tony? 'Hit the batter' I was telling you. Was that the right thing to say?"

Tony roared at her innocent question. "I guess it worked, Mary. Next time I pitch, holler the same thing." He gave her hands a quick squeeze and flushed when Spragg teased him.

"Not in public, Zoretek! Do yer hand holding when nobody's watching."

Little Armando Depelo offered his pencil and paper to Tony and Moose Spragg. His first baseball autographs brought wide eyes and a smile. "Will you teach me how to pitch the ball, Tony?"

Tony tousled Armando's hair. "I'd enjoy doing that, and this big fellow standing next to me might teach you how to hit the ball."

Peter watched the scene on the ball field in disbelief. It was glaringly obvious that he would not make any introductions, nor would he be taking Mary to dinner that night.

Later that evening after several whiskeys, Peter decided to do some further people watching and took a walk down Fifth Avenue to Garfield Street.

From the shadows of a dreary street corner, he watched the small Samora house. A light was on in the living room, but he was too far from the window to see anything inside. The chilly drizzle this night was an aggravation that the spirits in his flask could not alleviate. Still, he waited.

Moran's pocket watch read 10:30 when Tony Zoretek said goodbye at the front door and began walking down the street in the opposite direction from where he stood. "Mary and Tony," he cursed under his breath. In business, Moran had a credo that always served him well: Know your competition and undermine it! Life was business, and business was life in the Moran scheme of things.

Monday was a day off for Tony, but he was up early and on his way to Chisholm to see his Uncle Steven. So much had been going on in his life, and he was anxious to share the events with the one man he loved more than any other. Tony knew when Mr. Huber's creamery truck left Hibbing every morning, and he'd catch a ride with the milk man on this day, as he had many times before. Steven was off from work expecting his nephew's visit. He waited over his coffee at the table in the back corner of the familiar cafe on Lake Street.

Tony's arrival was met with Steven's typical bear hug embrace. Tony rambled from topic to topic with enthusiasm while his uncle sat back with the smile that always parted the thick beard below his straight nose. Tony's carpentry job was completed; he had made the baseball team pitching well the day before, but most exciting of all he was falling in love with the beautiful Mary Samora!

Steven gazed with pride upon the young man who was making a wonderful life for himself. "Tell me more about this Mary." Steven was most eager to know all that he could about this woman in Tony's life. Steven believed there was no greater satisfaction than to love someone.

After their breakfast, Tony told Steven about Senia Smith's inquiry at the Fourth party. "I told her that I'd ask you to give her a phone call. What do you think it's about?"

"I'm sorry, Tony. I have no knowledge of anyone by the name of Smith. That's an English name if I'm not mistaken. The English have always been on the other side from where I've been these past few years. Where did she get my name, I wonder?" Steven was curious. "She's been trying to find her husband for almost a year? That must be painful. I wish I could give her some information. Can you remember anything else she might have told you, Tony?"

"She said something about a secret she was hiding; that's about it. We only talked for a few minutes."

Steven was perplexed. "The name Senia might be Finnish. In fact, an old friend of mine, Martin Alto, has a daughter named Senia; I'm sure of it. Describe this Smith woman, Tony. What does she look like?"

"She's very attractive, Uncle. She has long blonde hair and bright blue eyes, a very light complexion, and speaks very good English. What else can I tell you?" Tony tried to think of any other characteristics that might describe Senia.

"You have described a Finnish woman, Tony. But, Smith?" Steven had a sudden insight. "Smith, I'll bet that's not . . ." He struggled to find the word he wanted, but it wouldn't come to him. "She is using a name that's not really her own. That must be it. I know of several Finns who have done something similar to that. 'Makis' have taken the name 'Hill', I think that's an English translation. It's hard for the Finns up here to get jobs of any kind—they're often labled as socialists."

Steven affirmed he would do anything he could to help her find her husband. He promised to call Senia at the Moran residence later that day. Afterwards, they might be able to get together and talk further. "You must tell her of my reputation, Tony. It's not safe for her to let anyone know about me. She could lose her job."

Tony left Chisholm promising to be discreet and thanking him for his willingness to help his friend.

It was just after ten in the morning on the clock in Senia's office. Downstairs, Moran's house was unusually quiet for a Monday morning, and she wondered if the staff had been given the day off for the holiday weekend . She didn't know if she was supposed to have the day off, too. No one had told her anything. Senia could only work and wait. Tony promised he would see his uncle and ask him to contact her when and if he could.

Senia heard Peter's heavy footsteps on the stairs then down the hallway. There was a rap on her office door. Without waiting for any response, Peter came into the room plopping down on an overstuffed leather chair across from her desk. He looked terrible. His thick hair was uncombed, his face unshaven, his clothes appeared to be slept in. "Got some things for you to do today." There was no "good morning," and his voice was hoarse. "I've got a little mess going on with Trembart." Peter explained the lie he'd told at his party to the village council president about the Alice land deal. Peter wanted Senia to call Jim and have him cover Peter's ass. He expected Mac to be in Hibbing later in the week and wanted him forewarned in case Trembart cornered Jim regarding the land transaction.

"Mr. McIntosh called this morning. I didn't want to wake you, but he won't be coming up to the bank this week," Senia said. "Wouldn't it be better if you called him yourself? Another thing, I think Martha had a bad weekend, sir."

"I told you to call him!" Peter snapped. "And, something else I want done this morning. Get ahold of Udahl. If he's not at the shop, get him at home. I want all the figures on the Anselmo job that Zoretek just finished. I want to know exactly how much time it took, what materials were used, and our bottom line profit on the project. Got that?"

Senia had never seen Peter in such a foul mood. She knew that his party had been a flop, but even that did not justify his anger of this morning. "Yes, sir. Is there anything else?" Then Senia remembered the report she had wanted to give to Peter. "I have completed a financial report on the hotel's first month, sir. You might be pleased to know it showed a profit."

"There should have been a profit. As far as I know, the place has been full every night. What are the numbers?" Peter questioned.

Senia hesitated before answering. "Not quite full, sir. Our occupancy was over seventy percent for the month. We had projected closer to ninety, and our expenses exceeded what we had planned."

"What's 'exceeded,' Miss Smith? It's not like you to give me generalities. How much over?" Peter scratched his unruly hair.

"About thirty percent over, sir. It cut into the profits, but we were still in the black." Senia cleared her throat. "I don't want to fault Mr. Sweeny, sir, but whenever I caution him, he gets quite upset with me. He doesn't . . ."

"He told me that you're on his ass all the time. Maybe you should just let him run things the way he sees fit. The guy's got a lot on the ball, you know," Peter snapped defending his manager.

"I'm only looking out for your interests, Mr. Moran. Perhaps I can be more sensitive, but let me be candid with you, sir. Mr. Sweeny wants to impress you. I want to give you the facts."

"For the present just leave Sweeny alone. Take care of those things I asked you to do and get the Anselmo information by this afternoon." Peter rose abruptly and left the room.

Senia had wanted to raise another matter with her employer, but she held back. Sweeny had not given her any insurance verifications on the hotel. She had asked him for the papers on several occasions, and all he would tell her was that everything was in perfect order.

"I won't do it!" McIntosh told Senia. "It's a shameless lie. I've worked hard to build a good reputation in Hibbing. How could Peter even imagine I'd deceive Trembart for him?" McIntosh gripped his phone in tight anger about Peter's outrageous request. "Why didn't he call me himself? You shouldn't be in the middle of this awkward situation, Senia."

"I don't know, sir. He's having a bad day."

"Senia, let me tell you something in the strictest of confidence." McIntosh had the highest respect for Miss Smith and hated to see her accountable for Moran's dirty work all the time. "Peter's been on the edge for some time. Maybe you've seen it, too. I worry about him. I've done some questionable things to help him out in the past, but . . ." Jim gritted his teeth, "Senia, this is the last straw. Tell him no for me. That's all there is to it, no. If he wants, he can call me himself. Sorry. I've had enough of his dirty work."

"I will pass along your refusal, sir. Thanks for being honest with me. And, yes, I've seen a lot of stress in Mr. Moran for some time now. Mr. McIntosh, there's no need for you to apologize."

When he hung up, McIntosh made an immediate decision. He would sell his Merchants and Miners bank in Hibbing and give more attention to his family in Duluth. With a sigh of relief, he began to outline his plan to put his bank on the market.

Later in the afternoon, Lars Udahl returned Senia's call about the Anselmo project. Puzzled by Moran's request, he had put all the numbers together. "Do ya want me to bring the figures over to the house or give 'em to ya on the phone?" Lars asked Senia.

"On the phone is fine, Mr. Udahl. Since it's your day off, you've done enough already."

Udahl found that Tony had used a higher grade of lumber than the specs called for, and he painted the interior walls. The painting was not in the contract. "From what I can see, Tony went about eleven dollars over the budget for the job. We had figgered a profit of fifty dollars, after labor and materials, so we made thirty-nine. I'm happy with that, and let me tell you, Miss Smith, Luigi is one very satisfied customer. You can tell Mr. Moran that."

Senia wrote up a brief report on the Anselmo job and put it in an envelope for Mr. Moran's attention. Like Lars, she was confused by the unusual inquiry. Was the real issue Moran's profit margin or Tony Zoretek?

Senia had two more calls that afternoon. A Father Patrick Foley from Duluth asking if Mr. Moran would be in that evening. "Please don't make an appointment, ma'am. I just wanted to know." The priest's call was another oddity in what was becoming a most unusual day.

Although the phone connection was fuzzy, the second call almost brought her heart to a stop. The accented deep voice on the other end of the line asked, "Am I speaking with Senia Smith?"

"Yes," Senia sensed from the question who was calling.

"This is Steven Skorich. Do you have the privacy to talk?"

"I do, Mr. Skorich. Thank you for calling." Senia tried to get a grasp on her composure. She had waited months for this call rehearsing what she would say a hundred times in her mind. But, now, she was all but speechless. "You have talked with Tony already?" Her mind stumbled for something to say.

Steven sensed apprehension in the woman's voice and a familiar trace of accent as well. With her few words, Steven knew that she was not a Miss Smith. "Yes, my nephew visited this morning. He said that you wanted to talk to me about your husband. I don't know of any Smiths, Senia, but if there's anything I can do to help, I will."

Senia had no choice but to trust this man. "My name is Senia Arola. My husband is Timo Arola. Do you know him?"

Steven felt a rush of anguish. What could he say and how might he say it? "Your husband . . . has been . . . a good friend of mine."

"Can you help me find him, Mr. Skorich?" Her words were a plea of desperation.

Steven formulated his thoughts before he spoke. "Yes, I can bring you to him, Senia," Steven said using her first name again. The sketch of a plan played in his mind. This would be difficult. How strong was this woman? Steven thought logically. If she came here from Finland to find Timo, she must have the same kind of courage that her husband had. "Can you meet me next Saturday morning? Early?"

"Yes, sir, Mr. Skorich . . . Steven. Yes, I can, and early is fine."

"Meet me at . . ." Steven considered where they would be going on Saturday, "meet me at the Drake and Stratton buildings over on the east side of Railroad Street. I will try to be there by seven." What else might he say? "Senia, wear comfortable clothing for hiking. We will be going some distance into the woods."

Senia smiled to herself. "I knew it, Steven. I knew Timo would be in the woods. Is he near a lake?"

"Yes," Steven fought back his tears, "near a lake . . . Saturday morning, then."

That evening, Peter was on the phone in his library. "Lars, I'm looking over the numbers from the Anselmo project that Zoretek did. Looks like we came in under the profit you estimated."

"Yes, Mr. Moran. About eleven dollars, sir. It's my fault, sir. I thought you wanted Mr. Anselmo to be real happy with the work," Lars apologized. "He's really pleased, sir; I'm sure of that."

"It's not so much me, Lars. Senia, you know, she's our numbers person. Things are slowing down now that the hotel work's done. Anyhow, she's giving me some ideas on where we've got to cut corners, you know," Peter said, shifting the responsibility for what he was about to do now onto his financial secretary.

Lars swallowed hard. He might lose his job over eleven dollars. "Lemme cover it, Mr. Moran, the eleven bucks. Or, I could bill Mr. Anselmo, if you'd rather do it that way."

Peter explained that there would be some layoffs. "I'm not blaming you, Lars. It was Zoretek who picked high grade lumber, and Zoretek who did the painting. That was irresponsible on his part. You don't need to cover for him."

Udahl was instructed to give Tony Zoretek a lay off notice the next morning. Moran would have Senia bring a final paycheck to his office. "Tell Zoretek that things are slowing down. No need to go into the Anselmo thing with him." Peter ended the conversation leaving Lars stunned.

"Mr. Moran." Senia was standing in the library doorway, her face drained of color. She had not wanted to interrupt his telephone conversation but had overheard Peter's last few words to Lars. "There is a Father Foley from St. James Church here to see you," she said announcing the tall priest standing behind her. "He says that you're expecting him."

Peter looked up from his desk and realized that Foley was looking at the open bottle of whiskey and his half-filled glass.

"Yes, Senia. I've been expecting a visit. Come in Father. Can I fix you an Irish whiskey?" Peter raised the bottle.

"That would be fine, Mr. Moran." Father Foley would not pretend to be the nice priest from out of town on this visit. He was angry. A whiskey might be good for him, "Straight up, thank you."

There were few pleasantries between the two of them. "It's been a long time, Mr. Moran, and you've not been answering any of my phone calls. Were it not for your monthly checks to the Schmitz family and an occasional monetary gift to my parish, I might have believed that you had fallen off the face of the earth."

Peter sensed Foley's frustration and was quick to lighten the atmosphere in the room. Peter held his glass in a gesture of a toast, "May the road rise up to meet you . . . ," he offered a familiar Irish sentiment.

" . . . and the wind be at your back," Foley acknowledged, taking a swig from his glass.

"This is not a social visit is it, Father? What do you want this time?" Peter's sour mood of the day was exaggerated by his drinking. He refilled his glass and slid the bottle toward the priest.

Foley would be blunt as well. "I'm here regarding your son, Kevin. I'm sure that would be obvious, Mr. Moran. You ought to meet him some day."

Foley explained his desire to find a reasonable closure to the issue of Kevin's welfare. He'd promised Art Schmitz he would get the adoption process going. "With your declaration of paternity and an authorization for me to act in your behalf, I can initiate adoption proceedings through the county. The Schmitz family would very much like to have legal custody of the child, and I assure you, do what is best for Kevin."

"I will do neither, Father. If this is the sole purpose of your visit to Hibbing, then I'm afraid you have made a long trip for nothing," Peter said matter of factly. "Your dear Schmitz family, may I remind you Father, has been *hired* to provide for the boy's care. Nothing more, nothing less."

The parameters of confrontation were drawn, and Peter felt a confidence in the position he held. "If, for argument's sake, the boy were mine, and I decided to get married, then what? Do I go to the county and ask them to give me the boy back? Just look around Father. Look at what I have to give. Concerning his best interests, the finest in life is mine to give."

"For the sake of argument, as you say, what if I take this matter to court?" Foley rejoined.

"Then we'll have our lawyers do all the arguing for us. I'll have mine, and the Schmitz'll have theirs. Is that what they want?" Peter smiled at the priest. "Are they willing to take me to court? It's a very expensive gamble for them—but not for me."

"They will not have to, Mr. Moran. It will be your lawyer against those of the Diocese of Duluth. And, if I can arrange it, counsel from the Vatican as well. I think I can assure you that it would be you against the Roman Catholic Church. We can afford it."

Peter's smile, like his confidence, vanished in the picture the priest had just drawn. He knew better than to pick a fight that he could not win. Where might he find any attorney that would take on the Church? Certainly his ambitious new attorney, Victor Power, (a Catholic himself) would counsel against such a confrontation. The publicity would be devastating! Hibbing, Peter knew, was a predominantly Catholic community with its large Eastern Europe population.

"You're a good fighter, Foley. I respect that in a man. Now, let's see what kind of compromise we can both live with for the time being," Peter offered. "Let me suggest that we keep the present arrangement for the next year. I'll even provide something extra for the Schmitz family, maybe fifty a month, with no strings attached. The extra money would be theirs to spend on whatever they choose. Will you extend my offer to them, Father?"

"No. I have papers along with me, and I'm not here to negotiate or compromise. If you don't sign them, then the next you hear in this matter will come from the court not from me. So, for the last time, will you sign the paternity and authorization papers, Mr. Moran?" Foley was adamant. He'd made his case and stood as if to leave.

"Relax, Father. Please sit down," Peter appealed. "This is all quite unexpected. I want to be fair, and I expect you'll be fair with me as well. You've threatened me with an ultimatum." Peter could see a way out of the predicament. "I'll tell you what. I've thought about Kevin every day for the past year. I was very fond of his mother Barbara, and we were intimate, Father. I'm sure that Barbara didn't have sex with other men, so, I think I'm probably the father. For Barbara's reputation, I will take responsibility for being the boy's father."

Peter believed he was gaining an edge and continued, "I'll sign the paternity papers, Father. If you'll leave the adoption papers, I'll look them over and get back to you. How's that?"

"You're a clever man, Mr. Moran. 'For Barbara's reputation,' that makes me sick! I'll leave no unsigned papers here with you. Do you have any other ideas? I don't." Foley took the papers from his lap sliding them into the briefcase he had set beside the chair. "I can't say that I'm surprised by anything you've said tonight, Mr. Moran. I'm beginning to see why you've done so well in the world of business. I'm one person, however, that does not believe that money buys people."

"Give me one month," Moran pleaded. "On my word of honor, I will either sign the papers or go to court for custody of the boy. One month, Father."

Foley recognized defeat in Moran's last appeal. "Within the next month, I will have initiated legal proceedings in behalf of the Schmitz family." Foley's statement carried a grave finality. "Before I leave, let me tell you that Kevin is a beautiful little boy, and I am the most available babysitter in the parish. As I said earlier, you might consider a visit some day when you're not too busy, Mr. Moran."

Peter signed the papers. If he wanted to countersue the Schmitz family for custody, he would tell his lawyer that he had signed these papers under extreme duress. He wondered again, what attorney would he ever find to represent him? "Here, take your papers." Peter was irate. "I hope you're happy."

Mary found it difficult to keep her thoughts on her work this Monday morning. The wonderful weekend replayed itself in her mind. Such a marvelous time it had been. The picnic on Saturday, the ball game on Sunday, and Tony! She wondered what Luigi and Tina would think if they knew she had invited Tony into her home the night before without a chaperone? Tony had kissed her again last night, and it was as wonderful as the first time.

As she looked around her new workspace in the back of the shop, she missed Tony terribly. Gone were those marvelous days when he worked on the addition with her watching him from the corner of her eyes. How often might she see him now? Mary envisioned him going to Chisholm to visit his Uncle Steven. How much she wanted to meet the uncle that Tony so respected and loved. Would he tell Steven about her? What would he say? Tony Zoretek was all that she could think about.

Luigi interrupted her reverie of the moment. "I ordered these for you, Mary. Come and take a look." He held up a pattern book and waved for her to join him at the table where he worked on some order forms.

"Luigi! These are from Paris!" Mary stared openmouthed at the book covers. "Where did you get them?"

Luigi enjoyed her appreciation and surprise. "You might find some new fashion ideas from these." He slid the books in her direction. "Sit down and tell me what you think."

Mary paged through the patterns with wide eyes. "I can make these dresses, Luigi. Look at this one." Mary pointed to a complicated design. "I would change the neckline here, where it's attached to the bodice, and I might choose a different sleeve style.

"I must show this pattern to Mrs. Bennett. She needs a new dress for an affair in Duluth next month. She'll just adore this. Even the Bazaar can't match the elegance of this Paris design." The Itasca Bazaar was Hibbing's finest ladies apparel store and Mary's greatest competition. Mary could only make two dresses each week on her new Singer machine, while the Bazaar had several racks of dresses and blouses from which their clientele could choose.

"Mary, I have another surprise for you. With the new space that we have, I am going to hire an assistant seamstress for you. She will do some of the material cutting for you and whatever other help you might need. What do you think of that?"

"Luigi, you dear man. Yes, that would be just wonderful. With help, I might be able to make a new dress every day. Maybe we could have a rack of dresses for women to choose from." Mary took the old man's hand in her own. "But, Luigi, you are as busy as I am, and you also could use help," Mary reminded him.

"I do just fine as it is, Mary. Now, tell me about your weekend. Tina told me that you went to the ball game with the Depelos yesterday and watched Tony pitch his first game." Luigi sat back in his chair and smiled. "I'm not a blind old man yet, and I think that my Mary has some romantic notions about a certain young carpenter I know. Could that be so?"

Mary's cheeks flushed as she and Luigi talked for nearly an hour about the weekend. Luigi and Tina did not have a good time at Moran's party. "It was the strangest feeling, Mary," he said. "We felt more like Italian immigrants that afternoon than American citizens. Both Tina and me, we didn't seem to fit in very well with the other guests. Only Lars Udahl paid us any attention, but his wife hardly said a word all day. I wish I'd taken Tina to the picnic as she had wanted. Oh well, Moran has quite a place, and the sight of his beautiful gardens probably made it worthwhile.

'A Gravesite by the Lake'

Tony walked along Fourth Avenue toward North Street between Walt Spragg and Tommy Pell. The three men were headed toward the lumber yard on a cloudy Tuesday morning following their long Fourth weekend. Moose boasted about his winning hit in Sunday's game, and Tommy talked about the girl he had met at Moran's party. "I think I'm in love, guys," Tommy Pell said. Slipping away from Moran's party, Molly Trembart and Tommy had gone for a long walk. Molly watched him play baseball on Sunday, then invited him to meet her parents at her house after the game. "I don't think Molly's father likes me," Tommy said. "First thing he asked me was about my educashin. All I could tell 'em was that I didn't have no schooling that amounted to much. He didn't like that at all."

"Love 'em and leave 'em," was Moose's philosophy on female relationships. "There were some ladies in town from the big city of Minneapolis this weekend. I had me two of em and broke the hearts of the other ones, I'm sure," Moose laughed about his exploits.

"Did'ja get their names?" Pell teased.

"One of 'em was Lucille. Can't remember the other one. Strange, but I think I liked the other one better than Lucille. She talked to me about things. Lucille just laughed and drank." Moose puzzled at the lapse of memory. "I'll havta get her name."

Tony kept his thoughts to himself. His weekend had been wonderful beyond description. He was in love.

"What'd you do this weekend, beside become the local baseball hero?" Moose asked his unusually quiet friend.

"Nothing, nothing at all," Tony would keep his activities to himself. "I did read a good book, fellas. Do you want me to tell you about it?"

Both Moose and Tommy laughed. Tony's explanation of his nothing weekend was bullshit, and all three of them knew it. "Did I ever tell ya, Tony? I read a book once," Moose said as the men continued their banter.

Tony was excited about seeing Lars Udahl that morning. He would ask the foreman if he could join the crew that was building houses over on the west end of Mahoning Street. He wanted to concentrate on learning all that he could about house construction. For weeks he had imagined himself designing a house with Mary. This would be the perfect house for them and the many children they would have. He laughed to himself over his fantasy.

Dreading the bad news he was ordered to give Tony that morning, Lars' stomach soured when he saw the men coming down North Street. Of anybody who worked in the lumber operation, Zoretek was both his favorite and his best employee.

"Hello, Lars!" Tony called to the man standing in the large warehouse doorway. "I want to talk to you first thing this morning if you've got a few minutes. I've got a big favor to ask."

Tommy split from his two companions and headed to Khort's Grocery where he worked. "See you guys at practice. Have a great day. How ya doin', Mr. Udahl?" He waved and turned down First.

Lars waited for the two men to get up to the building. "Let's talk right now, Tony. Walt, you can start unloading the lumber from the railroad flatbed, mostly two-by-sixes. Then check with me when yer done. Tony, you come with me."

Tony was puzzled at Udahl's uncharacteristic frown and gruff demeanor. "Mr. Udahl." Tony rarely used the "Mr." since both had become such good friends. "I want to build houses. Will you let me join the Mahoning crew this week? Please . . ." Tony smiled at his juvenile appeal to the boss. "Won't you . . . please!"

"Got some bad news fer ya, Tony. Com'on in and sit down." Lars gestured Tony into the office and closed his door behind them. When seated, Lars fidgeted with a pencil while explaining that business had slowed down since the hotel, and things were getting tight. He hated himself for the lie and hated Moran even more for demanding that he tell it.

"I don't believe it, Lars. Senia, Miss Smith I mean, wouldn't do this. Me? I'm the only one that's going to be laid off? No, I'm sorry. It's not Senia; it's got to be Mr. Moran." Tony hung his head in speculation. "I had a little argument with Mr. Moran about some stupid baseball bet he made. But that was a couple of weeks ago."

"Tony, I just don't know what to tell you." Lars' voice choked. "This came a coupla minutes before ya got here." Lars handed the familiar pay envelope to Tony. "I can't tell ya how badly I feel about this. Got my orders ta do this yesterday."

"It's not your fault, Lars. I'm sorry that you had to do someone else's dirty work. I'm going to find Mr. Moran right now." Tony got up from his chair.

"I think there's more; sit down a minute, Tony. Keep this to yerself." Lars explained the issue about the Anselmo project. "I tol 'em I'd make up the eleven bucks, but he wouldn't have none of it."

"I just wanted my first job to be perfect, Lars, you know that. It doesn't make any sense. Eleven bucks!" Tony was even more dumbfounded that he had been laid off over a few dollars.

"Don't go there, Tony, not now anyways. Moran's been in a really bad mood lately. Just let this blow over for a few days. I'll see what I can do fer ya," Lars appealed.

"Lars, I'm good at what I do. I've had the best teacher in the world. I'll find something. Don't get yourself in trouble with the boss over me. You're right though. I'll steer clear of Moran for a while."

Tony reached for Lars Udahl's huge, calloused hand, "I'll keep in touch. Thanks Lars, thanks for everything." Tony walked out into the gray morning carrying his last paycheck from the Moran Lumber Company.

Anger and confusion tugged at his thoughts as he walked aimlessly down North Street away from the warehouse. Where was he going? What was he going to do? Tony pondered the unexpected curve ball that had been thrown at him and laughed to himself over the baseball metaphor. "Think positive," he reminded himself. "Good things often come out of bad. He remembered something from a book he had read once about a *silver lining*. He glanced toward the cloudy sky and wondered if he might find one.

Tony walked down Third Avenue and crossed the busy Pine Street intersection that was the main artery of commerce in Hibbing. His gaze panned the long row of buildings on either side of the street. Wooden signs of every size and shape hung in disarray over the narrow sidewalk. He was amused by the hodgepodge scene . . . *Chinese Laundry* . . . *W.J. Ryder Home Furnishings-Cabinets* . . . *and* in smaller letters below, 'licensed embalmer and undertaker' . . . *Godfrey's Men's Shop- Hart, Shaffner and Marx suits* . . . *Elk's Club* . . . *E. J. Trembart- Attorney-at-law* . . . *Khort Brothers-* meat, fish, and poultry . . . *The Red Rock Tavern* . . . over a Fitger's Beer sign . . . the *Hotel Moran* sign loomed over the four storied building on South Street off to Tony's left.

Tony crossed the intersection and contemplated his former boss. In one way or another, Peter Moran's fingerprints were on almost everything in Hibbing. Until this morning, Tony had believed that he would be a part of the future undertakings of Moran's insatiable ambitions. That idea, however, had changed suddenly. Tony would somehow have to find a way to make a mark of his own on this city.

An ice wagon creaked slowly down the center of the avenue leaving its soft billow of red dust trailing behind. Tony waved at the driver who had given him a ride in the wagon on more than one occasion. "Need a lift before it starts to rain?" Larry Beckers waved back.

"Not today, Larry. Thanks anyhow."

Tony paused to read a cluttered corner kiosk . . . "Yankee Robinson's Greatest Show on Earth" . . . The notice advertised a coming circus. He pictured Mary and their children at the circus. "Three rings, two elevated stages, five bands- Tom Tom the world's largest elephant . . . lions, camels, and a monster airship! . . . an aerial ballet of the Tyball Family . . ." Tony read on, "thirty Salome dancers from Egypt, fifty clowns." Below the page in bold letters was the promise of a free street parade on July 24, 1908.

On another panel of the newsstand, "Wagner's Parsifal" was coming to the Power Theater in August, a wrestling match tonight, English champion Jim Parr would grapple with a local Norwegian named John Berg. Horse races on Sunday at the fairgrounds with one thousand dollars in purses. Newly attached to the board was a September ad featuring the "Buffalo Bill Wild West Show" coming to Duluth. Tony remembered reading that William Cody's sister lived in the port city.

Duluth reminded Tony of Jim McIntosh, the gentleman he had met once at Peter's office. McIntosh owned the Merchants and Miners Bank where Tony had his account. Tony would deposit his check sometime later this morning. He considered making an appointment with McIntosh. Maybe Tony could get a loan and start a little carpentry business of his own. The thought intrigued him. His own small business . . . Tony resolved to talk to Lars about the idea. How could things be slowing down in this hectic city? Moran was angry with him for something. That something was not the job he did for Luigi Anselmo.

The Sevenson Agency promoted 'exquisite property' for sale in one of the many new housing developments outside of Hibbing. South of the village was Silliman Addition where building lots required a down payment of fifty dollars. The advertisement attracted Tony's thoughts for the moment.

"Hey, Tony. Catch!" George Khort tossed a red fruit from his market across the street toward the walkway where Tony lingered. "Have yourself an apple. You pitched damn good on Sunday. I had no idea you were a baseball player, Tony."

"Great job, Zoretek," said a man at Khort's elbow. "Some fastball ya got," the stranger added.

Tony smiled at his celebrity status of the moment. Baseball was Hibbing's summer passion. "Thanks, Mr. Khort, an apple a day . . ."

"You're right about that. Maybe I otta send a bushel basket full of em to Brady. What d'ya think?" Khort laughed.

"Can't hurt," Tony agreed waving as he resumed wandering down Third Avenue.

An older man, bent over with his cane, stepped out from Max Friedman's confectionery store on the corner near Moran's hotel. "You gonna pitch next Sunday, Zoretek?" the man asked.

He nodded at the stranger, smiled. "I hope so, but that's up to Mr. Brady."

Tony was amazed at some of the contradictions of his city. Ahead was the Lutheran Church with its steepled edifice, freshly painted in white, and inspiring a holy dimension. Along both sides of the same avenue, however, were rows of saloons with upstairs brothels. The mine town was still a masculine, vulgar place.

A shaggy mongrel lazed on the board sidewalk several feet in front of him. The dog rolled over on his side groaning for some attention. Tony paused and scratched deeply into the thickly-matted fur. From the half-open window above Jendro's Barber Shop a baby was bawling. In an alleyway, three barefoot boys were scuffling over a coin one of them had found in the dirt. "Saw it first!" the larger boy shouted at the smaller lad.

"But, I picked it up!" protested the smaller boy.

"First ta see it gets it!" The bully grabbed the wrist of the small kid and forced him to surrender his coin. The loser sulked away fighting back his tears.

In the distance, Tony heard the chug and whistle and rumble of ore trains heading out of the city. The sounds and smells of this typical Tuesday morning mingled together. Tony passed the open doorway of a bakery, another laundry, a vegetable stand, and Canelake's Candy Kitchen.

Lightning arced a jagged slash across the dark rolling clouds, followed by thunder echoing a rippling clap. A heavy drop of rain splat on the dry boardwalk, then another. The downpour hit suddenly settling the red dust creating an instant mire in the streets. Tony looked up into the driven rain, feeling beads roll down his face, enjoying the refreshing coolness it brought to his morning walk down the busy avenue.

Luigi's shop was only a block away from where Tony stood below the canopy of the saggy-fronted, ill-reputed Central Hotel. He would not disturb Mary at her work although he was anxious to talk with her. "Maybe tonight," he thought to himself.

Stepping away from the building, he allowed the rain to soak him. With nothing to do for the rest of the day, he would find a good book and escape into the adventures of an author's imagination. Last week he had spent joyful hours in the western *Roaring Camp'* of Bret Harte. Moran's library might be off limits for now, but Hibbing's new Carnegie Library had recently opened, and Tony had not yet visited the stylish new public building. Maybe there was a book on starting a small business.

"What an unexpected surprise!" Mary gushed her happiness at seeing Tony waiting for her at the corner of Garfield Street. She was on her way home from Luigi's, and it was late in the afternoon. Mary noticed the dampness in his clothes. "Did your work get rained out? That was quite a storm this morning," she said reaching for his hand.

As they walked the last two blocks to Mary's house, Tony began to explain the events of his day. He was careful not to bring up the Anselmo issue that Lars had confided to him. "I just can't believe this slow down excuse Mr. Udahl gave me. Houses are going up all over town and most of them with Moran's lumber. It doesn't make any sense at all."

Unlocking her front door, Mary invited Tony in for coffee and a sandwich. As she listened to his story, she tried to frame the events of the past week in her mind. There was an obvious connection, but she did not know how to explain it to Tony. Peter, she knew, had seen her at the baseball game. She remembered that Tony came over to the railing, and that they had held hands. Peter Moran would have seen the two of them together. Their affection for each other was probably obvious to every one.

Tony interrupted her thoughts. "It's got to be an issue between Mr. Moran and me. We had a small argument one afternoon, but that was weeks ago. I left his party early to join your picnic, but he didn't seem upset over that. As I remember, he just told me to have a good time and to come back later if I wanted to."

"Did you tell him where you were going, Tony? Or, who you were going to see?" Mary winced to herself at the questions.

"I don't think so. No. I just said that I was going to meet a girl. He was happy about that." Tony shrugged his shoulders. "And I surely didn't embarrass him with my pitching in the game the next day." He paused, "Lars advised me not to see Mr. Moran right now; he said I should just 'let it all blow over for a while'. What do you think, Mary?"

Mary was slicing bread for sandwiches, with her back turned from Tony as he described his mystery. She wanted to cry for this man she loved. How would he react to what she might tell him about her relationship with Peter Moran? Her temples throbbed. Was she the real reason behind what had happened to Tony? Was Peter that jealous?

Tony got up from the table. "Let me pour us each some coffee, Mary. Where are your cups?" Tony asked.

Mary brushed bread crumbs from her apron. "You sit, Tony, I'll get the coffee and join you." Mary fumbled in the cabinet for two cups, then poured with an unsteady hand. She knew she must be honest and risk telling the truth. "Oh, dear God," she breathed to herself, "please give me the right words and let Tony understand."

Mary sat down across from Tony and reached for his hands. Her first words were more important than anything else she would say. "I love you, Tony Zoretek. With all of my heart, I love you." She began sobbing lightly and rubbing her eyes.

"Mary, what's wrong. I love you too; I can't even begin to tell you . . . I'll get another job, don't worry about that." He comforted her and softly kissed her hands. "Don't worry about me."

"I know you will," she sniffled. "I'm not worried about that at all. Please, Tony, don't let go of my hands while I tell you what is breaking my heart." Mary began her story with the episode back in January when Moran visited her house with his offer to pay off the mortgage. Later there were flowers and invitations. She choked on the words describing her excursion with Moran on that Saturday two weeks before. She told Tony how much she had wanted him to have been her escort that day; Tony massaged the back of her hands with his thumbs and squeezed softly.

She concluded her confession. "Then he saw us together, holding hands and talking after the game Sunday."

"I can't imagine any red-blooded man in Hibbing not being interested in you, Mary. My gosh, you're beautiful and wonderful and fun. I'm the luckiest guy in the world to be sitting here with you right now. That's the honest truth, Mary," Tony smiled widely. "You haven't done anything to cry about."

Mary dried her tears one last time returning his smile. "You're not upset about that day I spent with Mr. Moran?"

"Not at all. That happened before, you know. . . ." Tony let the thought drop. "But, I just can't believe that anybody would be as jealous as you think Mr. Moran might be. That's really sick, Mary. Fire me because he saw us holding hands? It must be something else." Tony shook his head in disbelief.

Mary gave Tony a questioning look. "How well do you really know Mr. Peter Moran, Tony? Maybe I see him a lot differently than you do. I don't think he's become powerful and rich by being a nice guy to everybody." She thought carefully about her next words. "I wouldn't be surprised if he offers you some kind of deal to stay away from me. That scares me, Tony. He scares me!"

"Don't give it another thought, Mary Samora. He would have to shoot me to keep me away from you." Tony laughed at the idea.

Mary could neither understand nor express what scared her about Peter Moran. Maybe it was his power over people or his belief that everyone had their price. Was he capable of doing something really sinister to keep what he wanted for himself?

Sensing an opportunity, Tony moved their conversation in a more positive direction. "I'm getting pretty hungry, Mrs. Samora. You promised me sandwiches an hour ago. While you're making them, I'll tell you about some business plans that I've been thinking about. I'm kinda excited about my ideas and want to share them with you."

Mary pushed his hands playfully away from hers, "Tony Zoretek, if you ever call me 'Mrs. Samora' again . . . I'll . . . I'll punch you in the nose. I will!" she said defiantly as she made a fist of her small hand.

Tony roared his delight, took her fist in his hand, and kissed her.

Steven Skorich spent Friday night in the secure North Street apartment of Bruno Moscatelli in Hibbing. His old friend was going through a bad time and welcomed Steven's company. "This past year has been hell for me!" Bruno confided. "I was lucky ta get my job back affer da strike, but everythin' else's been horse shit." The underground miner had been one of Steven's trusted companions during last summer's unsuccessful strike against the mining companies.

"Tell me about it my *Kum*." Steven used the Slovenian word for friend.

Bruno recognized the affectionate reference which Steven had used before with Timo, tried to smile but failed. "I ain't heard nothin from Maria in months."

Bruno's wife, Maria, had left him and moved with her sister to Eveleth thirty miles away. Her own shame and anguish over the deal her husband had made with his contract foreman, Barton Wick, were too much for her to cope with. Maria left Hibbing one Sunday while Bruno was at work. Her note said only that she needed to start a new life for herself.

Bruno had been a Judas and believed that he deserved his fate. Many times he had contemplated ending his life in the same manner of the Apostle who had betrayed Jesus. "It's so damn hard some days, Steven. I wonder what I'm living for?" Bruno fought back tears. "Anyhow, I'm happy to have yer company tonight. If ya can stay again tomorrow, I'll invite Bernie over, and we can have a little party here at my place. I've got the whole weekend off from the mine and nottin ta do."

Bernie was Bernie Ducette, another member of the former strike movement. Since being fired by Peter Moran from his job at the liquor warehouse more than two years before, the Frenchman had drifted. Ducette had spent a year back in St. Paul where he lived before coming to Hibbing then found a job in Duluth at the ore docks. He was fired for drinking on the job. Following this, Bernie made his way back to Hibbing a few months ago. He had become a hopeless, dangerous man! "I'd like ta burn dis fuckin city to the ground," Bernie said to Bruno one night when the two of them had been drinking. "That'd get rid of da rich pigs and all dose whores along with 'em."

Talking late into Friday night about the past, Steven consoled his dispirited friend. Before going to sleep on Bruno's sofa, Steven prayed for his friend and prayed for help with what he must do the following morning. He had mulled over the meeting with Senia Arola a thousand times in his mind during the past week . . . what might he say, how might he say it? Should he tell Senia of Timo's death before their trip to his grave site, or should he wait until they reached the lake where her husband was buried? Steven could only pray that he might say the right things at the right time.

The next morning, Steven bathed quickly in the metal tub in Bruno's kitchen, trimmed his beard in the mirror, and rubbed a dab of tonic into his thick black hair. He had brought a clean shirt and light weight trousers for the hike.

Early Saturday morning, Senia saw the large, bearded man waiting for her in the shadow of the brick fronted Drake and Stratton building. Her excitement was tempered with a tight anxiety. It had been nearly four years since she had seen Timo. What would he say? What would he look like? Had he tried to reach her in Finland during their time apart? What would happen to their lives now that they had found each other? So many questions with no answers.

"Mr. Skorich?" she called ahead of her. "Does Timo know we are coming today?" she blurted out before Steven had a chance to say anything.

"Call me Steven, please," he offered her his hand.

"And, I am Senia," she smiled nervously. "I hope I haven't kept you waiting."

"Not at all. I see that you're dressed for the walk, that's good. We have nearly a three mile hike, so we might get to know each other much better along the way. Are you ready, Senia?"

Senia realized that Steven had not answered her question about Timo but let it pass for the moment. "I'll look forward to the walk. It's a lovely morning to be outdoors." She had not done her hair in the tight bun of most days but tied it back with a blue kerchief matching her eyes and light cotton dress. She enjoyed the feel of her hair falling onto the back of her neck below her shoulders.

As they walked away from the village on a trail leading toward the woods, Senia told Steven about a hike she had made a long time ago. She told about how she watched Timo from the bushes on that spring morning by the Vaasa lake near their home in Finland. Her memory was vivid. "He was sitting on a rock ledge and dangling his feet in the icy water. He seemed so completely absorbed with the quiet solitude around him, but he knew I was there. Timo could feel my presence. I liked that . . ."

Senia laughed at the memory. "Later, I told him that the next time I followed him he would not discover me so easily. I told him I would surprise him. And now, four years later, here I am, walking through the woods again to find him." She brushed aside a pine branch overhanging the trail.

Senia could not help rambling, feeling more excited than she could remember. "These woods here are very much the same as those back home. I have such good memories of them. My brother told me before I came to Minnesota that Minnesota was very much like Finland, and that was why so many of our countrymen settled here." She talked in quick breaths as she tried to keep up with the long strides of the tall man who was leading their way along the narrow path. She enjoyed the birch and aspen trees which lined the trail creating a tunnel of green in places where the path narrowed.

Steven enjoyed listening to Senia's story and to the lilt of her voice as she spoke. They walked for nearly an hour in the morning sun, and Steven could tell that Senia needed to rest. When they had reached a small clearing surrounded by daisies and wild pink moccasin flowers, he suggested they sit down for a few minutes. They were now only a short distance from the lake. Steven felt that this was the opportune moment he had prayed for. He plucked a wild, white daisy from the side of the path and handed it to Senia who smiled warmly at the gesture. Then Steven said another silent prayer, "Dear God, bless my words, I ask this in Jesus' name. Amen."

Offering his hand to help her sit on a patch of long, green grass, Steven sat beside Senia without letting go of her hand. He needed to maintain his physical connection with her. "Senia, you asked earlier, if Timo knew about our coming out here this morning. I know I didn't answer you then. Quite honestly, I didn't know how." He paused, and met her clear blue eyes. She was a beautiful woman and he hoped, a strong one as well. She had not removed her hand from his while he spoke. It was as though she somehow knew that she would need it.

He continued, "I want to believe, with all of my heart, that Timo is watching us now as we sit here. Watching from a place where we cannot see him." He paused and felt the pressure of her hand as it tightened around his, fingernails digging into his palm.

Senia's eyes were tearing now. "From a place . . . ," she swallowed against her fear, "from a place above, Steven? Is that what you are saying?"

Steven fought his own tears, but failed. He nodded. "From a place above. I'm sorry, Senia." Releasing her hands, he pulled her close to him and cried softly into her blond hair.

"Oh my God!" Senia's tears spilled onto Steven's broad chest. They clung to each other releasing long pent up emotions. Senia was a strong woman. She allowed Steven a few moments of his own grief, then rubbed her tears away with her handkerchief. She released her grip on his shirt and dabbed at the tears that were in the corners of Steven's deep-set eyes. "The two of you were very close," she said in a halting voice.

Steven found strength in Senia's composure. "We became like brothers, Senia. It took some time for me to know him . . . but . . ." He looked away from Senia into the blue sky. "His passion for people was much like my own. I come out to this place and talk to him often."

"Tell me about Timo, Steven. Tell me everything about what the two of you did. Tell me how it happened." Senia's voice strained with emotion.

Steven related the story of the cause they shared, their times together, and the tragic night of his death. "The place where he's buried was a place where he would go to be by himself in those days. A place where, I'm sure, he told you about what was going on in his life.

"He might even have asked you to come to this faraway place and to find him. Just as you had done on that day back in Finland. I'm sure of it, Senia. He called out to you in his own quiet way. You must have heard him in your own way as well." Steven comforted her with a smile, "Once again, Timo has seen you coming, I'm afraid."

Senia stood offering her hand to a man who had been her husband's friend. "Like Timo, you're a man of great courage, Steven. This hasn't been easy for you, I know. You could have told me back in Hibbing sparing yourself the grief of bringing me out to this place. That would have been easier for you. I must thank you. You're a good man, Steven Skorich. Now, I'm ready to pay my respects. We aren't far away from the grave site, are we?"

Senia held Steven's hand for the remainder of their walk. In a few minutes they were at the lake. "Let's sit down again, Steven. Maybe Timo has something to say to us. We'll just listen."

The two of them sat beneath the tree branches that hung over the rock ledge. Without speaking, they gazed upon the blue-green waters which rippled musically upon the sandy shoreline below them. Each of them talked to Timo in their own private way for nearly an hour. The wind shifted to the west rustling the branches, swelling the waves, tousling their hair. Senia touched Steven's shoulder.

"Let me say goodbye one last time, Steven, before we return to town." Senia rose, walking over to the overgrown and unmarked grave site a few yards away from the lake. Steven blessed himself with a sign of the cross and walked slowly back toward the trail to town while Senia knelt in the soft grass above her husband.

It was mid afternoon when they returned to Hibbing. "This day has changed my life, Steven," Senia said. "I'm not sure what I will do now. The long search is over, and another chapter of my life must begin. I have no desire to go back to Finland, or anywhere else because my life is here now in Hibbing."

"This is a good place to live," Steven said. "You said that being here reminds you of your home in Finland. I believe there must be comfort in that feeling."

The two of them stood on the corner of the street. For the first time that day both felt an awkwardness. Senia hoped that one day they might be able to talk about his home in Slovenia. She had done most of the talking that day. She had become lost in self-searching thoughts as few words had been exchanged since visiting Timo's grave. She pondered the name of Smith, but her husband was the reason she was here, and it must be his name she would live with.

Senia realized her lapse and picked up the thread of words. Steven had been considerate of her reverie. "I will figure out what is the right thing for me to do, Steven." She smiled confidently.

"I know you will, Senia." Steven returned her smile. "I want to believe that. Although you have lost your husband, you have gained a new friend. I will do anything I can to . . . ," he was at a loss for words, "to help you, if you need me."

"Thanks, Steven, for being my friend. We have shared too much together to let this day pass without. . . ." Senia did not know how to finish the thought. "Will you call me again?" she asked before he would leave for home.

"I will," Steven promised. The tall man smiled as he watched her walk away. He stood for a long moment and said to himself, "I will Senia. God bless."

'CONSPIRACY TO COMMIT MURDER?'

STAN CLEARY WAS A PHYSICALLY imposing man. By reputation, only the legendary Hibbing policeman, Ole Nord, was stronger. Cleary, however, had no fear of Nord. The only man who intimidated Cleary was Peter Moran. Cleary's employer had power combined with a short fuse. On this Wednesday morning in mid-July, Cleary had some bad news for Mr. Moran. He feared for himself when he conveyed the message to his boss. For two days he had stewed about shifting the blame away from himself, but was not clever enough to come up with a workable plan. Moran's liquor business had suffered a huge financial setback, and it was Cleary's fault.

John Allison from Duluth had informed Cleary that he was going to supply a new distributorship owned by a group of businessmen in Virginia. As of the end of July, all of the Virginia and East Mesabi Range bars would be serviced from the Virginia outlet. Hibbing would be left only with the west Iron Range market. Allison's plan included the sale of hard liquor from the new operation as well. The economic consequences to Moran's business would run into the tens of thousands of dollars every year.

Stan Cleary decided he would pass the bad news to Moran through his financial secretary, Miss Smith. He hated dealing with women on *men's* affairs, but Moran would chew his ass on the spot. He might gain a little more time to organize his thoughts with this diversion.

Cleary's armpits were ringed with sweat when he picked up the phone. "Miss Smith, Stan Cleary talkin. How are ya today?" In nine words he had exhausted all of the small talk he was capable of making with her.

Cleary explained the Allison problem as best he could. Senia, pencil and paper at her fingertips, automatically calculated the potential losses and jotted them down. She was very familiar with this area of Moran's business, and her numbers came from her memory not the ledgers in her files. This half-year alone, the losses would approximate twenty-five thousand.

Senia's question to Cleary was an obvious one. "What reason did Allison give you, Mr. Cleary?" This would be the first question her employer would ask.

"I'm not really sure, Miss Smith. All he tol me was his new operashun would do better service to da East Range."

"I will have Mr. Moran talk to Mr. Allison personally." Senia knew that Cleary was an incompetent. Of Moran's many supervisors, only Lars Udahl was honest, capable, and trustworthy. "Would you like me to have Mr. Moran call you before he talks with Mr. Allison?"

Cleary's voice had a nervous edge. "No, I'm sure he'll be talking ta me later on today. But'cha might tell Mr. Moran that this ain't all my fault, ya know."

"One other thing, while I have you on the phone, Mr. Cleary. I'm doing a quick audit of the hotel expenses for June, and I do not see any liquor billings being sent to Mr. Sweeny. Is it your practice to give the hotel free liquor, Mr. Cleary?" Senia probed.

"I ain't never sent no bills to Sweeny, Miss Smith. I just give 'em whatever he asks me fo. Ain't that the way it's supposed ta be?" Cleary had never thought of billing Moran's hotel for his own liquor.

Peter was also on the telephone this morning. Lately, he had been working from his library office. It was more comfortable to be away from the annoyances of other people and close to his bottle. He thumped his fist on his desktop. "God damn it, Lars. That can't be!' Moran's anger was unmasked. "How did we fuck this one up? I've never lost a job like this one before! Never!" He poured a glass of whiskey to calm his agitation.

The new Oliver Club construction bids had been opened the night before. Bid numbers were supposed to be presented in sealed envelopes to ensure that the contractor with the lowest bid would be given the construction contract. The ethics of bidding required secrecy and fairness.

"Didn't Fred Bennett give you the numbers we had to beat, Lars? He's always given us the inside track on Oliver jobs." Peter wiped perspiration from his brow. "Who got the job? McHardy?"

"Yessir. Tom McHardy beat us on this one," Lars acknowledged. Udahl had cut his bid offerings so close to the bone that Moran's profit would be under fifteen per cent. "I did the best I could, Mr. Moran."

Peter contemplated the setback. Tom McHardy's lumber business had been growing in recent months. Since McHardy had been elected to the Village Council, his friendships with Elwood Trembart, Fred Bennett, and the other local politicians had flourished. Moran sensed a conflict of interest in the Oliver job but would never be able to prove it occurred. The Oliver Club job was estimated to be over one hundred thousand dollars, and this was a difficult pill for Moran to swallow.

"I'm disappointed, Lars. I thought we had this job sewn up." Peter scratched his head. The Oliver project was expected to be his biggest construction effort of the summer. "What are the major jobs we've got contracts on right now, for the rest of the summer, I mean?" Moran inquired.

"We haven't got none, sir, nothing major at the moment. We got some houses down on Mahoning Street, some warehouses at the Seller's Mine, and a few other things." Lars admitted to the slow construction schedule. "I was gonna tell ya, Mr. Moran. We gotta bid on everything that comes up now. I've got twenty carpenters, and I don't want them sitting on their asses. I've also got a yard full of lumber we ain't paid for yet."

"Gotta go now, Lars. I'll talk to you later this afternoon. Miss Smith just came in the office and she's not smiling." Peter hung up and turned in his chair. "I don't like the look on your face, Senia. I'd like to have some good news this morning," he said.

Senia could smell Peter's liquor breath from across the room and wrinkled her nose in disgust over his morning drinking. She reported what Cleary had told her about the new Virginia distributorship and gave him the numbers she had quickly calculated. "I've had one contract cancellation already this morning, Mr. Moran, from the Grant Tavern in Eveleth. I wouldn't be surprised if we were to get several more in the next week or two."

Peter cursed and grabbed his phone. "Get me John Allison at the Fitger's Brewery in Duluth," he snapped at the operator. His face reddened while he waited for the connection. When he got through to Allison's secretary, he fumed into the receiver, "What the hell do you mean he's in a meeting? This is Pete Moran calling from Hibbing. Tell him to pick up the damn phone!"

Moran waited. While minutes passed slowly, he drummed his fingers nervously on the desktop. He could use a drink right now. Finally, Allison was on the other end. "Peter, old buddy, where have you been keeping yourself? I've got some good Irish jokes to tell you, and I'll even buy you a drink next time you're down in Duluth." Allison did his best to be light and jovial with Moran.

Peter was in no mood for small talk. "Fuck you, John! But speaking of buying drinks, who the hell is it in Virginia that's been buying you drinks these days? I just heard about your Virginia operation, and I'm really pissed off about it. At least when I'm getting fucked, I want to enjoy it."

"Pete, cool down. Nobody's fucking anybody. Business is booming up there on the Range. More business than you can handle by yourself from what I've been told." Allison explained about the many complaints he had gotten from taverns on the east end of the Range. Moran's deliveries were often late, and his supply was short of what had been ordered. Cleary was over his head in this business and not taking care of his customers as well as he should. "They drink a lot of beer over in Gilbert, Biwabik, and Aurora. The east Range needs to be closer to their supply, and Virginia is the best location for them. Hibbing's just too far away to do the job, Pete."

"Cleary's fucking up; is that what you're saying? I'll have a new man on the job tomorrow, John. Let's work this thing out. We've done business together for years." Moran's bargaining was in vain.

"You've got Hibbing and Chisholm and the whole west end of the Range, Pete. You're still going to make a fortune. It's not like we won't be doing business together any more. On the contrary, you and me both have a lot of money yet to make. It's just business, Pete, you know that better than anyone else," Allison reasoned. He would not tell the Hibbing businessman about other plans he had been making. In a few months, Allison planned a similar distributorship for Grand Rapids to the west. He was diversifying his operations, and Peter Moran would be squeezed in the process. "Come on down one of these days, Pete. We miss you at the Club." Allison was finished. "I've gotta run now; you might think about talking to Cleary about what we've discussed. Maybe he's not the guy for the job."

Peter stared blankly at Senia who sat through the conversation. "Give Cleary a call. I want to see him in my office in thirty minutes."

Senia risked telling Peter about another matter that he might want to discuss with Cleary. "Mr. Moran, there is something else," she said. "It's a bookkeeping matter that concerns me." Senia explained that the hotel liquor was not being billed, giving a false representation of hotel solvency. "It's not a good practice. Mr. Sweeny's reports indicate liquor payments, and Cleary's reports don't show income," Senia advised Moran. "The liquor money is basically unaccounted for."

Moran gave Senia a cold look. "Do you have a problem with the way I run my business? I don't charge myself for lumber or liquor or anything else; I never have."

Senia realized that Peter Moran did not understand some basic accounting procedures. Money was missing! If he had a better awareness of his own operations, he would talk to Jerry Sweeny. "You have done very well with your management, sir. The issue here is not about 'charging yourself', Mr. Moran. It is just a matter of tracking figures. Profits and losses must show up somewhere on the balance sheets. I am simply trying to act in your best interest, giving you the best advice I can."

"This has been a lousy day, Miss Smith. I appreciate what you do, but I make the decisions here. Now, if you would get Cleary, write the asshole his final paycheck. That'll be all for right now." Peter dismissed his secretary and the financial problems he did not fully understand with a wave of his hand.

Back in her office, Senia focused on her own issues. She had been liberated from the stress of finding Timo and spent the weekend contemplating a plan for her life. Beginning with a name change to Senia Arola, the next step would be a confession to Peter Moran. She dwelt on loyalty to her employer, the economic comfort of her present job, but with an equally strong desire to get a new job and place to live. Moran was, as Mr. McIntosh had observed only days before, 'on the edge'. Senia knew that the edge was not only emotional but financial as well. Her boss's drinking also concerned her. When he dismissed her that morning, Peter had helped to make her decisions easier. Senia would talk to Jim McIntosh about a job at his bank. Peter would have to sort out his issues by himself.

Cleary knew he was in trouble when he got the summons to be at Moran's house in a half hour. He realized that he deserved to be fired for the lazy disregard of his work and for bungling many of Moran's accounts. His drawer was filled with letters of complaint from irate customers all across the Range. Cleary's thoughts were too often preoccupied by card games, horse races, and gambling debts. He did have, however, an ace up his sleeve. He wondered if he had the guts to play it today.

Two years before, Moran had paid Cleary to cause some work delays at the Grande Hotel site. "I don't want to know what you do, or how you do it, Stan. I just want it to be quiet between the two of us . . ." was all that Moran had said at the time. Cleary, in turn, paid some of this under the table money to three St. Paul masons who were doing the brick work on Markman's project. The cement workers agreed to 'soup' the mortar they used in both footings and walls. One of the three workers, a man named Billy Herrick, was carelessly killed when a weak wall collapsed on top of him. The accident was never fully investigated. Four men had blood on their hands. Peter Moran was one of them. None of the men had ever talked about the incident.

Before leaving, Stan Cleary wrote a quick note that he might pass to his boss if the situation was right to do so. In Moran's presence, he knew he would be tongue-tied so using a prepared note would be helpful. He wrote as carefully as he could, not wanting to upset Mr. Moran too much.

> *Dear Mr. Moran,*
>
> *Sorry about the liquor problem we got now. I might have been to blame for some of it. But we are friends. I remember how we worked together on the old hotel. Too bad someone got killed. I still feel bad about that and I bet you do. I never said nothing to nobody about the money. That is because I want to always be your friend.*
>
>

Sincerely yours,
Stanley Francis Cleary

He put the note in an envelope, folded it in half, and tucked it into his shirt pocket. Keeping this matter confidential ought to be worth something to his boss.

As Miss Smith showed him into Moran's library, Cleary wondered if his boss would want to make a deal. Moran did not stand up or offer to shake hands with him. "Sit down, Cleary. This meeting is going to be short and to the point. Allison told me that you did a horse shit job with my accounts, especially over on the East Range. Is that true?" Moran asked bluntly.

The powerfully built Cleary cringed uncomfortably in his chair. "Kinda. I mean we been damn busy ya know, and I always thought that we take care of our Hibbing customers first, ya know. So, sometimes we get a little short of stuff, and . . . it's damn hard to keep track'a things, don't ya think, sir. Ya can't keep everyone happy all the time, ya know?"

"You're fired, Cleary! You've cost me a hell of a lot of money. Clean out your office and be out by this afternoon." Moran reached into the drawer of his desk and took out an envelope. "I've paid you for the rest of the week and given you a week's vacation pay. Don't ask for a reference, and don't let the door hit you in the ass on the way out."

Stan Cleary's mouth dropped. He didn't know what to do but found his hand reaching into his shirt pocket. Everything was a blur to the intimidated man. He stammered, "I got this for you, too, this envelope here." Cleary handed it across to Moran. "Maybe ya wanna read it, maybe not. I don't know, Mr. Moran. This whole thing's got my head swimmin."

Moran tore open the envelope in obvious irritation. "What's this, Cleary?" When he read the scrawl, Moran realized that this note could be serious trouble for him. "Is this some kind of blackmail?" He spit the words. "What money? Have you got any receipts of money from me besides your paychecks? Did anybody ever hear me talk to you about the old hotel? I don't know what you're talking about?"

"No sir. It was cash money you gave me, remember? And, we wanted ta keep it quiet, between us. Ya didn't want to know nothin about it. I think I tol Sweeny bout it—can't 'member tho." Cleary tried to explain how he had hired the masons, and how the wall had caved in on Herrick. "I don't 'member the names of the other two guys I paid. They was from St. Paul, I think. But I did what ya wanted me ta do, d'int I?"

"This is all bullshit to me, Cleary. Who would ever believe such a stupid crock . . . ? If you want to make any noise about this accident, and that is exactly what it was, an *accident*, you might find yourself up to your ears in trouble. If you did what you claim, you'll wind up in prison for the rest of your life. Have you thought about that, Cleary?" Moran had his former employee cowering in his chair. "I ought to go to the police with this story myself. They call it 'conspiracy to commit murder', I think. Do you hear me, Cleary?"

"Yessir, I hear ya. I wouldn't a done what I did if you didn't pay me, ya know? But, maybe, we better not say no more about it you and me. You ain't gonna go to any police are ya, Mr. Moran?" Cleary's shirt was drenched from his perspiration.

"I'll have to think about that. In the meantime, you better be careful about keeping your mouth shut. This crap gets out and I'm not going to be able to give you any help. If you really did what you've told me this morning, you're one sick sonofabitch."

Totally defeated, Cleary said he was sorry for everything and left the room. As Moran watched him leaving, he wiped sweat from his own forehead. Cleary was a dangerous man. Who could he see about getting rid of a dangerous man? "Thank God," he breathed a sigh of relief, "the guy has no brains to work with." Peter wondered why he had placed this man in a position to run his entire liquor distribution network? Moran had made mistakes in the past, and mistakes were costing him money.

On this bright Thursday morning, Tony was up before his roommates even though he had no job to go to. He did, however, have a new ambition and a plan to accomplish it. Ideas of what to do with his life had been swimming in his head since losing his job the week before. On this day it seemed clear to him. He would explore the idea of a small carpentry business with the one person he believed might be able to help him the most. Although he did not know Miss Smith very well, he had a great respect for her intelligence. He knew that she was Moran's financial secretary, and in that capacity, must have considerable knowledge of business matters. He would go to Moran's house early that morning and visit with Senia. If Moran was there at the time, Tony was confident he could deal with it. He held no anger toward Moran. It was, after all, Moran who had rescued his life by giving Tony his start in carpentry.

Tony sat on the front steps of his apartment house with a pencil and paper. He would write down some ideas before talking with Senia. Tony wrote:

1. bank account balance ($518).

From that amount, he must purchase:

2. horse and wagon (Get figures from Swenson's Livery)
3. office space (check building on east end of Center Street- #420)
4. hired help (talk to Benny Madden)

He would ask Luigi Anselmo for a professional reference and check on the cost of having a telephone of his own. Senia might have other ideas, if she would be willing to help him with this undertaking. Tony's greatest concern was money. How much would he need? Would he be able to get a loan from the bank? Could he successfully compete with the other Hibbing builders?

Tony went back upstairs to his room. The guys were awake and making sandwiches for their lunch pails. He shaved, combed his hair, and put on the fresh white shirt that Luigi had made him as a gift.

On his way to Moran's house, he took a detour past the vacant building on Center Street. In the back was an undeveloped yard that would be large enough for storage. He made a mental note to inquire further about the cost to rent the property.

At Moran's house, Senia seemed delighted to see him. "We had a pretty miserable day here yesterday, Tony, so Mr. Moran is down at the liquor warehouse trying to straighten some things out. I'm looking forward to a pleasant visit for a change."

"So am I, Miss Smith. I've never been in your office before. You've made it very comfortable." Tony smiled his approval as his eyes surveyed the attractive furnishings. From the window in Senia's upstairs room, Tony could look out over the back yard flower gardens and lush shrubbery. "I'll bet you spend some time at this window. What a pleasant view."

"It's where I begin every morning. I'm not a very religious woman, but I find it easy to say a prayer when I'm looking out at the gardens," Senia smiled. "I suppose you've come to inquire about whether I have heard from your Uncle Steven yet. Am I right, Tony?

"Well, I have already met Steven, and speaking of prayers, he helped me find an answer to my most important one a few days ago."

"I'm happy to hear that. May I call you Senia? My uncle is a wonderful man, and I knew he would be more than willing to help you in any way he could. Have you found your husband then?" Tony asked.

Senia nodded that she had. "Steven is truly a fine man. We spent last Saturday together. Sit down, please, Tony. Let me tell you all about it." She explained their trip into the woods south of town and their visit to Timo's grave site. Her eyes moistened at times, but she was coping well with her grief. "Yes, it was a sad, but somehow, a wonderful day. I mean, now I have a closure to an important chapter of my life, and I can begin to be *me* for the first time since coming to Hibbing. That more than anything, is exciting."

"You aren't going to be Miss Smith anymore?" he asked. "That's quite a decision. I'm happy for you, Senia."

"I'll probably talk to Mr. Moran next week. From then on, I'll be Senia Arola. It feels so good to say my name again, you wouldn't believe," Senia beamed. "Now, let's talk about you. I know that you lost your job last week and I'm very sorry. I'll be candid. Mr. Moran is not making good decisions these days. I know how fond he was of you. He talked about you all the time: how bright you were, how well you were doing on the job, how very talented you were in everything you did. Then out of the blue, he wanted you fired. I wish I knew what was going on in his head." Senia looked concerned. "Mr. Moran has been as good to me as he was to you. Something seems to have snapped in his life. Lately . . ." Senia decided not to conjecture on her employer's reversals of late.

"He has some good qualities, Tony. I really believe that, but, there is a very dark side to him as well. It's a mystery to me and everybody else who tries to understand him."

Tony nodded. "He has been good to me, unbelievably so, and I am grateful for all he's done. But, now, I've got to find my own way. Like you, I'll need to make a new start in life. I guess we've got a lot in common, don't we?" Tony smiled, "including Uncle Steven, now that you've met him."

"Yes, we do. I hope to see Steven again some time. He told me he would call." Senia's eyes could not hide the pleasure of her thoughts. "I told him my life's story and didn't give him much opportunity to tell me about himself. Somehow, I believe that his story has been filled with the same heartbreaks as my own. Now I'm talking too much, again." She laughed at herself.

"Senia, I need some help, and I hope you might be able to give it to me." Tony took the paper he had scribbled on that morning and explained his hopes and ideas. He wanted to impress her with his preliminary plans and make a positive impression. "So you see, Senia, I think I've got the necessary skills, and I know I have the desire to succeed, but it's the money and the experience that I lack. I would like to talk to Mr. McIntosh about borrowing some of the money I'll need. Do you know Mr. McIntosh very well? Do you think I can qualify for a small business loan?"

Senia nodded indicating she knew him, then complimented. "I'm truly impressed with the thinking that you've already done. Mr. McIntosh is a very decent man; the best I've ever met at financial matters." Senia regarded the handsome young man sitting across from her. She looked for a resemblance to Steven. Tony had the same strong features, dark hair, and deep set eyes. She would do anything she could to help this young man. She was flattered that he had come to her and excited about what she would propose.

"Tony, how much help are you willing to accept from me? I mean financial and otherwise?" Senia inquired. "I'd like to take care of some matters on your behalf."

Tony was surprised by the question. "Anything you can do. I don't have much more than what I think is a good idea. Anything, Senia, I'd be most appreciative," he shrugged his shoulders and gave her a searching look.

"If you will allow me to, I'd like to prepare a business plan based on what you've told me this morning. I'd like to do some groundwork with Mr. McIntosh for you. I can call him in Duluth this morning." Senia looked for an acknowledgment from Tony.

Tony's excitement sparked in his eyes. "You would do that for me? Great! What do you think Mr. McIntosh might say, about a loan, I mean?"

"I think he might be as excited as we are. I'm optimistic he will be supportive. But, there is one other matter that I'll need your permission to do. I hope that you'll accept it in the good spirit that it's offered. You'll need something called collateral for a bank loan." Senia briefly explained the concept. "I would like to provide you with a personal loan that would serve as your collateral. I don't want you to touch your own bank account. Are you willing to accept that, Tony?"

Tony was dumbfounded by the offer. "How much of a loan, Senia?"

"Let me work on that with Mr. McIntosh. I'll see, and we can get to-gether again on Monday morning. Will that work for you?"

"I can't wait. What can I do in the meantime?"

"Since you are all dressed up this morning and looking quite handsome, I might add, why don't you go down to the newspaper and introduce your-self to Mr. Atkinson? He's a baseball fan, and I'm sure he'll enjoy meeting you. Ask Claude about construction jobs that might be coming up. He knows more about what is happening in Hibbing than anybody I know. He's another decent man, Tony. He'll be happy to help you out."

They shook hands and agreed to get together again on Monday. "Both of our lives might be quite a bit different by next week," Senia laughed as she led him down the stairs to the front door. "Give my best to Steven if you see him this weekend."

Senia had not told Tony about her private wealth. She was paid well by Peter Moran, lived frugally, and came from a well to do banking family in Vaasa Province in Finland. Senia could take care of the necessary finances and get Tony into business without any problem. Yet, she realized, Tony should get his start with a business loan and have that responsibility on his own. He was a confident and resourceful young man. Senia had no doubt that he was going to find success in his venture.

Senia called Jim McIntosh. In addition to Tony's proposal, she had a personal item of her own to take care of.

"Miss Smith, it's always good to hear your voice. How are things up in Hibbing this morning?" Jim McIntosh was in a typically good mood and had plenty of time to chat.

Senia explained Tony Zoretek's business plan with a detailed budget which she had drawn up before making the call. Her numbers were concise and contingencies well thought out. Her presentation was clearly articulated and meticulous. "I would like to personally guarantee a note for Mr. Zoretek in the amount of two thousand dollars, Mr. McIntosh."

"You are impressive, Miss Smith. I can appreciate all that Peter has said about your efficiency. I have no problem whatsoever with the Zoretek pro-posal as you've described it. I'll call the bank myself and have them pre-pare the papers for the young man to sign on Monday."

Senia thanked him, swallowed hard, then asked, "Mr. McIntosh, do you have a few more minutes? There is another matter that I would like to share with you."

"You've caught me at a good time. I suppose you've got some more Peter Moran issues. By the way, I did talk to Elwood Trembart about the land deal. Peter got caught in his lie, I'm afraid. I would not be surprised if Trembart gets some sort of revenge. He's pretty steamed up about it. Now, I'm getting kind of personal, aren't I? I apologize, Miss Smith. Peter will take care of himself I am sure."

"I think that Mr. Trembart has found a measure of his revenge, Mr. McIntosh." She explained Moran's loss of the Oliver Club bid.

McIntosh was less surprised than amused by the story. "I never want to get myself caught in Hibbing politics."

Senia had decided to leave the employ of Peter Moran. Her new life as Senia Arola would require many changes, and she was determined to make them one step at a time. She had to begin now and Jim McIntosh, she believed, was a man to confide in. Without getting into her husband's activities, Senia explained that she was a Finnish widow who had been living a double life of sorts since her arrival in Hibbing a year ago. She mentioned her education and training in banking before coming to America. "I have an impeccable resume, Mr. McIntosh," she concluded confidently.

"You will be leaving Peter within the month, then, Mrs. Arola?" McIntosh wanted to be certain of the fact.

"Yes, sir. May I add, Mr. McIntosh, you are the first person in America to call me by my real name. It sounded so good. Thank you."

McIntosh laughed easily. "Can I be honest? I always thought that Smith was kind of fishy."

Giggling at his insight, she paused. "Will there be any vacancies at your bank in the near future, sir? If so, I would like an opportunity to interview."

"We could surely use a person with your background in finance. We've been thinking of hiring another loan officer. It isn't much of a job to start with, in terms of pay, but you could certainly move up to something administrative in a short time."

"That would be just fine with me, Mr. McIntosh. A place to start is all I'm hoping for," Senia assured.

"Now it's my turn to share a confidence, Senia. I'm Jim by the way, the 'Mr. McIntosh' thing doesn't work now that we are confidants. Anyhow, only a few people know this, but I've been seriously thinking about selling the bank. All the trips to Hibbing are becoming hard on me and my family. If I do sell, Harvey Goldberg would be the person I'd feel most secure passing the business to. Harvey's been my president at the bank in everything but title for the past several years. I trust him more than anybody I know. There's a solid Jewish community in Hibbing, and he could get any number of partners to go in with him if we were to make a deal of any kind. I have been thinking about little else these past few days," Jim McIntosh explained. "It's a big decision."

As he described the bank situation, Senia wondered if she might ever be given an opportunity to become a partner. Surely, her father and brother, both successful bankers in Finland, would consider supporting her in a banking venture. That, however, would be something to think more about at some later time.

"You have built a fine reputation here and would be greatly missed by all of us who have worked with you, sir," Senia said.

"I'd like you to meet Harvey," McIntosh chuckled. "Please, don't take offense, Senia, but something humorous just came to mind. If you and Harvey . . . a Jewish man and a Finnish woman were working together at the same bank in Hibbing, Minnesota . . . What a revolutionary concept!"

"I would have to agree. But Hibbing can handle anything, Jim, even something like that. I'd like to meet Mr. Goldberg." Senia smiled at the notion herself.

"I'll set it up. You can expect to hear from Harvey this week. Let's plan for the three of us to get together for dinner sometime next week. Let Mr. Zoretek know that he will be in business and expect a call from Harvey soon. I've not enjoyed a conversation any more than this one in quite a while, Senia. I've got to run now, God bless."

Senia had two calls on that Thursday afternoon. Harvey Goldberg was anxious to meet with her and set up an interview for the following Monday.

Steven Skorich was also anxious to see her. He called as Senia was finishing her work for the day and invited her to dinner on Saturday night. "You've been on my mind all week," he confessed.

Senia Arola's 'new life' was off to a most interesting start. She would talk to Peter Moran after her interview at the bank. For reasons she could not fully understand, she did not have any measure of dread about what she would tell her employer. Would Moran be more upset with the confession of her ethnic heritage and the deceit that went with it or losing his best, most confidential, employee? In fairness to Peter, she would caution him about placing any trust in Jerry Sweeny. The hotel manager was in a position to do more harm to Moran than either the incompetence of Stan Cleary or the politics of Elwood Trembart. She would also give him a complete review of his ill-fated financial affairs.

'SOAKING WET CLOTHES'

ON FRIDAY MORNING OF PETER Moran's most miserable week, he made another firm resolution to curtail his drinking. This time he was serious about it. His whiskey habit of late was a sign of personal weakness, nothing less, he believed. He looked at himself in the mirror, noticing redness in his eyes, the lines in his face, the pallor of his complexion. He was only thirty-three but looked much older this morning. Drinking, business stress, and overwork had taken an unmistakable toll on his handsome features. "Maybe," he thought, looking away from the image which distressed him, "I don't know how to enjoy myself or appreciate the comforts I have worked so hard to achieve." He would give some thought to making a list of activities that might bring him pleasure and another list of people with whom he wanted to reestablish ties.

In the past several months, Peter had truly enjoyed his life on only one occasion that he could bring to mind . Even more than his triumph at his gala hotel opening, his Saturday excursion with Mary Samora had made him feel alive and given him great pleasure. Did Mary enjoy that day nearly as much as he had? Maybe he had given up her affection too easily? Was Tony Zoretek anything more than a casual friend whom she got to know while he worked on the Anselmo project? Surely, young Zoretek had nothing to offer her besides his good looks. Peter, however, was not a bad looking man and, of course, was in a position to provide her with all of the luxuries that life had to offer. She must be aware of that reality. He remembered giving her the cameo necklace while they sipped a fine wine at his hotel just a few weeks before. She had to have been both impressed and flattered by his timely gesture. How could an immigrant kid like Zoretek ever hope to give her such fine gifts?

Mary's wide-set eyes, perfectly full mouth, and shapely figure were a vivid portrait of beauty in Peter's memory at this moment. Perhaps, he had disappointed her by not having shown further interest since their day together. He felt a surge of his former self-confidence as he withdrew a sheet of fine stationery from the drawer of his polished mahogany desk. He penned a note in his bold stroke . . .

Dear Mrs. Samora:

I missed you at my garden party but hope that your picnic was a successful affair. Everybody here had a grand time, but your presence would have made the afternoon an even happier occasion.

As I remember our last time together, after that wonderful excursion, we agreed to have dinner at some later date. I must apologize for not asking you sooner but finally my busy schedule has given me pause.

Kindly accept this gift of flowers and my invitation to dinner on Friday, the 23rd. I would plan for about 7:00 if that is convenient for you.

Thank you for your anticipated acceptance and response.

Most sincerely,
Peter

He would stop by the flower shop on his way to the liquor warehouse that morning and have his note, along with an expensive bouquet, delivered to Mary Samora at Luigi's tailor shop. Peter looked at the large, antique grandfather clock that stood against the east wall between two shelves of books. It was still early, and the flower shop would not be open yet. He had an hour before he had to leave for his warehouse, so he contemplated his list of things to do.

Peter could not recall the last time he had written to his mother in Pennsylvania. Was brother Denis out there with her? What a pathetic man Denis had become! Peter had no regrets about having him roughed up and run out of town weeks ago. What about his sister Emily and her family?

Had he ever written to his brother Terrance? What was the oldest of the Moran boys up to these days? Peter frowned over his estrangement from family. He promised himself that he would write them letters but not on this morning.

On a shelf to the right of his cluttered desk, Peter regarded the over-stuffed teddy bear that he had purchased for his son. How long ago had that been? Seeing the bear made him think of Kevin and Barbara, as well as the Schmitz family, and Father Pat Foley. Peter had not heard anything about the adoption proceedings since Foley's visit weeks before. He withdrew another sheet of stationery. He had never seen his son, nor had he ever made any personal contact with the Schmitzes. What were their names? Peter searched his address book and found Art and Sarah Schmitz.

In his letter to the Schmitz family, Peter asked if he might be able to stop by and visit with them one day soon. Although he did not tell them of his intentions in the letter, Peter would ask that Kevin be allowed to have the Moran name. He would be willing to make a proposal that would insure Kevin's future education and well-being for years to come. Peter would talk to Jim McIntosh about setting up a trust fund of some kind.

Peter's next note was to McIntosh. It was just a short message. How was Martha's health these days? How were his teenage girls doing in school? When would the two of them get out and play some golf? Peter promised to visit them all in Duluth one day soon. "Let's plan to have dinner at the Kitchi Gammi Club, Jim; I haven't seen the guys down there in ages."

Peter looked at his calendar to find what, if anything, was on his week-end agenda. Sunday was a home ball game against Mt. Iron. When he thought of the baseball team, Tony Zoretek came to his mind again. Peter's thoughts were troubled about the talented young man whose companion-ship he had so enjoyed before the relationship issue with Mary. Had Peter overreacted when he took Tony's job away? A thought came to his mind. With the loss of the Oliver job, some carpenter layoffs were inevitable. That reality gave some justification to having released Tony when he did.

Peter penned a quick note to himself and placed it under the phone on his desk. Later, he would talk to Ed Grant in Duluth. Grant was a master cabinetry carpenter and had done most of the elaborate woodwork in Moran's home. He would ask Grant, as a personal favor, to apprentice Tony in his Duluth shop. Such a ploy would not only appease his relationship with Tony, but also get the young man out of Hibbing.

Peter wrote a note of apology to Tony explaining the construction slow down and his continued concern for Tony's welfare. He mentioned a marvelous opportunity to learn new skills under a master craftsman in Duluth. "Let me know, Tony; I'd be happy to set everything up for you."

Peter Moran sealed the envelopes and headed out on his morning walk. He would drop the letters at the post office, stop by the flower shop, visit with Jerry Sweeny at the hotel, and interview Norman Dinter for the liquor warehouse job. Dinter, Moran was certain, had the intelligence to do the job Cleary had failed to do. Revenues from his liquor operations had been greater than those from his lumber business for the past several years. With some ambitious planning and reorganization, Moran would overcome the setback caused by the new Virginia distributorship.

Mary was training her new assistant, Clara Solberg, when the beautiful flower arrangement was brought to her at the shop. Mrs. Solberg was a middle-aged miner's widow that Luigi hired to help Mary with her work. Before opening the envelope, Mary knew the roses had to have been sent by Peter Moran. "For heaven's sake," she mumbled under her breath as she read the note. She had done nothing to encourage this invitation and was determined to put an end to Moran's intentions, whatever they may be. Mary was still under the impression that Moran, because of some twisted jealousy, had fired Tony from his job over her. She would be candid with him.

"How beautiful these are, Mrs. Samora!" Clara exclaimed as she bent to sniff the rich scent of the bouquet.

"You take them home with you this afternoon, Mrs. Solberg," Mary insisted. "I have flowers in my garden at home." She handed the widow the vase. "Now, would you please excuse me for a few minutes, while I return a note? If you would cut fabric for the sleeve patterns of the two dresses we've started, it would be most helpful." Mary found paper and wrote a terse reply.

Mr. Moran:

I am afraid that your invitation to dinner cannot be accepted. Since our automobile drive, I have had the good fortune of meeting a fine young suitor. He is a former employee of yours by the name of Tony Zoretek. In order to respect my feelings of affection toward Mr. Zoretek, I must decline.

Mary Bellani Samora

She addressed and stamped the envelope and asked Luigi to give her letter to the postman who would be making his rounds within the hour. Luigi looked at the address on the envelope and raised his eyebrows. "It's none of my business, Mary dear, but I can tell when my Bella is upset."

Claude Atkinson, Hibbing's *Mesaba Ore* newspaper owner-editor, found his meetings this week to be most interesting. He reviewed the events and stories in his mind as he put the finishing touches on Friday's issue. The newspaper would feature a story on Hibbing's fifteenth anniversary as a platted township. A rare photograph of the early logging settlement's few structures in 1893 would appear on the front page. In August, Hibbing would officially celebrate the special anniversary in a big way.

There was also a story about the new liquor distributorship in Virginia about which John Allison had told him. Always sensitive to his own community interests, Claude had inquired regarding the impact on Hibbing's own operation owned by Peter Moran. In his article, Claude quoted Allison's assurances that the Iron Range had "plenty of business to go around . . . the impact will have minimal effect on Mr. Moran . . ."

The story of the new Oliver Club construction was also big news. Claude had interviewed Tom McHardy who had been given the building contract. McHardy was quoted as saying, "This will give my lumber company a big boost. We will be hiring more carpenters. Competition is what makes our business community strong." Comments and observations from village president Elwood Trembart as well as mining official, Fred Bennett were included in the story.

The local political scene was relatively quiet these days and Claude could think of nothing noteworthy to report. He considered a story on the brash young attorney, Victor Power. Power was quitting his association with his brother, Walter, and establishing his own law practice. "Young Vic's got more political saavy than Walt ever had, and Walt was elected mayor of this town back in '03. Young Vic kinda reminds me of Peter Moran—a forceful little guy with quite a gift for talking." Claude mused about the lawyer and decided to do more with the story later.

A front page article would feature the new Carnegie Library. The public facility with its collection of fifteen thousand books was "a magnificent addition to the community, and would enable Hibbing's adults and school children to explore new worlds."

Other local interest features were about horse racing at the fairgrounds on the weekend and a home baseball game against Mt. Iron. The Moran Hotel planned to finish four new bowling lanes in the lower level before winter.

Among his many visitors over the past week, none impressed him more than a young man named Tony Zoretek. He had met Tony briefly at Moran's party two weeks before, but most of their conversation included Tom Brady and baseball chit chat. Claude puzzled over Tony's being laid off because of slow business at Moran's lumber operation. He might want to interview Peter or Lars Udahl sometime next week about the matter. Claude's curiosity was aroused by Tony's lay off.

Young Zoretek had explained his desire to open a small carpentry business and presented a positive outlook about what he hoped to accomplish. Zoretek was both intelligent and amiable. Claude promised that he would be happy to pass on any information that crossed his desk once Tony was ready to start his new business. Then, the two men talked about baseball, always Claude's favorite topic.

Another former employee of Peter Moran had stopped by to interview briefly for a job in the circulation department of the Hibbing newspaper. Stan Cleary, whom Atkinson had not met before, cited his experience in distribution of merchandise, although in the liquor area, and mentioned his brother-in-law as a reference. His relative, Andy Zdon, the print shop foreman at the newspaper, was well respected by Claude and the other newspaper employees. Zdon was Cleary's only reference, and the editor promised he would talk to his printer later that day. Claude, however, had no interest in hiring Cleary.

Stan Cleary, despite his imposing appearance, did not impress Claude Atkinson in any manner. Cleary was not bright and seemed highly agitated during the interview. The man told him that his layoff by Moran was due to slowing business prospects. This did not jibe with what John Allison told him earlier. Claude puzzled about what was happening in the world of Peter Moran's enterprises. He had difficulty believing that Cleary was really in charge of all distribution as claimed. Assuredly, Peter had brighter people than Cleary in his higher level management positions. Claude made a mental note to learn more about this man and the circumstances of his former employment in Moran's business operation.

Senia puzzled over her feelings for Steven Skorich. As she brushed her long blond hair and applied a touch of rouge on her high cheekbones to accentuate her clear blue eyes, she contemplated the man she would see this Saturday evening. Was her date with Steven appropriate considering that, as a widow, she should be in a period of mourning? As so often happened, she felt at a loss over cultural standards in this new country. Senia had been taking American Citizenship classes for several weeks, but most of what she had learned concerned matters of government and language.

Had she shown too much enthusiasm in accepting his invitation to dinner? They had talked by phone a second time the night before about a time and place to meet. Steven, familiar with Moran's ardent support of the Oliver Company during the strike, was reluctant about coming to her apartment in the Moran homestead.

Senia, sensitive to Steven's uneasiness, readily agreed to meet him at the corner of Washington Street and Third Avenue about seven o'clock. The restaurant he suggested was not a fancy place, she knew, but it would be far more comfortable than dining at Moran's fine new hotel. Further, the Aspenwood Cafe was well noted for a variety of seafood and Finnish dishes. Steven's choice was a thoughtful one.

Senia guessed Steven was about the same age as Peter. She imagined that, under his beard, he was a ruggedly handsome man. His eyes were dark and soft, his voice deep and rich, his demeanor gentle, despite his formidable size. She believed he was a good and kind man.

Senia looked forward to learning more about him. Did he have family here? Were there other women in his life? Senia laughed to herself over that thought. 'How can I be thinking such personal things?' She looked toward her clock and realized she had better get dressed. Senia chose a soft green summer cotton dress and matching bonnet. Tucking some money, along with a new handkerchief and makeup into her straw purse, she put on fresh white gloves. Changing her mind, she took off the gloves, returning them to her drawer. After a final appraisal in her mirror, she left to meet Steven who would be waiting two blocks away. The early evening air was refreshing, and Senia looked forward to a wonderful time.

She smiled brightly as she approached the tall man dressed in a worn, but well-fitted, pinstriped suit. Steven had trimmed his beard more closely to his face and slicked his hair back along the sides. "My goodness, what a handsome man you are, Mr. Skorich," she said teasingly.

Steven blushed at the compliment, returned her smile, and handed her a cluster of wilting wild daisies he had gathered on his walk to Bruno Moscatelli's Hibbing apartment earlier in the day. "Thank you, Mrs. Arola, I'm glad you think so. I didn't know how to dress for this evening." Steven ran his long fingers over the suit and adjusted the knot of his paisley tie. "I haven't dressed up in so long, I didn't know if I could still knot a tie," he added with a laugh of self-concious male pride. He gave her a long appraisal, his eyes moving from her shoes to her bonnet, "You look just wonderful," was all he could say.

As they crossed the intersection on their walk toward the downtown restaurant, Senia held his arm . Before meeting her that evening, Steven had reserved a table away from the kitchen and had requested that fresh linen and a candle be provided.

After deciding upon a carafe of wine, Senia said to Steven, "Do not think I'm rude if I seem quiet this evening, but I so wish to learn about you, Steven. I've already told you my story, and now it is your turn."

Steven did most of the talking over a Slovenian pork and rice main dish, called *sarmas*, that Steven had recommended to Senia. He was an articulate man and had a marvelous sense of humor. Steven told Senia he was twenty nine when he first arrived in Hibbing and had been here for over four years. He had worked in the Burt Mine before the strike and was now working for the railroad. Like his nephew Tony, Steven loved books and was an avid reader. "I've been reading many of Jack London's stories lately, and I like his writing as much as Mark Twain, who's so popular these days."

He had left a sweetheart behind in Slovenia. She had married a close friend of his who owned land of his own. Despite her earlier reservations about being too personal, Senia had asked Steven about women in his life now.

He confessed that he had no experience with women whatsoever and was terribly shy. "I cannot believe," he said further, "that I'm having this wonderful conversation with such a lovely woman. I find you easy to be with."

For dessert Senia tried a slice of *potica*, a Slovenian walnut sweet bread, that was so delicious she had a second helping with a lavish topping of butter. She talked about her family and her village in Finland, being careful not to mention the banking tradition or her college education. Such things might wait for another time. She confessed that she would soon be leaving her present job and moving to an apartment of her own, but remained vague about the specifics of her work.

The two of them talked about Tony and his current ambitions. Senia learned that Steven had many close friends who were Finnish, and that he had met her own friend, Mrs. Niemi, on several occasions. She was surprised that they did not talk about Timo. That was another area that they might talk more about later.

It was after ten when Steven walked her home. Senia was almost embarrassed by the pretentiousness of Moran's mansion. "It's becoming almost too much for me, Steven," she said noticing how taken he was by the fine architecture. "I would like to find a small house of my own in Hibbing one day soon. Or, maybe," she added, "have your nephew build me one." They both laughed. After saying their goodnights, and thanking each other for the wonderful time, they promised to see each other again. On an impulse, Senia stood on her toes and lightly kissed Steven on his cheek.

Returning to Bruno's apartment, Steven felt lightheaded about his evening with Senia. He could not remember having such feelings of affection before, and the warmth of her fleeting kiss still lingered in his thoughts. The lovely Senia remained an enigma, however, despite all they had shared in their time together. She was very bright, spoke articulately which hinted at a formal education, and worked for the capitalist, Moran. Senia had not said anything about what she did for Moran, why she was leaving her job, or what kind of work she would be seeking. Steven was a curious, sensible man. His infatuation was tempered by his worry about how their two different worlds might come together. Steven hoped they would.

While Senia enjoyed her outing, Peter spent Saturday night in his library with a bottle of Irish whiskey. Mary's note brought on another bout of drinking despite his resolve to quit. Why had she mentioned Tony Zoretek by name in her refusal of his invitation? There was certainly more to her relationship with Tony than he had imagined. What might he do about it? When Peter was in his lonely mood, he remembered Barbara and the good times the two of them shared together on his weekly visits to Duluth. He often longed to have a woman to share his life with, but at the moment, Mary was preoccupied with Tony. That might change if Tony took him up on the offer to apprentice in Duluth, but Peter doubted it might happen. There were not many attractive, single women of good reputation in Hibbing. Only two such women came to mind.

Peter heard the front door close and realized that Senia was back home from her engagement of that evening. Miss Smith, he realized, was one of the two women he might consider as a suitable companion. Earlier, when Senia had left the house, Peter watched her walk down the street. She wore her long, blond hair over her shoulders and looked more attractive than he had ever seen her before. Her green dress and bonnet were tastefully expensive. At the corner less than a block away, Peter saw the figure of a tall man waiting to meet her. Who was the man? He realized that Senia's life outside of her employment was unknown to him.

Peter thought about asking her to join him for a drink in the library. It was just after ten o'clock, not too late for a Saturday night. He wanted to get to know this most striking woman better. Then he heard her footsteps going up the stairs to her apartment and realized that another opportunity had been missed. Beginning tomorrow, Peter resolved, he would begin to give his personal secretary more attention than he had in the past. Peter had another drink as he contemplated how lovely Senia had looked that evening.

Sunday morning bloomed like the yellow day lilies that bordered the gazebo and walkway in Moran's colorful back yard. Before going out to the garden patio with his cigar and coffee, Peter left a note on the kitchen table where Senia would be certain to see it when she came down for breakfast. "Please join me in the garden this morning for coffee, Miss Smith." He signed the invitation Peter. He had not been so informal with his name before this note.

"Good morning, Mr. Moran." Senia greeted him as she brought a tray with ginger cookies and a carafe of coffee out to the patio. This morning Senia was dressed in a modest gray outfit with her hair combed into a typical bun. Expecting that Peter had an assignment for her, she carried a notebook and pencil in the wide pocket of her dress.

"Miss Smith, how are you this fine morning?" Peter smiled. "Did you have a good time last evening? I heard you come in after ten."

Senia was taken aback by the personal inquiry and his reference to her time of arrival home. "Yes, sir, a wonderful time. Thank you for asking. I don't think I get away from my office quite enough, so it was most a most enjoyable evening."

Peter smiled knowingly. "I couldn't agree more, both of us get too wrapped up in business; there's much more to life than balance sheets, contracts, and the like. Now, take today for example, I was going to work on some of those hotel revenue projections you prepared for me, but it's just too beautiful outside to shut one's self in the house. I think that I'll take in the ball game this afternoon."

"That sounds like a good idea, sir. I know you're quite a fan," Senia replied curiously. Peter seemed unusually congenial this morning.

"What do you say about being my guest at the ballpark for the game, Senia? I could explain the game of baseball to you over some American hotdogs and lemonade." Peter leaned forward in his chair. "I think you'd have a marvelous time. I know you're taking those citizenship classes at the school, so this would be an opportunity to learn some of our unique culture."

Senia noted the 'Senia' reference in the invitation and was bothered by how inappropriate it sounded. What was Mr. Moran up to now? Had Jim McIntosh inadvertently told Peter of her plans to seek employment with his bank? No, Mr. McIntosh was too considerate of her personal life. This was something else. She was planning to tell Mr. Moran of her plans to leave the next day. This invitation perplexed her. Fortunately, Senia had already made plans with her old friend, Mrs. Niemi for the day. "I am so sorry, Mr. Moran, but I have a social engagement this afternoon."

"With that guy from last night?" Peter's question was sarcastic and rude.

"Mr. Moran, I am offended by that remark or question or whatever it was, sir. What gave you the impression that I was with a gentleman last night?"

"I only assumed." Peter backed off. "I'm sorry if I offended you, Senia." He used her first name again.

Senia would elaborate more tomorrow, but she would give him something to think about today. "I will be going to a Finnish bake sale at the Tapio Hall this afternoon. My friend, Elia Niemi, is doing a fund-raising activity for Finnish miners who have been, I think the word is *blacklisted*, from all of the mines in this area."

Peter sank in his chair. "That seems like a nice gesture, Miss Smith." Blacklisted Finnish miners? What the hell was this about? He was surprised but would not be intrusive again.

Peter let his invitation drop. "Perhaps, when we get together in the morning, you could provide me with some information on setting up a trust fund. Do you know much about that sort of thing?" he asked, as he moved their conversation back to business.

"Yes, sir, I've worked on trusts before. However, it will have to be early, because I have an appointment at the bank about ten o'clock tomorrow morning. If that's all, Mr. Moran, I must get ready for Mrs. Neimi." Senia rose and excused herself.

Peter watched both the game and Mary, who was sitting with her Italian friends in the same area of the grandstand as before.

Later in the game, Claude Atkinson spotted Peter sitting by himself and moved to the empty space next to him. "I met that young pitcher, Tony Zoretek, last Friday. He's quite an impressive young man, ambitious, too. I'm sure you know that better than most people, Pete." Claude initiated the conversation. "I understand he's planning on going into business for himself." At this disclosure Claude watched for any reaction in Moran's eyes. He recognized an unnatural blink and continued. "I'll bet you hated to let him go. The kid's pretty sharp and as pleasant as this afternoon. He'll do just fine for himself in the construction business."

Peter tried to hide his shock over this news. "What did he tell you, Claude? I mean about quitting his job? It was quite a surprise; we all liked Zoretek a lot. He's a good worker, and like you said, a very personable guy."

"He told me that he was laid off, Pete. That came as quite a surprise to me. He said that your business was slow, and that you had to let him go.

That was hard for me to believe." Claude was a keen observer of people, and Peter Moran was an interesting subject. He knew that the businessman was uncomfortable.

Peter did not reply to the newsman's innuendo.

Claude would take their conversation one step further. "Anyhow, I also met a fellow named Cleary, Stan Cleary, if I remember correctly. He said that he had been laid off as well. I was going to ask you about that next week. You see, he applied for a position at my newspaper."

Moran was squirming now, but Claude had one more observation to make. "Cleary told me he ran your liquor operation, Pete. I found that hard to believe."

"He wasn't laid off, Claude. He was fired. My advice to you is don't even give him a second thought for any job. Cleary's no good." Peter could not look Claude in the eyes. "I'm sorry to leave you, Claude, but I've got a meeting with Sweeny down at the hotel this afternoon. Damned if I can ever get a whole day off. Always seems there's something going on. You know how that is, Claude. See you later."

Claude left the grandstand a few minutes after Moran's abrupt departure and followed him at a distance. His reporter's curiosity was piqued. Moran turned left, down Third Avenue, away from the hotel. The meeting with Sweeny was a lie. Zoretek and Cleary were two people Moran did not want to talk about.

Tony Zoretek pitched three perfect innings in the Colts' 3–1 victory over the visiting Mt. Iron team. Claude returned to his seat in time to watch the young hurler strike out the side in the ninth inning.

After the game, Tony stood with Mary and the Depelos at the grandstand railing. "This is for you, Armando." Tony handed the boy a baseball with autographs on it from several of the Colts' players.

"Thanks, Tony!" The youngster beamed his delight. "Did ya get Moose to sign his name?"

Tony pointed out the large scrawl on the ball, "You can't miss it. Before the season is over, Armando, I'll get you a bat as well."

John and Lucia Depelo congratulated Tony on his game and thanked him for the unexpected gift for their son. Mary wanted to give Tony a kiss for his thoughtfulness, but instead, simply brushed his dripping forehead with her handkerchief. "You're soaking wet, Tony. How can you play this game in such terrible heat?" The afternoon temperature had surpassed ninety, and Tony looked drained from his efforts on the sun-drenched field. Mary had seen Tony only briefly on Saturday because she had an Italian Society meeting that went late into the evening. "Will I see you later?" Mary asked.

"How can you ask such a question, Mrs. Samora?" he teased. Tony always used a proper reference when her friends were present. "How about eight? I have to get home and clean up, then the guys are having a little dinner and celebration at Mr. Brady's house. I'll come by after, and we can go for a walk. Will that be okay with you?"

"A walk sounds like a wonderful idea, Tony. I'll see you later." She took Armando's hand and began to walk him toward the exit gate. She turned to wave back at Tony, but he was already off with his teammates.

Team manger, Tom Brady, hosted a midseason get-together with his players once every summer. The party had always been an out door pig roast with a keg of beer, but at six o'clock the skies opened in a deluge of rain. The event had to be moved inside Brady's house.

When Tony arrived, the revelry of his teammates was already well in progress. Tommy Pell hollered a loud, teasing, welcome toward his friend. "Tony Zee, the 'Zero Kid', has made his appearance, everybody. Let's drink to the pitcher!" Laughter and toasting followed the introduction. The Zee nickname had stuck to Zoretek like pine tar since his pitching debut a few weeks before. Moose and Tommy tried to get Tony into the beer-drinking merriment, but as usual, Tony found a jug of milk instead.

The afternoon victory was replayed many times with several different versions of whose stardom was most crucial. Good-natured bragging among the men was rampant, and Zee was often the center of the banter. Before Tony realized the time, it was past eight, and the rain had become a torrent outside. He endured all manner of teasing abuse as he excused himself from the party. "I'm in the middle of a great book, guys," he responded in good humor as he moved toward the front door.

"Bullshit!" Moose shouted above the noise in the living room. "It's that

dark-haired beauty from the ballpark, ain't it Zee? Let's not have any secrets from the guys. You've got a date tonight, don't you, Tony?" Spragg
gripped his friend's arm to keep him from getting out of the door.

"Okay, no secrets, I've got a date tonight. If I don't get there pretty soon
though, it might be the last one I have. Wish me luck, guys, and don't forget
you've got to go to work tomorrow. Try not to wake me up. I think I'll sleep
late," he ribbed his roommates.

Mary waited at her front window, staring out at the downpour. Obscured by
the sheets of rain was a black Buick parked one block down the street from
the Samora house. Tony was nearly an hour late, and Mary wondered if the
weather had changed his mind about coming to her house. It would be un-
derstandable if he stayed at Brady's party. She would blow out the candle
on her kitchen table and return the chilled bottle of wine to her ice box for
another time. However, as she was about to turn away from the window,
she saw Tony's lanky form splashing through the mud in the middle of
Garfield Street at a full run. Mary opened her front door as Tony raced toward the steps of her porch.

"Sorry, Mary," Tony panted his apology as he came inside. "I've kept
you waiting. My fault for not watching the time."

"I'll hear nothing of 'I'm sorry' from you, Tony. You didn't have to . . ."
Mary smiled widely, and let her thought fade as she regarded the soaking
wet man. Apologies for lateness were a black memory from her past;
something her married relationship had been built upon, and something
she hoped Tony would make her forget. Michael's impotence had made a
debacle of their marriage, and his drunkenness was his only escape from
that reality. Tony did not drink, and his apology for being late was sincere. This man, she knew in her heart, could love her as she needed to
be loved.

"All that matters is that you're here. Just look at you though, Tony
Zoretek; you're drenched to the bone!" She raised up on her toes and
kissed him lightly on the mouth, then stepped away, giving a playful frown
at the sight of his soaked clothing. "What are we to do about this?"

Tony grinned as he looked at the puddle of red drippings from the street
pooling on the polished wooden entry floor around his feet. "Is there any

English word that means wetter than 'drenched'?" He took off his soaked leather shoes looking at Mary apologetically for the mess.

"Give me your stockings, young man. They must be hung to dry, or you'll catch pneumonia for sure." She scolded mirthfully looking into his eyes. "And your shirt as well, if you wouldn't be too embarrassed, that is."

They laughed at Mary's reference to a favorite shared memory from last spring when Tony was working at the tailor shop. So much had happened between the two of them in the months since then. Mary held his stockings as Tony unbuttoned his shirt. "Better yet, go into my kitchen and take off your trousers, too. I'll get you a blanket, and a towel to dry yourself with."

Self-consciously, Tony undressed leaving everything but his damp underwear in a heap on Mary's floor. With the plaid blanket draped over his broad shoulders and falling only inches above his knees, he stepped from the kitchen into the living room.

Pulling the blanket together in front of him, he sat on the sofa and sipped the glass of wine Mary had set out for him. He watched her hanging his clothes on a rope line strung across the small room. As he often did, Tony contemplated the shapely figure under the cotton dress, her small bosoms, narrow waist, and slender hips.

Joining him on the sofa in the living room, she sat close enough for her knee to brush lightly against his. "I'm afraid you're stuck here with me for awhile, Mr. Zoretek. Just me, a candle, and a bottle of wine. What do you think about that?"

Tony held out his glass in a toast. "I couldn't be more content, Mary. Here's to the rain that soaked my clothes and got me stuck here with you, your candle, and your wine." As he turned toward her to clink her glass, the wool blanket slipped from his knee.

Mary could not help noticing the dark hair of his thigh. On an impulse, her left hand stroked his leg above his knee. She leaned her body into him for a kiss. "I love you, Tony." She breathed the words into his face as she opened her mouth for his deep kiss. "I love you . . . and . . . I want you." Mary could feel a heat racing from her breasts, down her stomach, and between her legs. Her body pressed across his. Then dropping her empty glass behind the sofa, she put her arms under the blanket, gripping the back of his bare shoulders.

Tony slid back into the sofa, kissing her deeply, and moving his hands from the small of her back to her firm bottom. "I want you, Mary," he breathed in gasps.

The blanket had fallen away from his body. "My room, Tony, my bed . . . undress me, make love to me." Mary's plea was driven by a passion she had never experienced.

Tony rose from the sofa and lifted Mary into his arms, "I can't tell you how much I love you, Mary. I want you, too . . . more than anything I've ever wanted in my life."

He carried her into the bedroom, slowly undressed her, and lay beside her on the bed. The lovers shared ecstasy that was beyond anything either might have imagined.

'A Teddybear For Kevin'

SUNDAY NIGHT'S RAIN LINGERED INTO the following morning. Peter was not feeling well after another sleepless night. His Garfield Street surveillance had kept him up until midnight when, tired and despairing, he returned home for a drink. In a dark mood this early Monday morning, he reflected. Zoretek must have spent the night with Mary Samora. He determined that she was a slut, no longer worthy of his attentions. "Women," Peter thought to himself, "are all sluts in one way or another." Senia Smith was probably no exception. Peter pushed his morning whiskey aside and contemplated the day ahead. There were calls to make, people to see, and business transactions to attend to.

From his library desk, Peter surveyed the room. His gaze fell upon books he had not read, on a signed portrait of President Theodore Roosevelt whom he had never met, and on a teddy bear he had never delivered to his son. Missed opportunities were everywhere, but now might be a good time to redirect his energy and resources. Once again he resolved to fill his life with more meaningful activities and let go of things that only depressed him. He took the bottle of whiskey from his drawer and dumped its contents into a planter behind his desk. "Enough of this poison," he told himself. "Think positive!"

That afternoon, Peter had a meeting scheduled with the other board directors of the Hibbing Commercial Club. On the agenda was a proposal by Elwood Trembart, supported by Fred Bennett, to name Tom McHardy to the board. McHardy was Peter's major lumber business rival, and McHardy's nomination was a slap in the face to him. Peter knew that Trembart still carried a grudge against him for the land deal, and that Elwood was bent on undermining the influence Moran held as the Club's president. "Fuck them all!" he said aloud.

Peter considered making an announcement during the meeting of his plan to build a golf course on his Alice location property. The golf course idea was only a pipe dream, but it would turn some heads. Club members had talked about the concept in the past, but no one was willing to carry the ball. Peter's proposal would remind them once again that he was the only farsighted person in Hibbing. He wondered about his financial reserves for such an undertaking and would talk with Senia about feasibility when he conferred with her later that morning. She would tell him he couldn't afford this, or any other major undertaking, until the hotel was solvent. Peter knew that his financial secretary's conservatism was a good check on his liberal spending tendencies.

He had a list of Monday morning activities to take care of before lunch. Finding a phone number, he asked the operator to place his call.

"Father Foley, Peter Moran here. How are you this morning?" Peter inquired about the progress of the adoption proceedings and reassured Foley that he remained supportive of his effort. He told the priest about his wish to visit the Schmitz family in Duluth soon to finally see his son. He explained his interest in establishing a trust fund for Kevin's education, and "whatever the boy decides to do with his life when he's eighteen." He further expressed a willingness to continue financial support after the adoption, but he emphasized, "Kevin must keep the Moran name."

Foley agreed to talk with Art and Sarah Schmitz about Peter's proposals. "I'll try to arrange for a visit next Saturday, if that's all right with you, and I'll tell them about your wishes for Kevin's well being. Art has the weekend off, so I don't see any problems with getting together then. I'd like to join all of you, for an hour or so, if that's okay with you?" Foley set a time for one in the afternoon, and said he would call Moran only if things would not work out as planned.

Peter marked his calendar for Saturday with his son's name, Kevin. He would have Miss Smith draft whatever papers were needed for a trust fund. His meeting with Senia he remembered, would be after the bank business she told him about the day before.

Peter placed another call. "Sweeny, Moran here. How was our weekend business at the hotel?"

Sweeny explained that the weekend had been slower than expected, but in the week preceding, occupancy had been near capacity again. "Like I've told you, Mr. Moran, in three years we'll be paid off, and in the black for good. We're still in the process of getting ourselves established. I wouldn't be surprised if the Northern Hotel folds before winter, and probably some of the smaller hotels will do the same. We're in a very good competitive position, sir," Sweeny assured his boss.

"I've got a question about our internal accounting, Jerry. I thought you might be able to explain it to me better than Miss Smith was able to do the other day. How do we handle our liquor billings? Do you pay the warehouse for the liquor you're getting at the hotel? Do you understand what I'm getting at, Jerry?" Moran had been confused by Senia's insinuations that he and Sweeny were not properly managing liquor money between the hotel and warehouse. Senia Smith was a thorn in Sweeny's side, and he desperately wanted to be rid of her constant intrusions into his hotel dealings. He knew exactly what Moran was inquiring about with regard to liquor billing procedures, but he needed to deflect Moran's questions momentarily. Sweeny remembered Senia's slip of the tongue about her ancestry from some time ago and decided to use that knowledge now in an effort to gain Moran's favor. "That woman never lets up on us, does she? Probably her Finnish nature, or the training she got back in Helsinki." He paused for a reaction. "Maybe she should have learned American business practices like you an' me have, don't you agree, Mr. Moran?"

"What are you talking about, Jerry? What's Helsinki?"

"I'm talking about Miss Smith, sir. Helsinki's a place in Finland. I thought you knew that she was from over there. She mentioned that to both of us one day back before the hotel opened. Don't you remember?" Sweeny probed. "She was talking about her gardens back in Finland."

"She's from England, or someplace like that, Jerry. I'm sure she told me so when I interviewed her. I can't remember anything about Finland or gardens. What are you getting at anyhow?" Moran puzzled over Sweeny's allegations.

'Well, sir, I hate to make negative comments about any race of people, but we both remember the strike last summer. It was mostly the Finns that were the rabble-rousers. The Oliver Company wouldn't hire any of them back after the strike. It seems to me, the Finns just like to cause trouble with all their anti-business feelings. I heard that Arola guy give a speech one day. God Almighty, that Finlander wanted to bring down our whole way of life with his socialism. He was one scary fellow, that's for sure."

"I remember that name, I think. But, Miss Smith? I think you're wrong about that. I'll have to talk with her about this one of these days." Peter had lost his original train of thought.

Sweeny sensed his ploy had worked. "I've got records on all the liquor, Mr. Moran. Don't worry about that. Was there anything else you wanted to know? The construction on the bowling alley downstairs is going along nicely, and we've made a killing on the hotel slot machines. Everything's going swell over here, sir."

"Well, that's good to hear, Jerry. Keep up the good work; I'll stop by sometime this week, and we can have lunch." Peter said goodbye and thought about what his hotel manager had told him about Senia. Only the day before she had mentioned something about a Finnish society and raising money for blacklisted miners. Indeed, Sweeny was mistaken. Senia was much too bright to be a Finn.

Senia enjoyed her meeting with a meticulously-dressed Harvey Goldberg at the Merchants and Miners bank. Mr. Goldberg was pleasant and sincere just as Mr. McIntosh had described the banker when he and Senia had talked about a job last week. Before sitting down for an interview, Goldberg gave Senia a tour of the bank, introducing her to many of the employees.

"Yes, Mrs. Arola, we could certainly use a loan officer here," Harvey Goldberg said from across his desk. "Mr. McIntosh has given you an excellent recommendation, and the financial work you have done for Mr. Moran is a pretty good background. As you well know, Peter has been one of our bank's major accounts. Let me review your resume quickly." Goldberg shifted his spectacles down his nose, scanning the neatly-typed sheet Senia had provided him. In terms of training and experience, Mrs. Arola was almost overqualified for the loan officer position she was seeking.

The two of them talked for nearly an hour about the details of the job and banking procedures in general. Goldberg also mentioned his meeting with Mr. Zoretek earlier in the morning. "I was most impressed by that young man and by his business plan. I noticed that you were going to guarantee the note, Mrs. Arola. With your account balance, there will be no problem whatsoever. I told Mr. Zoretek that his loan account would be ready later this week, so he could proceed with the business plan you helped him prepare."

"He will do well, Mr. Goldberg. I have no doubts about that. Thank you for giving him the loan."

Goldberg informed Senia that he would like her to start working in three weeks if that was feasible; Monday, August 11th was agreed upon. "I want to assure you, Mrs. Arola, with the changes ahead at the bank, a woman with your experience will have every opportunity for advancement. I am one of the few men in Hibbing who realize the importance of having women in positions of responsibility in its banking business."

Goldberg escorted Senia through the lobby area of the bank and offered her his hand before she departed. "I'm sure we'll talk again over the next three weeks, but I'm certainly pleased to have you joining our staff, Mrs. Arola."

When Senia returned to her office, she found a note from Mr. Moran tucked under her door. Peter wished to have a meeting about the trust information he had requested as soon as she returned from her appointment. She could explain the simple bank procedure without preparing any specific documentation for their meeting. She had a new job that renewed her confidence and was prepared for the long overdue confession. Her letter of resignation was already typed.

Senia found her employer at his library desk. Peter was dressed in an attractive brown suit with matching bow tie and fresh white shirt. Aside from the redness in his eyes, he looked better than he had in recent days. She remembered that this Monday was a Commercial Club meeting date. She would compliment him on his appearance.

"You look quite well this morning, Mr. Moran," she said cheerfully as she found a chair beside his desk. Senia placed the opened notebook with a page labeled 'trust' in her lap. Inside the notebook was an envelope containing the letter she would leave with Moran when she finished this meeting.

Peter stared at her without giving any greeting. "What have you got for me on this trust matter?" The stare made Senia feel ill at ease.

"If you will provide me with some basic information . . . the kind of trust arrangement you are considering, and in whose name, I can draft the paperwork, and set everything up through the bank for you, sir. There are several options, and the procedure is quite simple."

"I could do all that myself. Is that what you're saying? I could just call McIntosh or Goldberg down at the bank?"

"Yes, sir, you could have the bank set it up over the phone and just sign the papers afterwards. I didn't mean to suggest, however, that I wouldn't be happy to get something set up for you. I'm sorry if I gave you that impression."

"Sometimes I get false impressions, Miss Smith, mistaken or deliberate. Do you know what I mean about 'false impressions'?" Peter waited for his question to find its mark. "If the trust thing is that simple, I'll call McIntosh myself and save you the bother. That might be the best thing to do because the trust matter is kinda personal, wouldn't you say." Peter gave the word 'personal' a peculiar emphasis. All morning he had pondered what Sweeny had told him over the phone, and he was determined to get to the bottom of the matter. "I'm not much good with my geography, Miss Smith, but could you tell me where a place called Helsinki is located?"

Senia frowned over Moran's strange question and unnatural stare. She felt as if some kind of bizarre trap was being set for her. Very few people knew her true identity, and only Jim McIntosh could have told Peter Moran. Yet McIntosh, she knew, would never betray the confidence she had shared with him. "Helsinki is the capital city of Finland, sir," she answered in clear voice.

Senia's confrontation with Moran was an unexpected springboard for her. "I attended university in Helsinki and grew up in a small town called Jurva, just north of there. Why do you ask, sir?"

"You never told me that you were from Finland. You said you were from England or someplace like that. I remember that quite clearly." Peter struck a match under his desk and lit a cigar. He leaned back in his chair and blew a smoke ring into the space between them. "Have you lied to me, Miss Smith?" he asked bluntly. "It is Miss Smith, isn't it?"

Senia considered the detailed confession she had prepared to give Moran that day, but this turn of events had dramatically changed everything. She summoned her resolve to be brief, forthright, and show some mettle of her own.

She met his eyes. "With regard to your question about my having lied to you, Mr. Moran, I did not tell you that I was English, but I allowed you to have that misconception. If I had admitted to being Finnish, I would not, in all likelihood, have been given consideration for employment. So, the name Smith was contrived. That was a lie, and for that, I sincerely apologize, sir. Despite my deception, Mr. Moran, I have given you the best service and advice that I was capable of doing. I sincerely hope that you believe that." Senia paused, took the envelope from her notebook, and handed it to Moran. "It is ironic, sir, but I had every intention of telling you about all of this when I came to your office this very morning. So, before I am terminated, I want to give you my letter of resignation."

Moran put the envelope on his desk without opening it. "Who in the hell are you, 'Miss Smith', some kind of spy? You had me and everybody else fooled. What have you been up to around here?" Peter was incredulous. "I could have you arrested for something. You can't just go out and take another name. That's gotta be illegal."

"My name is Mrs. Timo Arola. My husband was murdered last summer during the strike here. That was before I came to America from Finland. I am no spy. Such a notion is preposterous. As to my identity, sir, I have been very careful about that. My bank records, like every other legal document, are listed under the name Senia Arola. I was Miss Smith while in your employ only, and I never signed the Smith name to a business record. If you want to check, you will see that only the initials "s.a." appear on any of the business matters that I conducted in your behalf."

"Arola? Are you a socialist, Mrs. Arola? Is it your purpose to destroy capitalism? Is that why you're here? Trying to undermine my business affairs? God damn, you are one clever woman. Have you been skimming money from my accounts, messing up my books?" Peter's forehead wrinkled, "You've got a lot more explaining to do. And, let me inform you about something else. Nobody was murdered during the strike. I would have known if anything like that had happened."

"I am neither a socialist nor a thief, sir, and I resent those accusations. Clever? I am complimented, Mr. Moran. Yes, I have been quite clever and enterprising as well." Senia had a rush of confidence. "Before I leave," she continued, "I want to thank you for the opportunities and hospitality you have given me. I have always considered you to be a decent, generous, and thoughtful man. Your attitude this morning, however, has been less than honorable. In my letter, you will find that I intend to give you a full report on everything I have worked on for you over this past year." Senia got up and walked toward the closed door, leaving Peter in disbelief. Before leaving the room she turned, "My thank you was sincere, Mr. Moran."

Peter felt betrayed. Of the many people in his daily routines of business and life, she was the only one he trusted implicitly. How could she have deceived him so? Peter was convinced that Senia had always acted in his best interests, given him honest counsel, and worked with an efficient diligence on every task he gave her. He held the letter in his hand but still did not open it. He needed her, he realized, and would somehow find a way to talk her out of resigning. "Senia Arola," he thought to himself. He could learn to live with that.

The only other friend Peter had was Jim McIntosh. Mac's friendship, however, had become estranged in recent months, and Peter was perplexed over the apparent rift. He would make another effort at repairing the bridge between himself and Jim. He placed another call through the operator.

"Jimmy boy, how have you been? Has the train from Duluth to Hibbing broken down?"

McIntosh reminded him that the train was fine and that it ran both ways. "You, my old friend, have not been down here in months. What's going on in Hibbing that is so important you can't even get out of town for a weekend?"

The two of them talked casually about family, golf, and business. Peter told McIntosh about his Fitger's setback, and how their mutual friend, John Allison, had stabbed him in the back.

Peter, never much good at small talk, soon became impatient. "Well, I called for a couple of reasons, Jim. One of them is going to bring me down to Duluth next Saturday. I need to trust you with something confidential, Jim, and get your advice as well. Aside from a Catholic priest down in Duluth, you are the only other person in the world I have told this to." Peter spent several minutes explaining his relationship with Barbara Chevalier, her tragic death in childbirth about eighteen months before, and his son Kevin.

McIntosh was sympathetic, "A hell of a burden to be carrying on your shoulders all this time, Pete. I had no idea. Is there anything I can do? It will be between the two of us, I assure you."

McIntosh would draft a trust arrangement for Kevin that would mature on his eighteenth birthday. It would provide Peter's son with twenty thousand dollars at maturity. At Peter's request, the papers would be delivered to Father Pat Foley for his review and for the Schmitz family to consider before Peter's arrival on Saturday. Peter could sign the trust documents at that time and a letter of understanding regarding the 'legal' name of Kevin Moran.

"I've got a confession of sorts to make as well, Pete. The twice a week trips to Hibbing have been wearing me down over the years, and I've decided to sell the bank." Jim McIntosh explained his family considerations and expressed confidence that Harvey Goldberg would assemble a group of investors in a short time. Jim planned to call Claude Atkinson at the newspaper, who would make his decision known publicly in a week or two.

Peter was devastated by the news. "I'm really feeling abandoned by my closest friends these days," he acknowledged. "I'm gettin squeezed by my business colleagues at our Commercial Club, and even my secretary, Senia. She wants to quit her job with me. Let me tell you about the Senia matter, Jim."

Peter explained his conversations with Sweeny, then with Senia. He told Jim of his shock about Senia's nationality and the deceit it had inspired. "I'll talk her out of it, of course, but our relationship will certainly be different than it has been in the past. I'll let her know, in no uncertain terms, that she will never find a job in Hibbing without my help. She will realize that a woman, a Finnish woman no less, is just not in much demand."

McIntosh could not, in good conscience, keep what he knew from Peter. The truth of the matter would certainly come out soon enough. "I've already talked with Mrs. Arola about her decisions, Pete. She called me last week and gave me pretty much the same story that you have. She wanted a job before she talked to you, and I set up an interview with Harvey Goldberg at the bank. Harvey hired her this morning. We just got off the phone a couple of hours ago."

"You did what? I can't believe what you're telling me. That's another stab in the back, Jim. You of all people, God damn it!"

"Pete, you've got to understand; this is not about you in any way. Senia asked me for a job, and I was only trying to help her. As we both know, she's one hell of a bright woman, Pete. Goldberg saw that right away. Senia has resolved the issue in her life, and she wants to start over again. She wants her true identity back and her independence. She made her decisions before that horse's ass, Sweeny, tried to undermine her character. I'm sorry you're angry with me, Pete, but I haven't done anything to betray you or our friendship."

Peter was appalled. "Mac, this was all done behind my back. You didn't have the decency to let me know what was going on. How can you tell me that you have not betrayed our friendship? Fuck you! My next call will be to Goldberg at your bank, or his bank . . . who gives a shit anymore! I'm going to transfer all of my accounts to another bank. That's the price of fucking a friend." Peter slammed down the phone and sat shaking at his desk. He felt as if his world was caving in about him. He got up, looked out his library window at the gray rain, and fought against tears.

Peter would not attend the Club meeting that afternoon. He had never missed one before. He would not transfer his accounts from McIntosh's bank as he had threatened, and he would not drown his sorrows of the moment in whiskey. Somehow, he resolved, he would regroup himself. Somehow!

McIntosh asked his secretary to call Senia at Moran's house and let her know that he would forward all of the trust documents to Father Foley as Peter had requested. "Ask Senia to pass that information on to Mr. Moran and give her my warmest regards," he instructed.

Peter had little difficulty in locating the Schmitz family home on West 57th Avenue, a few blocks up from the St. James Church. Father Foley greeted him at the door and introduced Peter to Art and Sarah Schmitz. Their home was a neat, tidy three bedroom bungalow, attractively furnished. Sarah's living room window faced to the east over a large front yard dominated by two stately pine trees. Inside, several leafy table plants caught the sun.

Art made a good living as a supervisor at one of the many St. Louis River shipbuilding facilities. Married for nine years, Art and Sarah had been unable to have children of their own. Peter found the couple to be most amiable toward him and realized he could not have picked out more deserving parents for his son. Kevin was napping when Peter arrived, so the four adults had an opportunity to visit over coffee.

Foley reviewed the trust papers that Jim McIntosh had delivered to his church on the previous Wednesday. Art Schmitz had reservations about the fund, including Peter's pledge to increase his monthly financial support. He had intended to explain to Moran that the money he was sending was no longer necessary. "May I be blunt, Mr. Moran? Kevin will be our son. That is the sole intent of the adoption proceedings. I understand that you are a man of considerable means, but Sarah and I do not regard ourselves as paid baby sitters for Kevin. We are his parents. Not yet legally, but in every sense of the word, we are Kevin's mom and dad."

Peter was uncomfortable with this truth. "Please, Mr. Schmitz, understand my intentions here. I want to be generous; I can afford to be generous, and we are talking about my son after all. I am his father."

Art Schmitz was not intimidated by the well-dressed, wealthy stranger from Hibbing. At the same time, however, he did not want to be rude or obnoxious. This would be, after all, the first time in eighteen months that the 'father' would see his son. Art had envisioned this meeting with Mr. Moran for a long time and would not be influenced by any proposed monetary windfalls.

At some risk to the amicable atmosphere that Father Foley had suggested, Art Schmitz responded to Moran's paternity argument. "Almost any man can father a child, sir. I happen to be one of the rare exceptions, but *being* a father is a whole different matter. I will be Kevin's father. Your money cannot buy you a son. I don't know your world, Mr. Moran, but in my world people cannot be purchased at any price."

Father Foley intervened. "Let's all of us step back for a moment. We all want what is best for Kevin. There is no argument about that. We don't have to be confrontational. And, we don't have to resolve all the issues in our first time together. I'd like to propose that we put these matters aside for the moment. I'll keep these papers at the church, and we can give further thought to trust funds, and the like, in the months to come. Can all of you be comfortable with that?"

Reaching an uneasy truce, Art nodded. Sarah followed her husband's lead, and Moran could do no more than give his own consent to the priest's compromise. "If you're willing to keep an open mind, Art—and Sarah, I would be more than happy to give this issue some more time. As Father Foley suggested, we are all most interested in what is best for Kevin."

After nearly an hour of awkward small talk, Kevin began crying from a bedroom down the hallway. Sarah was up in an instant to attend to her boy. Minutes later, Sarah presented Peter with the most beautiful child he had ever seen. "Meet your son, Mr. Moran," she announced with a pride-filled smile.

Peter was choked with emotions he was unprepared to experience. Settling the boy in his lap, he saw his own unmistakable ears on another human being. Barbara was in the shape of Kevin's face and in his eyes as well. Peter handed Kevin the teddy bear he had brought with him from Hibbing. The boy was delighted with the new toy. He bounced the boy on his knee, beaming at the lad's playful giggling.

Foley found the opportunity to excuse himself from what seemed to be a more relaxed situation. "I've got some work to do on tomorrow's sermon, so I'll be saying goodbye for now."

Art retrieved Foley's hat as the priest moved toward the door. Foley paused as if he had just remembered something. "Oh, Peter, why didn't you tell me that you had a brother living in Duluth? Denis has registered at our parish. He told me to say hello to you when I saw you and said you must come and visit him on one of your trips down to Duluth."

Peter almost dropped the child. He felt his mouth go dry. "Oh, I— I just didn't think of it. Too much on my mind all the time. Give him my best when you see him, Father."

Peter left Duluth on the late afternoon train and mulled over the effect of his visit. For the time being, he would be 'Uncle Peter'. He could visit Kevin as often as he wished but would have to make arrangements in advance through Father Foley. He would discontinue the monthly payments and give the Schmitzes time to think about any trust fund. In all likelihood, the boy would be Kevin Schmitz. Peter had been unable *to buy* anything in Duluth that day.

The most troubling event occuring that day was the frightening disclosure about his brother Denis. It had been almost two months since he paid Ole Nord to run his drunken brother out of town. Peter had given his brother enough money to make it out to Pennsylvania where their mother and sister lived. He had no idea that Denis would end up in Duluth. What was Denis up to, and how was Foley involved in this insidious scenario?

Peter Moran's footprints in Duluth were nearly two years old. Sam Lavalle, a street-smart hoodlum, and Denis Moran had become fast friends since the incident of Lily's beating weeks before. Both men liked liquor, whores, and gambling; both men despised Peter Moran. Sam found an old acquaintance named Karl Chevalier out in the Moran Park neighborhood of West Duluth. It was Karl who had given Lavalle the name of his granddaughter, Barbara, and it was Sam Lavalle who had passed the name of Barbara Chevalier on to Peter Moran. Karl told Sam of Barbara's untimely death and of her son, whom a priest named Father Foley had placed for adoption. From that lead, everything else fell neatly into place.

Lavalle had always been a two-bit hustler, but now he could smell something much sweeter. He outlined his sinister scheme to Denis Moran. "You gotta do everything I tell ya, Denis. This is gonna make us both rich if we can pull it off right. Just don't ask me a lotta questions, okay?"

Denis joined the St. James Church and introduced himself to Father Foley. Locating Kevin had taken a few weeks. Moran's connection to the boy was a long shot that would require tedious surveillance. Taking turns, the two men watched the Schmitz home for a few hours every day.

Denis had followed Foley up West 57th Avenue that Saturday afternoon. He watched from a nearby corner as his brother walked up to the front door of the Schmitz bungalow several minutes later. The connection between Peter and the boy named Kevin had been established. Now, the two conspirators could move on to the next stage of their plan.

Sam and Denis celebrated their coup over beers at the Central Avenue tavern. During the past few weeks, the two of them had been arranging a scheme. Both wanted revenge for what Peter had done to them, but each had a different approach to achieving their end. Sam wanted Peter Moran's money, while Denis wanted to 'knock the sonofabitch off his high horse'. On many occasions Denis voiced his desires. "I'll kick the shit out of him for my own pleasure and burn down the fucking lumber yard he stole from my dad." Denis blamed the death of their father, Daly, on his brother and couldn't forgive the treachery he had exaggerated in his memory for years.

"We can leave the burning to Ducette after we get the money," Lavalle reasoned. "You can kill the asshole if you wanna, and all of us can get a chunk of cash to boot."

Lavalle had met the drifter, Bernie Ducette, at one of his brothels a year before. Ducette had been fired from his job at the ore docks and was on a weekend drunk. Lavalle always questioned everyone about where they were from and what they were doing in his territory. There was always a payoff for the information he picked up over a few beers. Ducette was from Hibbing and had been fired by Moran from a pretty good job in the liquor business. The little Frenchman expressed his hatred of Peter Moran, rambling on about some friend of his who was killed in a freak accident "right in front of my own two eyes." He was drunk, and cried over the incident.

Ducette was living in Hibbing again but got down to Duluth every few weeks. Bernie met Denis at a brothel during one of these visits. Denis bought him a whore for the night.

Lavalle, the brains behind the conspiracy, had not included Bernie Ducette in any plans up to this point. When he wanted to involve Bernie, he knew where to find him.

"So here's what we're gonna do, Denis." Sam leaned over his beer at a corner table of the barroom, whispering behind his cupped hand. "We kidnap the boy early in the morning after Schmitz goes to work. Then we hide the kid in the basement of Lily's place on Raleigh Street. There's an old coal bin that ain't bein' used. I'll pay Lily to take care of him. Then we send the ransom note to your brother with a threat to kill the kid if he opens his fuckin mouth to anybody. We're gonna tell him twenty thousand in small bills. . . ." Lavalle explained the details of a scheme he had worked over in his mind several times. He was convinced it would work.

Denis listened impatiently. "So he drops off the fuckin money, then what? When do I get ta kick his ass, or better yet, put a fuckin bullet between his eyes?" His revenge was not about money. "And, what about Bernie? Ain't we gonna burn down my brother's lumber yard? How does that fit into this fuckin plan of yours, Sam?"

The two men argued for another hour then tucked some beers in their pockets and headed over to Lily's place.

'TELL IT TO THE GRAND JURY'

THE MONTH OF AUGUST OFTEN presents summer in all her majesty to those who live in Northern Minnesota. The days are comfortably warm, the humidity reasonably low, and the evenings refreshingly cool. Tomato and grape vines show lavish colorings of red and purple; vegetable gardens begin to yield carrots, beans, peas, and squash. Astilbies, cone flower, mums, and marigolds splash their colors like a painter's brushstroke upon the green landscape.

On Sunday, August 10, 1908, the village of Hibbing celebrated its fifteenth birthday with Mother Nature showering the day with her most glorious cloudless blue sky. There would be a long afternoon parade down Pine Street and Third Avenue, numerous picnics in Mesaba Park, a ball game, and sky shattering fireworks after dusk.

Claude Atkinson loved this town and its melting pot society. In reporting the events shaping Hibbing's early years, he always found positive perspectives to enhance his stories. The town had more than its share of crime, vice, and rowdiness, but to Claude these were only symptoms of adolescence. Hibbing had grown too fast without logical design or plan. The rapid pace of mining had recontoured the landscape into shapes that were at the same time ugly and awesome. Gaping mine pits were canyons gouged from the earth, while enormous overburdens of rock and dirt created artificial mountain ranges surrounding Hibbing. These very same features were common sights across the face of the Mesabi Iron Range. Despite the ugliness of mining, Claude found a majesty in the tumultuous resculpting of the countryside which brought something new every day.

As a reporter, Atkinson searched for the truth behind the stories he told in his newspaper. Sometimes the truth was a challenge for him to uncover, and sometimes the truth was never to be found. Whichever the case, Claude Atkinson was always a tireless and persevering investigator.

Peter Moran's hotel, like the perplexing businessman himself, was like a riddle within an enigma to Claude. Harold Markman's only comment often came to Claude's mind. "Sabotage." Before Markman's sale of the hotel, a freakish accident claimed the life of a young brick worker from St. Paul, named Billy Herrick. Tragic deaths were not uncommon to this mining town, but the unlikely collapse of an entire building wall had never been fully understood or explained.

Atkinson had arranged for another interview with Stan Cleary, whom he had first met in his office two weeks before. The editor planned to search for some thread in the patchwork of Moran's activities, but he wasn't sure what it might be. Cleary was waiting outside his office door as Claude found his familiar tablet with a blank page labeled only with the date, *'Tues. 8/12'* on the top and two quotes he remembered from his conversation about Cleary with Moran during the Mt. Iron ball game. "He was fired . . ." and "Cleary's no good!" Claude's elephant memory was positive these quotes were exact. What interested Claude, however, was Peter's slight twinge of anxiety when he first mentioned Cleary's name.

Claude had learned from Harvey Goldberg, at the McIntosh bank, that Moran's financial secretary had quit and was taking a bank job. Too many people were either jumping or being pushed from Moran's ship. What was the story behind all this?

"Come on in and make yourself comfortable, Mr. Cleary." Claude rose out of his chair and offered his handshake to the large man who smiled awkwardly at him from across the top of his wide desk. "How have you been? May I call you Stan?"

"Sure thing, Mr. Claude; I mean 'Akonsin'. I bin just fine. I ain't found no job yet though."

Claude sat down. "Why might that be, Stan? You had a pretty important job with Mr. Moran, before getting laid off. You did tell me you were 'laid off' didn't you?" Atkinson began his interrogative interview with a man he had no intention of hiring for the job in the newspaper's print shop.

"Ya, laid off, I told you before. Maybe Moran has somthin' to do with that. He din't like me. That's for sure! I been doin some bar tending though, part time at Rusty's Bar, and I applied with the railroad, too."

Claude leveled his eyes upon Cleary. In his experience, the reporter believed, a person's eyes would tell him his story. "I had a long talk with Mr. Moran about you the other day, Stan." Claude let the statement hang in the air for several seconds while he studied Cleary's green eyes.

"Ya did? What did he have to say about me? That I didn't do a good job or somethin else?" Cleary's eyes already showed a fright like those of a deer caught in a sharp beam of light.

"Can we be totally honest with each other, Stan?" Again, Atkinson let his question hang for seconds.

Cleary's memory of his last conversation with Moran was a blur, but he did remember something his former boss had told him, "You could go to prison . . . conspiracy to commit murder." He felt the sweat in his armpits. Moran, he was certain, was out to get him to save his own ass. That's what the newspaperman was getting at with his question about being honest. Cleary, however, was not going to let any big shot like Moran pin all the blame on him. He swallowed hard, "I'll be honest about it. I only did what I was told to do. None of that was my idea. That's the honest truth, I swear."

Atkinson had no idea what was troubling this man to the point of per-spiration. "I'm sorry, but that's not what Mr. Moran told me, Stan. Maybe you should tell me what happened in your own words. I think you're an honorable man. What is the real story about what happened?" Atkinson was, as always, open-ended in his probing. He assumed that Cleary would tell him he was fired, not laid off.

Stan Cleary, however, told Claude Atkinson a story more shocking than the reporter had ever heard. The newsman was taking notes so fast his writing became illegible on the pages he rapidly flipped. If what Cleary was telling him was true, and Claude had no reason to doubt him, this was a bombshell! From his wide experience, he knew this was much more than the babbling of a frightened man. Cleary was not smart enough to fabricate a lie of these dimensions. How much of this did Markman know about, Claude wondered? More than likely, Harold's suggestion of 'sabotage' was no more than a gut feeling. If he did know or had any proof about this,

Moran would have been in jail long ago. Claude was convinced that Cleary had no idea of the magnitude of his disclosure.

Claude sought to calm the troubled man. "It took a great deal of courage, Mr. Cleary, to give me your version of the story. I want you to know that I believe you and so will a lot of other people. I'm sure you know the seriousness of this matter and that you've placed yourself at some risk by coming forward."

"I'm in trouble, ain't I, Mr. Akonsin? I'll go to prison just like Moran says, won't I?" Cleary, close to a breakdown, fought back tears. "I got a wife, three kids . . . and some bills that keep piling up. What can I do?"

"Are you willing, Stan, to give this same story to what is called a 'grand jury'?" He explained the judicial system in the most elementary terms. "So you see, it's just a group of people who will decide what to do about the incident at the hotel site. These people would, more than likely, want to bring charges against Mr. Moran. Do you understand that, Stan?"

Cleary nodded. "That don't mean that I'm off the hook, does it? I mean, I did something wrong; I know that I did. What will I tell my wife?"

Getting up from his chair, Claude walked behind Cleary. He placed his hands on the man's huge shoulders and gave him some simple instructions. "It would be best for everybody if this conversation were kept between just the two of us for now. Do you understand? I will talk to a few people I know, and they can tell us what to do next. None of them will say a word about our conversation this morning until the time is right."

Cleary nodded again. "I understand, just shut up my mouth, right?"

"Right, Stan. Not another word about it," Claude advised.

"What about the job?" Cleary asked.

Claude was puzzled. "What job?"

"The job you wanted to hire me for, Mr. Akonsin."

"Oh, I'm sorry, the printing shop job. Well, we won't be filling that job for a few weeks yet. We can talk more about that later. I know things are tough for you now, Stan." Claude reached into his trouser pocket and found a ten dollar bill. "This might help a little with some groceries."

Cleary was grateful for the gesture and thanked Claude profusely. "Nobody never gave me ten bucks for nothin before."

Claude escorted Cleary out of his office and to the front door. "I have

your address, Stan, and I'll probably stop by to visit with you again sometime next week. Let me know if you need some help with your bills, okay?"

Peter had been unable to dissuade Senia from resigning and gradually came
around to accepting the reality of her departure. He would miss her more
than any other employee he had ever hired. The elaborate reports she had
prepared on his business operations before leaving were casually passed
along to Jerry Sweeny. Peter didn't bother to study them and asked Sweeny
to review them for him. Sweeny assured Peter, "If there's anything in her
reports that you should know about, I'll pass it along to you."

Before Senia Arola left her office and upstairs apartment, Peter provided her with a sizable bonus for dedicated service. He encouraged her to
take any of the furnishings he had bought to her new place and reminded
her, "If things don't work out, you've always got this place to come back
to." Peter was apologetic for some of his wild allegations about her socialism and spying, shaking her hand before she left his home. "I hope there
are no hard feelings between us, Mrs. Arola, and I hope that you will feel
comfortable about stopping by to visit from time to time."

Senia's new apartment was located upstairs of Fay's Furniture Store on
the northeast corner of Pine Street and Third Avenue. Her living room window overlooked Hibbing's major commercial intersection. The view was a
dramatic change from the gardens of Moran's back yard. Senia spent the
week before starting her job at the bank redecorating her new place.
Although her move was only temporary, the furnishings she purchased
would go nicely in the new house that she would build the following spring.

Steven and Tony helped Senia haul her furniture up the narrow stairway. Steven found himself in Hibbing more often these days, helping his
nephew with his new business two blocks from where Senia was living on
Pine Street. On several evenings, she and Steven would go for walks down
Third to Mesaba Park.

Senia was inspired by the freedom that her own apartment gave her. For
the first time since coming to America, only one year before, she was getting her life in order. She had already purchased a parcel of land on West
Lincoln Street, and Tony was drafting plans for the house he would be
building on her property next spring.

Tony Zoretek was Hibbing's newest building contractor. He had moved into a building on Center Street, installed a telephone, and made a substantial purchase of lumber and other building supplies from Tom McHardy's lumber yard. McHardy had given him the best price in town for his materials, and Tony had a sizable area in the yard behind his shop in which to store them.

Tony's old friend, Lars Udahl, had been more helpful than anyone else in getting him started on the right foot. Lars had given him a drafting table for the Center Street office, located a usable cart for hauling supplies, and helped him prepare specs and bids on some local jobs. Lars had always wanted to do what Tony was doing and got himself involved with the new business as if it were his own.

Once the loan had been secured at the Merchants and Miners Bank, Tony picked up his first job. Claude Atkinson, true to his word, had given him an inside track on a roofing project for a downtown merchant named Hymen Bloom. Luigi Anselmo then helped Tony get another contract. Roland Saccoman was going to build a two-story home south of the city. Tony would do the framing and roofing for Saccoman, and other contractors would do the interior work. Tony had talked with Benny Madden, who was the best carpenter in Udahl's shop, about working with him on a part-time basis. Madden had expertise in wiring and plumbing as well as carpentry. His friend would help him out as well as teach him some of the skills that Tony needed to learn.

"I've been in business for two weeks already and just look at this place, Mary." Tony and Mary were looking over the mess that was Tony's office at 420 Center Street.

"I couldn't agree more, but that's why we're here. We'll get this place looking like a real headquarters in no time." Mary smiled her encouragement. "I've got enough cleaning supplies in this box to put a shine on this half of Hibbing."

They were planning to clean and arrange the office on this beautiful August Saturday. Steven and Senia would be by later in the morning to help them. Mary was anxious to meet Tony's friends for the first time. "I'm nervous about meeting your uncle, Tony. Do you think he will approve of me?"

Tony gave her a long appraising look, "I don't know, sweetheart. Steven's impressed by people's appearances: their hair, clothes, things like that," he teased while wearing a serious expression.

Mary pouted regarding herself. "I'm wearing the absolute worst clothes in my closet, and my hair?" Mary's long tresses were tied back with an old pink colored 'kerchief.

"From what you've told me about your Uncle Steven, what I look like is the last thing in the world he'd care anything about. I'll charm him with my personality despite how I look," she laughed. "Now, Mr. Businessman, where do we start? I think we'll have to sweep and mop the floors before we get to the dusting and those filthy, filthy windows! What do you say?"

"Just tell me what to do, Mary. You're the foreman on this job." Tony took the broom in one hand and the swabbing mop handle in the other, shrugging his shoulders in pretended confusion. "Take your pick."

"We're teammates on this job, partner. I'm not wearing the pants in your office," Mary rejoined. "How about if I start sweeping from the back of the shop, and you mop along behind me?"

"I like that idea. Then you won't be able to watch me watching you!" Tony laughed. He and Mary had become so much closer since that rainy Sunday night when they first made love. Tony was even beginning to hate the baseball practices that took up so many of his evenings, stealing time that might otherwise have been spent with Mary.

The two of them had been scrubbing and mopping for nearly an hour when Steven and Senia came by to help. Tony did the introducing, after which they had coffee that Mary perked on the stove in a back room of the building. Within minutes Mary was completely at ease with the two people Tony had told her so much about. "This almost seems like a family reunion," she observed. "I feel as though I've known you both for most of my life."

Steven, knowing of Tony's affection for this lovely Italian girl, thoroughly enjoyed seeing their happiness together. Senia had often expressed her fondness for Tony, and Steven had quickly warmed to Mary's spirited personality. Perhaps all of them would be family one day. "We do have a lot in common, Mary. We're good people making new lives for ourselves here in Hibbing."

Senia smiled at Steven's observation. "How profound you are Steven. Mary, I think we are lucky to have found these two Slovenian men."

By one o'clock, the office looked like a new place. Tony took everybody out to lunch at a small cafe just down the street. Over sandwiches and milk, they talked about how nicely the office was shaping up, and about the painting that would be done that afternoon. "Tommy Pell and Walt Spragg might stop by later to help us out. They're my roommates. Mary has met them both at ball games," Tony told Steven and Senia. "We have a game tomorrow afternoon, and Mary wants both of you to join her. She can tell you a lot about baseball. She's always shouting for me to hit the batter."

Mary was embarrassed by the tease. "That would be wonderful. Can you join some friends and me for tomorrow's game? I won't be able to tell you anything about the game of baseball because it's far too complicated. But my little friend Armando Depelo has become an expert and he'll be there for sure."

Mary remembered another event coming up the next day. "And, let's not forget the anniversary parade after the game. We could all go over to my house afterwards and watch the fireworks." Steven and Senia agreed it would be a fun way for all of them to spend a Sunday together.

That afternoon the men painted the office walls with the beige paint Mary had chosen. Later, the two women decided to take a walk down to Second Avenue and visit Luigi's shop. Mary wanted to show Senia some of the Paris patterns she was working on and some new fabrics that had arrived from Chicago.

Senia would need to add some new dresses to her wardrobe and was anxious to get some ideas from her new friend. She would start her job at the bank the following Monday. "Let's go to my apartment first," Senia suggested. "We can change clothes there. I'm a little taller than you, Mary, but I'm sure we can find something that might fit. I don't think we want to wander about Hibbing in these clothes. Besides, it will give me a chance to show off my little Pine Street apartment. I'm so happy with the downtown location."

After changing and freshening up, the two beautiful women walked arm-in-arm down Pine to Second Avenue. Men doffed their hats, greeting both women pleasantly, and turning their heads when they passed by. Other women regarded the two ladies with typical female aloof showing more than a bit of haughty jealousy.

While Tony, Steven, and Walt Spragg painted, Tommy Pell worked on the project he had promised Tony he would do for him once the front window was clean. Pell was very artistic and cut his letter tinplates with exacting precision. In two hours, he was painting over the patterns he had glued temporarily onto the glass pane. In bold black letters, which were fringed in golden paint, Pell's finished product would cover most of the large front window.

The women returned about four bringing pastries and lemonade they had picked up at a bakery down the street. Having finished the painting, the men were cleaning up.

"Before taking a break, let's go outside and take a look at the window. And don't think I'm too modest for compliments. I love 'em!" Pell beckoned enthusiastically.

From across the street they all regarded Tommy Pell's art work. Commenting on the fine craftsmanship of Pell's lettering, each felt their own sense of pride for the young man whose surname crossed the glass. Looking at the sign, *Zoretek Construction and Carpentry,* stirred emotions for Tony.

Bernie Ducette met Sam Lavalle and Denis Moran at the Raleigh Street apartment of Lily Brown, one of Sam's whores. Ducette had received a letter from Lavalle telling him to meet them on Friday, August 15th. Bruno Moscatelli, who could read and write, translated the letter for him. "We've got an important job for you . . ." Lavalle had written, without giving Bernie any details. The three men retired to the musty basement and sat around an old table that Lavalle had dragged into the unused coal bin. A lantern in the center of the table gave the space a small glimmer of light. About the lamp were two ashtrays heaped with cigarette butts and several empty beer bottles. In the corner of the dank bin was a pile of old blankets.

"I've got this thing all figgered out," Lavalle said beginning the meeting. "Bernie, we ain't told you nothing about our plan yet, but we're gonna give you part of the action. Do ya wanna make some easy money?"

Bernie regarded the the shadowed face under the down turned brim of a rakish felt hat. "You kiddin me, Sam? I ain't never gonna pass up an easy buck. Whatta you guys up ta?"

"It's some dangerous shit, Bernie. If we fuck 'er up, we're all of us gonna do some big time in the pokey. If we pull er off, we're gonna be on easy street," Lavalle said regarding both men. "Me and Denis here done most of the planning already. Most of yer part of the job will be up in Hibbing after we get the kid."

Bernie puzzled. "Get the kid? Whatta ya talkin about?"

Lavalle explained his kidnapping scheme. As he detailed the plan, Denis sat anxiously, fingering the revolver he had tucked under the belt of his trousers. Denis had picked up the gun at a pawn shop and had been thinking seriously about using it on his brother. If he just kicked the shit out of Peter, which would be very satisfying, his brother might get him later. If he killed him, it would be all over once and for all; his revenge would be complete.

"Me and Denis will go in the back door of the house after the old man goes ta work, about seven in the morning. You'll have the wagon waiting in the alley behind their place, Bernie. Denis and me'll tie up and gag this Schmitz woman, then take the kid and run. Won't take more than ten minutes to get the kid down here. It's as simple as that." Lavalle pointed to the blankets. "Then, Lily keeps an eye on the kid and feeds him whatever he eats for a coupl'a days. In'na meantime, you head back up to Hibbing fer the other part of our plan."

Denis interrupted for the first time. "Me and Sam are stayin in Duluth, Bernie. But I wanna give my fuckin' brother somethin' else to think about. I owe 'im fer what he done to my pa."

Denis told Bernie Ducette about burning down Peter's lumber yard. "That should just about do it for that high and mighty sonofabitch. We'll get his ransom money and wipe out all his business at the same time." Denis did not mention anything about maybe killing his brother as soon as Peter turned over the money. Bernie's eyes lit up at the mention of a fire. The pyromaniac would like to burn down the whole town of Hibbing. "Now you're talkin. Nothin to it. Come through the fence off Railroad Street, get into the back of the warehouse, and poof, we got us some flame."

Lavalle took control of the conversation. "Let's not get too wrapped up in that fire stuff right now. We gotta get the main thing worked out first." Lavalle took the note he had written from his shirt pocket. "I'm gonna read this to you guys; tell me what ya think, okay?

dear mr. moran

  we got your kid. we want $20,000 in small bills like five's and tens. we wont hurt him if you give us our money. you will get the next letter tomorrow telling you where to bring the money to get your kid back. dont go to your police or else.

"I made it short, ya see? What do ya think?" Lavalle smiled at his clever ransom note. "He'll get this letter on a Monday."

"Ain't ya gonna tell him about the fire?" Bernie questioned.

"What the hell for?" Lavalle snapped. "This ain't about no fire, Bernie. I don't like the fire idea anyhow. That's Denis' thing."

"Ya, that's like, whatta they say, 'frostin on our cake'?" Denis smiled at the thought of this part of his revenge.

"Now, here's the other letter, you guys." Lavalle took out a second page. "He'll get this next letter on Tuesday; I checked the post office about that. So we'll be getting the money on Thursday night. We take the kid on Monday morning, so the whole thing'll be over with in a few days. Now you guys listen up ta this.

dear mr. moran

  in two days when it is dark out about ten at night you bring the money to this place. it is in riverside out in west duluth by a pond by the railroad tracks. that is below penton bullivard in riverside and we will be there. you can have your kid back then. dont tell the police or else. remember $20,000 like we said before.

"That's all der is to it, two letters and twenny grand," Lavalle smiled his satisfaction over the notes he had carefully crafted. "Is der anything that I mighta missed?"

"Why da two letters, Sam?" Denis puzzled.

"I dunno. Gives 'em time to think about it I guess. Don't worry, I know what da hell I'm doin— jus let me handle all da plannin stuff. Okay? Any other stupid questions?" He glarred at Denis and shifted his weight in the chair.

"When do I start da fire?" Bernie was confused about his role in the plan.

"How about next Tuesday or Wednesday? It don't make no damn difference ta me," Denis offered.

Lavalle passed around bottles of beer. "Let's us have a beer on this, fellas. A week from now we can all be drinking champagne."

"Hey, Sam. How 'bout my money? You ain't said nothin 'bout that yet. Should I come back down here after the fire?" Bernie would burn the lumber yard for nothing. He despised Peter Moran, who had fired him long before, with the same passion that he hated all capitalists. He remembered his friend, Timo Arola, who had promised a better world where everyone was equal. Maybe, if the whole city of Hibbing burned down, a new world could take its place.

Peter Moran rarely left his library office these days. His telephone became his primary means of communicating with the outside world. Without Senia to take calls and remind him of business matters that needed attention, he felt alone and isolated. On Sunday he had missed his first ball game of the season and hadn't bothered to watch the fifteenth anniversary parade that afternoon either. He regarded his calendar, Tuesday, August 12; no meetings or appointments had been penciled in for that date. He noted that, aside from a Commercial Club meeting, and a lunch with Sweeny on Thursday, the week was an empty hole in his life. Senia, he knew, would have found something for him to do on every day of the week. His former secretary had started her new job at the bank the day before.

The telephone rang, and the operator connected him with his new liquor warehouse supervisor, Norman Dinter.

"Mr. Moran, I'm sorry to interrupt what you're doing, but I had us written down for a meeting this morning. I called yesterday afternoon; do you remember, sir?"

"I got tied up here, Norman," he lied. "What was it you wanted? Hell, better yet, let me come on over to your office as we planned. I'll be there in half an hour." Peter looked out his window at the beautiful morning, "I've got to get out of this place and get some fresh air. Maybe the sunshine'll perk me up a bit."

At the warehouse, Moran greeted several of his employees who were busy loading shipments to be delivered. He noted that several of the wagons, which had been idled by the slowdown, were now being stored in the back yards. Six men were working on this morning, four fewer than the ten who were required for the loading only three weeks before.

Norman Dinter welcomed his boss with a handshake but wore a serious expression on his darkly bearded face. "You probably knew about this, Mr. Moran, but with me being new here and all, it kinda caught me by surprise," Dinter said.

The two men went into Dinter's office. "What's up, Norm? What did I probably know about?" Peter frowned.

"The Grand Rapids distributorship, sir. I got a letter from Mr. Allison, at Fitger's in Duluth, yesterday afternoon. It said as of the first of next month a new distributorship will be opening over there. The same kinda thing as what happened in Virginia."

Peter fumed. "That sonofabitch! No, this is news to me. We're getting a squeeze job here, Norman. We're getting fucked again."

"I was just looking at a map here, Mr. Moran." Dinter had the large chart spread across his desk. He pointed to Grand Rapids which he had circled in a black ring to this left. "It would seem to me, sir, that from Grand Rapids here, Allison's new place will probably sell both beer and booze to Coleraine, Bovey, Marble, Taconite . . . probably even to Nashwauk; that's a pretty big chunk of our territory."

Peter sat back in his chair scratching his head. "What do you propose we do, Norm? I can't think of anything. Allison is fucking us, for sure, but it's a free country. Dog eat dog, I guess."

"I've done some checking around, Mr. Moran, and made some phone calls before you got here this morning. I like what you said about dog eat dog, sir, because that's what I wanted to tell you."

Dinter had called the Grain Belt Brewery in Minneapolis, as well as a few other large liquor retailers in the Twin Cities. If Moran was willing to make a large order, and pay up front, Dinter could get both the beer and liquor from the Cities at half the cost of what they were paying to Allison. "I think Grain Belt is a hellava beer, Mr. Moran, a lot better than Fitgers. It should sell real well up here."

Dinter could tell he had his boss's attention as Moran leaned forward in the chair he had been slumped into only moments before. The new supervisor explained how he might be able to price both the liquor and the beer at a huge discount and still show a profit of about twenty per cent. He showed Moran his figures on the large notepad he held. "I can't imagine why any bar between Aurora on the east, and even Grand Rapids, wouldn't jump at these figures. Hell, they'd be crazy not to. They'd come out money ahead just like we would, sir."

Moran smiled widely for the first time in days. It was good to be talking with a man who had a good head on his shoulders. "Can we get something exclusive from Grain Belt? A contract that gives us the sole distribution for the Iron Range, Norm?"

"Yes, sir, we can. I asked about that as well. All we have to do is guarantee our orders for one year."

"Damn, let's do it then. We'll get our prices out everywhere, get the orders on the books, and start hiring some people around here." Peter was enthusiastic. "Can you get the ball rolling, Norm?"

"I sure can, Mr. Moran; there's only one thing, sir." Dinter looked embarrassed. "I don't have the money in my budget for the order they would need. We'd need about fifteen thousand up front. I've only got about three thousand, sir."

Where was Senia when he needed her advice the most? Peter did not know how much money he had to invest in this venture. His financial situation must have been detailed in the reports she had given him before she left. He had been too lazy to even look at the files, and now he would have to talk to Sweeny about it. He knew that his lumber business was only marginally profitable these days, that his liquor receipts were down from what they had been only months before, and the hotel was going to be in the red for some time to come.

"Let me figure this out, Norm. I'll get back to you by tomorrow. Thanks for doing a great job on this. I really appreciate it. Take your wife out to dinner at the hotel, and charge it to me. Okay?"

Moran left the warehouse with a bounce to his step. He would find the money somewhere and give Allison a dose of his own medicine. He recalled Senia's frequent caution about Jerry Sweeny and remembered how McIntosh mistrusted Sweeny as well. Now his hotel manager had all of

Peter's financial reports. Peter would have to give Senia a call at the bank and find out what to do. "God," he said to himself, "how am I going to make it without Miss Smith?"

Claude Atkinson met with the village council President, Elwood Trembart, behind a closed door in the Hibbing attorney's office.

"I can't believe what I'm hearing, Claude." Trembart concealed his elation over the editor's story with a serious face. "Can't say I would put such a thing beyond Moran. He wanted that hotel badly, that much I'm positive about, but to go to that extreme? Cleary's allegations will blow up this town, Claude. But, we've got to move on this; there is no alternative."

"Elwood, I know you are one of Peter's best friends; I hate to dump this horrible mess on your desk," Claude apologized. Although the reporter knew about most things going on in Hibbing, he was not aware of the rift between Peter and Elwood. The land matter was something that had been kept effectively under wraps by Trembart.

"It's got to go to the grand jury, Claude. With Cleary's sworn testimony there will be an indictment, no doubt about that. Have you been in touch with Harold Markman in St. Paul on this?" Trembart asked, seeing a noose tightening around Moran's neck.

"He was the next person on my list, El." Claude explained his curiosity about Markman's 'sabotage' comment shortly after the fatal incident at the hotel.

"Let's get him on the phone right now. Maybe he can free up some time this week and get up to Hibbing." Trembart had the operator connect him with the architect's office in St. Paul. "Somehow, I don't think Harold is going to be surprised by any of this. He'll certainly have some interesting things to tell to a grand jury."

Senia and Steven had been invited to Mary's house for dinner on this Tuesday evening. Along with Tony, they would celebrate Senia's new job, and belatedly, Tony's new business, also.

Steven had been staying over at Bruno Moscatelli's house more often during the past two weeks. He had been able to see Senia after work on most days and had been with her almost the entire weekend while working at Tony's office on Saturday, the ball game, and parade on Sunday afternoon. The more time he spent with Senia, the more he respected her intelligence and understood her ambitions. Steven enjoyed conversation, and Senia had a wide range of interests that he found stimulating. He learned about her education, her family, and her responsibilities while working for Moran. Senia's independent spirit intrigued him and often brought memories of Timo to mind.

Senia learned on her first day at the bank that Harvey Goldberg had more in mind than having her function simply as a loan officer. She would be acting more as a junior vice president or assistant to Goldberg, working on bank investment strategies. She explained her excitement to Steven and Mary as the three of them waited for Tony's arrival.

"It is so challenging, Steven, to be speculating on areas of the economy that might be growing, and how it's all interrelated," Senia said.

"The bank uses our money to make money for themselves; isn't that right, Senia? If they make good investments, I would think that they can give us better interest rates on our money." Mary caught on to things quickly. "Luigi has a good business sense, and we've talked about some stock investments he's made," she added.

"Since meeting Senia, I've come to believe that if the mine and railroad workers would put a small share of their wages into a common fund with a manager investing their savings for them, then they would share in the growth of the economy. As it is now, only those who have money make money. The wealthy prosper, but the working man never really gets ahead," Steven offered his insight. "I'd enjoy doing that kind of thing for the mine workers to help them ensure a better life for their children."

Tony arrived with the two loaves of fresh Italian bread which Mary had asked him to pick up on his way to her house. The pot roast and garden vegetables filled the kitchen with a marvelous aroma, and everybody was starved. Senia and Steven had brought two bottles of champagne for the occasion.

"Let's have a toast before we share our meal," Steven suggested as he popped the cork from a chilled bottle. Pouring some into glasses and passing them around the table, he toasted, "To Senia on her new job and new life, to Tony's new business and future success, and to our lovely hostess, the second most beautiful girl in the world!" Steven laughed at his reference. All of them brought their glasses together.

"Hear, hear . . . to beautiful Senia, my wonderful uncle, and Mary, the woman I love!" Tony offered his toast in good spirit.

Senia stood to offer a toast of her own. "To the happiness of Mary and Tony, may they have a wonderful life together . . . and to my man, Steven, who has made me so very happy."

Steven smiled at Senia, "It's you who has made me happy."

Mary flushed, knowing that it was now her turn to offer a toast, "I am so happy to have each of you at my table tonight. We are all immigrants to this place of so much opportunity. Let me offer a toast to our families back home in Slovenia, Finland, and Italy, to those friends and relatives who gave us support in our decisions to come to this country, and to this country that has become our new home." Mary paused emotionally. "We all have so much in common, don't we, and so much to look forward to?" Mary choked back tears at the memories past and the consuming happiness of the moment.

"I hope my pot roast is better than my speech," Mary said as she dabbed at her eyes. "Must be the onions."

Tony was on his feet and gave Mary an affectionate hug; then he kissed her forehead. "We think of our families all the time, Mary. What you've said is as beautiful as it is true." Then he whispered into her hair over her ear, "I love you."

Steven and Senia left after the dishes were done. After goodbyes and thank yous, Tony lingered at the door. "Mary, will you help me with something I've been working on for the past several weeks?" His voice was unnaturally tight.

"Anything at all, you know that, my love. You're frowning, though, what's the matter?" She stepped in front of him and put her arms around his waist.

"Will you help me design a house? I'm working on a plan for Senia, but I've got so many other ideas swimming in my head. Ideas about a house of my. . . . make that . . . *our* own."

Mary's eyes sparked at what she hoped his next words might be. "Goodness yes, I'd love to," was all that she could say.

"Part of my lateness in getting here tonight was another stop that I made," Tony tried awkwardly to explain. "I picked this up." He took a small, white piece of linen from his shirt pocket, and handed it to Mary. "There's a question that goes with it."

Mary opened the linen and saw the gold ring inside. Tears formed in her eyes. She looked up at Tony then pulled her body into his. Mary felt Tony's gentle kisses on her head as she clung to him.

"Mary, will you be my wife?" Tony whispered.

'Under the Dust Cloth in the Drawer'

On Monday mornings, Art Schmitz always left home a few minutes earlier than usual for his supervisory job at the West Duluth shipyards. Strolling down 57th Avenue, he waved at three strangers in a wagon coming toward him up the street. "Good morning, fellows," he greeted without giving them a second thought.

"God damn!" Denis Moran cursed after Schmitz was out of earshot. "He's seen us, Sam. Now what'n the fuck we gonna do?"

"We're gonna do exactly what we came here to do. He wasn't payin us no attention anyhow," Lavalle snapped at his nervous partner. "Now, let's just go up the alley as we planned and get the kid," Lavalle said looking toward Bernie at the reins of the horse.

Behind the Schmitz house, all three men pulled bandanas over their faces. Lavalle and Denis raced across the back yard to the rear door of the house. The door was locked.

"I expected this," Lavalle lied to Denis. "I'll break the window and open it from out here." Lavalle pulled his hand inside his shirt sleeve and smashed the pane. Inside he found the door handle and turned it. The door released, but an out of reach hook-latch kept it from opening. "Fuck this, let's go around the front."

Denis followed Lavalle around the house and onto the front porch. He was panicking. "Let's get out of here before it's too late!" Denis pleaded. "I'm scared. We ain't done nothin wrong yet; let's get the hell . . ."

Lavalle had already pushed open the front door and was stepping into the living room. A terrified Mrs. Schmitz was on the phone, "Yes, operator, the police."

"Hang it up, lady!" Lavalle commanded. "Put down the phone or you're gonna get yourself hurt."

"I have no money in the house," Sarah pleaded, dropping the phone.

"I'll tie her up, Denis. You grab the kid." Lavalle pulled two strands of rope from his trouser pocket and dragged Sarah Schmitz into the kitchen where he had spotted some chairs. Sarah flailed against the powerful man, scratched at his eyes, and pulled down his face covering. Lavalle cussed, twisted her arm behind her back, and forced her into the chair. He needed help to subdue and tie up the struggling woman. "Denis, com 'on and give me some help!" he shouted.

Denis stood in the hallway with the child in his arms. "What'sa matter, Sam? I got the kid here."

"Help me tie up this bitch." Sam put a lock on her neck while he tried to hold Sarah in the chair.

Denis set the boy on the floor and ran to Sam's aid. "Hold her arms back 'til I can get her wrists; then stuff a rag in her mouth."

Five minutes after entering the house, the two kidnappers pushed open the back door and raced to the wagon where Bernie was waiting. "Get goin, Bernie. Stay in the alley 'til we get to Grand Avenue, just like we planned."

Bernice Randall, from across the street, called the police when she saw the two men break into the front door of the Schmitz home. Martin Isaacson, the next door neighbor, also called the police when he heard the window smash and noticed the stranger waiting with a wagon in the alley. When he returned to his window, Isaacson saw the men running across the back yard with little Kevin in their arms.

Arriving about fifteen minutes later, the police untied Sarah Schmitz. She was hysterical. "They stole my son! They can't be too far. Please . . . go and find them," Sarah pleaded in short breaths.

"I've got five cops out there looking already, ma'am. They went down the alley toward Grand. We'll find 'em. Don't worry about that now. Just try to calm yourself down a bit. Let me get some descriptions, and anything else you can remember will be helpful," Police Captain Lewis Jakola held her trembling hands.

"The bigger man was called Denis," she explained. "He had a red beard under the thing he used to cover his face," she sobbed. "The other one was Sam; I got a good look at him. I pulled off his mask." Sarah described Sam Lavalle's every feature.

The three men pulled in behind Lily Brown's house on Raleigh Street. Eight year old Sadie Roberts was jumping rope on the narrow sidewalk in the back yard. As Sam and Denis ran to the back door with the screaming baby, they almost stepped on little Sadie, scaring her half to death. Sadie, crying from fright, ran into the house behind the two men to tell her mother what had just happened.

Sam took Kevin into the basement while hollering to Denis. "Get Lily to com'on down here and take care of this kid. He's screaming his damn little head off."

Taking the wagon to the end of the alley, Ducette tied the horse to a lamppost. Then he headed toward the ore docks where he could hitch a ride on one of the ore trains heading back to Hibbing. Although he was exhilarated over the kidnapping, Bernie was already antsy to get home and to start his fire.

Lily Brown fed Kevin some warm pabulum she purchased at the corner grocery store the night before. She sat in the corner of the empty coal bin feeding the boy and delighting in her maternal experience. "Ain't he just the cutest little thing?" she giggled at the two men sitting somberly at the table sipping their beer.

"Ya, he's a peach, all right. Just don't go gettin yourself too attached. Know what I mean? Just feed 'im and keep 'im quiet. That's all ya gotta do, Lil," Lavalle said.

"We fucked it up, Sam. I know damn well we did," Denis Moran was a bundle of nerves. "She saw yer face good. D'ya think we're gonna get caught, Sam? Maybe we otta get outta here."

"We're back here with the kid, just like we planned, so shut up with all the worry stuff. Now we just gotta wait it out for a while. That's all. Your brother gets his ransom letter today, and we get our money on Thursday.

Then we split from Duluth, maybe head down to the Cities for a while." Sam reached in his pocket for his tabacco, finding an empty pouch. "Shit, I'm outta tabakka; you got any Denis? I really need ta roll me a cigrette."

"I don't smoke. You otta know that by now. I tol ya before that my pa smoked and it kilt 'im." Denis was agitated. "I'll go get ya some, though. I gotta get out and get me some fresh air anyhow. I'll pick up sommore beer while I'm at it." Denis got up from the table, climbed the stairs, and left through the back door.

Sally Roberts, Sadie's mother, watched from behind her kitchen curtains as Denis Moran headed down the alley. She had called the police from a neighbor's phone a few minutes before and told them about the baby in the cellar below her apartment.

When Denis returned a half an hour later, he saw several police officers in Lily's back yard. He tossed the bag of beer behind a fence and started running as fast as he could.

Peter Moran's maid, Mildred Graham, knocked on the library door, then entered with Monday's mail. She placed several envelopes in the basket on the corner of his desk, curtsied as she always did, and left the room without so much as a hello. Peter only glanced at the basket which was heaped with three days' worth of unopened mail. The first letter from Lavalle was in his stack.

He thought about having a short glass of whiskey before making his phone call but overcame the impulse. He had not had a drink in four days and was confident this morning that he had kicked the habit. He chose a cigar from his humidor instead.

"Miss Smith . . . I mean, Mrs. Arola, please," Peter had the bank's receptionist on the line.

"Mrs. Arola, may I help you?" Senia said in her familiar accent.

Peter had a rush of memory. Senia had only been away for two weeks, but he missed her presence terribly. "Mrs. Arola, Peter Moran here." His words sounded strange and awkward. "How have you been?"

"Well, Mr. Moran! Good to hear your voice. I'm just fine, thank you for asking. Busy, but fine. What can I do for you this morning?" Senia asked cheerfully.

"Have you got a few minutes to talk right now?"

"A few, but I have a meeting with Mr. Goldberg in about twenty minutes."

Peter gave her a quick overview of his conversation with Norman Dinter at the liquor warehouse. Dinter had reworked his numbers and spoken several times with the Grain Belt people. In order to get a September shipment, Peter would have to send the brewers in Minneapolis a check in the amount of fourteen thousand five hundred dollars. "So what do you think? Miss . . . Senia, I don't care what's right or not. I've gotta call you Senia when we're on the phone. Anyhow, would you advise me to go ahead? I mean, I've got enough money in my bank account to do this, don't I?"

Senia did not answer his questions for a moment. Why would he be asking her if he had enough money? Her reports had given him a complete breakdown of all his assets, accounts receivable and payable, monthly revenues, and her projections as well. "Do you have my reports nearby at the moment, Mr. Moran?"

"No, Senia, I'm sorry, I passed them along to Sweeny to look over," Peter apologized, wrinkling his forehead in anticipation of what her reaction would be.

"You did what? Sweeny has my reports? This is very upsetting to me, Mr. Moran. Did you read them over before giving them to him?" Senia was furious.

"Sorry again. You know me, Senia. I'm not much good at financial reports. It takes a special kind of person to understand . . . anyhow, I'm not one of them. I take it from your tone that I made a mistake."

"A mistake! That sir, is an understatement. In those reports I outlined exactly how Mr. Sweeny is skimming your accounts. Not only that, but I raised serious questions about all your businesses insurance policies. With the information I gave to you, Sweeny has a blueprint on how he might cover his . . . excuse me, I almost swore. Mr. Moran, you have some problems." Senia looked at her clock. "I'm sorry, sir, but I have a meeting. Let me get back to you later, okay?"

Peter slumped in his chair. What was he to do? He told Dinter he would get back to him this morning so that the order could be placed on time. "What the hell, I've got to have enough money for this. I'm not broke by a long shot," he said to the empty room. Peter would write a personal check and deliver it to Dinter.

Jerry Sweeny told his assistant that he would not be taking any calls that day. "If Moran calls, tell him I'm at a hotel convention in Virginia for the day. Or, better yet, make it a convention in St. Cloud, and tell him I'll be back on Wednesday."

Sweeny thought to himself, "Thank God, Moran has not read Miss Smith's reports." In her analysis of Sweeny's financial management of hotel affairs, Miss Smith had disclosed each and every one of his diversions. She was brilliant; Moran was not. Sweeny had convinced Moran to retire the hotel debt as fast as possible. Toward that end, seventy five per cent of the profits from each of Moran's three taverns were designated for hotel loan reduction. Sweeny had been skimming half of those revenues, putting the cash in his office safe. His records showed twelve thousand dollars paid to Moran's liquor warehouse account while, in fact, that money was in his own bank account in Minneapolis. Sweeny's larceny from the hotel had netted him about six thousand dollars because his reports to Moran were always twenty per cent under actual receipts. In addition, the hotel's insurance reported to be at five hundred thousand dollars was really fifty thousand. Money skimmed from the false insurance records lined Sweeny's pockets with another three thousand dollars.

Miss Smith was Moran's personal financial advisor, and Sweeny thanked his lucky stars that he had convinced Moran to let him handle the hotel without her constant auditing. Miss Smith protested but lost. She was, however, too loyal to Moran to allow Sweeny's embezzlements to go unnoticed. If Moran had listened to her cautions earlier, Sweeny would have been fired, maybe even jailed, months before. As it was, Sweeny was a very rich man on this Monday morning.

"You are in St.Cloud this morning, sir," his secretary said from the doorway. "I thought you might like to know, because Mr. Moran just called. He asked me to reach you there and have you call him as soon as possible."

There was an afternoon train running from Virginia to Duluth, then arriving late in Minneapolis. Sweeny realized he had tempted fate for too long already, and that his larceny would soon be discovered by Moran.

Miss Smith's reports were burning in his small office fireplace. He had enough time to get over to the Virginia depot, board the train, and leave the Iron Range once and for all. His bags were already packed and loaded on the back of a carriage he had rented. Fourteen thousand in cash was in his briefcase. He stuffed some personal effects from his office into a satchel and bade farewell to his career as manager of the HOTEL MORAN.

Sweeny left the hotel through the back door, taking one last look at the towering hotel, before heading down Third Avenue east to Virginia. He would be traveling as Mr. John Smith; the irony amused him.

Mrs. Graham informed her employer of Mr. Sweeny's convention in St. Cloud and Father Foley's three calls already that morning. She said Foley told her his calls were urgent. Peter dismissed her suggestion to return the priest's calls. Waiting for Senia to call him back after her meeting, he resisted having a drink.

Senia called shortly before noon. "Mr. Moran, I've got your bank account records in front of me. You wanted to know if you could write a check for fourteen thousand five hundred today. Wasn't that the figure?"

"Yes it was. That's no problem, is it? I've got a personal check written out already," gripping the phone at his question. How could he have allowed himself to become so ignorant of his own finances?

"You paid off the balance of your house mortgage in March, and there's the Alice Location property you bought in April. Both were drawn from your personal account, sir. These two transactions alone came to over nine thousand dollars. You paid cash for the Buick and wrote a check for the fountain in the city park . . . so many frivolous things." Senia groaned over the decisions that she had advised against. "I had everything in those reports, Mr. Moran. Everything! You will just have to get them back from Mr. Sweeny."

"He's out of town today, but I told his secretary to have him call me as soon as he can."

"Somehow, I have my doubts that those reports will ever see the light of day again. As I told you, I raised some very serious questions about Sweeny's transactions at the hotel in those reports. I didn't use the word *embezzlement*, but I could have."

"I'll get to the bottom of it, Senia. Anyhow, about the liquor money, what do you think?"

"Your current checking balance is two thousand eight hundred sixty-four dollars, and you have eighty two hundred in savings. That's a lot of money, but most of your assets are locked up in your businesses. You've never kept much of your money fluid. If I remember correctly, you keep about a thousand in petty cash in your library safe at home. All together you've got over twelve thousand dollars. My advice, Mr. Moran, is that you take out a loan. That won't be a problem. In fact, we can get the paperwork done this afternoon. I can do it myself for you if you'd like."

Peter was agitated. "I know I can borrow money any time I want to. I'm looking at a check I wrote from my account right now. I'll have to tear it up I guess. What I'd really like to know is whether you think this Grain Belt idea is a good one. If you do, I'll borrow the money today."

Senia reconsidered the proposal from their earlier conversation. "I think that your Mr. Dinter is a good thinker, sir. My only concern is that Mr. Allison in Duluth is not going to sit back and let you beat him out of his market. He'll find a way to underprice you, even if he has to lose a lot of money in the process. You must be prepared for some stiff competition with Allison, and it may go on for months." Senia had remarkable business insights. "Another option is to stick with the liquor territory you have right now and make some stock investments with your liquid resources. The national recession is tapering off now, so there's money to be made on the market."

"Damn it, anyhow. I thought you might make this decision easy for me. Now, I don't know what to do. Let me think about what you've said. I'll call you back. By the way, can I offer you a job here at twice what you're making at the bank?"

"You've made that offer before, Mr. Moran, and I'm flattered. You know my answer to that, don't you, sir?"

Harold Markman arrived in Hibbing on the Monday morning train. The portly St. Paul businessman was scheduled to meet with Elwood Trembart and Claude Atkinson that afternoon. Harold's gut feeling about his Grande Hotel project had always been that Moran somehow sabotaged the operation. He had, however, kept his mouth shut all this time because he had no evidence to support his theory. Now, it appeared, an investigation would finally be conducted. Trembart asked Harold to try and find the names of the two brick layers who worked with the deceased, Billy Herrick. Harold found the names in old payroll records, but he had no luck in locating either man.

Claude Atkinson introduced Cleary to both Markman and Trembart when the four gathered in Trembart's law office.

"I've asked Mr. Cleary to tell you gentlemen exactly what he told me last week. Isn't that right, Stan?" Claude tried to relax the big man sitting next to him by using his first name. He noticed that Cleary was already sweating profusely.

"Yessir, I told ya that. But I never talked to no lawyer person before today, and I'm kinda nervous, kin ya unnerstan that?" Cleary regarded the intimidating men in suits. "It was all true, what I tol Mr. Akonsin before; I swore to him it was." He wiped at his forehead with a dirty handkerchief.

"Don't be afraid of us, Mr. Cleary," Elwood assured the troubled man. "All a lawyer wants is the truth. We're on your side."

Stan Cleary told the story of Moran's cash payment and his instructions that Cleary was to "make trouble at the hotel." He explained what had happened to Markman and Trembart in almost the same words he used when first telling Atkinson. "So ya see, I only done what Mr. Moran wanted. I was doin somethin wrong like I tol ya. It wasn't all his fault, but he's gonna say he didn't pay me or nothin."

"Did you put the money Mr. Moran gave you into a bank account, Mr. Cleary?" Trembart asked.

"Yessir, I done that, at first I mean, but then I took it out again to pay those guys I told ya about. Was that a wrong thing for me ta do?"

"No, that was the smartest thing you could have done, Mr. Cleary. Do you have your bank records?" Trembart was smiling. He would be able to trace the Moran payment by locating Cleary's deposit at the bank. Cleary's own records were not necessary.

"My wife Bessy does all that, sir. She's a perty smart ole gal about money. I didn't tell her nothin about this money though. She'da asked me 'bout it, she always does that, ya know."

After Cleary answered a few more questions, Claude sensed that they had all the necessary information. The newsman stood, thanked Stan for giving them his version of the story, and shook Cleary's huge hand. He pressed a ten dollar bill into the sweaty palm, "I'll get back to you later, Stan. The three of us have some talking to do right now. Remember, we are keeping this among ourselves for now."

"Thanks, Mr. Akonsin, I shut up about it before like I said I would, didn't even tell Bessy. But you guys ain't said nothin about the trouble in it for me yet. Spose I'm goin to jail, ain't I?"

"We will do everything we can to help you, Mr. Cleary. Turning state's evidence will go well for you when this gets to court," Trembart said as he stood up behind his desk.

Claude Atkinson escorted Stan Cleary to the front door. "Thanks for the money, Mr. Akonsin, d'ya think it all went pretty well in there with those guys?"

"You did fine, Stan. If this goes to a grand jury, just tell your story the same way as you did today. Okay?" Claude gave Cleary an assuring pat on the back as the man stepped out the door.

When Claude returned, the three men sat down to discuss the next step. Trembart told them that he would have the grand jury assemble on Thursday at the courthouse. "The instructions for the grand jury will be to investigate the fatality at the Grande Hotel work site. We will not be going after Moran, specifically, until the grand jury has heard all of the testimony."

"What do you want from me?" Markman asked. "I wasn't able to locate the other two workers."

Trembart stroked his face. "Harold, we will need a detailed report on every disruption at your construction site. Late deliveries, substandard materials, altered specifications, anything you can find."

"I brought all of that information along with me, as you asked me to, Elwood. What about the threats Peter Moran made when I first met with him about his interest in buying my hotel?" Markman remembered that unsavory meeting very well.

"The grand jury will have a lot of questions, and you'll be able to say everything and anything you want. I think we're going to nail him on this one." Trembart had a crooked smile, then realized the bitterness in what he had just said. Atkinson stared at him with a peculiar expression.

Trembart recovered. "We're going to get whoever it was. Billy Herrick left a widow and kids, a tragedy, as we all know. Peter will get a fair hearing. Hell, maybe this Cleary story won't hold up. He's not the most impressive guy in town."

"Elwood, it looks as if you're carrying the ball on this. Is there anything I should be doing?" Atkinson asked. He was still intrigued about Trembart's comments regarding Moran. There was some bad blood between the attorney and Moran that he didn't know about. "If the grand jury is going to hear this matter on Thursday, I'll write something for tomorrow's paper. I've always done that."

"That would be appropriate, Claude. There isn't any *if.* The grand jury *will* meet on Thursday!" Trembart assured him.

Claude thought for a moment. He would be as fair as he could be with Peter Moran, regardless of his belief in Cleary's story. "I will call Peter this afternoon. I'm not going to let him read about a grand jury investigation in my paper without having been forewarned. He deserves every opportunity to prepare for the subpoena that will probably be delivered tomorrow."

"You go ahead and do what you think is right, Claude. I have the greatest respect for your integrity. Now, I'll get in touch with both of you as soon as I get any more information on proceedings. Thanks, both of you, we're only doing our civic duty. The truth about what happened in Herrick's accident will come out when this is all over and done with." Trembart walked to the door with the two men and shook hands.

Peter was having a light lunch in his kitchen when Mildred introduced police captain Ole Nord from the nearby hallway, "Officer Nord to see you sir."

Peter looked up in surprise at the powerfully built cop. "I didn't do it, Captain!" he raised his arms and laughed at his timely remark.

The cop held his hat in his huge hands in front of him. "I've been asked by a Father Foley to give you some news, sir. He's been trying to reach you all morning." Nord explained the abduction of Kevin Schmitz earlier that morning. He had checked out the story with the Duluth police department before coming to Moran's house. "They've got a guy named Sam Lavalle in custody right now. Also a woman by the name of Lily Brown, sir. The police down there are looking for two other guys who were involved but haven't located them yet. The Schmitz boy is just fine they tell me."

Peter listened in disbelief. Sam Lavalle? Peter regarded Nord, "The boy is fine. You're sure of that, Ole?"

"Yes sir. He's back home with his parents right now. I don't know why this priest wanted you to know about it, sir. I'm just doing what he asked me to do, ya know. Anyhow, this priest Foley, he says that you can call him if you need any more information."

Peter thanked the officer, and told him that he would contact the priest that afternoon. "I know the boy's family, Ole, good friends of mine. My heart goes out to them, of course."

After the cop had left his house, Moran contemplated the name from years ago. Sam Lavalle was a pimp. Peter had met Barbara Chevalier through him at the Kitchi Gammi Club. He remembered his distaste for Lavalle and his demand that the Club fire him. What was this kidnapping business all about? Peter racked his brain but was unable to make any connection between Lavalle and Art Schmitz. Could Lavalle have been targeting *him* in this scheme? Peter wondered. Nord had reported that two men were still at large. Peter would talk to Foley later.

Claude would not give his information to Peter over the phone. The reporter called him at home and made an appointment for one o'clock. "Something serious, Pete," was all Claude would say. Peter suspected that Claude had picked up the kidnapping story from the Duluth press and had somehow found Moran's name connected with the news. He wondered if Foley had told the Duluth police about Moran's paternity. "That's nobody's fucking business!" he cussed out loud after hanging up the phone.

Peter decided to wait until after he'd talked with Claude before returning the calls Foley had made.

Shortly before one, Claude was escorted into Peter's library. The early afternoon sun streamed into the room, highlighting the richly colored Persian rugs. Peter was standing at the sideboard, looking out into the gardens, when Atkinson entered. "Is it too early for a light one, Claude?" Peter invited as he held a bottle of Irish whiskey in his hand. "I'm going to have another one myself."

"I never drink before five, Pete, but today I'm going to make an exception. Three fingers will be just about right." Claude came over to the bar to accept the glass. "Nice library. Do you do a lot of reading, Pete?" Claude surveyed the shelves of books.

"Not enough, Claude." Peter took a heavy swallow enjoying the warmth as the whiskey made its way down. "If you see anything you like, feel free . . ."

"Let's sit down, Pete. I've got some bad news for you. There'll be a story in my paper tomorrow that's going to really raise some hell in Hibbing. I want you to know everything that I know at this point. If you have any comments for the article, I want to give you a fair shake. Fair enough?"

"The Duluth thing, Claude?" Peter anticipated the reporter's story.

Claude looked perplexed. "Duluth thing? No, I don't know what that might be. Is it newsworthy, Pete?"

Peter was mistaken and felt relief. He recovered with another angle. "Some liquor pricing competition, between me and Allison in Duluth, that's all. I thought it might be something you picked up, Claude. I guess it's some other story you're talking about."

Claude's expression was grave. "Do you remember that interview we had back when you just purchased your hotel from Markman in October of '06 as I remember? Anyhow, it was just after that accident at the hotel where a guy named Billy Herrick was killed on the construction site."

Peter felt dryness in his mouth and swallowed the remainder of his whiskey. "Vaguely, Claude. I'm not much on dates, but if you say it was in October, I'd never argue the point."

"Well, Pete, this Stan Cleary fellow, we talked about him you might remember, at the ballpark, three weeks ago yesterday. Cleary has come forward with some pretty powerful allegations about the hotel accident. I've talked with the man on two separate occasions myself, and I've passed his story on to Elwood Trembart."

Peter felt like an avalanche was about to fall on him, but he would avoid it somehow. "Cleary? He's an imbecile, Claude. You've talked to him, so you must you know what I mean. He's pissed at me for firing him. He told me he was going to get back at me, whatever it took him to do it. Downright threatened me, Claude. There can't be any story in whatever he's told you. It's all bullshit."

"What's bullshit, Pete?"

"Anything he's told you is bullshit. He's got it coming out of his ears. That's why I fired him. He's dumb, and he's a liar to boot." Peter's voice rose. "If he has smeared my character in any way, I'll sue the sonofabitch! What kinda crap did he give you, Claude?"

Claude allowed a few seconds for Peter to cool down. Then he told Cleary's story in explicit detail. "This morning Cleary gave the identical story to Elwood Trembart and Harold Markman. Trembart has called for a grand jury investigation of the incident for Thursday, and both Cleary and Markman will give their testimony."

Peter could not avoid this avalanche. His enemies were out to have his ass. "Cleary has threatened me with his revenge; Markman hates my guts—always has; and Elwood Trembart has been fucking me over for months. Surely you can find some other people who want to get their pound of flesh, too, Claude. There's a lot of envy and petty jealousy out there, and I've stepped on some toes over the years, but this conspiracy against me. . . ?" Peter shook his head.

Claude felt bad for Moran. What Peter said was probably true. He might find out what was between Trembart and Moran, but that was another story. This was far more than sour grapes; of that fact he was certain. "Will you give me something for the article, Pete? I'm going to be putting a story together this afternoon. Elwood has set the grand jury hearing for Thursday, and I'm certain you will be getting a subpoena to appear before them."

"I'm not allowed to have an attorney in a grand jury hearing, am I, Claude . . . just me and them?" Peter asked a question to which he knew the answer.

"I'm afraid not. No attorneys— unless or until there's a trial."

Subdued by the prospects, Peter rubbed at the sharp pain throbbing in his temples. "Something for the paper, huh. How about Peter Moran denies any and all allegations? He says that it is simply a matter of character assassination. Will you print that, Claude?"

"Most assuredly, Peter, word for word."

Peter slumped over his elbows on the desk with his face cradled in his hands. He squeezed his eyes closed and massaged his temples. People's faces rolled behind his eyes, laughing faces. He was in his Shamrock Saloon on a Friday afternoon, drinking with his buddies Elwood Trembart, Con O'Gara, Tom Godfrey, and Fred Bennett. Jim McIntosh joined them later with news of Peter's purchase of the Grande Hotel. They all toasted triumphantly. Irish Pete, as his friends called him back in those days, had the Irish Luck. He remembered how they all drank to his luck that night. Old Riley Gillespie, the mine shovel operator, was a drinking companion, too. Peter had friends all over Hibbing. He pictured being with his friends at the Kitchi Gammi Club in Duluth, how his quick humor always amused the guys.

Always there for him was his oldest and closest friend, Jim. Mac was more than any brother could hope to be. Jim . . .

He remembered the face of beautiful Barbara Chevalier. What fun they had together in the night clubs of Duluth! The birthday cake surprise in his hotel room. Barbara's giggle while hiding in the closet. The cake dropping when she kissed him. In another flashback, Peter was holding his son Kevin on his lap in the Schmitz living room. The teddy bear so amused the child. Then he and Barbara and Kevin were playing happily together in his back yard. Kevin was trying to throw a baseball to his father while Barbara laughed, encouraging their son. The Moran family enjoying a gorgeous summer day.

The night the entire business community had come together at the Power Theater at his summons slipped into his mind. He strolled across the stage like a Napoleon that night. He was *the man* in Hibbing back then. His audience ate out of his hands with his stirring speech on economic development, his good humor drawing applause. Everyone praised his commitment to making his town a better place to live and do business. Yet, in retrospect, the grand opening of his hotel was truly his finest hour, his crowning glory. He had organized an entire weekend of celebration for all people regardless of their circumstance in life. He provided festivities on a scale the city had never experienced before. Hibbing was, undeniably, Peter Moran's town back then.

Hibbing. Moran's town. Would Daly have been proud of his accomplishment? Peter held a deep remorse that his father had not been a part of these past years. His eyes moistened, "I loved ya, pa. We had something special back when I was your sidekick. Didn't we?"

The handsome face of Tony Zoretek stole into his thoughts. Tony at the lumber yard, in his library, washing his new car. He imagined beautiful Mary Samora, walking by his side in Mesaba Park, then sipping wine in his hotel's lounge later that Saturday. Senia, bright, efficient, and lovely Senia. Miss Smith, as she would always be in his memory, sitting out on the patio in his flowered gardens.

All these people whose lives had meshed magically with his own. His life was in harmony with the orchestra that was his past. Sometimes he was the maestro, at other times, a sweet violin adding its singular, rich tones to the music that was everywhere around him. How quickly his symphony had become a hollow, discordant noise which only turned his former friends away from him.

Was this his darkest hour? Peter's reverie swept the past. When Daly left his office and Hibbing? Barbara's death? Watching Mary's house in the cold, late night rain? Ruptured friendships with Jim, Tony, Senia? He'd had his share of pain. Yet, through all of these episodes, his reputation in the community had somehow remained untarnished. Perhaps his worst experience had just occurred . . . when Claude entered his library only an hour before.

What lay ahead? Had he already walked over his pinnacle in this life God had given him? Was it downhill from here? Peter touched despair with black thoughts of the future. He tried to see something down the road which might inspire the enthusiasm that had always driven him in the past. Nothing came to his tormented thoughts. All was behind him now. "What is there *to bless* for all that I've done? What is *to blame* for this empty life I have now?" But deep inside he knew one word could answer both questions. *Ambition!* "I've got everything . . . and I've got nothing," he mumbled.

Peter lifted his head from his hands. The clock read three. Atkinson's visit was again a reality. What would he do about Cleary's charges? What kind of case would his adversaries make against him? Would it simply be Peter's word against that of Cleary? Who might he find to help him? Who might lie in his behalf before a grand jury? Could he somehow pin the 'accident' on Sweeny? Had Markman's former architect know anything about Cleary's activity? He doubted that. No, Peter realized; he was all alone in this moment—as alone in his life as he was in this room.

He rubbed his temples trying in vain to rid himself of the headache still pounding mercilessly. He was supposed to call Foley this afternoon. Sweeny was supposed to call him back from St. Cloud.

Peter called the hotel. Sweeny, he was told again, would not be back until Wednesday. What the hell was he doing in St. Cloud? Why wasn't he returning Moran's calls?

More than half of the whiskey bottle was gone. Peter pulled open the bottom desk drawer, regarded the small pistol he kept concealed under a dust cloth in the corner. "I don't have the guts," he mumbled to himself, pushing the drawer closed again. He would relax with another drink before doing anything else this afternoon. Foley, Dinter, and Sweeny, all of them could wait. Nothing was as important as it seemed at the moment. Nothing could change the chapters of his life. If he could rewrite the years, how might he have changed the course of events to this moment? From his childhood he wanted to build a city, and he had realized that dream. He wanted wealth and power, and had achieved both in abundance. His ambitions had shaped his character. How different might the man he had become be if he only had another chance to write the pages of his life?

Peter felt his tension loosening with the alcohol. Such thoughts were meaningless. The Irish whiskey would give him the solace he needed to find. Such thoughts were meaningless. "I am who I am, I guess. Nothing can change that . . ." he muttered into the empty room.

'THE FIRE AND THE FALL'

THE MIDNIGHT SKY WAS CLEAR and star-filled, as Monday turned over into another new day. The sky was awash in a Milky Way splendor of light that stretched across the endless black space to the west. Bernie Ducette marveled at the sight as he walked along the railroad tracks behind the fenced lumberyards. He didn't know what the night lights in the sky were, or where they came from, but he found them awesome to behold. He recognized only the Big Dipper from among the many constellations.

Bernie paused near a wooden fence surrounding the yard, noting several places where he might enter without being seen and gauged the distance from where he stood to the back door of the warehouse. This would be an easy job. Tomorrow he would buy the kerosene he needed. The thought of a fire released an exhilaration through his frail body and brought goose bumps to his flesh.

Bernie continued his walk along the tracks, peering again into the magnificent sky. Two blocks away, the illuminated sign of the HOTEL MORAN caught his attention. The new building had become Hibbing's landmark since its opening only months before. It was a magnet attracting Bernie's attention even more than the sky. An intriguing idea crossed his mind. He felt a compulsion to check out the hotel before returning home.

In a few minutes he was in the alley behind the four storied building. He tried a door and found it unlocked. Inside, he saw a stairway leading down a flight of stairs into the basement. The hallway below, lit with overhead bulbs, brought him to a large room that smelled sweetly of new lumber. Inside the room he found a light cord, pulled it, and marveled at the sight of bowling lanes which were being constructed across the enormous space. Bernie spotted piles of sawdust and maple lumber scraps which had been swept by the carpenters in their cleanup for the day. The air in the room was uncommonly dry for a basement. He turned off the lights, found the stairway, and retraced his steps back into the alley.

Bernie Ducette was inspired by his unexpected discovery. What an awesome fire this building would make! The location of the hotel near the center of town might ignite several nearby wooden structures and maybe even burn the city of Hibbing to the ground. The thought was overwhelming. Denis Moran wanted a fire for revenge against his brother; how pleased Denis would be with a fire of this magnitude! Torching the lumberyard was nothing compared to what Bernie might do here in the hotel. His share of the money from Lavalle for helping with the kidnapping would probably be increased if he made an even bigger fire than expected. Ducette's mind was locked into a grander scheme; he would destroy Hibbing.

Denis Moran made his way from Raleigh Street in West Duluth to the central hillside area north of downtown and a few miles to the east of Lily's place on Raleigh Street. Once he found himself in this busy neighborhood, he felt the safety of anonymity. Sally Slade was a whore he knew on East Fifth Street, and he arrived at her apartment by late afternoon. Denis planned on spending two nights with Sally before catching the Wednesday morning train to Hibbing. The failure of Lavalle's kidnapping scheme was no surprise to Denis Moran. He knew their plan was doomed almost before it started. Too many people saw too much. Lavalle would keep his mouth shut; he was certain of that, but Lily Brown would spill her guts. The Duluth police were probably looking for him already.

While at Sally's place, Denis shaved his beard and cut his hair shorter than he had ever worn it before. He hardly recognized himself in the mirror, and Sally agreed she couldn't believe he was the same man. Denis had twelve dollars in his pocket; he would need two for the train ticket. Giving Sally five bucks, he told her, "If anybody comes around here lookin for me, like the cops, tell 'em I headed out ta Pennsylvania." He wouldn't tell her where he was going after he left.

On the train, Denis considered what he would do when he arrived in

Hibbing. His loaded revolver was in the satchel he carried with him. Although there would be no ransom money for him now, he would not be leaving Hibbing tomorrow as broke as he was now. Ducette, he knew, would burn down the lumber yard- Bernie wouldn't fuck up like Lavalle had done- and Denis would kill his brother. He was certain of that now. He had to do it. If all he did was kick the shit out of his brother, Peter would call the cops, and the Hibbing police would have his trail.

On Tuesday, Peter Moran read the second ransom note from Sam Lavalle where he had found the first note from the day before. The letters were almost comical to him: twenty thousand in small bills, meet in a place called Riverside on Thursday night, don't tell the police. "How could that two-bit pimp ever expect to pull off a kidnapping?" he wondered to himself. What motivated Lavalle? Was it the money, or some sick attempt at revenge over how Peter had treated him years before? Probably both. Peter planned on turning the two letters over to Ole Nord and let the Hibbing cop pass them along to the Duluth police. Before doing that, however, he would call Father Foley. After that, Peter would give his condolences to Art and Sarah Schmitz. Kevin's parents must have been traumatized by the events of yesterday, and they might appreciate a call from Peter.

Foley was angry about Peter's failure to return his calls the day before. "I had to get the Hibbing police to reach you. Even then, you didn't have the decency to call me back. Thank God, Kevin wasn't harmed in any way."

Peter apologized, "Officer Nord up here told me pretty much the whole story, Father. That's no excuse though, and I'm sorry I didn't call you back. I knew this Lavalle character, Father." Peter told the priest about the connection between Lavalle, Barbara, and himself. "So that must have been the motive for the kidnapping. It's too bad that the Schmitzes had to go through what they did on my account."

"There were two other guys, Mr. Moran," Foley told him. "The police here think one of them might be your brother, Denis. At least they have the name Denis. Sarah Schmitz heard Lavalle call his accomplice by that name and described him as having a red beard. I remember the beard from meeting your brother at the church. Anyhow, the police are looking for him as we speak."

Peter had forgotten about Denis being in Duluth. His mind had been flooded with so many other things these past several days. Denis and Lavalle were two of a kind. "That would not surprise me, Father; my brother is a bounder just like Lavalle. He has no love for me; I can assure you of that."

"Where do you think your brother would go? The police have no record of him, and so far, neither Lavalle nor the Brown woman have told them much of anything."

"My mother Kathleen lives in Warren, Pennsylvania. The last time I saw Denis was up here in Hibbing back in June. I was certain then that he was heading out east to see ma. That would be my best guess," Peter told the priest. In his gut, however, he knew Denis would return to Hibbing. But Peter decided to keep his suspicions to himself and wait for Denis to show up. "I've got to call Art and Sarah Schmitz, Father. How are they doing after this nasty episode?"

Foley informed Peter that Sarah was still shaken over her experience. "I'm sure they would appreciate hearing from you."

Claude Atkinson's article appeared in the lower left corner of the front page in Tuesday afternoon's issue of the *Mesaba Ore*. The story was printed under the nondescript headline, *Grand Jury To Convene Thursday*. The news story which would attract most readers' attention was about the Oliver Iron Mining Company's announcement of record iron ore tonnage shipments from its Hibbing area mines for the month of July.

Claude would not bury the grand jury story on page three, nor would he give it a headline treatment. It was important news today but would be far more sensational when the findings came out after Thursday's testimony. The article read:

Village attorney, Elwood Trembart has called the St. Louis County grand jury into a session on Thursday of this week. The grand jury will be investigating the circumstances surrounding the death of Mr. Billy Herrick in October of 1906. Herrick was working for the Markman construction team on the former Grand Hotel as a brick-layer. On the afternoon of 9/14/06, Herrick was caught beneath a wall that caved above him and died in the Rood Hospital three days later from his injuries.

Stanley Cleary of Hibbing has implicated himself and local businessman Peter Moran in a conspiracy that resulted in the Herrick fatality. This newspaper has learned that Cleary, Harold Markman, and Moran have been issued subpoenas to testify on Thursday. Cleary has maintained that he was hired by Moran to 'cause problems' at the site, and that his and Moran's activity were responsible for the untimely death of the worker, Billy Herrick.

Reached for comment on this story, Peter Moran told this reporter that '{he} denies any and all allegations,' and that {it} is simply a matter of character assassination'. After hearing the testimony of all parties, the grand jury will determine whether indictments will be forthcoming.

Bernie Ducette cursed the rain. Maybe he should wait until tomorrow night. No, on Wednesday he would go to Duluth and join Lavalle and Denis Moran. It had to be tonight; this rain would not save the building. Bernie felt the twitching in his hands and shoulders. He always had the same sensation before a fire. His heart rate quickened and adrenaline pumped through his veins. Excitement shivered through every fiber of his body. When the twitch came, he could not stop himself.

He found the door in the back of the hotel unlocked again tonight. Lugging the heavy can of kerosene down the stairs, he saw the room just as it had been the night before with several piles of sawdust and wood scraps swept into heaps on the floor. Everything was perfect for the arsonist's match. Bernie spewed volatile kerosene across the walls in wide circles about him. Dousing some rags he brought with him, he hurled them toward the corners of the huge space.

He inhaled the fumes deep into his lungs realizing this fire would be his greatest achievement. He had thought of nothing else through the sleepless night before. The torch job was more than revenge for his mistreatment by Peter Moran and more than the satisfaction of Denis Moran's hatred of his brother. This fire was for Timo Arola and all who believed in their vision of a better world. His dead comrade had promised that the fall of capitalism would bring equality for all men. Bernie had never forgotten that promise.

With the strike of his match came a sharp crack then a roar. Transfixed by the leaping flames and the searing heat on his face, Bernie felt consummate exhilaration. He smiled into the widely spreading blaze, then screeched an unearthly laughter. In seconds, however, he began coughing and choking on the billowing smoke that was rapidly enveloping him. Realizing his own peril, he quickly turned to escape up the stairway and into the alley. From across the street, he could watch the fire.

John Pender, the night watchman, heard the back door slam before he smelled the smoke. Racing to the stairway, he saw the flames had already crept into the hallway. Pender began shouting his alarm, "Fire! . . . Fire! . . ." as he raced through the lobby and stumbled up the stairs to the first floor rooms. He banged on doors and yelled at the top of his voice . . ."Fire!" People filtered into the narrow hallways, and then helped Pender spread the alert to other guests on the floors above.

Room by room the patrons were roused from their sleep. Some panicked in their fright, but most moved in orderly fashion down the stairs. Within minutes the hotel was evacuated, with more than a hundred people spilling out into the growing downpour.

Ducette watched with wide eyes from the far side of the street. Flames cracked from the blown out lower windows and swept completely out of control. One corner of the roof began sagging as the wood-framed interior structure rapidly disintegrated. The north wall began to collapse onto the wooden walkway below and spewed its yellow embers onto the boardwalk. The intense searing heat exploded in convulsions fifty feet outward in all directions.

Ole Nord, like a shepherd with a spooked flock, moved people away from the swiftly charring building. Within minutes, Hibbing's fire wagons were on the scene, but their only hope was to contain the blaze to the hotel building. A second wall fell inward, and along with it, the upper floors toppled into the guts of the ravaged hotel. The gigantic HOTEL MORAN sign hung precariously to a fragment of roof, but when the north wall imploded, it also tumbled into the growing heap of scorched rubble.

Ducette's past fires had never held such a fascinated audience, giving him an arcane sense of pride. Bernie had been a nobody since his childhood in St. Paul. All of that would change dramatically tonight. Burning the lumber yard would only have been another fire, but this was something magnificent. He moved into the street, sidling next to the burly cop who was maintaining the safety of people huddled together in the rain.

"I done it!" Bernie shouted at the uniformed man above the fire's roar. "I started the fire." A smile of proud satisfaction spread on his narrow face.

Nord regarded the frail man nearby suspiciously. "You did what?" annoyed at this intrusion on his efforts to control the crowd. "Hey, folks, get back from there. Across the street all of you. We don't want anybody hurt."

"The fire, sir. I started the fire, got it going with some kerosene in the basement." Ducette, not to be ignored in the hubbub of the scene, pulled at the officer's sleeve.

Ole Nord, struck with confused disbelief over what he was hearing, put a firm grip on the man's thin arm. "Are you crazy or something?"

"No, sir, I *had* ta do it! For the people, ya know. It's all gonna be better now, you'll see." Bernie tried to shake his arm away from Nord's grip. "We'll all have a better life when we're equal with everyone else."

Nord did not understand what the stranger was babbling about. "What the fuck do you mean, 'for the people . . . a better life'? Johnny, com'on over here." Nord called to another cop nearby. "Take this guy down to the station. He's telling me he started the fire."

Johnny Matthews, grabbing Bernie by the arm, pulled him away from the street. "Don't give me no trouble," he warned. "I'll break your scrawny arms if ya try."

Bernie looked back at the fire. "Ain't it fantastic, officer? I ain't never done nothin better than this one here before."

The fire breathed like Hades throughout the night ridiculing every valiant effort by the cadre of confounded fire fighters. They pumped feeble sprays of water onto the roofs of the endangered buildings next door, praying they might contain the blaze. The rain was helping their efforts mightily, but the hotel would be allowed to burn itself down to its foundation.

Once everyone had been evacuated, John Pender ran the five blocks to Peter Moran's house on Washington Street. When he arrived, Peter was already up, talking on the phone with the police. He looked at Pender knowingly. "Did you get everybody out, John? The police seem to believe nobody was left inside."

"All one hundred and twenty four of them, sir. Mr. Wright saved the register from the front desk, and we counted heads out in the street. That's what took me so long in getting here. The only one we can't account for, Mr. Moran, is Jerry Sweeny. We don't know if he was in the hotel tonight.

One guy told me he heard that Sweeny was out of town at some business convention, but I don't know that for sure."

"Well done." Peter wondered about his hotel manager, and where he might be tonight. "Try to locate him for me, will you, John? I was told he was in St. Cloud, but somehow I have my doubts about that."

"I will do that, sir, as soon as I can," Pender answered anxiously.

"What's it like down there?" Peter asked the security man.

"It's just terrible, sir. Unbelievably terrible." Pender shook his head in disbelief. "Are you going to go down and see it for yourself, Mr. Moran?"

"No, John, I don't want to see it. Thanks for coming over. I'll talk to you later," Peter said dismissively.

When John left, Peter walked out onto his front portico and looked toward downtown Hibbing. The red glowing sky appeared like a halo over the city. With the driving rain, the scene was surreal. Peter stood disconsolate, subdued, and overwhelmed by the feeling that this catastrophe was the final blow. His hotel had been the epitome of his many achievements, the fruition of his greatest ambition, and the climax of his career. Thoughts from earlier in the day raced back through his mind.

He could hear the phone ringing again inside the house. There would probably be many calls tonight, but none that he cared to answer. He would mourn the loss of his hotel and contemplate this ultimate undoing of his life, locked in the privacy of his library.

Senia was awakened after midnight by the shouts of a mounting hysteria below her window on Pine Street. "The whole town's on fire!" someone shouted. "Moran's hotel!" came another scream from the street. She wrapped herself in a long cotton coat, slipped into some shoes, and raced downstairs into the rain. From the corner where she stood, Senia could see the tongues of flame rising high above the city. "It is Peter's hotel!" she cried out loud to anyone listening. "My God; That poor man! This will destroy him for sure."

Senia, like everybody in Hibbing, had read about the upcoming grand jury in that afternoon's paper. She knew better than anybody that Peter was on the edge and had been for some time. First the subpoena, and now the fire; these two things might push him over. Senia ran upstairs and grabbed her telephone. She must call Peter now, give him her support, and offer to help in any way she could. Senia hoped it was not already too late when her call was not answered. She quickly changed into some clothes, grabbed an umbrella, and hastened toward Peter's house.

Tony Zoretek and his roommates Tommy Pell and Walter Spragg heard the commotion outside their house on Cedar Street. They pulled on their pants and stepped outside where they could see the flames. "Let's get down there, fellas. Maybe we can help," Tony encouraged his bleary eyed roommates.

Most of Hibbing's population were out in the streets to watch the spectacle. Despite the rain, they wandered about in their night clothing. Police and firefighters tried to keep the hundreds of onlookers away from the raging inferno which rapidly consumed their city's most majestic landmark.

"You guys ain't gonna be any help to us here. Just stay outta the way," a firefighter warned Tony and his buddies as they approached the fire. "On second thought, maybe ya could push those folks over there outta the way," he gestured at the growing crowd. "Push them to the other side of the street. That might help us out some. Everybody wants to get up too close, and there could still be another explosion."

"I'm going to Moran's house," Tony called to his friends. "I owe the guy whatever help I can give him. I'll see you back at the house later." Tony made his way through the mob and ran toward Washington Street.

Arriving at Moran's mansion, he spotted Senia talking with Mildred Graham. "Tony, Milly says Peter won't talk to anyone. He's even locked the door to his library!" Senia exclaimed hoarsely, still out of breath from her run. "I'm going inside and see if he'll change his mind. Milly, would you please put on a pot of coffee."

Tony was soaked, and his nightshirt clung to his skin. "I'm going up to Moran's bedroom and find something dry to wear. I hope he won't mind."

Senia rapped lightly at first, then pounded on the sturdy oak door. "Peter, let me in, please. We can talk. I know how badly you must feel, but . . . we'll get over this. Please."

No sound came from the library.

Senia appealed again.

"Go away." Peter's words were slurred.

"Please, Peter, don't shut me out. You need a friend right now. I want to help. Tony's here, too. Both of us want to see you!" she pleaded.

"I said no, Senia. I'm not talking to anyone right now. Maybe tomorrow."

Upstairs, Tony rummaged through Peter's closet, found a clean shirt, and a pair of trousers that fit him. On Peter's dresser top, Tony noticed a framed photograph that made him pause. The picture was one he remembered from weeks ago. Tony, smiling into the camera, was posed in his Colts' uniform. He picked up the photo and remembered the day when Peter had taken the picture. How proud Peter Moran had been when Tony made the team. "We were good friends then, Mr. Moran. I hope we can be again some day. I'd like that to happen." Tony felt a lump in his throat.

Claude Atkinson came by Moran's house minutes later. The reporter wanted to help. "I'm not here for any newspaper interview," he assured. Tony greeted the reporter as Senia returned to the foyer where the two men were standing.

"He's shut himself in and won't talk to me or anyone else. He told me to go away. I don't know what anybody's going to do to change his mind." Senia shook her head in worry and frustration. "Maybe we'll just have to wait until he's ready. Milly has made some coffee in the kitchen. Let's just wait him out."

By three in the morning, several other people had stopped by the house to offer Peter their condolences. Tom Brady and his wife, Fred Bennett from down the street, and old friend, Con O'Gara visited. The unexpected crowd kept Milly busy making coffee. Father Dougherty, from the Immaculate Conception Church stopped with Tom McHardy, Moran's lumber business rival. In times of tragedy, Hibbing's townsfolk always came together.

Again, Senia tried to talk Peter into unlocking his door. She told him about all the people who had gathered, friends who wanted to give him their support in this difficult time. As he had before, however, Peter only told her to go away. "Leave me alone for God's sake, Senia. Go home, all of you. I don't have any friends. Just get everybody out of here. I need to be by myself. Can't you understand that? Maybe tomorrow."

Senia thanked the visitors for coming by the house and told them that Mr. Moran might see them all tomorrow. Senia stayed, catching three hours of sleep on a living room sofa, then called Harvey Goldberg at his home.

Before she could ask the banker for the day off from work, Goldberg told her to stay home. "Give my best to Mr. Moran," he told her.

Senia was awake and freshened up when Peter came out of his library in the morning. His eyes were red from his drinking and lack of sleep. "Why didn't you go home with everybody else?" he asked as if nothing had happened the night before.

"I wasn't going to go anywhere until I knew that you were all right," she answered. "Are you?"

"I will be. Thanks for staying; it means a lot to me. Can I ask you to do your old boss a favor before you go?"

"Anything, sir."

"I'm going to shave and clean up now. Then I'll want to go down to the hotel, or whatever's left of it. Will you come along with me?"

"Absolutely, Peter," Senia found using his first name came easily. "I'll be here when you come down. Maybe I can make us a quick breakfast before we leave."

In Wednesday morning's light, the once prestigious Hibbing landmark, the HOTEL MORAN, was only a heap of smoldering ruin. Max Friedman's confectionary, adjacent to the south side of the hotel, was also destroyed. Several nearby buildings had severe smoke damage, but the city of Hibbing had not burned to the ground.

"Nothing left is there?" Peter said to Senia, choking back the emotion he felt. "This will just about do it for me. I'm only glad that it rained last night, or it could have been much worst. Someone could have been killed. Maybe I'm the only casualty," he laughed at his attempted humor.

Peter struggled to comprehend the ruination before his eyes. "Hibbing will miss her, that's for sure. She was quite a sight to behold."

"We all will, sir." Senia sensed his heavy melancholy.

"She was like my woman, Senia. I even gave her my name. I thought about that all through the night. That's why I needed to be alone. I needed to put this whole thing into some kind of perspective, had to figure out why it hurts me so much," Peter dabbed at his eyes with his sleeve.

"Most people are lucky. They have other human beings to give their love to. That must be a wonderful feeling, fulfilling, and comforting. It gives those who have it something to want to live for. I guess I haven't been lucky enough ever to find that feeling, or that someone to share it with . . . I have my possessions though, those trophies of life that my money could buy. I think I've learned something important along the way, Senia. One of life's most important lessons finally got through this thick skull of mine. You can't buy friendship or loyalty; you just can't buy people!"

Peter mused as he looked from the charred ruins to Senia standing by his side. "Since I was a kid, I watched my pa plan one move after another, always beating his competition to the punch. I learned from Daly that you've got to take chances. It was his gamble that brought the Morans to Hibbing a lifetime ago." Peter's reverie had consumed his thoughts since Atkinson's visit the day before. He had struggled with his perception of the life he had led through his thirty three years. Now, he needed to share his conclusions with a person he knew would listen without judgment.

"I am who I am, and I can't change one bit of it. I've gambled and won more than my share, and now I've tasted the shame of defeat. Well, enough of my ramblings for one morning, don't you think, Senia?" Peter rubbed at his red eyes once again, then gave the smoldering site one long and final look. "Good bye, my lady." Peter removed his felt hat and held it over his heart. "You've left me with nothing to live for."

"Don't talk that way, Peter. That is nonsense! 'Nothing to live for!' You're far too young and have too much to offer to give up on yourself over this. Today, grieve your heart out, and cry your eyes out if you want. Do that today, then let go of it for good." She tried her best to console the man for whom she held such peculiar affection.

"Then there is tomorrow, and a thousand tomorrows after that. A whole lifetime of tomorrows to do all the things that need to be done. The things that only someone like Peter Moran can do. We need you; Hibbing needs you. Please get that in your head." Senia smiled and took his arm in her own. "Now, let's get away from here. It's all too depressing. Tell me. What do you most like to do on a beautiful summer day? You've never told me what those things might be. Whatever they are, let's do them, you and me. I want my day to belong to you, Peter."

"I think I want to go home now. That's all. Thanks for all your good intentions. You are a special lady; I've been lucky to have you in my life." Peter released his hand from hers. "I need some sleep, and so do you. Go ahead now, get some rest." Senia's question opened a wound in his heart. Had he ever done something fun on a beautiful summer day? Even now, with Senia's wonderful invitation, he was at a complete loss for anything to say.

"I hate to leave you by yourself," Senia frowned.

"Before I head back to the house, I've got another favor to ask, Senia. Will you take care of some business things for me? A little side job that I'd appreciate a lot?"

"I'd be happy to, just let me know what it is and when you want it done," she paused, waiting for Peter to explain.

Peter only stared absently beyond her without a reply.

"What is it?" Not getting a reaction, she shrugged. "Well, if you don't mind, I think I'll go back to my apartment. You're right, some sleep sounds like an awfully good idea. I'm exhausted." Senia gave his elbow a squeeze, "You could use a nap as well. Don't shut yourself up in the library all day." She wanted to add . . . "and don't do anymore drinking," but swallowed the thought.

"I'll leave you a note." Peter mumbled his last request as she was turning away. His eyes followed her as she headed away toward her apartment on Pine Street.

Senia was too tired to give Peter's parting comment any thought. The note he promised to leave for her failed to settle in Senia's mind.

Before going back to his house, Peter decided to stroll around his city. As he walked toward his lumber yard, he was greeted and consoled by many well-wishers. Hundreds of people milled about the fire site, exchanging various theories on the cause of the blaze. Moran's name came up often. The grand jury story from yesterday's paper was tossed about, the horrific fire of the night before with the arrest of a drifter named Ducette, the timing of Harold Markman's return to town, and Jerry Sweeny's whereabouts. All were intriguing events on the minds of Hibbing's citizenry that morning.

At the lumber yard he found Lars Udahl in his office. "Good morning, Lars." Peter could offer little more than a halfhearted greeting to his warehouse supervisor, a man he both liked and respected.

The two men talked about the fire. "Thank God nobody got hurt, and thank God for the rain," Udahl offered. "I heard Sweeny might have had something to do with it, Mr. Moran. I heard there ain't no meeting in St.

Cloud; that's what Sweeny's secretary is telling every one, anyhow. Did you hear that, sir?"

"We have no idea where Sweeny is, Lars. That's all I know. He's out there somewhere I guess." Moran was distracted by other thoughts at the moment and looked around the place one last time before leaving. "I just want you to know that you're doing one hell of a job, Lars. I really don't tell you that often enough, do I? Anyhow, keep up the good work." Peter shook the carpenter's hand. "I've gotta go now. Give my best to your wife."

Lars scratched his head as he watched Peter leave his office and head back out into the street. "Thank you for the compliment, Mr. Moran," he called out behind the departing figure. Peter heard the thanks and waved his hand without looking back.

Two blocks away, at West Pine Street and First Avenue, Peter wandered into the liquor warehouse so that he could say a quick hello to Norman Dinter. He found Dinter talking with two of the teamsters loading their wagons with oak beer kegs. "Have you got a minute, Norm?" Moran interrupted the conversation. The two teamsters, recognizing Mr. Moran, quickly took off their caps offering their humble sympathies.

Off to the side of the workers, Moran put his hand on Dinter's shoulder, "I'm going to sit on the Grain Belt order for now, Norm. It's a great idea, don't get me wrong. It's just that I'm a little concerned about starting a price war with Allison right now. You would have a hellava time dealing with that."

"I understand, sir, I thought about the same thing myself. He wouldn't just sit back. That's for sure. We'll talk about this some more later. I know you've got a lot on your mind right now, sir," Dinter said thoughtfully.

"I want you to know, Norm, I really appreciate the job you're doing here. You've got a bright future in this business. Keep up the good work." Moran shook the new supervisor's hand warmly. "I'm making the rounds this morning and just wanted to say hello to you and the guys here. Give them all my best for me, Norm."

At the corner of Pine Street and Second Avenue, Peter paused at the door of his Shamrock Saloon. He remembered so many good times with the fellows in this busy downtown tavern. McIntosh and O'Gara came quickly to mind and so many Friday nights after work. The Shamrock always had a first class clientele of mining officials, politicians, and merchants. He decided to have a whiskey at the bar before continuing his walk. The young bartender did not recognize Peter. "What can I get you, sir?" he inquired casually.

"Your best Irish whiskey, bartender, straight up please." He looked around the tavern for a familiar face and saw none. It was close to noon, and Peter thought some of his old friends might be there for the famous corned beef sandwiches his tavern served for lunch.

"That'll be fifteen cents, sir." The bartender set his glass on the rich mahogany bar in front of him.

Peter found a ten dollar bill and passing it across ordered a drink for the bar. "Keep the change, bartender!"

The young man smiled widely, "Thank you sir, who should I say . . . ?"

Peter swallowed the whiskey in one gulp. "Pete Moran, the owner of this place." He got up from his stool, smiled at the bewildered young man and walked out the door.

At Third Avenue and Center Street, Peter entered another of his liquor establishments and one of Hibbing's most popular saloons: The Red Rock Tavern. Inside he found Riley Gillespie, an old Irish friend, sitting at a table by himself. Riley stood and greeted Peter with a strong handshake. "Sorry about your hotel, Pete."

The two men had a drink together. Moran bought a round for the house, just as he had done at his other saloon, then excused himself. "I've got a lot to take care of this afternoon, Riley."

"Sorry I couldn't make your party on the Fourth, Pete. Wife wasn't feeling good that day," Gillespie lied. Riley was an old but estranged friend for the past two years.

Peter contemplated his conversation with Senia earlier that morning as he walked the six blocks south toward his house. He had mentioned to her how his father had shaped his own ambitions when he was still a boy. He recalled a day when he and Daly stood by a river near Marquette, Michigan, watching the lumberjacks skidding a sled of logs into the rapid current. Downstream was a sawmill that would process Daly's timber. Peter was only eight years old when he told his father that he would like to build a city some day. He laughed to himself over the memory. "Well, old man, your son did what he always wanted to do."

When he arrived back at the house, it was early afternoon. Mildred

Graham had a list of people who had called while Peter was away. "Milly, I'm retiring to the library right now and taking my phone off the hook. I didn't get any sleep last night, and I might take a good nap. You can have the rest of the day off. You've got to be as tired as I am with all the confusion of last night. Visitors must have kept you up 'til all hours."

Mildred was a woman of very few words and little emotion."Thank you, Mr. Moran," was more than sufficient for her.

In his library, Peter pulled the drapes against the afternoon sun and sat at his desk with a bottle of whiskey. He would write a note for Senia's attention while waiting for his brother Denis. These were the only two things remaining on his personal agenda.

Clean-shaven Denis Moran, traveling as Mr. Jones, arrived at the Hibbing depot at two in the afternoon. He wanted to find a woman at the Northern Hotel and have a few drinks before confronting his brother Peter after it got dark. Everybody he encountered at the station was talking about the hotel fire.

"How about the lumberyard?" Denis inquired of a baggage handler working out on the platform. "Did the fire start at Moran's lumber yard and then spread from there?"

"Ain't heard nothin about that, sir. The lumberyard's fine as far as I know," said the stout man as he tossed a canvas mail sack into the back of a wagon. "The hotel's a goner though. Hibbing ain't never seen a fire like that one before, I'll tell ya that much."

"Who done the fire, do they know that yet?"

"Hey Eddie," the baggage man called to a fellow worker. "What's that guy's name that Nord hauled in after the fire last night?"

"A little French guy's what I heard. Name's Dumet or Duvett, somethin like that. Guess he was out in the street braggin about burnin it down to Ole Nord. Kinda crazy if ya ask me. Proud as a peacock the Frenchman was, smilin and carryin on."

Denis Moran concealed his disappointment. "Everybody was fuckin up their jobs," he thought. He promised himself to do his part the way it was supposed to be done.

Peter sat at his desk considering his last two options. Adversity stared him in the face, and he lacked the courage and resolve to fight it any longer. He would not meet with the grand jury scheduled for tomorrow. His reputation in Hibbing would be disgraced, regardless of the outcome. He would not rebuild his hotel. She had been one of a kind, and he would never compromise her memory with an attempt at building another to replace her.

Peter could run. In the open wall safe, behind the Matisse copy, was one thousand dollars. He might slip out of town in his Buick that night and drive west to Grand Rapids where he could catch a train to another place. Any other place. All towns were basically the same, he reasoned. Same people, same opportunities for someone with ambition. He could start his life over again and make another fortune. Senia Smith had done well for herself by using an alias in a new place. Running was definitely an option to consider.

Peter slid open the bottom drawer of his desk and withdrew his revolver. He placed it on the desk next to the blank page on which he would write his final note. The gun would mercifully end all his misery; once and for all. This second option held the greater appeal. Suicide seemed more honorable but took a greater courage than Peter had at this moment. He could not make this decision yet. He needed a little more time to think about it. Peter poured another glass of whiskey and began to write:

Senia.

When I am gone, I will be leaving many loose ends . You are the only person who can take care of them for me, and I thank you for doing so. When you dispose of whatever is left of my properties, please be generous to my friends and my associates. Give something to Tony for his new business. Pay off Mary Samora's mortgage even if she protests . I'd like you to give something to Lars Udahl, Norman Dinter, and Mr. Pender from the hotel. Take good care of yourself as well.

As I told you earlier today, there is nothing left for me here. I have a son in Duluth. I have not told anybody in Hibbing about him and would like you to keep the matter confidential. His name is

Kevin Schmitz. Please talk to Father Foley at St. James Church about Kevin's future financial security and do whatever the priest and the Schmitz family deem best for my sole heir.

Thank you Senia, for this and everything else you have done for me. You will see that the wall safe is open. The thousand dollars inside is for you as a small expression of my gratitude.

Peter

After finishing the note, Peter slumped over his desk and closed his eyes. He tried to say a prayer but found there was nothing he might say to the God he had never really known. "I'm sorry, God! We've never talked before and I don't think . . ." he mumbled the thought and left it alone in the empty room.

Peter Moran's house was as dark as the moonless night. Denis watched the windows from across the street, looking for any sign of activity inside. He walked around behind the house and noticed a faint light glowing from a room to the left of the patio. Denis moved carefully through the gardens. The back door to the house was carelessly unlocked. As he stepped inside, his heel caught on the door casing, causing him to stumble to one knee. He waited a few seconds to hear if his fall had raised any reaction from inside.

Peter was startled from his sleep by a noise from somewhere outside. It was quiet for a minute, but then he heard the soft fall of footsteps in the hallway near his library door. He considered the pistol on his desk as he watched the door knob slowly turn. He would not, however, use his gun on the man he knew was behind the door.

"I've been expecting you, Denis." Peter said calmly before the intruder had even entered the room. "Come in and have an Irish whiskey. I have a job for you. We can talk about it over a drink."

Denis Moran had been drinking most of the afternoon. "How'd ya know it was me?" he asked from behind the half-opened door. "Whatta ya mean, expectin me? Anyhow, I don't much givva damn." Denis stepped inside and closed the door behind him.

"And, it's too late for any job except the one I come ta do right now. Do ya hear that, you smart ass?"

"I offered you a drink, Denis. I can see you've had plenty already. Another won't hurt," Peter said flatly.

Denis saw the revolver on the desk and drew out his own firearm which was tucked in his belt. "Don't get any smart ideas with that gun ya got there. I'll blow your fucking brains out before ya know what hit ya."

"Don't worry about that, Denis. Just sit down so we can talk."

"I ain't sitting down, and I ain't hangin around here any longer than I hafta." Denis aimed his pistol at Peter's head. "You can say your prayers cuz I'm gonna kill ya, brother. I'm gonna do it for me and for pa. Understand what I'm tellin ya? I ain't gonna have no guilty conshence about it either."

Peter regarded his tormented brother and the pistol aimed directly at his head. His decision had been made easy. "I know the police are looking for you, Denis, even here in Hibbing. You've got to make a run for it. I can make the running a lot easier for you."

"I know I gotta run, soon as I get you taken care of. You got anythin else to say?"

"One last thing." Peter carefully pushed his own revolver across the desk toward his brother. "Use my gun, Denis. There's some money in the wall safe, and the keys to my car are on a table next to the phone in the front hallway." He swallowed at the vomit that burned in his throat.

"Just shove the gun in my mouth and pull the trigger. When you've done that, put the gun in my hand. Then . . . get the hell out of *my* town."

PAT MCGAULEY is a former Hibbing High School teacher and worked for both the Erie and Hanna Mining Companies. He served as an historian for IRONWORLD in Chisholm before becoming the Commissioner of Iron Range Resources under Governor Al Quie. McGauley was born in Duluth, received his masters degree from the University of Minnesota, and has lived in Hibbing for the past thirty-seven years.

HOWARD STREET
BOOKSELLERS

To order:

Copies of *TO BLESS or TO BLAME* are available through Howard Street Booksellers. Cost of $24.50 includes Minnesota Sales Tax plus shipping and handling.

115 East Howard Street
Hibbing, MN 55746
218-262-5206
Fax 218-262-3361